# And Then There Was One

Also by Patricia Gussin

FICTION

*Shadow of Death*

*Twisted Justice*

*The Test*

NONFICTION

*What's Next . . . For You?*

(With Robert Gussin)

# And Then There Was One

A Novel

Patricia Gussin

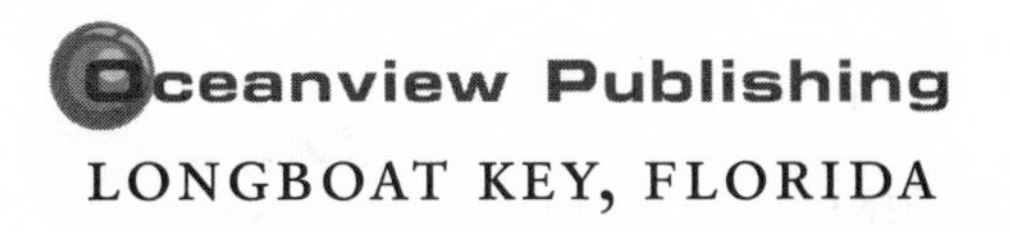


LONGBOAT KEY, FLORIDA

FIRST EDITION



This book is a work of fiction. Names, characters, places, and incidents either are the products of the author's imagination or are used fictitiously. Any resemblance to actual events or locales or persons, living or dead, is entirely coincidental.

ISBN: 978-1-933515-81-6

Published in the United States of America by Oceanview Publishing, Longboat Key, Florida
www.oceanviewpub.com

10 9 8 7 6 5 4 3 2 1

PRINTED IN THE UNITED STATES OF AMERICA

To my wonderful grandchildren

Melissa
Mike
Megan
Kris
Courtney
Connor
Will
Sal
Zack
Austen
Sonny
Luke
Nate
Joe
Nick
Rachel
Oliver

# ACKNOWLEDGMENTS

Thank you, Oceanview Team, for all you do: Susan Greger, Susan Hayes, Maryglenn McCombs, Mary Adele Bogden, John Cheesman, George Foster, Kylie Fritz, Joanne Savage, Sandy Greger, Joe Hall, and Cheryl Melnick.

A special thanks to my editor, Caroline Upcher.

And, the ultimate thanks to my husband, Bob, always my first reader and my twenty-four-hour inspiration.

# And Then There Was One

# CHAPTER 1

*Detroit Pays Tribute to Monica Monroe in Concert at Fox Theatre.*
*— Detroit News*, Sunday, June 14, 2009

"Scott, listen to me. We can't find Sammie and Alex!"

"Can't find what?" Scott Monroe shouted over the roar of Yankee fans as Derek Jeter approached the plate. The Yankees were pummeling the Mets, battering Santana. "Lucy, I'm in the dugout. I'll have to call you back."

"No. Don't hang up!"

Cell phone jammed against his ear, Scott left the game and headed to the players' lockers. "Hold on," he yelled, letting the door slam behind him, feeling his heart start to hammer, all the little hairs rising on his neck. His mother-in-law, level-headed and always composed, calling him during a game? Something had to be wrong. "Okay, it's quieter in here."

"Scott, it's about the girls — "

"What about them?" He squeezed the phone even tighter to his ear.

"Danielle took them to the movies today. At the mall in Auburn Hills. Sammie and Alex never came out. Danielle called me. I'm at the mall now and there's no sign of them."

Scott crouched against the concrete wall and forced a deep breath. *Didn't come out?* "Okay, Lucy, slow down. You said Alex and Sammie. Where's Jackie? Aren't they together?"

"No, they split up. Two different movies. Jackie went to *Star Wars* with Danielle. And Sammie and Alex went to *Night at the Museum* right next door. Both movies ended about the same time, but Sammie and Alex never came out."

How could two kids *not come out* of a theater?

"Just a minute, Lucy, I'm still having trouble hearing you." Scott moved deeper inside the hall. Lucy was telling him that two of his daughters were missing. Certainly they'd show up soon. They were nine years old, the age that girls like to hang around malls.

"Before I got here, Danielle asked everyone around," Lucy continued, breathless, "but nobody saw Sammie and Alex leave. Scott, we don't know where they are. I called mall security."

Scott felt his body go limp and he slumped lower against the wall. Where could they have gone? The New York City air was chilly for mid-June, but Scott felt the prickle of ice filling his veins.

"There're calling in the police," Lucy said. "Scott, can you come to Detroit? Now."

"Katie?" Scott hardly dared ask. His wife was a street-smart doctor, but when it came to their girls she had a sixth sense of paranoia — an obsession with their safety. Strange that Katie had let them go to the movies with their cousin, Danielle, even though Danielle was a responsible nineteen year old.

"Where's Katie?"

Lucy's voice faltered. "She and Sharon went into Detroit, that charity affair, guests of the bishop."

Scott remembered. Katie's sister was the chairperson of the posh luncheon event.

"Their phones are still turned off, but they'll be at my place soon. You know how Katie is about those girls."

Scott did know. Katie had grown up in Detroit, her early years in the inner city. Even though Lucy had moved her four daughters to the troubled city's outer borders and had sent them to a private girls' academy, Katie, the youngest, had never been able to shake the terror of those early years.

"The police?" Scott heard the echo of his voice in the empty hallway. Trying to think of logical solutions, he slammed into a wall of terror. "Did you check for a lost and found for kids?" he managed. "What about other exits? Don't they have emergency exits?"

"Yes," Lucy said. "But nothing."

Struggling for a sense of perspective, Scott squeezed his eyes shut, trying to focus on the diverse personalities of his identical triplet daughters. "If they are in the mall and lost, Sammie would never admit it. She'd hold out to the end before asking for help." Scott paused, "Lucy, you did say that Jackie is okay?"

"Yes, she and Danielle are in my sight. Jackie's scared, that's all. And of course, Danielle is devastated."

"I'm on my way." Scott opened his eyes and stood. "I'll charter a plane. I'm on my way."

"Let's just hope they're wandering the mall," Lucy said, but Scott had already disconnected.

Lucy Jones jerked to attention when the heavyset man in a rumpled brown suit barged into the cramped mall security office. She still gripped the phone on the desk with one hand while holding onto her granddaughter, Jackie, trembling at her side. Her other granddaughter, Danielle, stood back, her slim shoulders slumped, her head bent into tented hands.

"Clarence Plummer," the man announced. "Director of security. You reported a couple of missing kids?" Plummer swung his massive frame into the chair behind the desk, motioning for Lucy to take the lone client chair. She complied, pulling Jackie onto her lap, leaving Danielle standing. "Start at the beginning, ma'am. We're about to call in the local police, but — "

"Sir, my two granddaughters are missing. They're only nine years old." Lucy's words came out in a gush as she tilted Jackie forward on her lap. "They look just like this little girl here, only one has a ponytail. They're triplets. They were at the movie and didn't come out. They — "

"Slow down, ma'am." Plummer leaned forward, rubbing his shiny bald head, the color of mahogany. "What do you mean? They didn't come out of the show? That must mean they're in there. Why didn't you just go in and get them out?"

A familiar feeling started to settle in the pit of Lucy's stomach. How could she make him understand that she was not an ignorant black woman, unworthy of his time? When she was representing her clients as a social worker, Lucy felt empowered, but here, as an aging, overweight black woman, she suffered a surge of helplessness. The fact that Clarence Plummer, too, was black gave her little comfort.

"Sir, I'm afraid that they have been taken." Lucy struggled to enunciate, her voice was shaking so.

Gulping another deep breath, she prayed that she was overreacting, merely oversensationalizing the situation. Certainly the girls would show up any minute and she'd have to apologize for her hysteria. To her surprise, Plummer leaned forward, elbows on this desk, and fixed his eyes on hers. "Ma'am, please, start at the beginning."

"My other granddaughter, their cousin, Danielle," Lucy nodded to the older girl, "took all three girls to the movies in the mall. Danielle and Jackie went to *Star Wars* and Sammie and Alex to *Night in the Museum* right next door. When the movie was over, Sammie and Alex never came out."

"We were supposed to meet on the bench by the fountain." Danielle spoke for the first time in a voice strained and low. Her brown eyes were smudged with mascara, and when she spoke, one hand kept twisting the charm bracelet on her other arm.

Lucy's heart went out to her sensitive granddaughter. Danielle was spending her summer break from Vanderbilt with Lucy to help make sure her grandmother was okay after her hip replacement. Tears glistened against Danielle's caramel-colored skin, and Lucy wished she had a packet of Kleenex to give her.

"Could I have your names, please?" Plummer pulled out a pad and selected a pen from the cluster on his desk.

"Jacqueline Monroe." Lucy encircled Jackie with both arms. "Her sisters are Samantha and Alexandra. I'm Lucy Jones and this is my granddaughter, Danielle Evans." Lucy explained how she lived in Auburn Hills, that Danielle lived in Nashville during the school year, and the Monroe triplets in Tampa. She told him that the children were in town with their mother to attend their aunt's concert in Detroit last night. Their father, Scott Monroe, was on his way here from New York City.

Plummer, writing it all down, paused mid stroke. "Not *that* Scott Monroe, the Yankee catcher? His sister, Monica Monroe, my wife's favorite singer?"

"Yes." Jackie looked up at him, eyes brimming with tears. "Mister, can you find my sisters?"

There was now no doubt that Lucy had Plummer's full attention.

Scott Monroe was still a revered figure in baseball circles even though an injury at the plate had ended his catching career eighteen years ago. "Dang. Yankees beat the Mets fifteen to zip today. He was at *that* game?"

Lucy nodded.

"He's your dad?" Plummer scrutinized Jackie again. "Okay, let's start from the beginning."

"Danielle," Lucy said, "I want you to tell Mr. Plummer exactly what happened.

Through tears, voice shaking, Danielle repeated the same information, telling Plummer how the foursome had split up just before going inside the theatre. Since the movies were shown side-by-side, Danielle did not think that there was any risk. They planned to meet outside the entrance to the movie theater where there was a prominent fountain surrounded by benches.

After *Star Wars* let out, she and Jackie had waited for a while, and then she'd taken Jackie and they'd gone into the *Night of the Museum* theatre to search for Sammie and Alex. The theatre had been dark and empty, and she'd persuaded the ticket collector to turn on the lights. The space was completely empty. Then they'd gone around asking everybody, but nobody had seen the girls leave. The ticket taker volunteered that the emergency exit had not been breached. Then Danielle called her grandmother. As soon as she hung up, she and Jackie kept asking people in the vicinity of the fountain and movie entrance whether they'd seen the two girls. Nobody had.

"I got here fifteen minutes after Danielle called," Lucy said, "even though with my new hip I'm not supposed to drive."

"Jackie and I looked everywhere," Danielle said.

"Bathrooms?" Plummer asked.

"We checked. Every stall. They were not there. Not in the lobby. Not by the concessions. I figured they must be somewhere out in the mall."

"Oh, where could they be?" Lucy interrupted.

Plummer creased his brow and gestured for Danielle to continue.

"So I asked Jackie. 'Where would they have wandered off to?' Jackie said, 'Alex wouldn't wander off, but maybe Sammie. Sammie's always getting in trouble.' "

Jackie shifted in Lucy's arms, and Lucy pulled her closer.

"It's a big mall. Jackie said maybe they went to get candy. But why? There was plenty of candy at the movies. Jackie said that Alex likes animals, but there's no pet store in the mall. Jackie suggested a sports store."

Plummer raised his eyebrows.

"They're sports fanatics," Lucy said.

"I know this mall like the back of my hand," Danielle said. "I thought about the sneaker store, but Jackie said they just got brand new Nike's. That's when I called my grandmother. I figured that they had to be here somewhere, but if I was late getting them back, their mother would simply freak. Everybody knows how ultraprotective Aunt Katie is about her kids."

Jackie twisted again in Lucy's arms, "Where are they, Grandma?"

"Mrs. Jones, I need details." Plummer consulted his notes. "Alexandra and Samantha?"

"Alex and Sammie," Lucy said, gulping back tears.

Plummer got up and walked around his desk. He knelt at Lucy's side and directly addressed Jackie. His voice was firm, yet kind. "I have a couple of questions for you, Jackie. Okay?"

The child nodded.

"Can you tell me what your sisters were wearing?"

Jackie fingered the butterfly pattern on her blue slacks, then brushed tears from her eyes. "Yes. Sammie had on those awful pants, the ones with a lot of colors and a shirt I told her did not match. She said she didn't care."

"What color shirt?" Plummer asked?

"Yellow," Jackie said. "And the pants had a mix of colors, reds and greens."

"What about your other sister? What was she wearing?"

"A purple dress. Actually, violet. She likes dresses. And a barrette, like mine." Jackie fingered the fake jewel clasp holding the hair back from her forehead. "And Sammie had her hair in a ponytail with a red ribbon."

"I explained all that to the ticket guy," Danielle interrupted. "I told him, 'look at Jackie. Did you see two little girls who look just like her? One with a yellow shirt and multicolored pants. The other in a purple sundress.' And I explained that the one in the multicolors had her hair in a ponytail."

"Alex's dress was light purple," Jackie corrected.

" 'Miss, we see so many kids going through here,' was all he said."

Plummer got up. "Okay, timing is everything. I need to know exactly when you arrived and exactly when you separated."

Danielle said that they arrived at the mall at twelve thirty. They hung out for a few minutes then went inside the theatre to buy popcorn and pop. She and Jackie separated from Alex and Sammie at exactly the time the two movies were scheduled to start: twelve forty-five. New tears gathered as she faced Plummer. "And that's the last time I saw them."

Plummer patted Danielle on the back. "We'll find them," he said. Then he attacked the phone, spewing orders in a voice that bellowed: "monitor all access and egress; station security agents at each of the four mall exits; stop anyone with a child fitting the description of the Monroe girls — healthy nine year olds, black hair, one in a ponytail, the other shoulder length, brown eyes, dark bronze skin; nobody leaves the mall complex without scrutiny."

Plummer's next calls were to the Oakland County sheriff and the Michigan State Police. He urged the police not to wait to call in the FBI. The intensity of Plummer's tone terrorized Lucy as the security director repeated over and over that these first few hours were critical.

Lucy felt her heart race, and she broke into a cold sweat, pulling Jackie even more tightly to her chest.

# CHAPTER 2

*General Motors and Chrysler Bankrupt: Ford Next?*
– *Detroit News*, Sunday, July 14, 2009

Katie Monroe glanced again at her Piaget watch, an extravagant gift from her husband on the occasion of her forty-fifth birthday. She couldn't suppress the flicker of a smile even though at that moment annoyance was escalating to agitation. Her mother must have taken Danielle and the girls out for something to eat after the movies. She'd given the girls popcorn and candy and soda money. And she wanted them to have an early dinner so they'd get to bed on time. Their flight to Tampa left Detroit at seven thirty the following morning and they'd have to leave her mother's shortly after five a.m.

"Relax, Katie," Sharon said. "Stop trying to control every single minute. So they're a little late. Kick off your shoes. Let's have a cup of tea."

"So I'm a control freak," Katie laughed. "You've been telling me that since I was five, that's as far back as I can remember. I'll make the tea."

She and her sister Sharon sat in Lucy's cozy kitchen, drinking green tea, chatting about their kids, their nieces and nephews, getting caught up with the whirlwind of family gossip. Soon they were plotting the tactics of a surprise birthday party for Lucy. She'd be seventy-seven in December.

"My house in Tampa," Katie said.

"There you go again, little-sister-in-charge," Sharon shook her head with a gotcha smile.

"Who could object?" Katie started to sound defensive, then

grinned. "I promise perfect weather. The college kids will be on break. Mom's hip will be fine for travel by then."

"Just one thing," Sharon said. "Mom's birthday is the anniversary of Anthony's death. She won't leave Detroit because she goes to the cemetery. Every anniversary for Anthony, Johnny, and Dad. Remember, she always took us when we were kids?"

Katie nodded. She hadn't factored that in. She'd been just five when both of her brothers were killed in the Detroit riots. She didn't remember much about them, just how sad her mother and her older sisters were; how awful it was with all the flames and smoke and guns and sirens. A few years later, Lucy had managed to move her family to a house in the outskirts of Detroit, where Katie grew up, and after her daughters were married, she'd moved to a small townhouse in Auburn Hills.

Now Katie was forty-eight and lived with her husband and her identical triplet daughters on Davis Island in Tampa, a neighborhood that was as safe as any neighborhood can be. Katie thought of how different her life might have been. Before Scott, she'd had only one serious boyfriend, Keith Franklin. She still shivered, remembering the vindictive note he'd sent her from prison when he'd found out that she'd married a *white* man. And there had been that out-of-the-blue e-mail from him about a month ago. Just the thought of that made her cringe. She'd immediately deleted it, purged it from her system, and blocked the sender. She'd been more annoyed than concerned, but now...*Katie, I've changed. I need to be with you. I'll leave my wife. I'll take care of your daughters. All I think about is you —*

"Sharon, can you remember them?" Katie asked, getting back to her family, needing to escape the shadow of Keith Franklin on her life.

"Not much about Dad," Sharon said. "Even though I was seven when he died. You were only two. But, yes, I remember Anthony and Johnny. They used to tickle us until we cried. They had lots of friends. Johnny was always playing loud music."

Katie rarely allowed herself to think about her brothers. Now that she was a mother, she couldn't fathom the bottomless pain her mother must have endured. Losing a child had to be the ultimate in human suffering. Just the thought triggered in her a senseless rush of panic.

Not healthy, she knew, as a professional. Her psychiatric training had required a round of psychoanalysis, but that was before she'd become a mother herself, before she'd had any inkling of the intensity of a mother's love for her kids.

"Sharon, I'm getting scared." Katie said, again checking the time. "They should be back by now. And where's Mom? She shouldn't be out so soon after her hip replacement."

"She's probably visiting neighbors. She is supposed to get some exercise. Maybe she walked the girls to the Dairy Queen. You know how Mom spoils the grandchildren. Their every whim – "

"So why aren't they back?" Katie interrupted.

The sisters had migrated to the living room of Lucy's house. Sharon with her feet propped up on the ottoman and Katie perched on the edge of the sofa ready to pounce should the front door open. As the baby of the family, Katie had been more indulged than her three sisters, and they were used to her mild displays of histrionics.

"I just wish she'd get the girls back soon. Scott's flying back to Tampa from New York City tomorrow morning, and the girls and I have such an early flight out of Detroit. Naturally, Scott scheduled little league practice for them. He's fanatic about their baseball. The only girls in the league, and he makes sure that they're better than any of the boys – and I mean *way* better. And, I have to be back to testify in an ugly trial on Monday."

"What's up?" Sharon asked.

"Parental sexual child abuse. Dad's guilty as hell. I'll do my best to nail him, but the testimony of kids is always fragile. A guy with entitlement wealth. One of those narcissistic sociopaths. Charms the hell out of everybody. Anyway, he messed those kids up pretty bad."

"My little sister, the child abuse expert. Who would have thought? You do so much good, Katie. Plus, admit it, you like the theatrics. You always did like to be in charge."

"Give me a break. Growing up with three older sisters, I call it survival."

"Any way about it, you've got the best of all worlds, medicine and law. Or maybe the worst, considering the scum of the earth you put away, but it has to beat labor law. I get to spar with teamsters all day long."

"It does feel good to get back into the swing of practice," said Katie, positioning herself at the window. "I took too much time off when the girls were born. Once they started school, I lost my excuse."

"Seriously, those kids you protect — I know much of it is pro bono."

Katie got up and resumed her pacing, trying to stop her eyes from blinking the way they always did when she was scared. Sharon was right about the worst of humanity. She dealt with the scum — assaults on kids: physical, sexual, emotional. How could such horrors *not* make her overprotective of her children? That, and the ever-lingering fear of racial prejudice that her daughters might ultimately face. Racial prejudice comes in so many flavors, how well she knew that.

"We learned so much from Mom," Katie said. "She worked hard to get our values right."

"She worked hard for her clients, too. And for us. Imagine what it must have taken to send us all to Saint Mary-of-the-Woods Academy."

The phone rang and Katie ran to grab it.

"Scott?" Katie breathed a sigh that bordered on relief. She and Scott had one of those mutually supportive relationships where just the sound of each other's voice brought comfort.

"Scott, the girls are still out with Mom and Danielle," Katie rushed to say, twisting the phone cord. "We have such an early flight in the morning — "

"Katie — "

Katie failed to breathe as Scott told her that the police were looking for Sammie and Alex at the mall. That Lucy, Danielle, and Jackie were there. That everything would be okay. That he was on his way from New York City to Detroit. That he'd chartered a plane. That the police would be there soon to —

When Katie did take a breath, it came out as a gasp, followed by a muffled scream as she dropped the phone onto the carpeted floor. In an instant, Sharon was at her side, but by then Katie was on her knees, scrambling for the phone, moaning, "No, no, no."

Sharon grabbed the phone first. "Scott? What is it? What did you tell her?"

Sharon listened as she stood, then whispered, "Danielle?"

Katie, on her feet now, tried to grab the phone.

"Thank God," Sharon breathed deeply. Then she said, "Yes, Scott, I'll stay with Katie. What should we do? Go to the mall? Wait here? Oh, pray to God that this is all a mistake. I mean, what do you mean, *missing*? Couldn't they be lost in the mall? Maybe in one of those arcades? An ice cream shop? Something safe, innocent?"

"My flight is getting ready to take off," Scott said. "A police car will take you and Katie to the mall."

Sharon stepped back, shaking her head from side to side as she handed the phone to her sister.

"Scott, what should I do?" Katie's voice trembled as did her whole body.

The doorbell rang, followed by pounding, and Sharon opened the door.

Katie turned to find a fresh-faced police officer standing at the door, hat in hand. "The police are here, Scott. Please hurry." She grabbed her purse and rushed out of the door into the waiting squad car.

# CHAPTER 3

*Yankees Sweep Mets: 15–0.*
— Evening Sports, Sunday, June 14

It was nine thirty when Scott sprinted into the conference room at the Hills Mall, headed for Katie, and pulled her into his arms. Except for the movie complex and three restaurants, the shops in the mall were closed. By then every nook and cranny had been searched by both human and canine species. The girls had been missing for six hours and maybe as long as eight and a half. Hundreds of shoppers and clerks had been interviewed. Pictures of the Monroe girls were being circulated. The parking lots and the surrounding commercial areas were being canvassed. The media had gotten wind of the story and the mall was under the siege of camcorders, bright lights, reporters on alert. Nothing had gone out on the six o'clock news, but if the girls were not located within the next half hour, *Early News at Ten* would lead with the story.

Clarence Plummer, director of mall security, had hit the panic button early, and as it turned out, appropriately so. Local police, Oakland County sheriffs, and Michigan state police were now crawling all over one another. They were waiting on the FBI. Scott Monroe, still wearing a Yankee jersey with navy pin stripes on white, had to bully his way through clusters of them to get to his wife, athleticism and brute force serving him well despite his police escort. He'd been met by the state police at the airport and briefed en route to the Hills Mall. The whereabouts of two of his daughters was simply unknown.

"Scott, they still haven't found them!" Scott felt Katie's body shudder as he held her in a crushing embrace.

"I'm sorry it took me so long." Scott's naturally loud voice seemed to boom. "I needed to be here with you." Scott ran his hand over Katie's hair, something he did whenever he was upset and needed her near him.

"Where could they be?" Katie said through tears. "I just keep asking myself. Over and over, where could they be? They'd never go off with a stranger. After all we've taught them? But then how? Did someone force them? Just take them? The head security man found a lady who thinks she saw them near the fountain by the movie theater, but she got distracted by her own kids and didn't see where they went. She didn't see them leave the mall. Other than that one lady, the police haven't been able to find any witnesses, so maybe they're okay."

"Babe, where is Jackie?" For the first time Scott glanced around the room. "Is she okay?"

"Yes, I mean, *no*. Mom took her to the restroom. Scott, she blames herself. She and Sammie got into an argument about which movie they wanted to see. So Danielle let them split up. Danielle and Jackie. Sammie and Alex."

"What about Danielle?" Scott asked in a near whisper.

"She's distraught, blaming herself. Everybody's blaming themselves, including me, for going off to that lunch. Letting this happen."

Scott tipped Katie's chin up so he could look into her eyes. "Katie, promise me, no blames. We can't blame anybody, including ourselves. Hell, I ought to have come with you to Detroit." With a handkerchief, he wiped fresh tears off her cheek.

"Dr. Monroe. Mr. Monroe, I'm glad you got here so soon." A man with an authoritative voice appeared at the door.

Still holding Katie close, Scott turned.

"Special Agent Streeter, Tony Streeter, FBI." A man of Scott's height and build and age stuck out his hand. Streeter wore the predictable dark navy suit, a starched white shirt with a maroon striped tie, and smartly polished shoes. The ramrod straight stride, no nonsense crew cut hair, and a steel glint in his blue eyes projected an aura of competence that Scott found reassuring.

Scott reached to shake Streeter's hand.

"Sorry to meet under these circumstances, sir," his tone urgent, but polite. "I'm the agent charged with finding your children. Let me be up front. We suspect they've been kidnapped."

Scott felt Katie sag at his side. He tightened his hold, waiting for Streeter to continue, wanting to hear more, but aching to see Jackie. To see for himself that she was okay.

"Time is of the utmost importance. We need to go over every possible angle with you. We have Dr. Monroe's statement." A deferential nod to Katie. "But I want to review everything with both of you."

"I understand, Agent Streeter," Scott said, but my wife and I need a few moments with our daughter.

"Understood," said Streeter. "But quickly, please."

The mall manager had secured a secluded conference room for Lucy, Danielle, and Jackie. He'd sent in sandwiches wrapped in plastic, a variety of chips, and soft drinks. As Scott and Katie stepped inside, they all rose, one by one, and exchanged silent hugs. All except Danielle, who hung back. When Scott went to her, the sobs she tried to muffle poured out, "Uncle Scott, I'm so sorry. If only I hadn't left them."

"None of that, Danielle." Scott gathered her in his arms. "No blame, promise me?"

Danielle nodded, but didn't stop crying. Then Scott felt a tug on the pocket of his pants.

"Dad, you have to find Alex and Sam. Mom's really scared and so am I."

Scott bent down to pick up Jackie as if she were a toddler. She looked so fragile in her butterfly outfit, trimmed in blue. So alone without her sisters. His girls were always together. Had never spent a night without each other. Although he and Katie kept promising to let each of them, independently, spend a night with a friend, so far they hadn't. Much to Jackie's chagrin, she, ever the agitator for more independence.

"Everything will be okay, Jackie," Scott promised, praying that he was right. "I am so glad to see you, honey. I was worried about you, too."

"When Danielle and I came out of the movie, they never showed up. The policemen and a nice policelady asked me questions, and I told them the truth. Even though I had to say some things about Sammie — like how she's naughty a lot."

"Jackie, you were so helpful," Katie said, leaning heavily into Scott as he held Jackie in his arms.

"Honey, the FBI have to talk to Mom and me," said Scott, "so you can go home with Grandma. Okay?"

"Scott," Katie said, turning her face to his, "I think that Jackie should stay with us. For now, until we know more."

"I know everything about Sammie and Alex," Jackie said. "I want to stay here, with you."

"Tell you what," Scott said, setting Jackie down. "If the police have a question, they can call you at Grandma's."

"Okay," Jackie said, "but you and Mom just gotta find them. They must be so scared. Especially Alex."

"You say your prayers," Scott said, kissing Jackie on the top of her head as Lucy stepped forward to take her hand.

Katie took Jackie's other hand, gently tugging the child toward her. "She wants to stay with us, and I think it's best."

Lucy released her granddaughter's hand with a sad shake of her head. Scott knew his mother-in-law well. She did not approve, but she was not going to interfere.

On his way to Detroit, alone in the cabin of the chartered plane, Scott had racked his brain. Why would two of his daughters go off on their own? They were sensible nine year olds. He and Katie had always kidded about Sam's wild streak, but compared to other girls her age, Sam was well behaved and trustworthy. And Alex? Alex personified the obedient and loving child. He and Katie sometimes worried that she was too compliant.

Scott could not even contemplate a life without their three daughters. He and Katie had both been thirty-eight years old and married thirteen years before their daughters were born. He, a professional baseball player, a catcher for the Yankees, until a catastrophic collision at home plate and two cracked vertebrae in his neck ended his career. He'd been twenty-nine years old and devastated. He'd dedicated his whole life to baseball. But in the end, that fanaticism and his popularity with the players landed him a job with the Yankees as manager of spring training operations at George M. Steinbrenner, formerly Legends Field, in Tampa. Over the years, his popularity had not waned as he'd become a sports media personality. When baseball commentary was required, Scott Monroe was the favorite go-to expert. The reason he was in the Bronx today was to moderate the ESPN pregame show for the much touted subway series between the Yankees and the Mets.

But much more important than baseball to Scott had always been Katie. He'd met her during her medical school surgical rotation when she'd diagnosed his hernia. She'd just ended a long-term relationship, and after their first date, a Detroit Tigers baseball game, he'd known that she was the woman for him. Neither had a problem with the concept of an interracial marriage, and they married a year later. Now, Katie was a forensic pediatric psychiatrist in Tampa. They lived on Davis Island in Tampa and, to their eternally incredulous delight, were parents of nine-year-old triplets. Even more incredulous, the triplets were identical. Identical triplets, conceived without the aid of fertility treatments; the chances of that, an astounding one in two hundred million pregnancies.

Wherever they went, the girls attracted attention. "Are they triplets?" "Are they identical?" "Do multiples run in the family?" "Did you have fertility treatments?" and on and on until Katie and Scott would just laugh and say, "Yes, yes, no, no."

Neither Scott nor Katie minded these questions, but they'd always been wary that their daughters attracted attention in another sense, too. Scott, of European descent was six foot two, muscular, with light, freckled skin, hazel eyes, crew cut brown hair, and a brilliant toothy smile. Katie, an African American, was trim at five foot five, with shoulder-length black hair, creamy dark brown skin, brown eyes, and a gleaming smile. They realized that they were a handsome, but unusual, couple and they'd adopted a nonplussed attitude as they accepted as inevitable the omniscient stares and double takes when they were out and about with their three identical little girls whose skin tones exactly blended Scott and Katie's. But as complacent as Katie was about attracting attention, she was adamant about not letting the girls out of her sight. She'd seen enough atrocities to convince her that evil can lurk beneath a thin veneer of assumed innocence.

Agent Streeter was waiting for the Monroe parents in a small office off the mall manager's suite. Head bowed, he massaged his temples, trying to dispel the irrational. Two nine-year-old girls were missing. How would he react if they were his? How could he comfort Marianne? Or were the missing girls' parents somehow involved? Too many times things were not as they seemed. Too many times with missing children the parents had been implicated. He tried to recollect details of the Madeleine McCann case, the four-year-old British girl who had gone missing while vacationing in Portugal several years ago. Her parents had been considered suspects, of that he was quite sure. He even recalled the Portuguese term, they'd had *arguido* status.

A knock at the door and Streeter jumped up, smoothing his wiry crew cut, straightening the maroon striped tie, not bothering to button the suit jacket. He was facing two choices. Step up his fitness program or move up to size forty. He acknowledged the Monroes politely, noting that Scott still had that athletic build, lean and buff, the look he used to have back when Streeter and Marianne were still together. Back before a steady diet of junk food.

As the Monroes gathered at the conference table, Streeter hesitated a moment to see what they'd do with Jackie. Dr. Monroe proceeded to settle the child on her lap. Scott Monroe pulled his chair close to them, and Jackie reached out to pat him on his arm, a tender, natural gesture. Could these parents be behind the abduction? Had they for some perverse reason wanted to eliminate two of their three kids? For a long moment he just observed, all his senses tuned to the Monroe parents. All he could feel was their profound distress and Jackie's total trust. His impression: these parents were not faking. How could the confusion and grief etched on their twisted, tear-stained faces not be genuine?

He needed to get started despite his discomfort with exposing the child to uncomfortable questions. Streeter began his interrogation gingerly, then moved to rapid fire: Who would want to do this? How much were the Monroes worth? Answer: comfortable, but not wealthy enough to make them a ransom target. Any enemies? No. What about professional motives? Anything to do with baseball rivalries? No, everybody loved and respected Scott Monroe. How about Katie? Her pediatric psychiatry practice? Testimony in child abuse cases – physical as well as sexual – sending perpetrators to jail, removing children from abusive parents? Sex offenders exposed? How many vengeful adversaries had she accumulated? Plenty.

But nothing in Michigan, Katie insisted as she kept twisting her daughter's hair in and out of a braid. All that was in Florida, and much of it before a five-year hiatus between the birth of the triplets and when they'd started kindergarten four years ago. Wasn't it too much of a stretch to think that a child abuser or sexual pervert would track her to Detroit to abduct her children?

Streeter wondered. The evil he'd seen in human beings defied logic and exceeded the worst horrors that most people could not even dream. Except for Katie Monroe, she'd seen that kind of evil. He could imagine the desperate scenarios that must be playing in her mind.

Streeter's first impression of Katie had been admiration. A woman with the guts to go up against the scumbags of the world in order to protect little children. Tough, raising a family and holding down such an emotionally demanding job. She was different from his ex-wife, Marianne, who seemed exhausted just taking care of their kids.

To him it seemed cruel to keep hammering Katie with questions, but he had to be relentless if he was to find her daughters. After two solid hours, a faraway look crept into Katie's eyes and Streeter realized that he'd hit the point of diminishing returns.

"Let's take a break," he suggested.

As Streeter headed for Plummer's inner office, he knew he'd need to uncover the worst of the child abusers that Katie had helped put away. He'd have the Tampa field office pull court records to generate leads. But his interrogation did identify one glaring person of interest. Dr. Monroe was scheduled to testify in a child sexual abuse case the following week. Guy by the name of Maxwell Cutty.

Streeter picked up Plummer's phone and called the Tampa field office. He spoke to the special agent in charge and asked that Dr. Katie Monroe's cases, whatever was in the public domain, be pulled with immediate attention on Cutty. He asked for subpoenas to access whatever was sealed. It would be a long night in Detroit and in Tampa, too.

Could the abduction of the Monroe kids be racially motivated? Streeter wondered. The Monroes were a mixed-race couple. Could there be a maniac bigot out there who would do the unthinkable? Detroit was a fanatical place and Streeter knew his history; riots in 1943 and in 1967. The city never had recovered from them, and now with the collapse of the auto industry who could predict what might erupt? Hate crimes were on the rise. He searched his memory for details of the bureau's recent briefing on white supremacy organizations and grimaced. The National Socialist Movement (NSM), one of the country's largest neo-Nazi groups, was based right there in Detroit.

# CHAPTER 4

*Two Tampa Children Missing in Detroit Suburb.*
— *Tampa Morning News*, Monday, June 15

Maxwell Cutty tossed and turned, the silk sheets cool against his skin. He hated sleeping alone and craved the warmth of a young body, male or female, either would do. He hit the muted light on his night stand and reached into the drawer for his bottle of Ambien. He shook out two tablets and gulped them down with the bottled water he kept by his bedside. No wonder he had trouble sleeping. His life had spun out of control. First Olivia, his wife, had screwed him over big time when she found out that he was gay, or bisexual, as he'd tried to explain.They could have lived together in the house with their sons. They could have remained partners in the business they had built together. But no, Olivia had freaked. Kicked him out of his own house — at least temporarily. Damn near bankrupted him, demanding her share of the business. Then that bullshit about the boys — way over the edge even for that vindictive bitch. Oh yes, Olivia deserved what she got.

But Olivia's revenge was in the past. Maxwell's most hurtful betrayal still stung. Adam Kaninsky, his young lover, had been penniless, loaded with student loans after he'd graduated with a degree in architecture. And Maxwell had taken him in. Taken him as an intern into his firm, taken him into his home, taken him into his heart. Only to be betrayed, to have Adam tell that Monroe shrink hideous lies about him and his own sons. How could such a beautiful creature be so unappreciative?

Maxwell tossed off the light blanket. Then suddenly chilled, he pulled it back over his naked body. Adam, that self-righteous ingrate, was far out of reach by now. So why not just try and get some sleep? Adam would not show up at the hearing. That doctor-bitch would not get away with her fucking lies and innuendoes. Hell, more than innuendoes. That bitch was trying to put him on a public pervert list. Even worse, she wanted him behind bars. No way that was going to happen. He knew what inmates did to child molesters. He'd made fucking sure she would not testify in tomorrow's trial.

Having finally drifted off to sleep, Maxwell awoke to the intrusive ring of the phone. Groggily, he searched the inky blackness for the luminescent dial of his clock. 1:33 a.m. He picked up the receiver and mumbled a hello. Nothing. Must be a wrong number. With a jerk, he disconnected the phone, planning to bury his head back under the blanket, when he stopped. Was that the doorbell?

Maxwell kept a pair of velour shorts at the foot of the bed. Hesitating long enough to make sure he was not hearing things, he slipped out of bed, donned the shorts, grabbed a robe, and headed for the front door. By then the pleasant ring of the bell was accompanied by insistent pounding. What the heck? Should he answer it or call the police? Subsequent shouts of "FBI!" settled his dilemma. What the fuck was going on? This was a prestigious neighborhood. What would the neighbors think?

Again, Maxwell hesitated. This time to take a deep breath. Did this have to do with Adam? Another deep breath and a gulp. Did this have to do with Olivia? No, impossible, he determined, flipping on the array of porch lights.

With an expression of sleepy bewilderment, he inched open the front door. Badges flashed. Several of them.

"What the fuck?" flew out of his mouth.

"FBI. Are you Maxwell Cutty?"

"Yes," Maxwell shrunk back far enough to allow them to enter. "What do you want?"

The agents introduced themselves. Rather politely, making Maxwell relax just for an instant before they told him they needed him downtown to answer some questions. They wouldn't tell him why. Shouldn't he call his lawyer? Or should he appear innocent and just go with the pricks? Shit, he had a court appearance that day, and he needed his lawyer well rested. He decided to comply, see what the feds wanted, and go from there. One of the agents waited by the door and the others followed Maxwell into his bedroom and stood there, watching him change into khakis and a golf shirt. That must be a violation of his rights, Maxwell thought, but he said nothing, just gave the impression that he was willing to go along with all their crap even when they patted him down for weapons.

On the way to FBI Headquarters, few words were exchanged. Once there, the agents led Maxwell into a brightly lit rectangular room. Inside was a conference table around which were placed four chairs. They motioned for him to sit in one, the one closest to shackles bolted to the floor. Then the agents left. When Maxwell heard the bolt slide shut behind them, he felt a sick panic. He couldn't help suppress a scream, "I want my lawyer."

But the agents did not return for a very long time.

# CHAPTER 5

*Search for Missing Monroe Children Intensifies in Auburn Hills.*
— *Morning Detroit News*, Monday, June 15

Every light in the Hill Mall shone bright through the early hours of the morning. The cleaning crew had been scrutinized by the police as they reported for work. Then they'd been told to report any sign of the missing girls. No one reported anything. Not a single scrap of evidence that Alex or Sammie Monroe had ever been in that mall. Special Agent Tony Streeter mopped sweat off his forehead, as he returned to Clarence Plummer's office.

"Looks like you could use a pop." The big man grimaced as he held out an ice-cold can of Vernors ginger ale.

Streeter had recently relocated from the Los Angeles office to Detroit, and still hadn't gotten use to the way Michiganders called soft drinks "pop" and how they loved their Vernors. Thirteen years ago, he had joined the FBI right out of Georgetown Law School. He was assigned to Chicago, and three cities and three children later, his wife, Marianne, could take the life no longer. The irreconcilable issue: she'd been no competition for her husband's total dedication to the job. Three years ago she packed up his daughters, now eight, six, and four, and moved back to her hometown, Grand Rapids, Michigan. That's why he'd requested a transfer to Detroit. Tony missed his girls and was gunning for the SAC job for the Detroit office, special agent in charge. Maybe then he'd go to Marianne, ask her to reconsider. At the very least he'd stay in Michigan, only 150 miles from his daughters. Streeter figured that if he solved this apparent kidnapping case quickly and efficiently, he'd have a crack at that promotion.

"Only ones left here are the mom and dad and the poor little kid," said Plummer, slapping Streeter on the back like they were old buddies. "The grandma and cousin and the aunt were reluctant to leave, but I convinced them that there's nothing they can do here. Just wish the parents had let the girl leave, but tell you the truth, I can see why they want her by their side. Just in case — protective instinct."

Tony thought of his own girls. How Marianne would react? How he would react? He'd be insane with fear, he knew that. "You have kids?" he asked Plummer.

"Yeah, a daughter. Grown. My pride and joy. How about you?"

"Three daughters. Oldest just a year younger than the Monroe girls."

"We'll find them, Agent Streeter," Plummer said. "You just let me know what more I can do. I'll work day and night."

"Call me Tony. Okay? You did a fine job tonight. Nobody could have jumped on this faster. You found the only lead we have."

"Didn't pan out to be much. Just that Davis woman with two little kids who 'thinks' she saw the two Monroe kids walk out with a middle-aged woman. Nondescript, useless description. Not fat, but overweight. Medium height. Musta been a few thousand of them in the mall. Teased auburn hair, gray streaks. In 'frumpy' dark blue housedress."

"We'll take another go at her tomorrow."

"Hopefully without her screaming brats," Plummer said. "Makes me wonder if I really do want grandkids."

"She did seem pretty stressed out, our lone witness," Streeter said. "First thing tomorrow, I want to set up an interview process for all your employees that worked the afternoon shift yesterday. I know that's a tall order, but somebody must have seen something. We'll especially squeeze those working in and around the movie theatre. Meantime, I'm going to talk to the parents, then head back to the field office. I'll have an open line for you to call in anything. I'm not one of those Feds that take all the glory. I'll take all the help I can get."

Streeter found Katie and Scott in each other's arms, sobbing with abandon. What else could they do?

Thankfully, the little girl was asleep on a bench, her head resting on her mother's purse.

"Uh, excuse me, Mr. Monroe, Dr. Monroe. Why don't you go get some rest?"

"Not until you find my daughters," Katie said, her voice hoarse from crying. "I just can't."

"I'm leaving for my office now," he told them. "It'll be easier for me to work the system there."

"Then we'll go with you," said Scott as he and Katie stood.

What could Streeter do? Of course he'd let them accompany him. They'd be dead on their feet as would he, but if they were up to it, he'd keep pushing them, especially the doctor. He was sure there was more to be learned about her past, and the shady people that she'd pissed off as a forensic psychiatrist. He wondered what had possessed her to chose such an unseemly career. Treating the children of abuse and kids with all kinds of mental illness, that he could understand, sort of. But going head-to-head with abusers, pitting her expert opinion against the lowest rung of human deviants? It took a special person, and from what he'd been hearing from the Tampa district attorney, Katie Monroe was a special person, indefatigable, tough, yet compassionate. But what he was seeing now was a woman unraveling, faltering, unsure of herself. Streeter had seen this before and he'd seen the opposite, too, with mothers, passive and meek, who'd transformed in a crisis threatening their children into aggressive tigers.

During the ride into downtown Detroit, Streeter sat up front with his driver and the Monroes in the backseat. All were quiet on the ride as Jackie slept in her father's arms and Streeter contemplated the most difficult of questions. Had either parent played a role in Sammie and Alex's disappearance?

The Sunday evening news had reported the missing Monroe children, but by Monday morning the story exploded throughout Detroit, across Florida, and was going national. Despite their lack of sleep, Streeter had advised the Monroe's to tape an appeal. Scott wanted to spare Katie, but in the end they both sat in front of the cameras, teary eyed and in voices hoarse from endless crying, pleading for the safe return of their daughters. Both parents had experience with the media, but huddled together, they looked like innocent children themselves, so pathetically scared were they. The networks lobbied for an interview with the third triplet, Jackie. Katie and Scott refused. Yes, they would provide photos and videos of the triplets if that would help.

By mid-morning, the viewing world had become obsessed with the triplet images, trying to decipher which was which. Friends and teachers were approached for interviews by the media, soon followed by the Tampa police, looking for any clue. By afternoon, stories of the girls' individual personalities became talk-show fodder. Sammie, the feisty one; Alex, the shy one; Jackie, the friendly one. Added to that was a rehash of Scott's baseball career, all the old pictures, the replay of the injury that took him out of the sport. The local Tampa station ran video clips from the girls' baseball games. "Condors" in red letters against white uniforms. Sammie, the pitcher; Jackie, shortstop; Alex at third. Startling, the alacrity of media access to show-and-tell video content.

With all the publicity flack, it was after one o'clock when Agent Streeter called each parent, one at a time, into his office for another interrogation.

Streeter had spoken to the manager of the New York Yankees just prior to leading Scott into his office. Don Plese pretty much corroborated what Scott had told him. Scott was a stand-up guy. Players liked him. Managers liked him. Hell, even opposing teams liked him. Type of guy that transcended cultures, races, social strata. Any enemies? No, but a qualified no. His job did require decisions. Who would move up to the majors. Who wouldn't. Any vendettas against him? None known. Any family troubles? No, the guy was a dedicated husband and father, devout Catholic. Gave out Communion at Mass. No girlfriends hiding in the closet, or boyfriends for that matter? An adamant no, that Streeter believed credible. Any racial problems? After all, the guy was white married to a black woman. Any inkling of threats or taunts from bigots, racists, ordinary rednecks? Not that anyone in the Yankee organization knew about. Scott had white friends, black friends, Asians, Hispanic, you name it. Did Scott Monroe qualify for sainthood? Streeter had asked. The answer came back, "yes."

Streeter interrogated Scott more about Katie than about himself.

About the nature of her job. The creepy people she helped put away. And there were plenty. Sexual predators and monsters who abused kids both physically and psychologically. But, Scott admitted, much of what Katie did was covered under doctor-patient privilege and had to remain confidential. But Streeter could see that this line of questioning scared the hell out of Scott. That his wife was exposed to horrors so heinous that she could not even divulge.

The bottom line for Streeter, "Would any of these creeps want to hurt Katie so desperately that they'd take her kids?"

Scott could not answer that. He could only stare ahead and finally mumble, "I don't know."

When Katie replaced Scott in his conference room, Streeter could see that she was fading into uselessness.

"Dr. Monroe," he began, "I do need to talk to you about Maxwell Cutty, but I'll keep it brief. The FBI questioned him during the night. You were supposed to testify in his trial today?"

"Yes," she said, looking up at Streeter, eyes so swollen that he wondered if she could see.

"As you know, he made a threat of sorts toward you and toward the judge the last time you were in court. Remember?"

"Yes. He said something like, 'How would you like someone – fucking – in the head of your kid?' Those were his actual words to me. The judge threatened him with sanctions." Then Katie leaned forward, a sudden pulse of energy flashed in her eyes. "Agent Streeter, are you telling me that he took my daughters?"

"His hearing on child abuse charges has been postponed because you won't be there, but no, we can't link him to your daughters. We have nothing to hold him on."

The temporary spark went out of Katie and she slumped forward, fresh tears brimming. "I'm sorry, I can't think about anything but Alex and Sammie. About what might be happening to them? Where they might be?"

"Getting back to Mr. Cutty, Dr. Monroe, knowing his psychological profile, do you think he would try something like this? Take your children to keep you from testifying? He certainly has motive. Of course, he did not do it in person, but he has financial means."

"He's a sociopath who needs to be in jail, at the very least, isolated from children. But kidnapping my kids? Twelve hundred miles away?"

"We have to be thorough. What do you know about his live-in boyfriend, Adam Kaninsky?"

"Adam?" Katie sat up straighter, a wariness in her tone.

Katie stood up and started pacing. She asked for a glass of water. Streeter poured her some iced water. She drank slowly then sat back down. Settling her head in her hands, she began, "Here's what happened. Several months ago, Adam came to me in a professional setting. He said he had an ethical dilemma. He told me that he was gay and that he had a partner, an older man, a man with money and style, a man with two young sons, Aiden, seven, and Jake, five. He told me that he had witnessed his partner's sexual abuse of his sons."

"He was a witness?" Streeter tried to get her back on track.

"Adam said that Maxwell would take the boys in the shower with him. Adam didn't think there'd been anal penetration, per se, but he definitely used the kids as sex objects. The kids seemed to accept it as normal. Adam described them as submissive. I don't need to get into all the details."

"So why did he come to you?" Streeter asked.

"He felt bad for the kids. Adam wanted it to stop, but he didn't want to jeopardize his golden status with Maxwell."

"What did you tell him?"

"I told him to make an anonymous call to the Child Protection Agency. To use the hotline. That the call could not be traced to him. Then I also called the agency. Anonymously. Just to make sure."

"And now you're officially involved in the case. Isn't that a conflict, a breech of ethics?"

"Suppose it is?" Katie looked up, staring straight ahead, but avoiding eye contact. "I wanted to help keep those little boys safe."

For his fifty-fifth birthday, Pamela Spansky had treated her husband to a concert. They'd seen Evan's favorite female vocalist, Monica Monroe, at a sellout performance at the Fox Theatre Saturday evening. Being from Detroit, Monica reminded native Detroiters of the raging popularity of the Supremes back in the old days. Pamela's favorite was Celine Dion, a Canadian, and for her fiftieth, Evan had taken her to Las Vegas. That time they'd taken their two sons and flown from Toronto. This time they'd left the boys at home and driven from Toronto to Detroit. They'd booked two nights at the Renaissance Hotel to give them a day to recuperate. All had gone well, Monica had put on a spectacular show, but Pamela knew that Evan was anxious to head back home to check on their two sons, Craig and Tim. Not exactly children any more, at age fifteen and sixteen, but Evan was ever watchful, bordering on paranoid, she thought.

"Check out time's noon," Pamela called to her husband. "We told the boys we'd be home for dinner, but we have plenty of time for lunch before we leave."

Just as they were getting ready to leave their hotel room Monday morning, Evan called Pamela to take a look at the TV. "There's been a kidnapping. Right outside Detroit. Two little girls." Evan paused for a moment. "Geez, they're Scott Monroe's kids. He grew up here and he's Monica Monroe's brother. How awful for him."

Pamela joined him in front of the TV set. "His wife is black?"

"Guess so," Evan said, "that I didn't know. Cute kids. They were in town for the concert, too. How sad is that?"

"We have to check out, honey. Birthday's over."

With that, Evan clicked off the television.

# CHAPTER 6

*The U.S. Government Bailout Pits "Get's" vs "Get-Nots."*
— *Business News*, Monday, June 14, 2009

Maxwell Cutty paced the length of the great room. Back and forth. What he needed was a massage, a deep one. Sitting alone in that over air-conditioned holding room for hours stiffened his neck. No one had checked on him or asked if he wanted coffee. Then the agent in charge, a total prick, showed up, wanted to know about Adam. Where Adam was, specifically. And that line of questioning made Adam his first problem. Adam, the ingrate, was the root cause of this unacceptable situation. If he hadn't butted in, and told that shrink lies about how he treated his sons, Aiden and Jake, none of this would have happened. But, even so, Maxwell couldn't think of Adam's Adonis body without wondering who he was with? Just thinking of Adam gave him a hard-on. That distraction, he didn't need.

Maxwell wrung his hands, still feeling the rage that had erupted that night when Adam had spilled his guts. They'd gone to Bern's Steakhouse, just the two of them. Adam had been quiet, even moody, during dinner. For an after dinner drink, Maxwell had ordered the most expensive port on the legendary wine list. A real treat that would certainly cheer the boy up, but no, Maxwell watched as Adam's first tear trickled into the deep purple drink.

"What's wrong?" Maxwell had asked.

"I did something today." Maxwell had to lean forward to hear him although there were few remaining diners. "I went to see Dr. Katie. Dr. Katie Monroe, my old therapist," he'd confessed. "I needed her advice." Maxwell knew that Adam idolized this Doctor Katie. "I asked her, 'What should I do?' he'd said.

At first Maxwell had no idea what Adam was talking about. "Do about what?"

"About what I saw in the shower." Maxwell remembered how shaky Adam's voice had sounded and how Adam had refused to look him in the eye. "I didn't feel right about what you did to those two kids, Maxwell."

"I never hurt Aiden or Jack." His words came out too loud, and he'd glanced around the room.

"Dr. Katie used to tell me that men are not supposed to do that to kids," Adam had said. Maxwell had been grateful that he spoke in a voice so low it was difficult to hear. "That it's child abuse, sexual child abuse. I learned all about that. I'd never, ever, touch a kid."

Adam's body had started to tremble as he tried to steady the crystal stemware. "Maxwell, I don't want you to get in trouble, but—"

Maxwell's mind had been calculating. Okay, what if the boys were questioned? What would they say? All he'd done was rub his prick on their naked bodies. He hadn't stuck it inside, though he had wanted to, and would someday, once he got them back.

Whatever Adam had told that doctor would be in confidence, but Maxwell knew he could not take a chance. Adam wouldn't be testifying at the hearing. Neither would Dr. Katie.

The phone interrupted as Maxwell lingered on the consequences of Adam's unfortunate choice of a confidant. An organized, methodical person, he needed to think things through in stages. Too many things were happening too fast. He had to focus.

"Maxwell, I'm calling about your hearing."

Shit, his lawyer. Why had he picked up? But now that Greg Klingman was on the phone, should he tell him that he'd spent the night at FBI headquarters? While he was there, had the feds searched his house, taken his hard drive? He'd look stupid if he didn't mention it and Klingman already knew. But what would he say? That the feds thought he had something to do with the missing Monroe kids? What can of worms would that open up?

"Now that Dr. Monroe is unavailable, the judge wants a postponement. What a tragedy about her kids."

"Uh, Greg, now's not a good time," Maxwell mumbled. "Didn't get much sleep last night. Worrying about today."

"There's a lot we have to talk about — "

Maxwell hung up the phone and put it on "make busy." What he said was true, he did not do well with less than eight hours of sleep. He'd take an Ambien. When he felt refreshed, he'd go over everything. Was there anything on his computer that could tie him to Olivia or to Dr. Katie Monroe? He didn't think so, but just in case, he'd have to take action.

Maxwell slept four hours, awakening at two p.m. only because he'd set an alarm. Still groggy from the sleeping pill, but with clear priorities. First, scrambled eggs, microwave bacon, and strong coffee. Deal with Adam, permanently this time. That was clear to him now. He'd have to use a pay phone and hope that his contact got back to him quickly. After he took care of that, he'd decide whether to call his attorney and raise hell about the FBI questioning him last night. Surely hauling him out at that hour was an invasion of his civil rights? And, had they said anything about a search warrant? One thing at a time, he told himself.

Maxwell never left dirty dishes, and he felt his eyelids twitch when he forced himself to leave the house less than perfect. As an architect, he had to have his showcase house ready to impress potential clients, and he could not tolerate one article out of place. Here's where he and Olivia had seen eye to eye. As much as he did not like to admit it, the splendor of the house had just as much to do with her interior design talent as his architectural genius. For sure, one thing that he didn't miss about Aiden and Jake's temporary absence was their untidiness. On his way out the door, he glanced at the framed cover of *Architectural Digest* with a full-color spread of the elegant Cutty home. Too bad about Adam. He'd have been a perfect partner in this house. Those deep brown eyes, so expressive when they were making love. Longish black hair, very silky, so erotic. Just the thought aroused Maxwell, making him dizzy with desire.

As Maxwell climbed into his Lexus, he tried to decide from where to place the call? Not Carrollwood, where he lived, but Ybor City, where the guy who called himself "Vincent" hung out.

The call went to voice mail. "This is Mr. Justice," he said, using the same name he'd used before. "Call me as soon as possible. I have something for you." Maxwell gave him the pay phone number. He did not see the forest green minivan with the dark windows lurking at the corner of the block.

He waited fifteen minutes before the phone rang. "What's up?" asked the familiar masculine voice.

"We need to talk. I have a job. Has to be done immediately."

"No way. I'm outta here on a long vacation. Out of the country, man."

"Good. My job's out of the country, too. Nevis. Island in the Caribbean."

"I know where Nevis is," the hit man said. "Look, I got no time to haggle. You say Nevis. Yeah, it might work. Meet me tomorrow morning eleven sharp with details. Same place, but come with the money. You know the drill. Seein' it's a rush job, it'll be complicated. Bring a hundred fifty, all up front this time."

Before Maxwell could protest at such an exorbitant price, the connection was severed, leaving that buzz in his ear. Last time he had hired Vincent – the only time – it had set him back one hundred grand. Cash in hundreds. Then he'd had more time to plan.

Maxwell slammed down the receiver and considered his limited options. He had to get his hands on a hundred fifty grand. He checked his Rolex: 3:05. Enough time to get to the bank. Premonition told him to get the money now, not wait until morning, just in case the feds decided to freeze his accounts. Although he didn't think they could do that. If they had anything on him, they wouldn't have let him go. He didn't have that kind of cash in his personal account, so he'd have to take it from the firm. Shouldn't be a problem with a half-a-million line of credit, but there'd be scrutiny by the fucking accountants. No big deal, he'd have time to replenish the money once he could get at his brokerage account and sell enough stock or go with a margin loan, whatever. He was a professional architect and a damned successful one. But the man called Vincent was right about this job, it could be complicated.

Streeter picked up the call from Special Agent Emmitt Rusk, his counterpart in Tampa.

"Cutty went into a bank? What the heck did he do in there?" Massaging his forehead with the palm of both hands, he took a deep breath, then pinched the bridge of his nose. He needed sleep. He'd been awake for almost forty hours.

"Can't be sure," said Rusk. "He went into a private office at the Bank of America with one of the vice presidents. Went in and came out with a canvas case. Without a warrant, we're not going to get anything from the bank."

"Follow him. Let's get a warrant to access all his financial accounts, personal and business. Meantime, I'm going to crash for a couple of hours, but call me if you get anything."

Streeter had sent Katie and Scott home empty. Without a scrap of information. There'd been no ransom note. No trace of the little girls. His only lead, Maxwell Cutty. Not much to go on there, but he'd milk it for all it was worth. As the Tampa field office held Cutty for questioning, they'd gotten a warrant to search his house and seized his computer. They'd found zero evidence of the missing Monroe girls, but they were still going through his hard drive. It was obvious that he had not personally snatched the girls in Detroit, then made it back to Tampa to be found alone in his own bed in his night clothes in the wee hours of the morning. But a man of his sophistication, financial means, and deviant personality had ways and means and motive. Dr. Kate Monroe had been about to nail his ass in court. To what extremes would he go to prevent that?

Exhausted as he was, Streeter took one last look at the e-mailed photo of the elegant architect. Age forty-two, dark brown hair, feathered with a tinge of stylish grey just at the temples, so perfect that Streeter suspected he had it colored. The eyes were deep blue and just a touch too sunken as they peered vainly at the camera. Katie said he was narcissistic, and his image fit the bill.

Streeter then picked up two other photos. In his right hand, Adam Kaninsky, a candid shot outside the Cutty home, looking smug and coquettish in shorts and a tank top. Dark hair, too long in Streeter's opinion, large soulful eyes, and a buffed smooth body. In his left hand, he held an image of the late Olivia Cutty. Same age as Maxwell, they had graduated together and worked side-by-side in the business they built. Streeter studied Olivia's photo. She had aged faster than her husband, not usual for a woman. In the black tailored suit she looked sallow and too thin. A fragile appearance that didn't match the tough business personality her friends described. The "brains behind the firm" was the refrain that kept reappearing in her file.

Streeter resolved to dig deeper into the investigation of her death. A death ruled accidental by Hillsbourgh County authorities, a death entirely too convenient for Mr. Maxwell Cutty, surviving partner, single father, out-of-the-closet gay man.

What had caused the Cutty marriage to break up? According to the file: When Olivia Cutty found out her husband was homosexual, she insisted on a divorce. Judgment of divorce gave her the house and typical joint child custody with Mrs. Cutty named custodial parent.

Seemed straightforward, Streeter thought. Just like Marianne and him. He had every other weekend with his girls — unless the job got in the way. He had every other holiday, too.

Then Olivia Cutty drowns, falls off a yacht cruising Tampa Bay. The boat belonged to Olivia's date, who was also her sister's boss and editor of the *Tampa Tribune*. Streeter rubbed his eyes, forcing them to scour the accident report one more time. There was a fire on board, a faulty fuel pump. While her host and the two couples on board hustled to find the fire extinguisher, call for help, scurry about, and do whatever had to be done to put out the fire, Olivia, a weak swimmer at best, simply disappeared. Once the fire was contained, the remaining five people started to look for her. Several days later, her body washed up on shore. Cause of death: drowning, confirmed on autopsy. Boys' custody reverts to Maxwell, and they all moved back into the big house. This time with Adam. Case closed.

Had Olivia suspected or even known that her ex-husband was molesting her sons?

Streeter put the case file down. His heart went out to the Cutty kids. Hillsborough County Child Protective Services had placed them temporarily with Olivia's sister, Roberta. What would happen to them if their father went to jail? But that was not his immediate problem.

He couldn't let anything distract him from finding the Monroe twins. He corrected himself, they were not twins. Exhausted, Streeter slipped off his jacket, laid down on the floor, and was asleep before his head hit the carpet.

# CHAPTER 7

*Former Yankee Catcher, Scott Monroe, in Detroit Following Abduction of Two of His Triplet Daughters.*
— Sports News Networks, Monday, June 15

Cliff Hunter crushed another sheet of lined yellow paper in his big hands. The thin tablet was almost used up. He had to get this right. At first he'd made an outline. First, tell Scott Monroe that he had his daughters; second, decide on the amount of money; third, warn the parents not to call in the law; fourth, set a timetable; fifth, threaten to take the third girl. He wanted to get the language just right. He didn't want to sound too smart, as if he could even if he wanted to; he didn't want to sound too dumb. He wanted respect and he wanted money and he wanted payback.

Cliff's biggest problem was how to make the demand. He'd considered his options, but hadn't yet decided. The FBI would naturally be monitoring Monroe's house, his wife's office, probably both of their parents' places, but maybe not Scott's employer, the Yankee's central office in New York.

Next, he had to decide how to deliver the demand. His first choice would have been to do it by e-mail. Quick. Convenient since he had access to the e-mail addresses of both parents, work and home. But Cliff knew his limitations. He was not technology savvy, but he knew that the feds could track e-mails, so he ruled out cyberspace. That left the post office, or a delivery service like FedEx or UPS, or the phone. He was leaning toward the phone, but he wasn't sure which number to use. He could disguise his voice on a phone message, either in person or if it went to voice mail. Voice message would be preferable, and he knew how to use the Yankee organization's voice messaging system.

There was the matter of where to set up the exchange – money for kids – and since he'd already scouted out potential sites, he could finalize that in a hurry. The precious little girls for the big bag of money. But of course, he would not disclose that until the last possible moment.

His last problem was what would happen next. He'd have to leave the country. He was no fool. With the FBI swarming all over this case, they'd find him one way or the other. By then he'd be in Portugal. He had relatives there, and he'd stay as long as he pleased. He wondered if he'd take up Portuguese. Probably not, he'd never been good at languages, not clever enough. Not even English, he'd been told. Fuck them all. They'd find out how fucking smart Cliff turned out to be. Or maybe not. If all went perfectly, maybe no one would find out at all.

His cell phone rang just as he was about to pen another draft.

"Yup."

A buddy reminding him that there'd be pick-up baseball at the park at five that night.

"Be there," he said. *Once I get this fucking message the way I want it.*

# CHAPTER 8

*Detroit Staggers Under the Recession and the Auto Industry Crisis — Auto Suppliers Aid Request Refused.*
— National Financial News, Monday, June 14

Scott and Katie and Jackie had returned to Lucy's townhouse in Auburn Hills. Throughout the day, relatives came and went. All trying to prop up Scott and Katie's hopes, but with tears in their eyes signaling unfathomable grief. What could they do? Nothing but pray. Except for Scott's sister, Monica, who could and would offer any amount of money for the safe return of her nieces. World renowned vocalist, Monica Monroe's concert Saturday night at The Fox Theatre was the reason that Katie and the girls had been in Detroit. That, and the fact that Katie loved to spend as much time as possible with her mother, Lucy.

When Scott carried Jackie upstairs and laid her down on a pile of comforters on the floor next to their bed, he and Katie had tried to rest, but neither drifted off to sleep. For each other's sake, they each kept quiet, but they were too terrified for sleep. Too terrified for Sammie and Alex. *Where were they? What was happening to them. Were they safe?*

Finally Katie sat up, followed by Scott. "There must be *something* that we can do," she said. "We can't just lie here and do *nothing.*"

"It's the helpless feeling," Scott said. "I'm their father and I can't protect them. All I can think is what might be happening."

Katie propped herself up on two pillows and leaned in close to Scott, relaxing just a bit as he stroked her hair. "We're so used to being in charge, being in control."

"Mom? Dad? Did they find Alex and Sam yet?" Jackie stirred on the floor below them. Just hearing her voice tore at Katie's heart. The triplets each had their own special way of speaking, but their voices sounded so alike.

Both parents avoided Jackie's question.

"Let's go downstairs and get a snack, Jackie," Katie suggested as she and Scott climbed out of bed.

Lucy turned up the volume of the television as the three of them came downstairs. "Here you are," she said, "on TV. With all the commotion outside, I can hardly hear anything." She pointed to the throngs of reporters staking out their ground, congesting access to the residential community. "I want to keep the door open for the spring air, but it's so noisy out there."

All the Jones and Monroe relatives gathered in the living room paused, silent, as Katie and Scott and Jackie joined them just in time to watch the televised appeal.

"Mommy, you did good on TV and, Daddy, your voice sounded so loud," Jackie said after the reporter repeated the hotline phone number and Web site and the video cut to footage outside Lucy's house. She walked over to the window. "Why don't all those people just go away?"

Scott blinked away a tear. How long had it been since any of the girls had called Katie "mommy" and him "daddy"? For years it had been just "Mom" and "Dad."

"They all want to find Alex and Sammie," Lucy said, patting Jackie's head. "They don't seem to be stopping my neighbors from bringing over all that food. How are we ever going to eat all this?" Lucy drew Jackie over to a table laden with casseroles, cakes, pies, cookies, and pitchers of lemonade.

"Katie, I wish you'd let Jackie come home with us." Sharon joined Jackie at the window, putting her arm around her niece. "She could practice piano, swim in the pool, play tennis, get her mind off — "

"Thanks," Katie said. "but I think it's best if we all stay here. We're closer to the mall, should we get word — "

All the while the talking head on the TV kept going on and on about the Monroe triplets, Jackie, who was safe, Alex and Sammie who were missing.

"You want me to turn that off?" Lucy asked. "Or change channels?"

"It's okay, Lucy," Scott said, getting up to turn down the volume.

The story of the two missing triplets dominated the TV news, talk TV, sports TV, and the radio. At first Scott and Katie had tried to shield Jackie from the most dire of scenarios as channels out-hyped each other. Kidnapping "experts" filled the airwaves, titillated by the lack of a ransom note, the looming threat of racial prejudice, their Aunt Monica – an idol among music fans – Scott's baseball notoriety, Katie's work with the sleaze of society, the rarity of identical triplets, and the biology of such, and the fact that the three little girls were simply adorable. The fact that four-year-old Madeleine McCann had not yet been found. That the parents had been suspects, and that the mother's name was Kate.

"All that talk mobilizes volunteers." Scott nodded at the flickering screen.

"Lots of people are looking. Right, Dad?"

"Yes," said Scott, taking Jackie's hand as a collage of his daughters danced across the screen. He wondered where all those images had come from. The triplets as infants, the triplets in white First Communion dresses, the triplets in their parochial school uniform, the triplets playing baseball. Their little friends had been interviewed, playing into the reporters' hands as they described the three distinct personalities. Alex: shy, sweet, always in the shadow of the other two. Sammie: aggressive, opinionated, outspoken. Jackie: friendly, helpful, energetic. And endless speculation as to how Jackie, the *safe* child would fare.

How could it be healthy for Jackie to see all this? Yet, how could they keep her away?

"Mom, could I go home with Aunt Sharon?" Jackie had turned her back to the TV and was munching on an oatmeal cookie. "Danielle and I could play Monopoly and do other stuff. We could take some of these cookies."

Jackie's innocent request made Scott cringe. He knew that Katie was not comfortable letting Jackie out of her sight. But was that fair to Jackie?

"I think we're going to need you today," Katie said, accepting one of the cookies Jackie offered.

"Katie, let's not bring her to the bureau." Scott gave Jackie an I'll-take-care-of-your-mother look. "If you don't want her to go with your sister, let her stay with Grandma."

Katie put down her half-eaten cookie and took both of Scott's hands. "Baby, I'm so scared," she said, her brown eyes brimming with tears. Can't we keep Jackie close to us — just for now? Please?"

Scott's resolve melted. He want to say, "You're scaring her. Let the family distract her." But he kept his mouth shut, understanding her reaction, fright was overriding compassion.

"We told Agent Streeter that we'd be back later tonight," Katie said. "Can we get going?"

Scott struggled, his spirits sagging. What good could they do? Hadn't they told the FBI everything? Checking his watch, he felt his heart sink. Twenty-four hours ago he'd been at Yankee Stadium. Twenty-four hours ago Lucy had called from the mall. Twenty-four hours without a clue. Where could Alex and Sammie be?

Then the cell phone that the FBI provided rang. The sound and vibration coming from his shirt pocket penetrated his skin and stopped his heart. For a moment he and Katie stood, paralyzed.

"Scott, answer it!" she said, dropping her purse and Jackie's hand to go to him.

"Mr. Monroe, this is Agent Ellen Camry. I wanted to catch you, just to let you know. We don't have anything specific for you here, and Special Agent Streeter asked me to call and ask that you come into the bureau tomorrow, not tonight. We'll have a lot to go over once we finish tearing apart both yours and your wife's hard drive and once we check out all the Florida leads."

"Katie and I are on our way. There must be something —"

"You and your wife need some sleep, sir. She's a doctor, so I'm assuming that you can get sleeping pills or sedatives if need be."

"I see," said Scott, torn between the agent's sensible advice, and wanting to be there to personally keep up the pressure to find Sammie and Alex. "Please do everything you can to —" He couldn't finish, his mind flooded with images of Sammie and Alex, his two little girls. Where could they be? The possibilities were endless, each more horrific than the next.

When Scott told Katie, she slumped against him. "Tomorrow," she mumbled. "Another night. I don't know if I can do this."

# CHAPTER 9

*Detroit Red Wings Lose in Stanley Cup Finals:*
*Pittsburgh Wins Two Major Pro-Sports Titles*
*Already This Year – Penguins and Steelers.*
– Sports Radio, June 15, 2009

At nine o'clock on Tuesday morning, Scott and Katie, Jackie between them, were ushered into the conference room adjoining Special Agent Streeter's office. Scott noticed dark shadows under his eyes. Gone was the ramrod posture, the jaunty gait. He and Katie had had no sleep and he guessed that Agent Streeter had not, either.

After an exchange of amenities, Streeter offered to have his secretary take Jackie for ice cream. Scott saw Jackie's eyes light up.

"In a little while," Katie said, settling Jackie in the seat next to her.

As other agents filed into the room, Streeter tried again. "Dr. Monroe, we need to focus on your contacts," Streeter said, waving a sheaf of paper. "Hillsborough, Manatee, and Sarasota counties have put together a portfolio of people with motive to do something to – and something's come up on your hard drive. Are you sure that you want your daughter to stay?"

"Jackie will be just fine," Katie said, pulling a tablet and a pen out of her purse. "Here, sweetie, draw some pictures."

*Like that would hold her interest*, Scott thought, bitterly resenting that Katie had not let the girls travel with their video games. Obediently, Jackie sat down, staring straight ahead at the bare wall.

"You have my patient records?" Katie seemed incredulous at the array of folders spread in front of her. "But they're confidential."

"Not what's on public record," Streeter said. "Where you've testified."

Scott stayed focused on Jackie. Afraid to confront her mother, he felt he'd let Jackie down, and his chest contracted when she looked up at him as if to say, "that's okay."

The triplets were used to Katie's protective nature, which bordered on paranoia. They all reacted differently according to their personality. Sammie, with her rebellious streak, would challenge her mom. Alex, would comply, no questions asked, and Jackie tried to reason everything out in her logical, practical way. Scott told himself that he didn't have favorites, but truth be told, he felt closer to Jackie than the other two. He, rather than Katie, had always been Jackie's confidant. She was so like him. Congenial, but capable of a certain toughness. She might sit here in submission, but she'd take it all in and ask him about it afterward. Scott had always understood how Jackie at times resented being a triplet. He knew that she longed to be more independent, to have her own friends. That's why she and Sammie were always going at it. Sammie, so determined to corral the other two into a tight threesome clique.

"This is not going to be pleasant." Streeter scanned his five colleagues seated around the conference room and gestured for one to turn on the projector.

There followed a parade of unseemly characters. Katie seemed familiar with them and the atrocities they'd committed. Growing up in the Grosse Pointe suburb of Detroit, Scott lacked firsthand experience with bloodshed and brutality. Hurting a child was beyond his comprehension.

When Streeter projected a toddler with its naked torso scarred by cigarette burns, Scott stood abruptly. "Katie, give me Jackie. We're going to get that ice cream."

This time, without protest, Katie nodded her assent. Scott took Jackie by the hand and left the room.

"Dad, did you see those pictures?" Jackie asked once they were out in the hall. Her voice shook and a trickle of tears appeared. "Of those kids who were hurt? Is that what's happening to Sammie and Alex?"

Scott flinched, horrified. Of course, what else would a smart child like Jackie deduce after exposure to Katie's mutilated patients? "No," he said as firmly as he could.

"Dad," she said, "where do you think they are? I keep thinking and thinking. We know not to talk to strangers. You and Mom are always telling us that. So where did Alex and Sammie go? Why can't you find them?"

Scott had to swallow hard to choke down the surge of acid. The anguish in his daughter's voice, her fear for her sisters was destroying him. "We'll find them, Jackie." He felt he would gag on the promise, but he had to be strong for his daughter's sake. "Now let's find those vending machines."

Once Scott and Jackie left, Katie sat straighter in her chair, steeling herself to focus on her former patients and their abusers as Streeter continued the slide show, a parade of her forensic career. Those men and a few women whom she'd testified against in child abuse cases dating all the way back to the early nineties when she'd completed her residency at Columbia University, left New York City, and started a pediatric psychiatric practice in Tampa. She hadn't intended to do forensic work, but the need was there and she had boards in pediatrics and psychiatry. Katie pressed her fingers against her temples. Why hadn't she declined? Why had she let her professional ego drive her to these high-profile challenges? She'd taken a break after the triplets were born. But once they started kindergarten, she'd jumped back in.

And why had she overstepped a professional ethical boundary in trying to help the Cutty boys? She couldn't help thinking that Maxwell Cutty was behind this. He had taken Sammie and Alex away from her to prevent her testimony, preying on the worst fear of a mother. Wasn't this the only scenario that made sense, what with no ransom demand?

When Streeter left the room to take a call, Katie rested her head on the table. Exhausted, terrified, she just couldn't shake the image of Maxwell Cutty locking her daughters up — or worse. Wading through her professional knowledge, she tried to determine whether he would sexually abuse Sammie and Alex or whether they'd be protected by his preference for young boys.

Then there was the lingering specter of Keith Franklin. She'd intended to tell Agent Streeter about him last night, but she'd been too exhausted. Why after so many years had he sent her that e-mail? Naturally, she had not responded, but could his ego have become so fragile that a rebuff could have set him off? Triggered an act of retribution of such drastic proportions? Could her old boyfriend have Sammie and Alex? His email had said *I'll take care of your daughters.*

Katie's head stayed down until Agent Streeter returned. She had no choice. She had to tell him, and in doing that, she'd have to disclose to Scott the only secret that she'd ever kept from him. How he would react she didn't know, but the lives of their daughters were hanging in the balance.

"You okay?" Streeter he asked.

"Agent Streeter, I have something to tell you." She nodded at the other three agents still in the conference room. "Just you, please, and Scott?"

# CHAPTER 10

*Monica Monroe Cancels European Tour to Be With Family.*
— *USA Today* Tuesday, June 14

Early Tuesday morning, two FBI agents pounded on the front door of the Franklin home on the east side of Detroit. Keith himself came to the door. He looked his age, fifty, had skin a shade darker than the tan coveralls he wore, sleeves rolled up to emphasize impressive biceps. The agents had approached the home cautiously. Could this be the lead they so desperately needed? Through an open window, they heard the canned laughter of a sitcom rerun interspersed with the strident shouting common to marital combat.

The feds had tracked Franklin as he left his job at central sanitation. He'd put in his eight-hour shift, driving the truck, helping to wrestle garbage cans, a messy job, not a pleasant one. No wonder he followed his shift with a beer or two at a local bar before heading home.

"Mr. Franklin, we're from the FBI," the senior agent announced, hand on holster. "We would like you to come down to the field office. We have some questions we'd like to ask you."

A woman inside, whom the agents assumed was Penny Franklin, his wife, was still shrieking expletives nonstop.

Franklin stood slack jawed and mute and opened the door more widely.

"What's it about?" Franklin asked as a slender, attractive woman, several years younger joined him.

"What are they doing here?" The woman tossed her hair and pointed to the two agents in suits.

"Mr. Franklin, we need to question you about the Monroe children," came the response. "You need to come with us."

Franklin's face gave nothing away, but his wife's glare was pure hostility. Turning, she slapped him, hard on the face. "What the fuck have you been doing with that bitch?"

"Nothing."

"I thought so. You are seeing her! Do you have anything to do with those missing kids? Are you in this with her, you piece of shit? Because if you are, I'll see you burn in hell."

"Come with us, Mr. Franklin." The agents flanked him, separating him from his wife and three boys who stood gawking in the background.

Keith Franklin responded without a word.

Streeter acquiesced to Katie's request that the agents in the conference room give them a few moments. As they filed out, Katie asked, "Could someone keep Jackie while we talk?"

"Ellen," Streeter called, "come back. Can you locate Mr. Monroe and bring him in here? Then could you keep an eye on Jackie?"

A few moments later, Scott walked into the conference room with Jackie. He already looked like all the life had drained out of him. And now, she had to deepen his anxiety. What she was going to tell him would not be the problem, it was just that he'd be hearing it for the first time, and she and Scott had vowed never to harbor secrets between them.

"You okay, Mom?" Jackie asked. "Do you want one?" She held up a melting Eskimo Pie. "Dad said not to get you one. That it would just melt, but I wanted to."

"No, sweetie." Katie knew she should smile, but only a grimace appeared.

"Katie, what's wrong?" Scott asked. "Something about Cutty?"

"No," Streeter answered for her. "He hasn't left Tampa. We're still looking for his ex-companion, Adam Kaninsky."

"I still can't understand why you just don't arrest him," Scott's voice boomed louder than usual, then lowered as Jackie left with Agent Camry. "Guy like that, you have to put the pressure on. If he knows where my daughters are —"

"Scott," Katie said, "I —"

"Those are my daughters out there, man. Some sick fuck has my little girls and what are you all doing, strutting around, talking into your walkie-talkies, typing on your computers. You need to *arrest* that bastard."

"Scott," Katie interrupted again. "I need to tell you and Agent Streeter about something – someone –"

"Mr. Monroe, let's hear what your wife has on her mind."

Streeter leaned back into his chair and waited. He had a new line of questioning for Dr. Monroe, too, but he'd hear her out first.

Katie began, "Scott, what I have to say – it could be important. It's about an old boyfriend, Keith Franklin."

Scott's eyebrows rose, he twisted in his chair, but he said nothing.

"Before I met you, I dated a guy, Keith Franklin. The one in some of the family photos at Mom's. I dated him in high school and all through college. He was good to me, but he turned out to be a drug dealer. He tried to involve me in hiding drugs, and I testified against him at his trial."

"Good lord, Katie, how terrible for you." Scott looked puzzled, but agitated, too. "What does that have to do with Sammie and Alex?"

"I received an e-mail from him. A couple of weeks ago."

Streeter reached into a folder and pulled out a sheet of paper. "Yes," he said, "I was about to ask you about that. We found it on your hard drive, deleted, but we found it. He pushed it across the table, centering it between Scott and Katie. Katie squeezed her eyes shut as Scott read silently.

*Katie,*

*I think about you every minute of every day even though it's been twenty-four years. I made such a stupid mistake and I lost you, the only good thing that ever happened to me. My mother sees your mother and keeps track of where you live and what you're doing. I know that you are still married to that white baseball player and I'm sorry that I sent you that one note. I have nothing against the man, except that he has you and I don't. I know that you have three daughters and I want you to know that I have three sons. Katie, I've changed.*

*I need to be with you. I'll leave my wife. I'll take care of your daughters. All I think about is you. Please say that you'll have me back. I love you and I can't forget you and what might have been.*

*Yours forever,*
*Keith*

As they read silently, Scott's face turned a bleached shade of white. Streeter noticed that he squirmed just a fraction of an inch away from Katie, and he kept his eyes focused straight ahead.

No one spoke for a moment. Streeter finally said, "Katie, start at the beginning. Tell us everything you know about this man. And why he is appearing in your life again."

Katie spoke in a husky monotone. She began with her senior prom where she'd first met Keith Franklin. She'd gone to St. Mary-of-the-Woods, an all girls academy run by nuns and catering to the rich. She, following in the footsteps of her three sisters, had a scholarship. She was one of three black girls in the class, and since it was a boarding school she'd had little opportunity to meet nice black guys. She'd been so excited when her mother's friend suggested her son as a prom date. Keith was two years older than Katie and a student at Detroit Community College. He was fun, attractive, with lots of friends.

They'd started dating exclusively almost immediately after the prom. Shortly thereafter, Keith quit school and got a job with FedEx at the Detroit airport loading and unloading planes. She and Keith were a couple through all four years of her college and into her third year of medical school. Had she been in love with him? She honestly didn't know. She'd never dated anyone else. She'd had no frame of reference.

About the time she started med school, Keith started to give her expensive gifts: a Rolex watch, dangling diamond earrings, even a car, not a new one, but a Mustang convertible. He shopped for her at designer shops, always pulling out plenty of cash. But he never made demands of her, understanding when she had to study, taking her to lavish parties only when she was free. They'd never talked of marriage, which suited her just fine as she was preoccupied with medical school.

Her problem with Keith started abruptly. Keith had been brutally beaten and dumped along the road not far from the airport where he worked. A Good Samaritan had picked him up and taken him to a pay phone. She was the one he called to come get him. It was the night before her pediatric exam, but she went. He asked her to take him to a buddy's house and to say nothing if anyone asked about him, especially the police. She begged him to let her take him to a hospital, but he refused. She took him to the address on the west side of Detroit, a place where she'd never drive on her own. She'd wanted to tend to his wounds, but he sent her away immediately. He shoved a shopping bag into her arms and told her to take it to her house and hide it in the back section of her closet behind a panel he knew was there.

When she got home, she inspected the bag, found it full of white powder she suspected to be cocaine. Behind the panel, she found three other such bags.

"My God, Katie," Scott's eyes had widened and his mouth gaped. "A dealer."

"I didn't know, Scott," she said. "I was home alone that night. I didn't know what to do."

"Go on," Streeter urged.

Katie explained that her mom had been out of town visiting Katie's oldest sister, Stacy. She called, got Stacy, and told her the whole story. Stacy left her mother at her house, took the next plane to Detroit, and together, they decided to call the police. It was the toughest decision she'd ever had to make, betraying Keith.

She'd testified at Keith's trial, her mom and Stacy by her side. But Keith's mother had been devastated, and Katie had never been able to erase the look Keith gave her as they read the verdict, a look, not of hatred, but deep disappointment.

Katie had been twenty-four, and she hadn't seen Keith in the intervening twenty-four years. He was sentenced to fifteen years for dealing drugs. His mother stayed in touch with Lucy, but Katie had never seen her since that day in court.

"Did Franklin keep in touch?" Streeter asked.

Katie explained that at first Keith wrote her from jail, begged her to visit him, said he'd forgiven her. In letters she'd tried to explain why she could not. How vehemently she was against drug use. He promised to turn his life around. That she'd always be the woman for him, and he the man for her. How the thought of her was what got him though each day. She stopped writing back. Shortly thereafter she met Scott and never looked back.

"How did Franklin react to your marriage to Scott?" Streeter asked.

"He sent one ugly letter. I destroyed it, but he used obscene language that was racist in nature."

"Katie, why —" Scott started to speak, then dropped his head into his hands. "I never knew —"

Katie lifted his head in her hands. Facing him she said, "You've always known that I had a long-term boyfriend and that we'd gone our separate ways. I was just too ashamed to tell you the whole story."

"Secrets — our pledge — Katie, I just don't know."

"Baby, after meeting you, it was like my life with Keith had never existed."

"And now, he's back. He wants you so bad that he'd take our little girls. *My* daughters, Katie, does he have *my* daughters?"

"I don't know — I don't think so." Katie said. "And Scott, they're *our* daughters."

"We have him in custody now," Streeter said. "He served nine of those fifteen years. And, we know that he attended Monica's concert Saturday night. Stalking you, Dr. Monroe? Maybe. He went alone, didn't bring his wife."

Katie couldn't help but feel a sliver of relief. If Keith had taken Sammie and Alex in an attempt to get her back, he would keep them safe, wouldn't he? So many atrocities had been circling through her head that she almost wished that Keith *had* abducted them.

"Katie, I just don't know." Scott lowered his head. "I'm so confused, I just don't know."

"Let's take a break," Streeter said. "Go find Jackie. Get something to eat. Meantime, I'll check out what we're learning from Franklin."

Streeter left the conference room. Katie and Scott made no move to leave.

Fifteen minutes later Streeter returned with Camry, Jackie between them. He hoped that Katie and Scott had used that time alone to mend any rift in their relationship that Katie's story might have triggered. It wasn't so much about what had happened between Katie and Franklin, Streeter knew, but that Katie had never shared that episode in her life with Scott. He and Marianne had gone through something similar. His pregnant wife had gone ballistic when she found out that he'd shared a room at a posh Chicago hotel with an old girlfriend during a surveillance assignment. Not wanting to upset Marianne, he hadn't told her. Then she read about it in a newspaper story. He blamed her overreaction on hormones, but he worried that she could never really trust him after that. With the intensity of emotions enveloping the Monroes, who could know whether Scott would harbor a grudge?

"Mom?" Jackie headed toward Katie, who was slumped head down on the conference table. "Are you okay?"

Katie raised her head, brushed strands of hair from her face and held her arms out to Jackie. "I'm okay, sweetie. "What about you?"

"Agent Camry got me some paper and more crayons," she said. "And we had a Sprite and cheese crackers. The yellow ones that come in a package."

"Thanks." Katie wiped tears from her eyes before lifting Jackie onto her lap.

"Shouldn't there be a ransom?" Scott's abrupt query took Streeter by surprise. "Is this normal, I mean, no ransom?"

"So far, nothing," Streeter said. "We're monitoring your phone at home, your two offices, your parents' homes."

"Whoever took them must know that Katie and I could get the money. Everybody knows that Monica is my sister, and that she's a multimillionaire. She could have a billion, for all I know. She'd part with all of it to get Sammie and Alex back."

"She wants to put out a reward, but we've asked her to hold back for now," Streeter said.

"This is about me," Katie said, squeezing Jackie so tight that the little girl started to squirm. "Even after talking about Keith, I think it's Maxwell Cutty. He'd do anything to stay out of jail. With me sidelined — "

"Then arrest him," Scott said, pounding a fist on the table, glaring at Streeter. "If there's even the slightest chance that he knows where my daughters are, this is bullshit."

"Scott's right." Katie shifted Jackie so she could focus her glare on Streeter. "What are you doing to find them! We're not living one more day without them! Find them! Sammie and Alex are out there. Find them!"

"We're doing everything we can." Helpless words, he knew, but as he said them, Streeter observed the Monroe parents closely. He wished that he could totally dismiss them as complicit. He wished that Jackie had not had to endure such emotional torture. He wished mostly that he could find Alex and Sammie.

During Katie's outburst, Jackie had squeezed out of her mother's grasp and gone to stand by Scott, tugging at his shirt. "Daddy, can't we find them? Ever?"

Scott drew Jackie into his arms. "We will find your sisters. I promise."

"You two need a break," Streeter said. And he needed a break from them. "You can go back to Mrs. Jones's or stay here in another room."

Katie stood, smoothing her dress, calmer now. "What about an appeal? Didn't you suggest another one? This time with Jackie? Agent Streeter, we have to do *something*."

Streeter rubbed his eyes. Too many balls in the air. He'd almost forgotten. "We have the television studio scheduled for two o'clock. So why don't you go out for some lunch?"

"We can eat here," Katie said, getting up, reaching for Jackie.

"Jackie might like the food outside better," Streeter tried. They had to give the kid some slack here.

"The cafeteria in the basement is okay." Katie took Jackie by the hand and Scott followed. As the Monroes left the conference room, Streeter's agents filed back in. "Give me everything you've got on Cutty," he demanded. "Tell me all about what he did in that Tampa bank and where he's been so far today? Cutty's our first priority. Then tell me what we know about Keith Franklin."

Why was Ellen Camry's face an ashen shade of gray as she approached? "We have a new suspect," she announced. "Come with me."

Norman Watkins sat ramrod straight in the metal chair, trying for an innocent look of calm acceptance. Seven days out of the joint. A hefty man, no longer the skinny shit he'd been ten years ago. His wife joked that he looked like a professor with horn-rimmed glasses and hair trimmed to just below the ears. He'd picked up decent slacks and a sports jacket with patches on the elbows at the Goodwill Store. Except for the worn sneakers, he felt like he looked the part of a decent middle-class citizen. And it wasn't just the upscale threads. He had changed in so many ways. Clean, born-again, determined never to go back inside, no matter what. But right now, the most important thing was to keep his cool.

"I told you before, officer," he was saying as the woman officer walked in with the boss officer named Streeter. "I got the call in the middle of the night." Respectful like, the way he'd counseled his former prison mates. "My sister called. Told me my mother had a massive stroke. Like she didn't expect her to make it. You can check that all out, man. Henry Ford Hospital."

"We're checking." Camry, the woman officer working on him wore a sour, mean-spirited sneer when she spoke, but so far nobody had shoved him around. Must not want to mess up their pricey suits. The government paid those assholes way too much. Wary, expecting a sudden assault, Norman concentrated on his breathing.

Norman explained everything to the head agent, Streeter, who now sat fidgeting with his shoulder holster, as he'd listened, almost politely, to Norman's sincere-sounding answers as to his whereabouts yesterday. But Norman knew this was just good-cop bad-cop. Ten years in the pen, you hear lots of stories.

"Tell me again when the call came through," Streeter said.

"One in the morning."

"That'd be Saturday morning. What were you doing?"

"Sleeping with my wife, just like I told you before." Norman poured out thanks to God that Connie had stuck with him. All through those ten years. And she'd raised Tina just fine. Never put the bitterness in her about how her old man beat the shit out of her when she was just a baby. Now was his time to make it up to Tina.

"So?" The bitch agent sat back like she was bored. Shit, Norman had told this story six times already. He'd have to be extra careful not to screw it up.

"Me and her talked it out. We agreed that we'd drive to Michigan. Connie's got a sister livin' in Detroit. Ain't seen her since we moved to Florida twelve years ago. Did I tell you we was both from Michigan? The wife was born in Livonia. Me, in Hamtramck even though I don't got a Polish name." *Feed 'em the bullshit*, Norman thought, then he stopped himself. Now that he had religion, did that mean he'd have to give it to them straight? Here's where the rubber hit the road. Inside, he'd preached trust in the Lord.

"Your wife's sister, that's the address where we picked you up?" Agent Camry asked, diddling with the tape recorder.

"Yeah, the girls were out shoppin'. Then we was gonna head for home. Did you know that my wife is the assistant manager of health and beauty aids at the Winn Dixie? She's already used a vacation day and we was gonna drive all night. Just like we did comin' in. That way we don't have to pay for no motel."

Agent Camry put down the tape recorder to inspect her fingernails. "Your probation?"

"It's not like I could call my parole officer in the middle of the night." Norman sat up, deciding to look this cold-faced bitch right in the eye. "Officer, I knew it was a violation. But I hadn't seen my mother in twelve years and she was dyin'." "Fuckin' dyin' " almost came out, but Norman caught it. Stick with the new image he hastily reminded himself. "So I took a chance. I'd seen my P.O. earlier that day so I didn't think he'd be lookin' for me 'til the middle of the week. I wasn't gonna be stayin', just long enough to just check. You know, say good-bye if she was dyin'. Let my wife catch up with her sister. My little girl ain't never even seen her aunt. Now that ain't right."

"So how's your mother?" she asked.

Norman smirked. The bitch — Agent Camry — kept asking him the same shit over and over again. They both knew damn well that his mother was just fine. No stroke as it turned out. Hadn't even got admitted to the hospital. When he went to see the old lady at her place, she refused to let him in. So he had wasted the whole trip. And worse, the feds were fucking with him. Big deal, he skipped the state, a parole violation. He'd had a damn good excuse. So why were they feeding him all this shit?

"Turned out to be a false alarm," Norman said, not caring if he sounded sheepish. Sounding sheepish would be natural, wouldn't it?

"So you get a call. You figure you have to be in Detroit. You spend the night in your car?" Now tell me again why you would sleep in that ratty station wagon when you could have stayed at your mother's place?"

Norman resented the sarcastic tone. What right did she have to call Connie's car "ratty"? The Ford wagon was rusty inside and out. There was a hole in the front floorboard big enough for Tina to fall through. He'd fix it up as soon as the money came though. Norman sat rigidly upright and repeated his mantra. The same one he'd taught his fellow inmates: Don't let them get inside your head. Stay calm. Look innocent.

"That's pretty much it. I was embarrassed that my own mother wouldn't let me in. Old lady said she was ashamed of me for having a criminal record. So I just hung out in the wagon. You know, to keep up appearances."

"Appearances? Give me a break. What am I missing here?"

"It's the truth," Norman said lowering his eyes modestly. He figured that the feds would have his prison file. They'd know he'd been a model prisoner. That he was like a religious leader in the joint. Almost as good as a chaplain. The cons even called him "Reverend."

"How old is your daughter?" Agent Camry leaned into Norman's face. He was particular not to let anyone in "his space" but this time he'd have to suck it up.

"She just turned eleven, ma'am."

"Eleven years old. Do you remember what she looked like when she was nine months old?"

The obnoxious bitch pulled a pack of color photos out of a folder. He hadn't seen those pictures since the day he was sentenced. Why were they putting him through all this? All Norman could do was shield his eyes as Agent Camry painstakingly pointed out the limp, twisted arm of his baby girl; the bandaged head after doctors drained blood from inside the skull; the red, peeling feet and legs all the way to her waist; and the cigarette burns. With a twitch he remembered his anguish when he'd recently discovered that Tina still had scars on her arms and legs.

"You did that?" Camry's face was just inches from Norman's. He could smell the shampoo in her short brown hair. "Look at this," she shouted. "Look at what you are capable of doing. You despicable bastard."

Norman glanced at Agent Streeter who sat, staring at him. He didn't know how to react. He wanted to slug the woman. He struggled to recite his mantra — stay calm, breathe deep — but those photos were getting to him. *Yes, he'd done that.* Tina was born premature. She cried all the time. Connie couldn't make her stop. Connie quit her job, and he'd had to work as a night watchman. He wasn't getting any sleep so started to take speed. The drug had a terrible effect on him, an adverse reaction, he now knew. Amphetamines made him so horribly angry. He took more drugs. Uppers. Downers. Then cocaine and heroin. His brain was fucked up. He had never meant to hurt his baby girl. His mind had been messed up trying to support his family.

"Stop it," Norman said after a glance at the heinous photos. "Take these away."

Before Camry could react, the door to the interrogation room opened a burly, pasty-faced male agent entered, a wad of clothing in his big hands. "Sir, we found these in a plastic bag under the back panel of the suspect's station wagon. Kid's clothing."

"Why were these in your car?" Agent Camry grabbed the garments, inspecting them.

Norman came close to shoving her back, but held back. "Can't say," he said. "Must belong to my daughter, Tina. Yeah, she musta put them in there."

"Hidden behind a panel?" Agent Streeter reached for the girl's clothing, examined each garment, and handed them to Camry.

"I didn't know they were there. Connie must have stored them in there."

"You bastard," Streeter shoved back his chair. On his feet, he towered over Norman, grabbed a hank of his hair and jerked him to a standing position. "You tell me now. Where are the Monroe girls?"

Norman Watkins slumped forward and faked an epileptic seizure.

# CHAPTER 11

*Thousands Protest amid Call for Annulment of*
*Iran Presidential Election.*
— International News, Tuesday, June 14

Jackie had never been in a TV studio. She'd heard the adults talking about doing the TV show at the studio or doing it at the FBI. She was sure glad they decided to leave that horrible FBI Building. It scared her. People looked mean and some of them even had guns. The only ones she liked were Agents Camry and Streeter. They were nice and really cared about her, too. But so far they had not been able to find Alex and Sammie and that was making her more and more scared.

When they'd first gotten to the television building, she'd been excited, but when they put her in a room and left her alone, she started to cry. Not out loud, just sniffles. She was very, very scared. Maybe whoever took her sisters would come to get her, too? That was worrying her more and more. That must be why Mom made her stay with her all the time.

She was sitting, staring straight ahead at nothing when her dad came into the room and knelt down in front of her chair. He had a serious look on his face.

"Jackie, the FBI wants you to go on television with Mom and me. Sure that's okay?"

Before she could say, "Yes, that was okay," he said, "You don't have to talk. Just let the camera take your picture with us. But if you don't want to — "

"I want to, Dad." Being in there with Mom and Dad would be better than sitting out here.

"It won't take long. Come along. I think Mom will want to brush your hair."

Jackie didn't care how long it took. Afterward they had to go back to the FBI. She'd have to listen to more grown-up talk about finding her sisters. They didn't think she could understand because she was just a kid, but what they said made her stomach hurt. Last night she threw up two times, but didn't tell her parents.

Jackie was surprised how hot it was in the studio, and she was embarrassed when a lady in a pink suit offered her a lollipop. She was nine years old, not a baby. When the taping was over, they returned to the FBI building. As they walked through the cool lobby, Jackie noticed a girl a couple of years older than her sitting next to Agent Camry. Jackie slowed to smile at the girl, but she looked aside as if she were shy.

"Come along, Jackie," Mom said.

"Can I wait out here?" Jackie asked, reaching into her backpack for the set of crossword puzzles and mazes that Agent Camry had given her. Maybe she could share the puzzles with the other girl.

Agent Camry said, "I'll be happy to look after Jackie, Dr. Monroe." She got up and held her hand out to Jackie for an adult-like handshake.

"She'll be fine, Katie," her dad said, patting her on the back, making her feel like a nine-year-old rather than a baby.

Her mom did not argue, and bent to kiss her on the top of her head.

"Thanks, Mom," Jackie said, squeezing her eyes shut so she would not cry. Whenever her mother left, she always kissed all three of them like that.

Agent Camry led Jackie to the chair next to the girl. She was very thin with long black hair and white skin with freckles. That was the one thing Jackie always noticed, the color of people's skin. She always compared it to hers. She considered her skin "medium." Halfway between her Mom's and her Mom's relatives and her Dad's and his relatives. She and Alex liked this halfway color. It made them feel comfortable with white people and black people. Lots of people had their color; people who were half black and half white like them, people from

Mexico and lots of other places, like Vietnam and Korea and China. But Sammie was different. She always wanted to have darker skin, like Mom's. She told everybody that she was African American. She disobeyed Mom and even lied about it when Mom made them put on sunscreen. "I want to be black," she always said. "The best athletes are black." Jackie always worried that Dad would feel bad, since he was white, but he just laughed and said in his loud voice, "All my daughters will be good athletes, no matter what color they are."

As soon as Jackie sat down, she reached into her pack and pulled out a book of mazes. She loved mazes and word games, could do them faster than any of her sisters.

"Want to work at this?" Jackie handed a booklet to the girl. Then she pulled out two pencils.

The girl nodded and took one.

"What's your name?" Jackie asked.

"Tina Watkins," the girl said.

"I'm Jackie Monroe. Are your mom and dad in there?" Jackie pointed to the door her parents had passed through.

Tina nodded and asked, "Did your mom or dad get arrested?"

"What?" Jackie stared at her. "Arrested? Why would they arrest my mom and dad?"

"Don't worry," Agent Camry broke into their conversation.

"Don't make my dad go back to jail," Tina said.

"Your dad was in jail?" Jackie was curious. She'd never known anyone who'd been in jail. "What did he do?"

Tina looked away, but said, "A long time ago, he did some things. I was just a baby."

Then Tina turned to Agent Camry. "Why did you FBI people take him? He didn't do anything wrong. He's a Christian just like me and my mom. Why are you people all so mean?"

"Tina, I can't talk about that," Agent Camry said. Jackie didn't think she sounded mean, but she could understand why Tina would be upset.

Jackie couldn't help wonder what bad things Tina's dad had done. And that made her think about bad things happening to Alex and Sammie. She'd heard that expert man on television say that if they didn't find kids in the first two days, something bad had happened and they might *never* find them. What if Sam and Alex never came home? Would her parents still love *her?*

Jackie had always been sure that that her parents loved her and her sisters very much. But she knew that, if they had to make a list of who they loved the most, that Alex, always so sweet and obedient, would come first. That would only be fair. Sammie would come in last because she was so bratty. That left Jackie in the middle. Fine with her. She'd never been jealous of Alex, and she did not feel sorry for Sammie. Now everything in her world had changed. She wasn't so sure anymore. She did know one thing: it was all because of her that Sammie and Alex had been taken. She should have just gone with them to the stupid museum movie. But if she had, would the bad person have taken her, too?

Connie Watkins had arrived while the Monroes were taping their plea for the safe return of Sammie and Alex at the television station. Waiting to be recognized at the bureau reception desk, she'd shivered in her tank top and adjusted her floral print stretch pants, wishing she'd grabbed a sweater. Why was it that federal buildings always cranked up the air-conditioning to near freezing? Shy by nature, easily intimidated by authority figures, Connie, in awe of her own boldness, had marched up to the imposing desk, her twelve-year-old daughter, Tina, in tow. "I want to see my husband," she'd announced.

A man in a suit had been engrossed in reading a file. When he looked up, Connie's voice faltered, her course in assertiveness training failing her. "You arrested him an hour ago at my sister's house on Outer Drive. Neighbors saw you take him out in handcuffs."

"Make them send my dad back home," Tina said, obstinate, challenging. "He didn't do anything wrong." She stood, shoulders slumped, so frail she looked like a waif with straight black hair, parted in the center, her pale skin in stark contrast.

"Whoa, ladies." The man looked back and forth at mother and daughter, standing shoulder to shoulder. Both five foot two; both in tank tops with matching flip-flops; the older in maroon; the younger in canary yellow. "I don't even know who you're talking about. Name?"

"Norman Watkins," said Connie. "I'm his wife, and this is our daughter, Tina."

Connie observed the deskman's eyebrows rise. He was very young. An agent? A male secretary? Did it matter? Then she noted his name tag. Agent, somebody, a long Polish or Slavic name she couldn't pronounce.

Without a word the agent picked up the phone and buzzed a number. "Tell Streeter that the Watkins woman's here. With her daughter."

"Turns out you're saving the taxpayers gas money," he said. "They were going to bring you in. And here you are — "

"I'm here to see my husband." Connie tried to sound polite, which she was by nature. But she was so scared for Norman. She had to get him out of here. She knew how the cops treated ex-cons. She'd tried to help some of Norman's buddies when they'd gotten out of the joint. She'd seen how they'd been slapped around. Cops were all alike. Didn't matter if it was Florida or Michigan or local or the FBI. At least she knew a good lawyer. Had his phone number in her jeans' pocket. But he was in Florida. This was Michigan. But certainly Norman wouldn't need one. There had to be some horrible mistake.

Tina now squeezed Connie's hand and she'd started to sob. Sweet Jesus, not after she and Norman had worked so long and hard to make it up to Tina. All they wanted for their daughter was a normal life with two parents in their little house. No more weekly visits to jail separated by a bulletproof wall, with only a phone line, like an umbilical cord, connecting Tina with her father.

Tina was considered by social workers as an "at risk" kid. Poor academic skills, an attitude problem, the school counselor had complained, using words like "antisocial" and "apathetic." But Connie was convinced that all Tina needed was her dad, and now that Norman was home, she would be just fine.

"Why do you have him here?" Connie asked, afraid of the answer, yet not knowing why.

"Ma'am, he's violated his parole, so . . ." the desk agent was cut off as a tall man in a suit approached.

"Mrs. Watkins?" The man extended his hand to her. "Agent Streeter. I have questions for you. First off, does your husband suffer from a seizure disorder? Is he taking epilepsy medication?"

"No." Connie's hand flew to her throat. Or was he? And she didn't even know? "Uh, maybe they put him on something when he was away?"

"Not in the record," Streeter said. "We need to take your statement." He shifted his gaze to Tina and seemed to hesitate. "They took your husband to the hospital."

Connie drew Tina closer to her.

"Mom, what's wrong with Dad?"

"I don't understand," Connie said. "I have to see him."

"Not now, ma'am. Your husband violated his parole. At the very least, he's going back inside once the doctors get though with him."

Connie slumped, propping herself against the desk with one hand, letting Tina's hand drop from her other. "He's done nothing wrong," she gasped. "His mother — "

"Come with me," Streeter said. "Best your daughter wait in reception."

What could she do? Should she leave Tina by herself in this hostile place? But if she took her with her and they started delving into Norman's past with Tina? Yes, Tina had been told that her father had "hurt" her when she was a baby; she knew that he hadn't meant to; that he'd been on drugs that blurred his judgment. Indeed, she had used this story to scare her daughter away from drugs. She and Norman hadn't started on drugs until their last year in high school, but now even sixth graders were exposed to drugs at school. Norman was always after her to keep their daughter drug-free. So far she thought she'd been successful.

"I want to go with you." Tina said, trying to be brave, trying to hold back tears.

"No, you wait out here. You'll be okay." Connie opted for the safer option, or so she figured. She could not count on an iota of sensitivity from these hard-core government types. Turning toward Streeter, Connie asked, "You sure she'll be all right?"

"Agent Camry will stay with her," Streeter promised. "She'll be close, in case we need to question her, too."

Agent Camry asked Tina to come with her as Connie followed Streeter into a small square conference room dominated by a round table. The only décor an American flag on a pole in one corner. Connie sat when he indicated a chair. Streeter turned on a tape recorder and started asking questions. He didn't sound friendly, but he didn't sound angry, either. What had Norman done?

"When did you leave Florida?"

"Saturday. Early morning," Connie drew the words out, her mind frantically trying to figure out why they had her husband.

Questions kept coming. She told Streeter about the call Norman got about his mother. That he'd been upset. His mother was very ill, and he wanted to see her before she died. Show her that he had changed. Let her see Tina, her granddaughter. Connie explained that she had a sister living in Detroit's east side. That Norman wanted her to stay with her sister until he'd made the first contact with his mother. But Connie knew that she'd faltered when Streeter kept insisting on exact times. Who talked to whom when, from where? Connie asked for a drink.

Streeter paused the tape recorder and got up to pour her a glass of water. While up, he made a call. He asked only, "Are they back yet?"

Connie began to sweat and the water was warm, not refreshing. Streeter kept hammering her on timing. Where had he been since he dropped her at her sister's? Who would Norman stay with in Detroit? Connie started to smell her own sweat. Had she forgotten her deodorant? She was tempted to sniff under her arms just to check, but she didn't. Streeter continued to badger her. Was Norman a vindictive man? Did she know of any plans he had for retribution, having to do with Dr. Monroe?

Goddamn. These idiots think that Norman's connected to the Monroe girls' kidnapping? Shit, that's what this was all about. As the questions kept coming, Connie knew that the only way to help Norman was to keep her cool. What good would it do if she broke down? She couldn't let these bastards sense her fear. Norman had been at the hospital with his mother. He'd called that morning to say that his mother was going to make it, and that they'd head back to Florida right away. No mention of whether he'd be taking her and Tina to see his mother. Had Connie thought that odd? To tell the truth, yes.

When Katie and Scott returned to their usual conference room, Streeter was all business. No chitchat. No "how did it go." "Something new just came in," he said before they'd even sat down. "Dr. Monroe, does the name Norman Watkins mean anything to you?"

Katie swallowed and grasped the edge of the table to stop her hands from trembling. "Yes," she finally said. "He tortured his baby daughter. Scalded her, twisted her arms right out of their sockets. Threw her against a wall. Fractured skull, concussion. I still remember her name. Connie. No," she corrected herself, "that was her mother's name. The child was Tina."

"He's the one that scared the hell out of you." Scott moved his chair closer, a protective gesture that Katie appreciated.

"Bastard," Streeter spoke through clenched teeth. "How were you involved?"

"Hillsborough County Child Protection called me in," Katie said, "but there wasn't much I could do as a psychiatrist other than to observe the child's development, which amazingly was okay once Norman went to prison."

Katie stopped suddenly and looked up. "Why are you asking about Norman?"

"Did you testify?"

"Yes. I did."

"Reason we bring him up," Streeter said, "is that he was released from prison last week. He served ten of a fifteen year sentence in Starke, Raiford State Penitentiary – Florida State Prison."

Katie stared at Streeter. They'd put him away when she was pregnant with the triplets. Could it be possible that he was back in her life?

"Geez, Katie, I remember – Agent Streeter, I'll never forget how frightened Katie was that day."

"Nine years ago. You know, I can hardly remember life before the girls." And she couldn't. The triplets were her life. Back then, she and Scott had given up on having children of their own. Then all of a sudden, triplets. She'd been in seventh heaven. Scott, too.

"Did he threaten you?" Streeter asked.

"Yes. In court." Katie felt she would choke. Same sensation she'd had then. "I was pregnant. It was my last day before maternity leave. My friends at the courthouse were having a baby shower for me that day." Katie felt her muscles tense and reached down with one hand to pat her flat abdomen. "Then Norman Watkins shouted out a terrifying curse. Everyone in the courtroom heard it."

Agent Camry had stepped inside and leaned in to take the papers from Streeter. She flipped to the second page, pointed to a section, and handed it back. Streeter read verbatim, " 'The child of the devil grows inside you. Let it be born dead and go straight to hell.' Nasty stuff for a pregnant woman."

"It totally freaked me out. As a professional, I realized the guy's brain was fried from drug abuse, but I still have nightmares about it." Katie's voice escalated in alarm. "Do you think he has anything to do with Alex and Sammie?"

"We almost missed him on our radar screen," Streeter admitted. "He was released just last week. Seems the locals take their time to update their databases. We sent an agent to check on his whereabouts, and we found that he was not at home."

Scott blurted, very loud, "What the hell? Where — ?"

Streeter continued, "A neighbor saw him leave Saturday morning with his wife and daughter in their station wagon. Later, the neighbor got a call from Connie Watkins asking if they could feed and walk the dog. We were able to trace the call to a pay phone in Gainesville. But here's the important part. Mrs. Watkins said that they were traveling to Detroit. That Norman's mother was in the hospital there."

"Where is he *now*?" Scott was on his feet, glancing around.

"We have him in custody. Hospital prison ward. He had a seizure after we apprehended him. We have questioned his wife. That was his daughter out there."

"What?" Katie, too, stood. "He's here? Jackie's out there!"

"I'll get her." Scott rushed to the reception area and Katie followed.

They found Jackie deep in conversation with the young girl they now knew was Tina Watkins.

"Dad, Mom," Jackie said, "this is Tina. Her dad got arrested and it's not fair. He didn't do anything wrong. Right, Tina?"

Katie took a better look at the child. Horribly thin, shivering in that flimsy halter. Then she saw the telltale scars. Scars she'd seen only too often among her small patients — multiple circles the size of a cigarette on the girl's left arm.

"Tina?" she asked.

"Tina Watkins, ma'am," Tina said, looking up with sad brown eyes.

Could this be the toddler she'd protected in court? The pitiful child, scalded, broken bones, cigarette burns on all four extremities. Katie stepped forward to look closer at the scars. She had seen to it that this child had been placed in foster care. Months later, she'd concurred with the guardian ad litem that Tina be returned to her mother once the mother successfully completed rehab. And that was the last she heard until today.

"Mom, why are you staring?" Jackie asked. She'd gotten up to stand next to Scott. "Is something wrong, Dad?"

"We're happy to meet you, Tina," Scott said. "I'm Mr. Monroe, Jackie's dad and this is her mom."

Tina's eyes got very big. "I saw you on television." She pointed to Jackie. "You must be the triplet that didn't get kidnapped."

"That's why we're here," Jackie said. "To help the FBI find my sisters."

"I hope they find them soon," Tina said. "Me and my mom and my aunt said prayers for them."

Katie was about to ask Tina where her mother was when a woman was buzzed though the security gate into the lobby.

"Here's my mom," Tina announced. "Mom, this is Jackie, the triplet that didn't get kidnapped. And her mom and dad."

Katie and Connie Watkins stared at each other.

"Dr. Monroe," Connie spoke first, one hand on her chest, the other tightly clutching her tote bag.

Agent Camry moved to a position between these two women who had such a bizarre history.

"Where are my children?" Katie felt Scott's hand press down on her shoulder.

"How would I know," Connie said, shrinking back. "And neither does my husband. He's in the hospital, for God's sake. Why are you trying to destroy my family?"

Agent Camry spoke for the first time. "Easy, now, Mrs. Watkins."

Tina now stood protectively in front of her mother.

"Mom? What's the matter with you?" Jackie asked. "Tina's mom doesn't know where Sammie and Alex are."

"Your husband knows," Katie challenged. "He must. Make him tell us." She tried to soften her voice. "Please?"

"Norman has nothing to do with your children, Dr. Monroe. I swear it. He's a good man. I know he made mistakes. God knows he's paid for them."

"After all these years, he still wants to get back at me?" Katie tried to blunt the hysteria creeping into her voice. "Tell him that I'll do anything! Anything. Just tell me where they are. Tell me they're okay. Please!"

Then Katie felt a surge of hope. They had Norman Watkins in a Detroit hospital. They were questioning him. Right now. It must he him. She'd been wrong about Maxwell Cutty as well as Keith Franklin.

"I need to see him," Katie said, "to ask him —"

"Not possible, Dr. Monroe," Camry said. "We'll let you know as soon as we have anything. I promise."

Connie took a step forward. Shifting her bag to her shoulder, she grabbed both of Katie's hands. "I swear to you, Dr. Monroe. Norman is a born-again Christian. He would never hurt a child again. My husband is innocent!"

Connie dropped Katie's hands and grabbed Tina, spinning the child to face Katie. "You remember how much my little girl has gone through. Now her dad is back. He's gonna make it all up to her."

Katie stared at Tina. Then she turned to Scott. She did not know how to react. Leaning into Scott, she felt her knees buckle.

"Come on Jackie, let's take Mom home," Scott said.

"Bye, Tina," Jackie turned, and she and Tina exchanged a feeble wave.

As soon as the three of them had climbed into the black Suburban, Jackie had started with the questions. She'd been fascinated by Tina's dad being arrested, and she wanted to know how Katie and Tina's mom knew each other. Katie, helpless to respond, sank into an inky void. Scott compensated and he and Jackie held a two-way conversation about who-knew-what. Once they were in the house, Scott released Jackie to her grandmother downstairs and took Katie upstairs, insisting that she lie down.

"You know what, Scott?" Katie said as she accepted a glass of water. "I'm of no help to the FBI. I can't concentrate. I just feel like I'm dead inside."

"Katie, I know. I'm so scared that I almost can't breathe, but we have to be here for Jackie."

"I feel like I'm failing her, too."

"Here, take this." Scott shook a mint green capsule out of a brown prescription bottle. "What you need is some sleep."

Katie accepted the pill, wondering how Scott, who avoided all drugs, had gotten ahold of a scheduled medication. She'd ask him tomorrow. Eventually she did drift into a dream-filled sleep.

Dreams of Maxwell Cutty and Norman Watkins; dreams of abused children; dreams of evil; and dreams of Keith Franklin.

After three hours, Katie awoke, still groggy from her drugged sleep, but determined to wake up and find out whether there was any news. She was reminded of that time nine years ago when she'd awakened following the birth of the triplets. Just as he was now, Scott had been sitting in a chair by her side. His face had been grim, his voice hesitant as he'd told her about their tiny, premature daughters.

"We have three daughters and we think they are identical," he'd said. Baby A, who turned out to be Sammie, 3 lb. 15 oz; Baby B, Jackie, 3 lb. 9 oz; and Baby C, Alex, just 3 lb. 3 oz. "They're in the neonatal intensive care unit."

She'd been scared then, but she was terrified now.

"Babe, you awake?" Scott whispered.

"Scott, has anything — "

He shook his head. "Nothing."

"Jackie?"

"She's downstairs."

"Oh, Scott," Katie held out her arms and he moved to sit with her on the bed.

They held each other for a long time, letting their tears mingle, and their sobs merge.

"So there's nothing," Katie finally whispered. "I am so sorry, Scott, I'm to blame for this. My career — all those sick perverts. I never thought — "

"Stop right now." Scott leaned over and held her head between his hands. "None of this is your fault."

"And that stuff about Keith. I should have told you before. I was just so ashamed that I got into something like that. "

Katie watched Scott's face as he hesitated. "I just don't want any more secrets between us. Ever."

"I swear to you, Scott."

"Then that's it, babe. But Agent Streeter does want to talk to you."

"About what?" Katie was already sitting up, swinging her legs off the bed.

"About Norman Watkins. Something's going on with him. Streeter didn't say what. Do you think he took them, Katie?"

"I can't trust my judgment," Katie said. "My first impression was yes, but now I just don't think so."

"So you don't think he's capable of that kind of retroactive vengeance?"

"No," Katie answered from her heart. Deep inside she didn't think that a woman like Connie would have stuck by a man that evil. Connie wouldn't have raised her daughter to love and respect Norman unless he'd become a decent man. Connie said that he was now a different person. The FBI had verified that he'd been the ideal prisoner. Actually helping fellow inmates straighten out their lives.

"But he was in Detroit at the exact time that Alex and Sammie were taken," Scott said. "How can that be a coincidence?"

Katie didn't know. Could he have repressed all that hate for ten years and then focused it on her children? God, she was supposed to be a psychiatrist, yet she seemed to have no grasp of what was happening to her family.

# CHAPTER 12

*Nine-Year-Old Sammie and Alex Monroe Missing with No Clue.*
— Radio News, Tuesday, June 14

Spanky was working his hand hard and fast over his crotch when the angry blast of a horn interrupted. With a jerk of the wheel, he pulled the eighteen wheeler back into the center lane, flipping the middle finger of his left hand to the unattractive female driver of the Lexus passing on the right.

"Slut," he growled over the background of the Tampa news station, a sexy female radio voice had been going on and on about those missing girls. Nine year olds; one wearing a lavender outfit and the other a multicolored pattern. They had black, wavy hair and one had a ponytail. The reporter sounded sexy with a southern drawl that was too much. She was saying that the young girls had light brown, almost golden skin. What was that all about? He listened more carefully now.

Spanky knew that Scott Monroe had been a catcher for the Yankees and that he was white. He'd seen him in person one time when the Yankees played the Tigers, that time Mom had surprised him with a ticket to Tiger Stadium for his birthday. So if these missing girls were "brown" then Monroe musta married a black woman or maybe an Asian or even Hispanic. So what? Spanky was not prejudiced. Truth be told, he'd only had white girls, but he'd have nothing against taking a black girl or half-black in this case. And he'd never had two at once. Just the thought made him sweaty with anticipation.

Spanky — his real name was Samuel Spansky — was midway through the tedious Detroit-to-Miami haul. Couple days off and he'd be heading back. He could have driven I-75 in his sleep and sometimes he almost did. But anytime his boss had asked him if he wanted another route, like to Texas, he'd turned it down. Miami was a hot city and Spanky knew where to go for action.

Spanky liked his women young. Usually he had to settle for teens on the road, but he preferred little girls. Girls the age of those missing triplets. Just the thought made him salivate, not to mention how hard it made his throbbing cock. Spanky prided himself on his discretion. He wasn't one of those perverts who messed with real young ones. He liked his little girls old enough to know that he had something special for them and still young enough to be too scared to tell. And if they did? He'd be long gone.

By the time the Lexus had disappeared out of sight, the news was over and he started flipping the dial around for another one talking about the girls. What he was thinking about was their panties. He wondered whether they were cotton or nylon. Were they the same color as their outfits? Just pondering that question made his erection even stronger. He just had to jerk off. He'd need to pull over.

No, not now. He forced himself to keep his rig on the road. Pulling over would attract the Florida State Police. But tonight at the truck stop, he'd find negligent parents, ones that let their kid wander while they go to the bar for a couple of beers. Spanky knew that if he ever had kids of his own — and he did want them — eventually he'd find a good woman and settle down — he would watch them constantly.

Moving his right hand from his huge erection, he reached down under his seat. He pulled out the sandalwood box he kept there, well hidden and secured with a padlock. He couldn't open it while driving on I-75 through Tampa, but just the sweet smell of the wood made him nearly ejaculate. Inside the scent would be overwhelming and he craved the smell and the touch inside. The silky, soft touch and the indescribable smell — not musky, like a woman's, but more earthy or cloying or spicy, he never could exactly place it — of the mementos he'd collected from his little playmates. Tonight before he went out hunting, he'd touch each of them. There were nineteen now.

In his mind Spanky could remember each pretty little thing, how they'd struggled and tried to squeal through the monogrammed handkerchief he stuffed in their mouth. The same one he now had ready in the pocket of his pants. The initials were not his, but his stepfather's, the only memento he had of the son of bitch. Pulling it out to finger it, Spanky could feel the wetness of the tears that he'd wiped off their little faces when he was done, and he could see how big their eyes got when he threatened to strangle Mommy and Daddy if they ever told. Still fondling the ratty piece of cloth, with the chatter about the Monroe triplets in the background, Spanky knew he would take another tonight.

Twenty, a nice round number.

# CHAPTER 13

*The Big 5 Health Care Dilemmas.*
— *Time* magazine, Wednesday, June 15, 2009

Norman was not sure why he'd done that. Faked a convulsion. Now as he lay shackled to the bed in Detroit General Hospital, he knew that it had been a mistake, offering him only a temporary reprieve. He should have waited to make his move. His brain wave test and the MRI would be negative, and then they'd know. He'd done this once before, after he'd been inside for a year, and needed to escape an attack from the cell block bully. Copying the jerking movements and tongue lolling from his first cell mate who had authentic epileptic fits, Norman had plunked to the floor and violently contracted his right side in a rapid rhythmic motion, tighten, release, tighten, release. He'd held his breath and bit his tongue until it bled. His attacker held back, but not before kicking him viciously in the flank. After that he'd peed blood for days, but did the penal system get him any medical aid for that? No. He was convinced that he must have a bum kidney. Today he planned to ask that foreign doctor to be sure to check out his kidneys as long as he was in the hospital anyway.

"Mr. Watkins."

Norman rolled over on his side so suddenly that his left wrist restraint ripped the skin on his wrist. "Shit, get this thing off me. It's tearin' me up."

The dark-skinned doctor — neurology resident according to his name tag — with an unpronounceable name and a singsong voice nodded.

Encouraged, Norman said. "Hey while I'm here, can you check out my kidneys?"

"All your tests are negative." The guy had ignored his question.

"So what's wrong with me, doc?"

"No seizure," the doctor said as he wrote in the chart. "Soon as my attending gets here, you go."

"I asked about my kidney. I got a bum kidney. Pee blood, that sort of thing." Not true about the blood. That was years ago.

Norman wondered what language he was writing in. Pakistani? Iraqi? Did he even comprehend the word, "kidney"?

"My kidney?" Norman repeated.

The freaking doctor didn't respond. Didn't even look at him. The asshole simply walked out of the room.

Shackled to the bed by one ankle manacle and two leather wrist restraints, Norman could not even take a leak without calling one of those hags at the nursing station. Not for a minute did he think any of them were real nurses. Except for the one massive stud of a male nurse, the rest were just minimum-wage bag ladies they pulled in off the streets.

Then there was a tap at the door and a tall, black man, dressed in black pants and a black button-down shirt walked in. "Chaplain Henry," he announced in a booming voice. "Okay if I come in for a chat?"

"Yeah, sure," Norman said, wondering if a visit from the chaplain boded well for him. Maybe his reputation at the prison was paying off. "Sure, Reverend."

"Your wife suggested that maybe you'd like to pray with me," said the man of the cloth.

"Uh, sure. Hey, Rev, you know when they're gonna spring me outta here? All I did was skip parole to see my ma? You know?"

"Your wife says you're in real deep. Those missing kids. Daughters of Scott Monroe. I remember when Scott played for the University of Michigan. Fine catcher. Nice man. Too bad he got injured. But Norman, if you know something about those little girls, I pray to Jesus that you tell the police where they are."

"I'm not saying nothin' about that bitch's kids."

"For your wife's sake and your daughter's, if you tell the police where they are, it'll go easier for you, son."

Norman gaped at the preacher. So Connie suspected? She'd sent the reverend in to get him to talk. Well, it wasn't going to work that way. No one could prove that he was *not* just driving around or sleeping in his car.

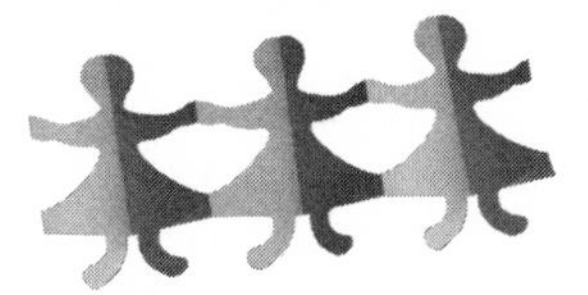

# CHAPTER 14

*FBI Press Conference Not Encouraging –*
*Where Are Sammie and Alex?*
– *Morning News*, Wednesday, June 15

Katie and Scott did not return to the FBI field office Tuesday evening. Instead, they'd participated in a conference call led by Streeter and included agents from Detroit and Tampa. At the end of the call at nine p.m., they could not detect even a trace of optimism. The team kept repeating that as time passed, so did the hope of finding Sammie and Alex alive. Fifty-three hours: no ransom, no concrete connection linking any suspects to the Monroe girls, no new witnesses, lots of unsubstantiated sightings all the way from Florida to Michigan, from California to New York.

Scott had asked for an update on the prime suspects. Maxwell Cutty: continued surveillance in Tampa, no evidence linking to Alex and Sammie other than he'd recently withdrawn a large sum of money, no sign of his boyfriend, Adam Kaninsky. Norman Watkins: seemingly faked a convulsion, being held in a hospital prison ward for observation. Keith Franklin: admitted an ongoing infatuation with Katie, would leave his wife in an instant if Katie would have him, admitted to an extramarital affair with a white woman, no evidence to hold him, released but under surveillance in Detroit.

Jackie had fallen asleep in her grandmother's arms, and Scott had carried her into their room, laying her on the makeshift bed on the floor. Lucy had an extra bed in her room, but Katie would not allow Jackie out of her sight. Before they went to bed, Scott slipped the contents of one of Lucy's post-surgery sleeping pills into Katie's ginger ale. Scott hated all drugs, but Katie had slept so well with the pill he'd given her earlier.

When Katie awoke Wednesday morning, she was surprised to find that it was already eight thirty and that Scott was not in bed. How could she have slept so late? The usual question for one accustomed to be up before dawn. But as she rolled over and saw Jackie asleep in her cocoon on the floor by her side of the bed, reality struck, erasing any trace of sleep, jolting her awake.

*Sammie and Alex*? Had there been any news? It was all she could do to refrain from crying out. She looked down at Jackie, needing to see Alex and Sammie lying there, too. Just thinking about them made her heart pound so violently that she felt that she might be having a heart attack, and she struggled to breathe. *Where could they be*? *Were they safe or not?*

Despite the sunlight pouring into the room, Katie's world became totally dark and her body went still. She'd heard their voices inside her head last night, voices so familiar in their individuality. One loud, demanding: "Mom, wake up. You have to take care of Jackie." The other, shy and trembling. "Mom, please, Jackie needs you."

Katie felt her body stiffen, but her eyes remained closed and she stopped even trying to breathe. Sammie's voice, Alex's voice. Both mingling, pleading with her, and finally fading.

Katie sat up, trying to understand what Sammie and Alex were trying to tell her. The triplets had been so close, anticipating each other's every move. Were they telling her that something would happen to Jackie, too? Ever since the triplets were born, a piece of Katie's brain had been set in triplicate. Like an equilateral triangle she often thought, three identical angles making up a whole. An equal proportion allocated to Alex, Sammie, and Jackie. Holding her breath, Katie peered down on the floor to the nest of comforters. Jackie was still asleep, her head buried under the Yankee logo sheets that Scott had given Lucy for Christmas last year.

Katie climbed out of bed, lowered herself to the floor, and lay down by Jackie, placing her hand over her child's chest just to make sure that it was moving, up and down.

"Please stay with me," she whispered.

Jackie stirred and turned to face Katie, so close that Katie could feel the brush of air with each breath of her child.

"Mom, are you okay?" Jackie reached out to stroke Katie's hair.

"Yes, sweetie, as long as you're here with me."

"I'll never leave you and Dad."

Katie was still cradling Jackie in her arms when Scott walked into the bedroom, a steaming cup of coffee in one hand and a mug of hot chocolate in the other.

"Thought I heard voices up here," he said. "Now let's get you two up off the floor."

Scott set down the hot drinks and offered his hand to help Katie, then Jackie, up.

"Is everything okay?" he asked, his gaze lingering on Katie as he handed her coffee.

Should she tell Scott about the dream? *You have to take care of Jackie.*

When Katie did not answer, he repeated his question to Jackie as she sipped hot chocolate.

Before Jackie could answer, Katie said, "I think we should get Jackie a puppy."

Both Scott's and Jackie's jaw dropped, and Scott had to help Jackie steady her hot drink.

Jackie was the first to speak. "A puppy? Mom, you've got to be kidding."

"You've always wanted a dog. Remember that golden lab puppy you and Alex adored?"

"Mom? Sammie hates dogs. She got bit by one. Don't you remember? On her leg. She still has the scar." Jackie stared at Katie, "Hey, Mom, are you okay?"

*No, I'm not okay. Maybe I'm going about this in the wrong way. In my dream, Alex and Sammie each said to take good care of you.*

"What do you think, Scott?" Katie said.

Scott said nothing, just shook his head.

# CHAPTER 15

*Experts Probe Similarities of the Monroe Kidnapping to That of Madeleine McCann in Portugal.*
— Talk Show Circuit, Wednesday, June 17

Manny Gonzalos, beloved by his neighbors for his random acts of kindness, lived alone in a Spanish-style villa on the shore of the Gulf of Mexico in Clearwater Beach. He mostly kept to himself, but there were rumors that he was the anonymous philanthropist behind the many projects that benefited the beach community. There had also been rumors that he was gay, but they'd been squelched when his Clearwater neighbor ran into him at a restaurant on the island of St. Bart's with a voluptuous dark-haired woman. Manny had graciously introduced her as Monique, and it was clear that their relationship was not platonic. No one knew how old he was, but with the spring in his step and his well-muscled physique, the guess was mid-fifties.

Whenever asked about his line of business, Manny simply answered, "financial advisor." All his mail went to a P.O. Box in Clearwater where he kept a façade of an office. Manny had served his profession for forty-five years. Now, at sixty-two, he planned to sell the Clearwater property and retire. Only he would not be applying for Social Security benefits. He'd be off enjoying life in the islands with Monique, who seemed to get more beautiful and sexy with each passing year.

Like most professionals at this stage of his life, Manny wasn't sure how well retirement would sit with him so he had a backup plan, a career adjustment. Something different, but related; a business plan he could implement from anywhere in the world.

Manny would always look back on his career with a surge of professional pride. In all honesty, he considered himself the smartest and the most resourceful pro in the business — even with his one fuck-up, now many years ago, for which he'd paid by absenting himself from the country for seven years. Despite that one exception, he'd always prided himself on his work and endeavored to exceed his customers' expectations.

Manny attributed his success to three factors: client selection, meticulous planning, and ingenuity. The way he worked was to cluster several cases close in time and then disappear to the islands and into the arms of Monique for a few months. When he returned he would entertain the next schedule of hits. For each client, a different identity — different name, different physical appearance, secure contact. About this he was meticulous.

Manny found scrupulous client selection the trickiest part of the job. The actual killings were easy. There were endless ways. All you had to do was treat the job like any profession, stay focused, and be reasonably smart. For Manny, smart was his calling card. The hallmark of his talent was taking the time to figure the strategy that fit each case perfectly. He'd been successful in every case but one and that still gnawed on him — and it was a kid. Well, he was smarter now.

In the dark corner of the office in his uncle's Ybor City club, Manny checked his Rolex and patted his jacket pocket. The thick wad of airline tickets felt good. No e-tickets for him. A master of disguise, Manny had chosen the ponytail and a jeans and sports coat look for the meeting with his client. The wig was the same he'd used in the past dealing with Maxwell Cutty, but the threads were different. And the name Vincent, the same as last time. Thinking of Cutty made him grin at the prospect of overcharging the bastard. He'd charge the faggot double the going rate. The creep was a pedophile. So despicable he made Manny cringe. But a job was a job. Good guy — bad guy, he didn't care. As usual, Manny had been briefed by his high-level cop informant inside the Tampa Police. Manny always checked his clients out. He couldn't afford surprises. And he always wore a wire for client meetings.

When Maxwell Cutty had tried to withdraw money from the bank Monday afternoon, the assistant manager had balked. "Very irregular," he had responded to Maxwell's request for one hundred and fifty thousand dollars in hundreds.Normally when some lowlife jerked him around, Maxwell would demand to see the manager and threaten to take his business elsewhere. But, instead, he'd had to kiss the prick's ass and politely point out that he did not have to explain his use of his own company's funds.

Now that he had the money, all he had to do was wait. Vincent said it would take a day to set things up in Nevis, and they'd meet in person at noon in Ybor City. In the meantime, Maxwell did not leave the house. The feds had already searched the place. They had his computer hard drive, but what could that do? Maxwell was not stupid enough to leave trace evidence. By tomorrow, Vincent would have eradicated the last trace linking him with the Monroe family, any child abuse charges, and even to his wife's death.

# CHAPTER 16

*European Union Summit in Brussels to Focus on Climate Change Policies and Tightening Financial Supervision.*
– International News, Wednesday, June 17, 2009

Unable to come to grips with Katie's bizarre suggestion of a puppy for Jackie, Scott simply left the room, shaking his head, descending the stairs, heading for the kitchen. Lucy had gone out for her morning walk, longer every day now as she rehabbed from hip surgery. Danielle had moved back in with her parents to make room for Katie and Scott and Jackie. Scott needed to be alone, alone with his fear, his anguish, and now, his confusion over his wife's reaction.

While Katie had slept the sleep of the drugged, he had lain beside her and cried all night. He'd never believed a man could sob so uncontrollably. He felt drained, his throat was dry, his head foggy. All night long, every scenario, one worse than the next, kept playing in his head. Finally, he'd had to squeeze his head with both hands to try to make them stop, but they wouldn't because the truth was that Alex and Sammie were out there somewhere, but nobody knew where, and he was powerless to find them. Scott knew they were alive. Certainly, if they – he couldn't even think the word – he'd know, he'd be able to feel it, sense it. He missed them so and was so scared for them. Every minute without them was the worst torture he could imagine.

Scott realized that he was losing confidence that he would be able to endure. Katie, too, seemed at the breaking point. What was going on inside her head? Between them, did they have the strength to get through?

Scott went about making coffee and more hot chocolate then sat in Lucy's breakfast nook cradling his mug, waiting for Katie. He planned to talk her into staying home, but when she appeared, one look at her trim mauve business suit dismissed that possibility. He recognized that determined look that she usually reserved for court testimony, that take-no-prisoners look that her colleagues teased her about.

When she came over to sit next to him, putting her arm around his rounded shoulders, he slumped even deeper. He didn't know if he could take another day of agony, another day of uncertainty, another day of abject helplessness.

"Scott, I had a dream last night," Katie said in a near whisper.

Scott looked up, his glance unable to avoid the window facing the gauntlet of reporters camped out on Lucy's lawn and pouring out into the street.

"What about?" He stared out the window, unable to meet her eyes.

"Alex and Sammie. They —"

"Katie, I don't want to hear it."

"In my dream, Alex and Sammie each said, 'To take care of Jackie.' What do you —"

"Stop it, Katie. It was a *dream.*" Scott's voice got louder, "Dreams are *not true.*"

"Dad, are you okay?" Jackie's call came from the top of the stairs.

Scott's head jerked up. "I'm sorry, honey." He summoned the energy to climb the stairs. He picked Jackie up and carried her into the kitchen as if she were a toddler. Jackie, too, was dressed for a day at FBI headquarters. Resigned, obedient, a role model for her collapsing parents.

"I'm okay," Scott said, setting her down by the kitchen table. "What about you?"

"I'm ready to go in to see Agent Streeter," Jackie said. "Did you know that he has three little girls?"

Scott was barely able to nod, so intent was he on holding back the brimming hot tears.

"You know, Dad, what Mom said about me getting a dog, it did cheer me up. But once Sammie is back, she'll talk Mom out of it, I'm sure of it."

Scott said nothing, put Jackie on his lap, but was unable to focus on her, only thinking about Katie's dream. He didn't want to hear it. What was happening to Katie. What was happening to him?

When he'd met Katie, she'd been so innocent. She was a medical student and that did make her automatically smart, but how could he ever have imagined that such a sensitive and wholesome woman would end up with a job dealing with despicable perverts? Isn't this what the kidnapping was all about? Some twisted maniac's idea of retribution?

Why couldn't she have gone into dermatology or orthopedics or basket weaving? Why forensic child psychiatry? But Scott knew the answer; Katie's heart went out to the small victims of such unspeakable violence. She felt compelled to protect them from the child abusers and sexual perverts under whose custody they suffered. If she didn't help them, who would? To whom would the court turn to get these kids to a safe place? Scott felt his face contort when he considered what her Pollyanna attitude had cost. Nothing, nobody's children could balance the loss of Sammie and Alex.

"No." Scott said aloud. Stop thinking. He would go insane if he allowed himself to dwell on the stream of atrocities that kept invading his mind. Atrocities that he knew might be worse than the outer limits of his imagination. "No," he repeated.

"Dad?" Jackie looked up from her position on his lap. "You mean about the dog?"

"No what, Scott?" Katie scrutinized him, her eyebrows arched.

"Okay, everybody, I'm going to make breakfast," Lucy announced from the front door. "I walked a half a mile today and no pain. I nodded to all those reporters, but didn't say a word."

"That's great, Mom, but —" Katie started.

"Scrambled eggs and sausage," Lucy interrupted. "Jackie, could you butter the toast?"

"Sure, Grandma."

When Jackie hopped off his lap, Scott stood. Wanting to avoid a confrontation with Katie, he walked into the living room. Another glance out the window, television reporters and journalists waiting. Waiting for what? For a glance at the bereaved parents? For a glimpse of the *safe* triplet? Desperate for any glimpse of parental reaction.

What if Katie's dream — he couldn't think about that. A dream is a dream, nothing more. Looking up, he saw the Jones family collage, Lucy's pride and joy. Lucy's four daughters at their respective college graduations. Stacy, Sharon, Rachael, and his Katie. All overachievers, the result of Lucy's insatiable drive and her bottomless devotion. On either side of this collection was a high school graduation photo of Lucy's two sons. Each of the boys had a different father, different from the four girls. Each had died tragically, each a victim of the Detroit riots, now more than forty years ago. Anthony and Johnny. Unlike Lucy, Scott did not think he could survive the loss of two children.

He inspected Katie's graduation photo closer up. She stood proudly in cap and gown, in front of the maize and blue University of Michigan banner. Lucy on one side, and a tall lanky boy close to Katie's age, with skin a few tones lighter than hers, on the other. Keith Franklin. Was this whole thing about Keith's obsession over Katie? If so, why couldn't the FBI nail this guy and find his daughters?

"Scott, come get something to eat," Lucy called just as he was setting the photo composite down. "Oh, that reminds me," she said.

When they got back into the kitchen, Lucy handed Scott a plate loaded with eggs and sausage. "You can serve your dad the toast, Jackie."

Then turning to Katie, Lucy seemed to hesitate. "Katie, I think I need to mention this to you."

"What's that, Mom?" Katie asked.

"Daisy Franklin stopped by yesterday. She said that the FBI had taken Keith in for questioning and kept him overnight. They pretty much tore up his house, searched his car, and searched Daisy's house, too. She wanted me to tell you that her son had nothing to do with Alex and Sammie."

"He went to Monica's concert and sent me a recent e-mail, Mom." Katie pushed aside her plate.

"You see, Keith never got over you. Daisy admitted that she'd been passing information about you that she got from me to Keith. That Keith is always holding you up on a pedestal. That his obsession — that's the word she used — angers his wife. That it's driven a wedge into their marriage. He's even admitted to having an affair, but that's not because —"

Katie began to massage her temples. "Keith was so long ago. All that was so long ago. I can't believe it"

"Grandma? Who are you talking about?"

"I'm sorry," Lucy said, bending to pull Jackie into her arms. "Just a man that your mom used to know."

"A bad man?"

"Yes," Scott said, "a bad man, but you do not have to worry about him, honey."

"Is that where Alex and Sammie are? At his house? Why can't we go there and get them?"

"Agent Streeter is checking all that out," Katie said. "Now we'd better get going downtown."

"I know that you said I could stay with Grandma today," Jackie said, "but I decided I want to go with you."

"I thought you didn't want to come with us?" Scott said. Had he missed something?

"Tina goes with her mom so I want to go with you," Jackie said. Jackie was holding together pretty good, Scott thought. Better than he and Katie were.

Maxwell Cutty awoke the next morning groggy from the pills and booze, but horny. Flipping over, he half expected to find Adam lying naked beside him. That was before he remembered that by tomorrow night Adam would be sacrificed. Unfortunate trade-off, but necessary, to eliminate all traces. Maxwell groaned at the realization that he'd have to find the boy's replacement. Adam had been diligent as well as sexy. He would have had coffee ready, using that automatic feature on the coffeemaker that Maxwell could never figure out. Now he'd have to fix his own. Instant would have to do.

Maxwell eased out of bed and shuffled in the nude to his bathroom. He'd forgotten to set an alarm, but a glance at the clock told him it was only ten thirty, plenty of time to make his noon meeting in Ybor City. He found a bottle of Tylenol and downed three gelcaps with the bottled water he kept nearby. That should calm the nagging headache that plagued him every morning after he'd had more than a couple of drinks.

His erection had not subsided and Maxwell felt a particular longing to call Adam just to hear his sweet tenor voice for the last time. And, to make sure that the boy was ensconced in that villa in Nevis. Maxwell took out his wallet to find the phone number of the isolated house on the beach. As he pulled it out, a photo of him with Adam on a sailboat on Tampa Bay fell out. Maxwell bent to pick it up. They looked so perfect together. Both tan and lean. Adam trimmer, but he *was* twenty-plus years younger. Adam was gazing at him with those expressive gorgeous turquoise eyes. The kid looked so hot that Maxwell felt a delicious pulse harden his erection. Too bad that that gorgeous specimen of a boy had to be destroyed. But the stakes were high, and there'd been no choice.

Heading toward his dressing room, Maxwell slipped on yesterday's underwear and pulled on sweat pants and a polo shirt from the dirty laundry. He was usually meticulous about his grooming, but today he was not himself. No wonder, he thought, it was midmorning and he needed a caffeine fix. So he merely brushed his teeth and ran a comb through his thick head of auburn-tinted hair.

As he passed a mirror on the way to the kitchen, a silly smile appeared on his face. Still a stud, he said to himself. The smile turned to a grimace when he searched his cupboard and realized that he was out of coffee of any type and that the bread on the counter was marbled with blue mold. At least the orange juice was fresh, so he poured himself a glass and tried to read the newspaper. The story of the missing Monroe girls dominated the news, and he read every word. He felt exhilarated that Dr. Kate Monroe was reduced to begging for the life of her daughters, but he also felt worried. The job was not yet done.

"Have to have coffee. Have to think this through." He spoke aloud to no one as he ran his fingers through rumpled hair. "Go to Starbucks."

Once he had his brain fired up, he'd consider his other problems: how to replace that money he'd taken from his company to pay the hit man, soon his accountants would start asking questions; figure out what the FBI might have learned from searching his home; find out whether he could get his lawyer to bring some kind of charges on the feds for invading his privacy; make plans to get his sons back home.

He'd been too exhausted to think about it last night, but he'd have to do a careful mental inventory of his computer hard drive. Had he left anything that could implicate him? Were there other precautions he should take? But he wasn't overly worried. He was smarter than them all.

But first things first. He retrieved the money from his safe and packed it in a large plastic shopping bag. A guy in sweats hauling a Kmart bag would hardly be worth a glance.

On the way to Starbucks, Maxwell found a pay phone near a strip mall. Needing to check on Adam, he dialed the Nevis exchange using an untraceable phone card. No answer. He let it ring fifteen times. Tampa summers are blistering, and sweat started to pour down his face. Thinking he may have misdialed, he tried again. Still, no answer. Adam should be there. He wasn't supposed to leave. It was critical that no one on the island see him. Maxwell had been precise: arrival by boat at night, avoiding all immigration and passport checks. Why wasn't the boy answering the phone? Then with a start, Maxwell tapped his head. He'd specifically told Adam not to respond to the phone or the door. And no way could he risk e-mail.

Maxwell breathed a loud sigh and cursed himself. He should have set up some kind of code so they could communicate. Still, he couldn't dismiss Adam from his mind as he drove through Tampa to his meeting in Ybor City. What if Adam couldn't keep his pecker in his pants? What if he was out walking the beach, picking up another rich patron? The fucking boy knew that he was Adonis personified.

Scott and Katie and Jackie arrived at the FBI field office on Michigan Avenue at ten thirty a.m. They did not have a specific appointment, but Streeter told them that they could spend as much time at bureau headquarters as they wished. He'd been careful to emphasize that they need not come in, assuring them that he'd make immediate contact if any information came in. They were now heading into the third day without a sliver of helpful information as to the whereabouts of Alex and Sammie Monroe.

Why had no one come forward with a ransom demand? That did not bode well. If nothing happened today, he'd put the Monroe parents back on television for a renewed plea. And he'd make a decision on whether the family should offer a reward. Scott's sister, Monica, was pushing for a very significant one. The woman had huge financial assets and wanted to go for at least a million dollars. Ridiculous, Streeter knew, but he was considering one hundred thousand. That amount should stimulate anyone who had knowledge of the girls to come forward. It would also trigger an avalanche of fake sightings.

Yesterday with the help of Katie and Scott, they'd sifted through the barrage of sightings everywhere from Detroit to Florida to Alaska. Streeter vowed to follow up even the most ridiculous reports, but so far neither his agents nor the Monroe parents had seen anything that triggered suspicion. The sightings were vague and nonspecific and none had panned out.

By the time the Monroes arrived, Streeter had evaluated the latest call-in, a clerk at a Kmart, suspicious because an old woman checked out on Sunday with "two of everything." How remote was that? But he'd committed to the Monroes and to the media. Every lead would be followed up.

All Streeter could tell the Monroes was that there was one possible witness — Courtney Davis, the mother of the crying kids — the woman had been so distracted that her description was vague. Of all the people in the mall, only one person reported seeing two little girls leave with a middle-aged, overweight white woman. She'd seen no struggle, nothing that would indicate foul play. Nothing more could be squeezed out of anyone at that mall. Clarence Plummer had not given up. He had personally organized ongoing surveillance of all shoppers and moviegoers on the outside chance that someone may have been there Sunday afternoon and noticed something of interest.

Once in their assigned conference room, Katie handed Jackie her book of crossword puzzles. Jackie fidgeted, shifting from foot to foot like his daughters did when they had to go to the bathroom. Before the Monroes sat down, Jackie, her voice noticeably louder than usual, said, "Are Sammie and Alex dead, Agent Streeter?"

"Jackie, no —" Scott's loud voice only a whisper now as he pulled Jackie against him. For a moment, Streeter thought Scott was going to cover the little girl's ears.

"Jackie," Streeter said, we haven't found them yet, but everybody's looking for them."

"Why haven't you arrested the bad man that hates my mom? Did he kill them?"

Streeter tried to say something soothing, calming, but he couldn't come up with the words. "I have —" he started.

Katie's voice was soft as she interrupted, "Jackie's talking about Cutty. What if he hired somebody to come to Detroit? That would divert the attention from him in Tampa. Right?"

Streeter remained silent. No response percolated to his tongue.

"I'm sorry. I know that you and everybody are doing everything —" Katie gestured toward Jackie and Scott. "We're just all beside ourselves with worry and fear."

All that psychiatric training means nothing when you're a mother and your own kids are involved. Streeter watched Jackie inch closer to Scott. How cruel to make a child endure such extreme tension. Streeter didn't know what to do. Could he order them to take Jackie and not bring her back, for the child's own good?

A banging knock interrupted the tableau, and Agent Camry barged into the conference room.

"Ransom demand," she said, shoving a printed sheet of paper at Streeter.

"That means they're alive," Katie breathed.

Streeter scanned the note, then looked directly at Scott. "Mr. Monroe, we need to talk to you about this. The surveillance that we put on the Yankee organization paid off."

"We've got agents all over this," Camry said. "Tony, you want to go check on things and I'll brief the Monroes?"

Camry must have sensed the background tension in the room and Streeter accepted her offer of temporary escape.

"Dr. Monroe, Mr. Monroe, Jackie," she said, "why don't we all sit down and I'll tell you everything we have. She waited for the three of them to take a seat, and she did too. "Ten minutes ago," Camry began, "Don Plese, manager of the Yankees, got a phone call that went to voice mail. Here's what it said." She read verbatim: "*I have the Monroe girls. They are alive. I will keep them that way as long as you do exactly what I say. You call Scott Monroe and tell him that he can save his precious daughters, but it will cost him one million dollars. Cash. That's all I'm gonna say right now. I'm going to leave a message tomorrow, or maybe the next day. I'm going to tell you exactly what to do. I'm just calling now so you can tell him to get the money ready. If anybody calls in the cops or the FBI, I will know. And I will kill these two little bitches and go after the third kid, too.*"

"A million dollars," Katie breathed. "We can do that. Right, Scott?"

"Yes," Scott said. "But why the Yankees? Somebody I know?"

An agent poked his crew cut head into the room. "Traced back to a pay phone. Auburn Hills. Less than a mile from the mall where they were taken. Credibility undetermined at this time. Could be bullshit."

"And all the time we were looking at Dr. Monroe as the target," Camry said. "Yes, the team will need you for several hours, Mr. Monroe. Dr. Monroe, do you want to take Jackie home, or somewhere?"

# CHAPTER 17

*High Risk Profession: Forensic Pediatric Psychiatrist?*
*Dr. Katie Monroe.*
— Tampa Newscasts, Wednesday, June 17

Keith Franklin knew what he wanted and who he wanted. And he wanted Katie Jones. She belonged to him. How many times had they whispered that *they belonged together*. And she had belonged to him for how many years? Had it been six or seven? Back then they were just two kids in love. Matter of fact, he loved her so much that he took advantage of the system so he could buy her expensive gifts. She loved jewelry and hot rides. She'd been so proud of him back then. One good looking dude with a full-time job, extra bread on the side. He loved her so much that he'd forgiven her, actually forgiven her, for turning him in and testifying against him in court.

Most people didn't appreciate deep love like that. They were all into payback, retribution, they called it. Not him. He'd served his time in the Jackson state prison like a man. Parole after nine years. Never nobody's bitch. Decent parole record. Nothing worse than the occasional drunken binge. Currently employed by the city of Detroit; union job, riding a garbage truck. Decent benefits.

Keith was smart enough to know that he'd have to bide his time to get Katie back. He made no secret about wanting her. His family, his wife, and even his sons knew that. But until now they'd all laughed him off. What would hoity-toity Katie Jones Monroe, living the rich white husband life want with him? Well they weren't laughing now. Even the cops were taking him and Katie seriously. Once this was all over, he'd have Katie back. Only her name would be Katie Franklin, not Katie Monroe.

Was his wife jealous? Damn straight, she was. Like he gave a shit.

He may have put on a show, letting Penny rant and rave, but he'd walk out on her in a New York minute. The boys, too. Unless they *wanted* to come live with him and Katie and her triplet daughters. His boys were ten, nine, and seven. Given a choice, they'd go for Katie over Penny. Who wouldn't?

Keith had given a lot of thought about how to get Katie back. Matter of fact, Katie was about all he thought about these days. His solution: through her daughters. Through his mother, he'd kept track of Katie for all these years, but only recently had he made his move.

Down at the FBI, he'd been Mr. Cool with the asshole agents. Treated them politely, refusing to let himself be baited. Behavior that had worked for him in the joint. Eventually, they'd let him go, but only after he'd given up a piece of information that he hadn't intended to. While waiting for Katie, he'd started an affair – with a white woman. Jane Wise. Poor bitch, she was married, too. And now the feds were gonna be all over her. Up until now, he'd kept his white girlfriend from Penny, but now all hell would break loose. He didn't give a rat's ass about Penny, but Katie, what would she think?

# CHAPTER 18

*Swedish Car Company Agrees to Buy Saab from General Motors.*
– National News, Wednesday, June 17

The Detroit FBI field office is located in the Patrick V. McNamera Federal Building in downtown Detroit, not far from Tiger Stadium. The building occupies a full city block on Michigan Avenue and is twenty-seven stories high. Jackie, for some reason that Katie could never understand, did not like large buildings. Whenever Katie took the triplets into the courthouse in Tampa, which was rare, Jackie had always protested. "I hate big buildings," she'd say. Sammie and Alex would laugh and tease her, all in fun.

When they'd arrived this morning, Jackie had come to a full stop before entering. She'd looked up at Scott. "Dad," she'd said, "I just wish we could see the Tigers play. Do they have a game today?"

"I don't know," Scott told her. Scott, who had every major league team's schedule etched in his brain, had not spoken one word of baseball since this had all begun. And now, he'd have to refocus. Whoever claimed they had Sammie and Alex was connected to baseball. Why else would the kidnapper contact the manager of the Yankees?

Leaving Scott in the conference room, Katie took Jackie's hand and walked toward the elevators. As they descended from the seventh floor, heading toward the food court in the basement, Jackie tried to ask Katie questions. "Mom, did Agent Camry say that they found Alex and Sammie? Are they okay? Who was that old boyfriend that Grandma was talking about? Did Daddy know that you had a boyfriend? Do you think Tina's dad will be okay? Why did you yell at Agent Streeter and use that very bad word?" On and on. Katie had no answers, just two gaping holes in the triangle that used to be her life. Jackie's questions went unanswered and ignored.

As Scott walked into the large, rectangular conference room, the air was warm and musty. Too many agents with too many laptops and several big screens to display team rosters and lists of staffs. Names and faces of his professional contacts over the years. Was his daughters' abductor on these lists? To find out, he'd need to focus, to concentrate even though he felt drained of every bit of logic and reason. For the past sixty-six hours, he'd been blaming Katie and her career, and now it seemed, the blame was on him.

Could this be all about him? Not Katie? Not her perverts? Not her jealous ex-boyfriend, but him? Scott felt his heart hammer and sat down, grasping his head tightly between his hands so that it wouldn't explode. Could there be something from his past, so heinous that payback meant taking his little girls? Or was this all about money? He and Katie were well off and the whole world knew about his sister's wealth. Monica would part with every one of her dollars for Alex and Sammie's safety, of that Scott was sure. So if it was about money, didn't that mean a ray of hope? Scott hadn't realized, but he'd started to cry, right in front of a roomful of federal agents.

Streeter spoke first. "Mr. Monroe, we know how difficult this is for you, but we need your help here. We hope that you can shed some light on why this ransom demand came through the Yankee organization? Why would the kidnappers use the Yankee manager to get to you? Please, let's start with your career as of now and work our way backward."

Streeter started probing the Yankee organization. The Bronx, Tampa, the majors, the Grapefruit League, George M. Steinbrenner Field and before that Legends Field, Scott's home base. Was there dissent? Altercations, verbal or physical? Scott denied any. For two ruthless hours, agents rotated through team players with whom Scott had worked in the American League. As players and staffers clicked on, then off the screens with their bios and stats, Scott searched his mind for any connection or any clue that could trigger his daughters' abduction. He failed to make a connection. Scott had always prided himself on getting along. Sure, a lot of jerks and losers had crossed his path, but he'd made the most of everybody's positives and didn't let the negatives stick in his craw. Or at least that's how he'd thought of himself. Had he been that wrong? Somewhere in his career he must have antagonized a player or a coach or somebody to the point that his daughters would be used to get back at him.

# CHAPTER 19

*Tampa Little League to Hold Candlelight Service on Davis Island.*
— Local Tampa News, Wednesday, June 17

Maxwell pushed the image of Adam aside as he walked into the appointed room at precisely noon. A bulky man with a gray ponytail — looking the same as he had the last time — sat at a square table. The man he knew as Vincent did not get up, and as usual, he wasted little energy or words. But he was dead-on efficient. Maxwell wondered how Vincent would choose to eliminate Adam.

"Got the money?" Vincent asked. No pleasant chitchat.

Maxwell set the shopping bag on the table and continued to stand.

Vincent grunted as he opened the bag, fingered the bills.

"It's all there," Maxwell said. "Just take care of it, fast."

"It'll be my pleasure to meet your friend and conduct my business," Vincent said, apparently satisfied that the required one hundred fifty grand had indeed been delivered.

Maxwell turned toward the door. Feeling nauseous, his headache returning.

"The details that I asked you for?"

"Oh, yeah," Maxwell fumbled in his pocket, found the package and handed it to Vincent. Photos of Adam. A photo of the villa in Nevis as well as the address and phone number.

"You say that he'll be here?" Vincent stabbed the image of the looming white villa.

"Anywhere else he might hang out?"

"He's there to hide out. He's not going anywhere."

Vincent pocketed the photos. "You better be right about that."

"Just get it done now," Maxwell said. "Like before, do whatever you have to do. You hear?"

"Oh, yeah. I'm good on meeting my commitments, Mr. Cutty. Now you stay out of trouble."

Streeter had left the conference room, returning at noon to call for a lunch break. "We will need to continue this, Mr. Monroe. You've had a long career and we'll move to the National League and then to the minors. Maybe something will trigger suspicion. Perhaps?"

"Katie and Jackie?" Scott asked. "Are they still here?"

"Yes, we've been going over the call-in leads. Dr. Monroe insisted, but I wish she'd take Jackie home. I have daughters of my own and I wouldn't want — "

"I've tried. Katie has some kind of paranoia," Scott tried to explain. "But who can blame her? She's always been the best mother with the best instincts that I've ever seen, but now — "

"Let's get you out to them. It's a nice day, maybe you could take a walk. Go to the stadium. Tigers are in St. Louis today, though."

"I'm just too beat up and confused, I don't know what to do."

Scott tried to get up, but felt his knees buckle and he slumped back in the chair. Suddenly his vision blurred and his heart raced. He grasped the edge of the table to check the surge of dizziness. His doctor had suggested that he cut back on caffeine. Today he'd had too many cups of coffee to count and had eaten little.

"Maybe if I got something to eat?" He tried again and this time stood without getting dizzy.

Streeter took him to Katie, who was speaking quietly to the agent monitoring incoming calls reporting Alex and Sammie sightings. Jackie sat limp beside her, her crossword book open and unattended.

Katie left her post and the three of them headed to the cafeteria, hand in hand. Just feeling Katie's touch immediately made Scott feel stronger, more physically stable. She asked if anything was new.

He shook his head. "I know what you've been going through, babe. Lots of questions. No answers. No leads whatsoever that I could identify. Anything come up here? All this — " Scott said over the top of Jackie's head.

"Dad, does anybody know where Alex and Sammie are?" Jackie asked. Her tone held no hope and her question was ignored.

"So many people calling in," Katie sighed. "So many false reports. So many sightings; so many disappointments; so many nothings. Last caller said a lady bought twin beds at her garage sale. Lady looked suspicious. Nothing else. Just bought twin beds and looked suspicious. Believe it or not the FBI will check it out."

Manny Gonzalos donned a muddy brown sweat suit, changed into sneakers, exchanged his gray wig for a dark brown one with a bald patch, and followed Cutty. This prick of a client had no remorse. Just kill the wife. Just kill the boyfriend. Just kill. But who was he to pass judgment? He no longer kept count of his hits. For him, it was a job. No emotional entanglements.

From a window, Manny observed Cutty walk out onto the busy street, keeping him in sight, sweeping the small binoculars in a circular pattern. This was his routine, and today he was taking every precaution. His sleazy customer had not mentioned anything about the missing Monroe children. Through his police informant, Manny knew that Cutty was a person of interest in their disappearance, and he knew that the feds had nothing on him. Maybe he shouldn't have taken this job; he'd vowed to never get involved when the hit involved kids. And now, as two men in dark, conservative suits, which screamed FBI, followed Cutty at a conservative distance, he knew he'd made a mistake. Had this been about the hit he'd done on Olivia Cutty, the cops would be local, not feds, and Manny would have had a heads-up from his man in the Tampa force.

No matter, the feds had followed the stupid fuck to Ybor City. That made Cutty a liability that Manny could ill afford. He had no choice. It was not the first time he'd run into complications and had to take out his own client. Manny could not risk the fed's interrogation of a coward like Cutty. The die was cast; he had only to choose the means. His arsenal of methods started to cycle though his mind as he logically evaluated his options. Cutty had gotten into a white Lexus sedan. The guys in suits got in a plain black sedan, and Manny followed in his tan paneled van.

Adam Kaninsky would have a few more hours added to his life, but Manny would get to him. A deal is a deal. And loose ends are loose ends.

# CHAPTER 20

*Obama's Health Care Plan Sidetracked by Economic Woes.*
– National News, Wednesday, June 17

A male nurse, burly and bearded, barged into his hospital room just as Norman Watkins had drifted off to sleep. Why were hospitals so noisy at night? And why had they refused his request for a sleeping pill? And now, what did they want?

"You're outta here." The nurse unlocked the manacle on his ankle, and removed the straps binding his wrists to the rail of the hospital bed.

The nurse wasn't alone. Two men in dark suits, one tall, one squat, hovered at the foot of the bed.

"Put these on, dude." The nurse tossed a bundle of puke green clothes at him. Prison issue.

The squat one, not yet identified but an obvious federal agent, pulled out a set of cuffs and jangled them as Norman picked up the ugly, wrinkled pants and shirt. "You're coming with us."

The taller man checked his watch. "Hurry it up, man. Streeter wants you now."

"Can't I see my wife?" Norman figured the request was worth a chance. By now, Connie must know where he was. She'd be royally pissed. After all the promises he'd made. And he'd meant them. And now it all came down to this. He was headed back to prison. He'd made the wrong choice, again. He supposed that made him a defective person. His life had turned back to shit. He was not worth a goddamn. Of no use to Connie. And Tina? She'd be better off without him.

For Norman it was like an epiphany. Like when God came down and struck Paul, or Saul, as he was called, off that big white horse. Like a clear message. Only for Norman, he would not be going forth and speaking in tongues. The only use for his tongue was to tell Connie and Tina that he was sorry. That he had screwed up their lives one more time.

Neither of the suits bothered to respond to his request to talk to his wife. The agents had launched into an animated discussion of the Detroit Tiger's standing in the American league. The squat one just kept jangling the handcuffs. The tall one deliberately brushed his jacket back just far enough for Norman to see the gun. For a moment Norman stared at it. Despite time in the joint, he didn't know much about guns. Never even had held one. Didn't know the difference between a pistol and a revolver or even if there was a difference. He seemed to recall that one had a safety; the other didn't. He pondered that uncertainty as the male nurse followed him into the bathroom, watched him whiz, and supervised the removal of the polka-dot hospital gown.

"Speed it up, man." The bearded nurse vainly flexed his biceps as Norman changed into drab green prison gear.

Securing him by one arm, the nurse led Norman toward the waiting agents near the lobby. Norman kept his head down, trudging as if sedated. Now close to the two agents, the nurse dropped his hold. Like a good con, Norman extended his hands to be cuffed.

All baseball banter came to a violent halt when Norman, hands pressed together and extended, lurched toward the taller agent, the one with the open suit jacket and exposed weapon. Intimidated, scared, but committed, Norman grabbed for the gun. It was easier than he thought to yank it out of the shoulder holster with one hand as his other grappled with the stunned agent. For an instant he held the weapon solidly in his hand and stared. It was heavier than he'd expected. But time was not on his side, and Norman did not hesitate. A dedicated family man, he could not put Connie and Tina through this again. With an expression of awe, Norman lifted the gun, bringing the barrel perpendicular to the agent's chest.

No one knew whether Norman heard the blast as his body jerked backward against the bulky male nurse before it slumped onto the dusky gray tile, a gaping hole marring the forehead.

Uneaten sandwiches and an open, nearly full potato chip bag remained on the table when the three Monroes left the cafeteria. Mostly they had remained silent. Even Jackie had given up trying for answers to her unending questions. After thirty-five minutes, Katie checked her watch and suggested that Scott return to the conference room to complete his interrogation. Katie said that she would spend time with Jackie in the reception area. But both she and Scott knew that she wouldn't stay. Within minutes, she would rejoin the agents going over new sightings.

"You sure you don't want to go back to your Mom's, take Jackie?" Scott posed the question, again. "This could take a long time."

"No, we'll wait here. Scott, I'm so scared. I don't want to be away from you."

"Okay, babe, but they want me to go over almost everybody in professional baseball."

Scott hugged Katie and Jackie before he disappeared back into the conference room. On the way back to the reception area, Jackie spotted Tina and Connie Watkins coming out of a small room.

"There's Tina and her mom," she pointed out. "They look so sad. Do you think her dad is still in jail?"

"He's in the hospital," Katie said.

"What happened to him?"

"I don't know," Katie said, unwilling to explain the suspected faked convulsion.

Then Katie stopped short. Should she try to talk to Connie? Would it do any good? Connie might know something. She decided to approach her.

"Mom, please, don't get into another argument," Jackie said, tugging on Katie's shirt sleeve. "Look, they're both crying, real hard."

As Katie headed toward Tina and Connie, Connie grabbed her daughter, shielding her with her body.

"If he dies, it's because you killed him," Connie shrieked. Her tear-stained, bloodshot eyes stared at Katie. "As surely as if you'd pulled the trigger. You put Norman away once. Maybe now you put him away forever." Connie spun Tina around and shoved her forward, close to where Jackie stood, riveted. "See my little girl. All Tina wanted was to have her Dad. You bitch, you murderous bitch. You deserve what happened to your precious daughters." Then she yanked Tina back into her arms.

Katie's eyes started rapid-fire blinking, but all she could do was gape at Connie dragging Tina away from them.

"Tina, I'm sorry about your dad," Jackie said loud enough for all to hear.

"Thank you, Jackie," Tina said through tears. "It's not your fault."

Agent Camry appeared at that moment. "I think you should go now, Mrs. Watkins," she said.

Katie turned to Camry. "Can't you keep her here? What if she knows where Sammie and Alex are? You're going to just let her go?"

By then Tina and Connie Watkins had turned the corner, and Camry ushered Katie and Jackie back into the conference room.

"Tell me how this could have happened!" Streeter yelled, waving the paper in front of the task force as every ashen face turned downward to inspect the surface of the cluttered table. Camry repeated what he'd already heard. "The suspect faked a seizure while in custody. The docs pronounced him perfectly healthy. Our agents were with him as he changed from hospital to prison garb. Then the guy flipped out. Grabbed a weapon off an agent. Aimed it. Our guys had no choice, sir. They had to take him down."

"Shit. What's his status?" Streeter demanded.

"He's in neurosurgery," Camry said. "Critical, they say. Bullet entered the head." She pointed to the middle of her forehead.

"So he's not dead?"

"No, he's not dead, but the prognosis is bad. Even if he lives, the neurologist says he'll be brain dead.

"With this guy's brain may go the whereabouts of those little girls," Streeter said. He had moved Norman Watkins up to being his strongest suspect. Why else would the man be in Detroit on the exact day the kids were taken, and for what? A lame "sick mother" excuse?

"The guy was either crazy or intended to take himself out," Camry said. "No way was he going to escape from a hospital prison ward without getting whacked."

"A suicide right in front of our eyes – a *police* suicide." Streeter's blue eyes blazed with anger. "How the hell did we let that happen?"

No response, but there'd be hell to pay for the Norman Watkins screw up. Streeter could well pay with his job.

Streeter had had only two suspects, three if he counted Franklin, which he did not. Watkins and Cutty. Of the two, he'd liked Watkins better. Now Watkins wouldn't be talking anytime soon, if ever. That left Cutty. It was time to interrogate him in person. That meant going to Tampa. Despite Katie Monroe's insistence, they hadn't had enough incriminating evidence to haul him up to Detroit.

In no mood to face the Monroes after the Watkins debacle, Streeter was about to duck into an empty office when he saw them walking straight toward him.

"We need to talk to you," Katie said, "about Norman Watkins."

"In here." Streeter led them toward an empty conference room down the hall.

"What was his wife screaming about?" Scott asked.

As Streeter updated them on Norman's status, he could see them struggling to process what had gone down. He waited for an outburst of frustration or anger. It didn't come. Instead, Scott said, "I'm going to wait outside with Jackie. Katie wants to go over something with you."

On the way out, Jackie gave the tiniest of waves and Streeter's heart went out to the child and for a moment all he saw were images of his own three daughters.

"I'm struggling to be logical, less hysterical," Katie began. "First, I want to apologize for my inappropriate outbursts. Out there with Connie Watkins and earlier with you. I know that you personally are doing everything you can to find Sammie and Alex and the entire law enforcement team is supporting you. I promise you that I will try harder to help. I was just telling Scott that I've been more of a hindrance, getting in the way. Not acting like a trained professional."

"Katie, I understand, your daughters are missing, you have a right – oh, I'm sorry," Streeter stammered. "Dr. Monroe."

"I like Katie better," she said. "And it's driving Scott crazy that you keep calling him mister. He keeps looking around to see if there's a mister in the room. You are the closest ally we have right now. And we want you to know that we appreciate all you're doing. How long has it been since you've had any sleep?"

Streeter's eyes misted. "A long time," he admitted. "And do me a favor, too. It's Tony. Okay?"

Katie gave up a minuscule grin, the first he'd ever seen cross her face.

"But," she said, "I do want to talk about Adam Kaninsky. I'm trying to be logical here. I've been thinking a lot about Adam. When he first told me what Maxwell was doing to his sons, I was under doctor-patient confidentiality – which as you know, I have broken. Adam was adamant that Maxwell would do anything to keep from going to jail. And I believe that to be true. As a narcissistic personality, he knows he couldn't survive in jail. So he fixes it. He takes my kids to get me off his case. What might Adam know? They were very close, Maxwell and Adam."

"We have Cutty under surveillance," Streeter said. "But we've been unable to locate Kaninsky, and that bothers me."

"Adam was abused as a kid," Katie explained, "by an older brother. Child Protective Services referred him to me eleven years ago. My testimony put his brother in juvenile rehab, and I tried to guide Adam back to a normal childhood. Now he's dedicated to doing whatever he can to prevent other kids going through what he did. That's why he came to me in the beginning of this sexual abuse thing. I don't see Adam hurting my daughters, but he well might know what Maxwell did with them. If you can find Adam –"

"I'm going to Tampa myself, tonight. I'll do what I can," Streeter said.

"If you can find Adam –" Katie repeated.

"I'd better be on my way." Streeter headed into the hall, heard the click of heels in the hallway, and looked up. His secretary was approaching with a dark green shopping bag and a navy blue overnight case. "You're packed for Tampa," she told to him. "And Dr. Monroe,

I have a few things for Jackie, puzzles and games. That's what I get for Agent Streeter's daughters to keep them occupied when they visit him here."

Katie accepted the bag with a sheepish expression and peeked inside. Jackie would love the Harry Potter maze

"But, frankly, Dr. Monroe," the secretary continued, "do you think it is such a good idea to bring her in here with you?"

"I'm so afraid," Katie said. "I'm afraid to lose Jackie, too."

"I understand, Dr. Monroe. God bless you."

Scott noticed a change in Katie when she returned from her private talk with Streeter. He'd known that she'd intended to apologize and he surmised that it had gone well. She seemed more together, less panicky. He wondered how he could be supportive to her when every fiber within him was unraveling. Leaning over, he said to her, "Babe, I love you."

He was rewarded with a sweet smile.

"Katie, let's take a break. Take Jackie to your mom's. Just hang out there."

"Okay." Katie grabbed for Scott's free hand.

"Mom? Are you going to be okay now?"

Katie gave Jackie no response, neither a "yes" nor a "no."

# CHAPTER 21

*Person of Interest in Sammie and Alex Monroe Kidnapping Critically Injured in FBI Custody.*
— Evening News, Wednesday, June 17

Streeter prided himself on his ability to go long periods without sleep, but after nearly seventy-five hours, sleep deprivation was taking its toll. Katie Monroe was right. He needed sleep, he was losing his edge without it. He'd never been so physically exhausted. After calling his ex-wife to say that he'd be going to Tampa, he'd been relieved when she advised against the girls visiting him in Detroit until the Monroe case was closed, one way or another. Marianne knew his limits better than he himself. As much as he missed his daughters, he would be no good to them in his condition. Marianne had put the girls on the phone, and he could detect disappointment in their sweet voices, reminding him of life with Marianne, a life for her full of disappointment.

But Streeter knew he could not dwell on Marianne, and he pushed his own family to the back of his list of priorities. Every hour that passed without finding Sammie and Alex escalated the chances that they would not be found alive. To stay awake, he'd been taking Provigil, a drug used to treat narcolepsy and people with sleep apnea. Shift workers used it to stay awake and Streeter had been on it for three days now. As he climbed into the FBI aircraft at eight thirty p.m., he hoped for an uninterrupted three hours.

Prudence prevailed and Manny had waited until dark to commence his vigil. In his business he was loath to compromise on any details. His job was all about precision. You get the minutiae laid out right and then back it all up with contingencies. Manny prided himself on his professionalism and he very much appreciated the simple, isolated life that his career had afforded. Every once in a while, he was amused when he overheard a conversation or saw a movie about "terminators." People assumed it was a dangerous job, but if the details were carefully worked out, assassinations weren't that tough to pull off.

He felt confident with the cover of night, not much of a moon, and his prey lived in a neighborhood with large lots, plenty of foliage for cover, and, of course, Manny had the best of the best when it came to equipment. He'd had to fight down the urge to move earlier in the day, realizing that his customer was under FBI surveillance and that the feds could pull him in at will. But his police mole had assured him that the bureau had no plans to move on Cutty until the morning arrival of the lead agent working the Monroe kidnapping in Detroit. So it was mandatory that he do the deed tonight.

Lucky for him that he spent the last night — executing his contingency plan — with night goggles, scoping out concentric perimeters around the Cutty Mediterranean-style estate. An ostentatious pad, but no wonder, the guy was an architect. And his unfortunate late wife, an interior decorator. Must be just glorious inside, but Manny had no plans to go in there. He had, however, been disappointed in the landscape. When he had settled into position, just before dusk, Manny realized that the property needed more color. In his head he laid out the beds of flowers and the arrangements of palms that he'd have added.

But more important than the less than acceptable landscape was the surrounding terrain. He was most pleased to find a wooded knoll overlooking the precise spot where his target would emerge to reach his Lexus, conveniently not parked in the garage. From his perch, lying flat on his stomach, Manny kept in his line of sight the FBI players as they executed their own brand of surveillance of his client.

Unless Cutty went out for the evening, he'd live until morning. Then pop. Didn't matter how many feds were in the swarm.

As it turned out, Cutty did not live until morning. Right after ten thirty p.m., Manny saw his target exit his side door. He also saw a head pop up in the unmarked cop car parked on the street. With no hesitation, his powerful laser scope found Cutty's left temple. With a steady gloved finger, Manny pulled the trigger. As the shot reverberated, Manny paused only long enough to see Cutty's body jolt.

Before the victim's body dropped to the cement apron outside his door, two agents in dark suits leapt from their vehicle, talking into radios.

Calm, efficient and practiced, Manny zipped his weapon into its leather case, swung it over his shoulder, and headed for the Honda cycle waiting across the sparsely wooded lots of two neighbors. Two blocks from the Cutty mansion, he bounced the bike over the curb, slowing at the strip mall two blocks ahead to deposit the rifle into a Dumpster. He hated to part with it, but he'd learned the hard way. Ever since a screw-up with a deaf girl many years ago, he vowed never to use a weapon twice. Another two blocks and he turned into an alley, dumped the cycle, and jumped into the waiting Toyota Camry.

Once in the car, Manny changed into a grandfatherly disguise, complete with the bulging belly he aesthetically disliked, but found quite effective. Calmly he drove to the Courtney-Campbell Causeway and when he found the turnoff, he maneuvered the car into a tiny space surrounded by clumps of palmettos. Then he walked across the street to the dock. Carrying two duffel bags, he headed for the marina's men's room. There he changed into shorts and a golf shirt and a shaggy dark brown wig. He'd now stuffed one duffel bag inside the other, the one weighted down with a large rock containing the changes of clothes he'd used. He smiled pleasantly as he boarded the modest cabin cruiser that would take him to Fort Myers. From there, he'd drive to Fort Lauderdale, then board the flight that would get him to Nevis. All Manny had to do then was find Adam Kaninsky, exterminate him, and move on to St. Bart's and Monique. What happened to the Monroe girls would no longer be his problem. Business was business. Collateral damage, an accepted component of the business model.

# CHAPTER 22

*Photos of the Monroe Triplets Dominate the Media:*
*Are Children Being Exploited in America?*
– Online Public Opinion Poll, Wednesday, June 17

When Katie and Scott arrived with Jackie, Lucy promptly, but politely, dismissed the well-wisher visitors except for her daughters, Sharon and Rachael. Scott headed upstairs to take a shower, leaving Katie with her sisters around the kitchen table while Lucy warmed a casserole of macaroni and cheese, Jackie's favorite. The rest of the kitchen was loaded with salads, sandwiches, fried chicken, chips, and snacks of every description. "They all keep bringing food," Lucy explained, "and Monica's caterers have dropped off huge spreads every day."

"Stacy's on her way home," Sharon told Katie. "She didn't know anything about the girls until she finished the Milford track and got to her hotel in Queenstown. Well, you can imagine her reaction."

"How long will it take Aunt Stacy to get here?" Jackie asked.

"New Zealand is far away," Lucy responded. "But she'll get here just as fast as she can."

"We'll all be together. Oh, God, will we ever be all together? Will we get Alex and Sammie back? Ever?" Katie slumped forward, elbows on the table, head in her hands. She couldn't prevent the sudden gulping sobs, so she just let go. Sharon and Rachel rushed to her side, but when Katie looked up she saw her mother, standing over her with that faraway look in her eyes. Katie knew that look. Mom, thinking of Anthony and Johnny. *No*, was the answer to her question. The Jones family would never be together, not in this life.

Jackie had taken only two bites of mac and cheese before pushing her plate away. How could she eat with Mom crying so hard? She thought about her sisters in some horrible place with nothing to eat. Were they being tortured? Could they even be dead? She didn't think that they were, but she had so many questions. There was so much she didn't understand, but no one wanted to talk to her. She knew they all must hate her, even Grandma, because she had such a funny look on her face. Jackie wished she was with her sisters, even if they were in a terrible place. Sammie would make her laugh, and she'd be there for Alex. If all three were together, they'd be okay, but with her alone, without her sisters, nobody would love her.

Mom was crying even harder now, and Jackie couldn't stand it so she accidently-on-purpose knocked over her glass of milk. Mom might be angry, but it might make her stop crying.

A hefty black man in a dark, crisp suit met Streeter when the FBI aircraft landed at Tampa International Airport. It was eleven thirty, and Streeter rubbed his raw, red eyes as he walked toward his Tampa counterpart. He'd never seen Special Agent Emmitt Rusk, but they'd developed a decent relationship working the Monroe case on the phone and in cyberspace. When Rusk introduced himself, Streeter recognized the polished voice.

But as Rusk approached, he seemed to be motioning for Streeter to go back on the plane. "Best to talk in there," he called out. "Don't know whether you'll be staying or what."

"I just want to get some shut eye," Streeter said, continuing in Rusk's direction, eyeing the waiting Suburban that would take him to his hotel.

"I hear you, but that's not in the cards," Rusk said. "I've got some real bad news for you, Streeter. Best we go on the plane, sit down, and discuss."

Rusk did not beat around the bush. He came right out with it. Maxwell Cutty had been assassinated one hour ago. Leaving his house. Long-range sniper. Bullet to the head dropped him dead.

Streeter was glad he had taken Rusk's advice and sat down in one of the plush seats. He wasn't sure his legs could have supported him through the rage that surged through his being. Rusk's Tampa team had lost forever the last credible link to Katie and Scott's little girls.

"What about the surveillance? You guys had Cutty surrounded."

"Our guys were in place. Whoever did this was a pro. High-powered rifle. Night vision. The works. The question is who had him taken out?"

"Shit." Streeter pounded his fists on the table in front of him. "Where are those little girls?" All the suspects paraded through his mind. Watkins. Franklin. The ransom note. Cutty. And all the kooks that still kept calling in. And what the nondescript middle-aged white woman that their lone witness had seen. That woman was the link to whoever took the girls, but finding her, a needle in a haystack. Sammie and Alex had gone with her, voluntarily, not kicking and screaming.

"Sure you've eliminated the parents?"

Streeter's grimace strained his facial muscles. "I ask myself that at least once every hour. Bottom line, I cannot believe anyone can fake their kind of grief."

"Except it happens."

"I can't see a motive."

"What kind of people are they, the parents?"

"According to everybody, they were a happy, well-adjusted family. Personally, I like them both. Scott's a man's man, an athlete with a winning smile, one of those big, booming voices, easy going personality." Streeter paused before going on. "Katie's more complex. More edgy, less warm and fuzzy, more controlling, won't let the third daughter out of her sight. Funny, the psychiatrists I've known seem like that, more emotionally detached, sort of erratic. On the other hand I've only seen her under extreme stress. She could be totally different under normal circumstances."

"So you're not following the parent angle?"

"I can't totally rule them out, but nothing leads in that direction."

"Tough call," said Rusk. "Hey, we're going to work the hell out of the case here, but I wasn't sure whether you would want to go back to Detroit, or stay here. For me, it'll be an all-nighter, but you look like hell."

Streeter was too exhausted to be making critical decisions. What more could he be doing in Detroit? And Detroit meant facing the Monroe parents with this devastating news.

"Rusk, I'm going to a hotel. I can't function without some sleep. Maybe things will come together for me in the morning."

"Then let's roll," Rusk said. "I've got to get back to the field office, but I'll drop you at a hotel. I just wanted to tell you face-to-face how we fucked up. Let you decide whether to go or stay."

# CHAPTER 23

*Vendetta Against Mom? Can Law Enforcement Protect Key Witnesses Who Protect the Most Vulnerable of Children.*
— *Tampa Daily News*, June 18

Streeter awoke Thursday morning with the weight of the missing Monroe children preying so heavily on his mind that a pounding pressure began to squeeze his temples. He needed Tylenol and caffeine. He made coffee in his room, swallowed two geltabs, then took a hot shower. Feeling better, the pounding headache gone, he made the first of three calls. The easy one: arrangements for the jet to take him back to Detroit. He could leave at eight, putting him downtown before noon.

Next, he called Special Agent Rusk. Nothing new about the Cutty assassination. Sniper placement was confirmed as a clump of trees atop a knoll on neighboring property. Nothing left behind. A clear getaway. Nothing in the Cutty house or car or office relating to the whereabouts of the Monroe children. Rusk did not elaborate, but implied, based on scrutiny of Cutty's financial records, that Cutty had played a role in his ex-wife's death. He also confirmed that he'd pulled one hundred fifty thousand dollars out of his firm's bank account on Monday. The money had not been found.

Streeter didn't care about Cutty's dead wife. "Was Maxwell Cutty responsible for the kidnapping of Sammy and Alex?"

"He's a credible suspect, but without evidence — " Evidence that would now never surface. But what about that missing money? Did it relate to Katie's theory of a professional hire?

Streeter's last call was to Ellen Camry. He asked her to go directly to Lucy Jones's house and inform the Monroes that Cutty was dead, that they were still looking for Adam Kaninsky, and that Streeter would be back that afternoon should they wish to see him. Camry was a trooper, but Streeter could tell by the tremble in her calm, steady voice that she was badly shaken.

With time still left to get to the airport, Streeter ordered a room service breakfast, dressed, packed, ate, all those ordinary things normal people do. He missed his kids. His heart ached for Katie and Scott. In the light of the day, he dismissed the lingering suspicions about them that he and Rusk had discussed the previous night.

Camry rang Lucy's doorbell at seven thirty in the morning. She had not called to forewarn them. Scott answered the door in a tee shirt and sweatpants. Immediately, he wished that he had not. Agent Camry would not be there at that time of the morning with good news. He opened the door and she followed him inside.

"Katie's not up yet," he said. "Should I get her?"

"Yes," Camry said.

Scott ascended the stairs like a robot, passing Jackie at the landing, turning back only when she spoke.

"Dad? Are you okay?"

He didn't stop to respond. He needed to get Katie. He needed to protect Jackie. He needed to protect Alex and Sammie, but he was incapable of doing that.

"Hi, Agent Camry," Jackie said, still in her nightgown, her hair hanging down, not yet brushed. "How come you're here?"

"I came to talk to your parents," Scott heard Camry say. He wished that he'd let Lucy take Jackie on her morning walk, but Katie would have gone ballistic if he'd let their daughter go outside. And Katie would have been right this time as the number of reporters camping out on Lucy's street had multiplied. Poor Jackie was in a prison.

"Did you find my sisters?" Jackie asked.

Scott listened for Camry's response. "No, honey, not yet," she said.

"Thank God," Scott said aloud before resuming his course up the steps. *They can't be dead. She didn't say that they were dead.*

Katie, dressed in slacks and a tunic top, came into the living room just as Lucy returned from her morning walk. Scott had served Camry coffee and he'd fixed oatmeal for Jackie. As he poured coffee for Katie, he tried to conceal his annoyance. When he'd told her that Agent Camry needed to speak to them, together, Katie had said that she'd be right down. Half an hour later she appeared. Scott guessed why it had taken her so long. Like him, she was terrified of what the agent might tell them.

"Mom, can you take Jackie upstairs and get her ready to go out?" Katie asked.

Not saying a word, Lucy took her granddaughter's hand and urged her up the steps.

"Why can't you tell me what's happening?" Jackie repeated.

Neither parent responded, nor did Camry.

"Come on, Jackie," Lucy said. "Everything will be okay."

Katie and Scott sat beside each other on the sofa.

"What is it?" Scott moved closer to Katie and she took his hand and placed it on her lap.

Camry took the last sip of her coffee and informed them what had happened in Tampa last night.

Surprisingly, Scott thought, Katie did not explode. She listened quietly, analytically, asking a few pertinent questions. She was mostly interested in Adam Kaninsky. Scott could see her shoulders slump and the life go out of her eyes when she was told that he was still missing. Scott couldn't help but wonder what kind of a relationship his wife had had with that kid. Until this week, he'd really had no idea of the secrets that Katie kept, the sordid relationships that her forensic practice forced upon her. Yes, he was in awe of her talents, but he was now vividly resentful of the inherent evilness she faced in her practice. Yet, that ransom demand had come from his profession, not hers.

Agent Camry was getting ready to leave when Scott tuned back into the conversation.

Katie was saying, "From the beginning I was sure that Maxwell Cutty was behind this. I was so sure, but now with Norman Watkins, I don't know. And the ransom note? How does it all connect?"

"You know we have hundreds of agents working the case, Dr. Monroe, a SWAT team on standby, all our resources — "

"Still, you don't know where our daughters are!" Gone was Katie's initial calm, her voice rising an octave, but shaking. "We have absolutely no idea. All those people working, yes, we know, but why can't you people find them? And now Maxwell Cutty is dead. And Norman Watkins is on life support. The only connections to our daughters — get assassinated right in front of you or gets their brains blown out by one of your agents!"

Worried about Katie's abrupt change from calm to hysteria, Scott's first reaction was to try to calm her, but everything she said was true. The FBI had let the two most viable suspects slip though their hands. He was about to back her up, but before he could speak, Katie's shoulders slumped, and she asked, "What about Aiden and Jake Cutty? Their mother's dead — "

*Who cares about that pervert's kids? We need to find our daughters!* Scott wanted to yell, yet did not. But he did withdraw his hand from Katie's grasp. The palpitations in his heart were constant now and he felt a surge of lightheadedness. He leaned back on the sofa and took slow, deep breaths. He was so close to the fatal ledge. So close that a single blast of wind would send him over. He needed to control his escalating fear.

"No, there's no *apparent* connection to the ransom demand."

Scott must have zoned out again. What had he missed? "Ransom?" he repeated.

"The FBI doesn't think that the ransom demand came from Cutty," Katie said.

"I don't give a damn about what anybody *thinks*," Scott said, his voice even louder than usual. "My little girls' lives are at stake. And with all your *resources,* you have nothing. You haven't even moved on the reward that my sister wants to offer! Are you all so smart that you *know* it's not about money? And, you can bet your ass that we'll have the money for whatever bastard called in that ransom offer."

"Scott — "

Scott sensed that he'd gone too far, but he didn't care. Katie started to get up, but he pulled her back and jerked her head to face him.

"God, Katie, I can't help it. I'm on an emotional teeter-totter. I'm sorry. I'm letting you down. Anger goes up. Fear goes down. Back and forth in my head. I can't make it stop."

"I'm going back to the field office," Camry said. "Agent Streeter will be back by noon. I will impress on him your sister's desire to post a reward, *again*. Personally, I think it may be the right time. We may want you two to televise the offer. Maybe Miss Monroe, too."

*It's about time you get your head out of your ass and start doing something*. Scott did not say that. Jackie had appeared at the stair landing. Long ago Scott and Katie agreed never to use unseemly language in front of their daughters.

"Mr. Monroe, we would like you to come down to continue going over professional baseball contacts," Camry said. "We'll be ready when you arrive."

"Yes, but I wasn't much help —" Yesterday had been a literal parade of players he'd worked with over the past twenty-odd years. The slide show started to click in his head, then stopped on a guy. Yankee uniform. A hefty guy with thick, blond hair, very curly. What was his name? What was there about him?

# CHAPTER 24

*Fourth Day and Monroe Triplets Still Missing – FBI Stumped.*
– National News, Thursday, June 18

At first Jackie had thought that maybe, just maybe, her sisters were goofing off. Playing a trick on Mom and Dad. Sometimes Sammie yelled at Mom that she treated them like babies. "We're *nine* years old, not kindergartners," had been her usual line. And on this, Jackie had always agreed with Sam. But on Monday morning when she woke up and Alex and Sam were not home, Jackie had changed her mind. Something very bad was happening to them, and it was all her fault. If only she and Danielle would have given in and gone with them to see *Night at the Museum.*

Jackie had tried to figure out if Alex and Sammie were dead like some of the television people were suggesting. She knew that Dad didn't think they were, but she wasn't sure about Mom. Mom had had a dream right before she promised to get her a puppy. What did that mean?Everybody kept asking Jackie if she was *okay*. No, she was not *okay*, and if they didn't find her sisters she could never be *okay*.

At first, Jackie had tried to stay close by her dad. He'd always understood her the best. But now he was not acting like her dad anymore. She'd heard him yelling at that nice Agent Camry. She'd heard him say two bad words, *ass* and *bastard*. Dad never talked like that even though he was an athlete and everybody knew how bad they talked. "Trash talk" they called it.

And sitting at the top of the stairs, waiting for Grandma to take a shower, she'd listened to the grown-ups talk. A bad man in Tampa had been killed. And he had two little boys, Mom had said. That made her think of Tina, the nice girl she'd met at the FBI. Something bad had happened to her dad, too.

When Agent Camry left, Dad came up to get dressed.

"Dad," she'd said, "I heard Agent Camry say that you have to go to the FBI today. Do I have to go, too? Can I stay with Grandma or go to Aunt Sharon's?"

"Afraid not. Aunt Sharon has to take Grandma to a doctor's appointment."

"But, Dad —"

"I'm in a hurry, Jackie, I have to jump in the shower." She started to follow him into the bathroom, but he shut the door in her face.

Tears trickling down her cheeks, Jackie sat down on a step. She didn't want anyone to see her cry, so she waited. She heard her Aunt Sharon arrive and go into the kitchen with Mom. Jackie inched down a couple of steps so that she could listen to what they were saying.

Sharon asked Mom all kinds of questions and Jackie was surprised at how calm Mom sounded as she explained about what Agents Streeter and Camry were doing, about how Aunt Monica was giving a lot of money for Alex and Sam.

"Katie, are you going to be okay," Aunt Sharon asked.

"Yesterday, I had what I think was a hallucination." Jackie wondered what that was. "Alex and Sammie spoke to me. At first I thought that meant they were, you know, *dead.*"

"Like a dream?" Aunt Sharon asked.

"Yes, just a dream, but when I tried to tell Scott, he wouldn't even listen. I am so worried about him. Last night I crushed up a Valium and put it in his drink. He did sleep better, but he was awake by the time the FBI agent got here this morning."

"You did?" Aunt Sharon sounded surprised. "You know how Scott feels about drugs. That guy won't even take a Tylenol." Jackie did know how her dad felt about drugs, he was always volunteering for antidrug programs. She wondered what Valium was. Would it make Dad a drug addict?

"I had to do it. Scott is falling apart. I don't know how else to say it. You know how he's always been so strong, so steady. Throughout everything. Even when he got hurt and had to drop out of baseball.

Throughout all the stresses we've had to face as a couple. Well, you know what I'm saying."

Jackie kept listening. "Yes. We've often said, both of us Jones girls married stalwart men. Men with inner strength, strong values, 'self-actualized' men. Isn't that what you called Scott and my Fred?"

"Yes," Mom said.

"But with what you two are going through —"

Jackie felt a little guilty, knowing that eavesdropping was not polite, but she just had to know what Mom was thinking. About *her*. So far Mom had not mentioned *her*.

"Each day that passes," Mom told her aunt, "I keep thinking that it'll be *today*. That Sammie and Alex will come skipping into Mom's house. I just can't let myself sink into hopelessness."

"I sure agree with that," Aunt Sharon said. "But what about Jackie? How's she holding up?"

Jackie almost leapt off her step to join her mom and her aunt, but she held back. What would Mom say. About *her*?

But Mom said nothing. That is, nothing about Jackie.

"More coffee?" Aunt Sharon asked.

"Sharon, I'm convinced that they are with a woman, not a man. That belief is the only thing that keeps me sane."

*What about me, Mom. Don't I matter to you?*

"Katie, I just don't know if you're being —"

"I've had enough coffee. And where is Scott? We have to get downtown. But, Sharon, I feel it in here, in my heart. My Alex and Sammie are okay. They're off on an adventure. Making a joke out of leaving Jackie behind. Jackie's always plotting to be an individual, deep down, she resents being a triplet. That's why the girls split up at the movie, squabbling over which movie to see, Jackie wanting her own way."

Jackie stayed riveted to her seat on the stairs. Now she *knew* that Mom — and Dad, too — blamed her. Whatever had happened to her sisters *had* been her fault.

"We have to think positive thoughts," Mom told Aunt Sharon. "That's what I tell my patients," she said. "Negative thoughts are just that, negative."

"No suspects, only a ransom note," Aunt Sharon said. "What about Keith Franklin, Katie, anything new there?"

"Jackie, what are you doing sitting there?" Grandma tapped on her shoulder. "Come on, let's go downstairs."

Jackie felt her body begin to shake all over. She hoped that Grandma wouldn't notice when she took her hand, and together they went down the rest of the steps.

Mom didn't even look up as they walked into the breakfast nook, but Aunt Sharon did. Jackie heard her whisper to Mom, "Look at Jackie. You didn't give *her* any drugs?"

"Of course not," Mom said, blinking her eyes like she did when she was mad.

"Katie," Aunt Sharon said, "let me take Jackie with me today. After Mom's appointment, she can swim in the pool; I'll take her to the club for tennis. Her Monroe uncles can keep her busy with baseball. She'd be distracted with constant activities."

Aunt Sharon had gotten up and she put her hands on Jackie's shoulder. "Look, I'll get her away from all those reporters out there."

"You may be right," Mom said, but then she stopped. "But they need Scott downtown, and I can't let him go alone and if Jackie —"

"I think it's a good idea, Katie," Grandma said.

But Jackie didn't really care what happened. *Her parents hated her.*

Pulling her hand out of Grandma's, Jackie took a step back, squirming out of the hold that Mom and Aunt Sharon had on her shoulders. "My sisters are dead," she said in a normal tone of voice. "And it's all my fault, Mom said so. *It is all my fault.*"

Jackie stepped farther back as her mother came toward her with her eyes blinking very fast. "That's not true, Jackie," Katie said. "I did not say that!"

Jackie backed up two more steps onto the landing of the stairs. "I heard you, Mom!" Her voice so loud now that she sounded like her sister, Sammie, challenging Mom.

Mom reached to grab her shoulders, but Jackie took a step backward. "Jackie, please, I never, ever meant that. Come here, sweetie."

"I heard you tell Aunt Sharon. You don't want me any more. Do you?"

Katie stopped. "That's not what I meant," she said with such a strange look in her eyes. Jackie couldn't tell if she was angry or scared or what, because her face looked so twisted. "Jackie, you're everything — "

For an instant, Jackie wanted to step forward, into her mom's arms, but when she heard footsteps from the top of the stairs she turned to see who it was, then she took a step back, lost her balance, and fell backward off the two-step landing.

Jackie's head hit the hardwood floor with a thud. Katie gasped, seemingly frozen as Sharon rushed to the child. Just as she did, Scott came bounding down the steps.

"What was that noise?" he asked, almost stumbling over Jackie's body on the floor, curled in the shape of a comma.

"Katie, what happened?" he shouted, now on his knees, a hand over Jackie's chest, his hazel eyes wide with dread.

"Don't move her," Katie managed, still standing, unable to move, unable to breathe. "Her neck — "

Not sure she wanted to take another breath, ever, Katie remained frozen. *What have I done*? "My fault," she mumbled. "My fault."

Lucy was at the phone, dialing 9-1-1.

"Katie, you're a doctor," Scott's voice came out as a croak. "Get over here."

On the 9-1-1 call, Lucy asked them to contact Agent Camry at the FBI. Within minutes an emergency team had arrived, and Camry called to say that she'd meet them at Children's Hospital.

Alex and Sammie's voices warning reverberated through Katie's head. *Take care of Jackie.*

# CHAPTER 25

*Monica Monroe Offers One Hundred Thousand Dollar Reward for Return of Nieces.*
– National News, Thursday, June 18

Spanky's rig jostled over the rough spots on I-75. Radio blasting seventies tunes, static interfering. He'd be fifty in two years, but he was still a teenager at heart. Stuck in adolescence some shrink had once told him. His stomach growled and he decided to pull over at the next stop for a burger and fries.

He knew the truck stops on the Detroit-Miami run like the back of his hand. Could tick them off in order of his chances to score a little pussy. The one ahead near Knoxville had promise, but not at noon. Besides, his needs had been satisfied last night down in Valdosta. A real Georgia peach. Said her name was Kiki. Now what kind of a name was that? Hawaiian? Her skin was kind of brown. Not black like an African American, more like Mexican or Indian or one of those stinkin' Middle East countries. Kiki'd been hanging by the vending machine. He'd bought her a candy bar and promised to show her a nest of baby birds. He hadn't hurt her. He never did hurt them. He just rubbed his willy all over those soft spots. Well, he *had* licked. But nothing that hurt or left a mark. And he was careful not to let his cum get on her clothes. When he was done, he'd given her the usual warning not to tell mommy or daddy, and he'd kept her panties. White nylon. He'd been hoping for something more sexy for number twenty. Oh, well. He couldn't wait to ceremoniously add it to his collection.

Shit, he'd missed his turnoff. Now he'd have to wait another hour for a decent place to eat. He was sick and tired of McDonald's and all those chains that lined the interstate. Give him an honest to goodness truck stop any time. He shifted his attention from food when some jerk in a Porsche tried to pass him on the right. "No you don't," Spanky said, cutting abruptly into the right lane. He laughed at the panic on the rich lady's face. One day a driver wasn't going to see him in time. Oh well, he was bigger than them. Trucking firms had insurance. Maybe that'd be his signal to retire. Hang up the keys to eighteen wheelers. Maybe do odd jobs in his pickup around his hometown until he had enough moola to move to Alaska. Now that was a dream worth savin' for.

His stomach kept on growling, made worse by the Dorito commercial on the radio. He changed stations, looking for a local twelve o'clock news and weather channel. Weather was important in his business and since he didn't read newspapers, how else was he supposed to keep up to date?

The lead story was the missing triplets. He figured that something bad musta happened to those kids. He was curious, and yes, he had to admit, turned on. He'd followed the story. His opinion: it was all about money, but why no ransom demand? Maybe it was one of those perverts who the mom sent to the joint? That's what the cops thought. Like it was payback. Vindictive. Retribution. Mentally he slapped himself on the back. Ma would be proud of him using such big words. Just because he was a truck driver didn't mean he was ignorant. No sirree.

Shooting the breeze with the truckers last night, he'd had a few too many beers. "Pervert got those girls," he'd said. "Shit they were grabbed out of a mall. That's where those guys hang out. Rape 'em. Kill 'em. Toss 'em where nobody's gonna find 'em." When the guys around the bar just stared at him, he'd known he'd gone too far. The assholes were all staring at him.

He'd shrugged his shoulders. "Hey, man, just tellin' it how it is."

The big ape on the end of the bar got up and stomped over to him. Got his ugly white face so close Spanky could smell the stink of booze mixed with smokes. Spanky had flexed his muscles for a fight, but the asshole just said, "Sir, shut your fuckin' mouth. You can think whatever the fuck you want, but you're in the South 'n we don' talk about women like that."

"Amen, brother," the others said, slumping over to lift their drinks.

Spanky hadn't been too drunk to know he'd best get the hell out of that bar.

What did those fuckers know about human nature? Spanky figured that he knew about perverts. Perverts had something sick wrong with them. Spanky, he had morals. Sure, he liked little girls. He could admit that to himself, but why would he have to kill them? That just didn't make sense. As long as he could scare them enough so they wouldn't tell. He'd found that little girls were easy to scare. Most, anyway. If he thought one acted too tough, he'd just let her go. There would always be another, like Kiki last night.

Spanky had taken his mind off the news report long enough to finger Kiki's panties. "Oh, yes," he purred. This was followed by "Fuckin' A," when reconnecting to the news, he heard how some skinheads got arrested in Gainesville for writing shit on a barn wall. Disgusting how Florida was so fucking redneck. He ought to know, driving fourteen hundred miles up and down I-75 three times a month.

"Yeah, man," he snarled, hearing that the shitheads were members of the Klan. "Fucking assholes think they're better than any other asshole. Throw them in the joint, that'll teach them who to fuck with."

When Spanky was a kid he'd wanted to be a cop. His mom used to buy him all those toy guns and badges, but that was before she married that pansy jerk-off. Evan may have taken away the toy guns, but now Spanky had the real deal. Yes siree.

Driving on, Spanky had to piss. His stomach growled louder, and he felt a surge of heartburn, so he grabbed a swig of Mylanta. "What the hell, a Denny's. Good enough." He pulled off the next exit. He'd call Ma from there. Let her know that he'd be home tomorrow. She'd been bitching about needing a new car. Tomorrow was Friday. He'd scout one out for her. Take her out on Saturday, her day off.

Spanky parked the rig off to the side, but as he walked toward the men's room, he saw the lady in the Porche crawl out of her car. Too bad he couldn't get one of those for Ma. He laughed so loud that the woman veered off to avoid him. Now, that was a picture, his Ma crawling out of one of those hot little cars. As a joke maybe he'd take her for a test drive in one this weekend.

He emerged from the men's room to a buzz among the customers at the counter in Denny's.

Monica Monroe, one of his idols, had offered a fucking hundred thousand bucks for two of those triplet girls. The thought made Spanky salivate. What he wouldn't give for that kind of money. *What he wouldn't give to have those two little girls.*

# CHAPTER 26

*Yankees Play the Nationals at Home: Time Out to Pray for the Safe Return of Scott Monroe's Daughters Planned.*
– *New York Daily News*, June 18

Scott and Katie hovered over Jackie as she lay perfectly still on the small gurney in the emergency room of Detroit Children's Hospital. She'd been seen by the neurosurgery team, neurology, and, of course, pediatrics. She'd had an electroencephalogram, skull X-rays, an MRI, and a CAT scan. All were normal. No skull fractures, no bleeding inside the skull, no swelling of the brain, no sign of brain injury. Her vital signs were stable. Her blood chemistries and her complete blood count were in normal range. But she had not regained consciousness. Her body lay supine and limp, her chest rising and falling as if she were merely asleep. All of her reflexes were normal, and they could identify no neurological focus to account for her being unconscious. The blow to her head, stumbling off only two stairs, should not have been severe enough to cause prolonged loss of consciousness. But it had now been five hours. The doctors admitted her.

The media had followed the ambulance into the inner city hospital and were doing everything in their collective effort to find out what medical calamity had struck the remaining triplet. The ensuing chaos had stalled Lucy's arrival at the hospital, and it was only after her mother and sister joined them that Katie accepted a modicum of consolation and stopped repeating *all my fault*.

Scott couldn't understand what was happening to Katie. Why did she keep rambling about *her fault*. Wasn't it enough that two of their daughters had been missing for four days and the third was in a coma that the doctors could not understand?

And what *was* wrong with Jackie? He'd heard the doctors huddled outside her hospital room discuss psychiatric syndromes where kids under stress just shut down. *Shut down*? What did that mean? Katie, with all her psychiatric training should know, but Katie seemed helpless. She just stood by Jackie's bed, staring at nothing, saying nothing.

Finally, when Lucy accompanied Katie to the restroom, Scott pulled Sharon to the far corner of the room and asked, "What's wrong with Katie?"

"She's under too much stress, Scott. I can't imagine anything more devastating to a family. I keep putting myself in her place, you know. I don't think that any parent can predict how they will react to something like this. It's like every time you think about Alex or Sammie, not knowing, it's like they're dying over and over. You just don't know. You and Katie just have to do what you can to get by, minute by minute. Jackie's been under that stress, too."

Scott rubbed his eyes. "My own emotions are all over the place. I can't seem to focus. And this morning I feel so groggy that I don't know if I'm capable of processing information. The news that the main suspect was gunned down last night — I just can't imagine —"

"The stress is just too intense, Scott. I don't know what to advise. Stay here at the hospital, go to Mom's for some rest, spend time with the FBI agents? I just don't know."

When Katie and Lucy returned, Scott and Sharon stepped apart, and Scott went to Katie's side, putting an arm around her waist. They stood silent until there was a knock on the door.

An attractive, dark-skinned woman in her sixties stepped inside. She carried a patient chart, but she was dressed in a turquoise silk dress and matching jacket, not a white coat.

"Dr. Monroe, I'm Dr. Susan Reynolds, chair of child psychiatry at Children's Hospital," she said, approaching Katie. "I'm a friend of your sister, Stacy, and I'm here to see your daughter." Dr. Reynolds turned toward Scott, "And I feel like I know you, Mr. Monroe. I'm a baseball fan, the Tigers, naturally, not much of a Yankee fan, I'm afraid. Tigers are in first place in their division. Yankees are a couple of games out in the east, if I'm not mistaken."

Scott simply nodded. Baseball, nothing more than a remote memory. Pensive a moment, he shook his head, failing in an attempt to remember the name associated with that curly haired blond guy that lingered on the fringe of his consciousness. He needed to focus. He needed to be here for Jackie. He needed to be downtown, helping the FBI find Alex and Sammie.

Katie turned to face Dr. Reynolds, but said nothing.

Dr. Reynolds introduced herself to Sharon and Lucy and expressed her prayerful wishes that Alex and Sammie would return safely and quickly. Then she turned to Jackie.

"I'm sure pediatrics told you that they can find no physical basis for your daughter's prolonged depressed level of consciousness," she said. "The child's been under so much stress that naturally we have to look for psychiatric causes. Do you agree, Dr. Monroe?"

"I guess so," Katie said, sounding lost and helpless.

Lucy spoke, "Dr. Reynolds, what do you need. How can we help you?"

"I'll need to examine Jackie," she said. "And I'd like to ask the parents some questions."

Katie just nodded.

"Anything, Dr. Reynolds," Scott said.

"I'd prefer that you call me Susan," the psychiatrist said.

"Please, Susan. Katie and Scott," Scott said.

"Stacy will be in later tonight," Lucy said. "She'll be so glad to see you. I just wish Dr. Nelson was here, too. I know you two were close. Same medical school class, if I recall."

"I'm glad Stacy's coming. Speaking of Laura, how is your father, Scott?"

"Recovering from heart valve surgery at the Mayo Clinic, and devastated, of course."

Scott had planned to fly to Rochester, Minnesota, this week to visit his father after his surgery. Was that a lifetime ago?

"Of course," Susan said, stepping around Katie and Scott to begin her examination of Jackie. The child had not opened her eyes or made any movement that seemed purposeful.

No one spoke as Susan performed a series of neurological tests aimed at evaluating neurological versus psychological dysfunction.

When she was finished, she suggested that Katie and Scott sit in the chairs arranged in a semicircle around Jackie's bed. Sharon and Lucy excused themselves and Susan began. "What we have here is a conversion disorder. A reaction to extreme stress. Layer on layer of stress: Perhaps influenced by the survivor syndrome, why was she saved, and her sisters were taken? Perhaps overlain with guilt, blaming herself that they did not all stick together."

"What can we do?" For the first time, Katie's voice joined as one with Scott's.

"I'm admitting Jackie to the psych floor. The rooms are comforting there, conducive to recovery. Serenity is key. No contention. Just loving acceptance. I'll have them put in two cots so there will always be loved ones there. I know you two may have to spend time with the FBI, so if Mrs. Jones, Stacy, Rachel, Sharon, and perhaps some of your relatives, Scott, could stay with her around the clock, that would be good. But whoever is with her must maintain a serene, supportive, atmosphere. Jackie's room is a sanctuary. It is not the place to discuss her sisters. Whoever can't commit to these ground rules should not be included in Jackie's inner circle.

"Naturally, our staff psychiatrists and house staff will oversee her treatment, as will I, personally. So we'll be in and out. But a family member needs to be by her side at all times. In the event she *wakes up*, we'll instruct you what to do. And if you have any information about her sisters, tell me immediately so we can discuss options of how to handle this with Jackie." Susan hesitated. "She's most vulnerable right now, but she will get through this, if we handle this right. Katie, as a child psych professional, as well as a mother, are you okay with this?"

"Yes," Katie answered, "And thank you, Susan."

Scott felt his heart lighten at the tone of sincerity in Katie's voice. She sounded *rational*. As Susan made arrangements to transfer Jackie to the psych unit, he longed for a moment alone with Katie, just the two of them. He needed to reassure her and to be reassured by her. They'd been sinking into a dark bottomless hole. They were both crumbling. They needed a touchstone. They needed each other.

An orderly, flanked by security, had just arrived to transfer Jackie to the fifth floor when an FBI agent squeezed by the stretcher to announce, "Mr. Monroe, there's an urgent call for you at the desk."

For an instant, Scott froze, his heart standing still, then Katie touched his arm and said, "Take the call, I'll stay with Jackie."

Scott picked up the phone at the nurses' station, his shoulders hunched forward, supporting himself with one hand on the plastic partition.

"Mr. Monroe, this is Agent Streeter. I am sorry to interrupt you at the hospital. I can't tell you how distraught we all are about Jackie. She'll be okay?"

"I don't know," Scott said, and he didn't know. Dr. Reynolds had said she was catatonic.

"I'm back in Detroit. Matter of fact, I'm on my way to Children's. I have something to go over with you and Katie."

"Yes, of course, but they're just getting ready to take Jackie to the fifth floor," Scott said. He couldn't bring himself to say *psychiatric* floor.

Scott and Katie accompanied Jackie up to her room. On the way they passed rooms with cribs and small beds. At the end of a corridor Scott almost walked into a treatment room full of crying kids. Katie had been a pediatric resident before going into psychiatry, and Scott wondered how anyone could cope with the chaos of bawling babies and crazed parents.

Streeter waited for the Monroes near the nursing station. Scott arrived first, saying that Katie would be along in a moment. As they waited, Scott asked to be briefed on the status of Keith Franklin.

Streeter told him that Katie's former boyfriend had been held for questioning well into Wednesday morning. They'd determined that the ex-con had been paroled for acceptable behavior, having served nine of a fifteen year sentence for drug trafficking. He had a string of odd jobs before landing a position with the Detroit Department of Sanitation. For nine years he'd ridden a garbage truck and had recently moved up the pecking order to driver. His parole record and his employment record had been adequate. If one was grading his report card, he'd be a C minus.

"What did he say about Katie?" Scott asked.

Streeter relayed that Franklin admitted that he carried a torch for her. He confirmed that Katie — that is, his infatuation with Katie —

had driven a wedge into his marriage. He and Penny had been married for twelve years and they had three sons."

"Happily married?" Scott asked.

"'*Hell no*,' were his exact words. Described his wife as a bitch. Nothing ever good enough for her. Her spending has him on the edge of bankruptcy, that sort of thing."

"So he needs money?" Scott asked.

"That may be true," Streeter said. "Franklin admitted that he'd never stopped fantasizing about Katie. About how their life together might still be."

"Shit," Scott said, "like that would ever happen."

"I'm just telling you what he told us," Streeter said. "Delusional for sure. He said that he was sure that she still had feelings for him. The guy did not hold back. He put it all on the line."

"Great," Scott said.

"First, he sent her that e-mail. Then he managed to siphon a hundred bucks from the stack of bills he owed and he'd bought a ticket for your sister's concert. He'd learned from his mother that Katie would be there without you. He'd expected her to sit up front, and had gotten a glimpse of her when she entered with the triplets and her mother. He'd waved, but he didn't think that she'd seen him. After the concert, he waited outside, meaning to walk up next to her and strike up a conversation. But she didn't come out through the main entrance. Katie had left by the back door and stepped directly into Monica's limo. After that, he went off to his local bar and stayed until closing. All those details have been confirmed."

"So you believe this guy?"

"On Sunday," Streeter continued, "Franklin took the family to the Detroit zoo. And that, too, was confirmed. We had no grounds on which to hold him, and he was allowed to return home."

"So nothing."

"He did tell us something. He admitted to an affair. An affair with a white woman. Woman by the name of Jane Wise. Mean anything?"

"White woman?" Scott's heart started to race. Had Franklin sent his girlfriend to take the girls out of the mall? "Could it be the woman that the witness saw in the mall?"

"Franklin had her picture in his wallet." Streeter showed him a photo of a middle-aged white woman, plump, pale in complexion, brown eyes with too much makeup, and what was probably bleached blonde hair in an old-fashioned pageboy cut.

"Recognize her?"

"I don't know this woman."

"We're showing her picture around, but she has an airtight alibi for Sunday, at a family affair with her husband. She's fifty years old. Works in the automotive industry, no criminal record, seems like a nice lady. Don't know what she saw in Franklin. He even told her about Katie. Go figure what women put up with."

Scott's shoulders slumped. Another dead end.

"We do have Franklin under twenty-four-hour surveillance."

"Thanks for being so honest with me," Scott said. "I guess I'm still having trouble coping. And about this morning — Katie and I were pretty rough on Agent Camry. We know how hard everyone is working."

"Maybe you should go get Katie." Streeter glanced at his watch. "I need you and your wife. This can't wait."

"She's getting Jackie settled, but I'll get her."

During the flight from Tampa that morning, Streeter had second-guessed every decision he'd made on the missing girls. He had requested a meeting with his boss, the special agent in charge, as soon as he arrived at the field office, and on his arrival, the SAC and a roomful of FBI abduction specialists listened to Streeter's summary report. They asked lots of questions, but no one had any useful ideas. The SAC was not happy. In the words of his boss, "Maybe not your fucking fault that Cutty took the hit in Tampa, but our own guys shooting the brains out of Watkins? Get your shit together and get those girls. The director's on my ass. Obama himself is on his. And I'm on yours. No more screwups."

While Streeter had been in flight, Agent Camry warned him that both the Monroe parents were bordering on hysteria. She'd also taken the initiative to have Monica Monroe tape a poignant reward offer, already all over the airwaves and into cyberspace. Monica as the spokesperson had not been his preference, but Katie and Scott were far too preoccupied with Jackie to focus on a script. Maybe Camry was right, Monica's star power would grab worldwide attention and maybe shake somebody into action. There had to be people out there who had seen the two Monroe girls. Unless. He didn't want to think about the unless.

Reviewing Monica's video reminded Streeter that he needed to intensify the investigation of Scott Monroe's family, so he assigned one of his best agents, Juan Ortez, that task. On Katie's side, he'd personally met all of her family except the sister who was now on her way back from a vacation in New Zealand. He'd detected no complicity with them, but Scott's family might be a different matter.

Upon leaving the SAC and still licking his wounds, Streeter headed to his office, locked his door, and called Marianne. Yesterday, when he'd discussed the Monroe family dynamics with Marianne, she had predicted that Jackie would collapse, warning, "No nine-year-old should have to endure the stress that Doctor Monroe had put that child through, and she, herself a child shrink. Those two parents had better get their act together," she'd said, "if they were going to survive as a couple after this was all over, one way or another."

The thought of marriage and marriage counseling made Streeter grit his teeth. When Marianne had suggested they go to a therapist, he'd rejected it outright. Their problem was his job. He loved the job. And if she couldn't handle it, so be it. But where had that gotten him? He was miserable, all the time, everyday. He missed his wife and he desperately missed his own three daughters, even more so with the missing Monroe girls consuming every iota of his energy and the question that would not go away: What if it had been his daughters?

When he was honest with himself, Streeter was forced to admit that he had lost his edge. There was a vacuum inside him and it was affecting his work. Sammie and Alex had been missing for four days, and he had nothing but one dead and one brain-dead suspect. He had a ransom note that sounded phony. He had the mom's boyfriend from the past who'd produced nothing helpful. A reward scenario that he hoped was not too late. Career-wise, there'd be hell to pay if something didn't break soon. He'd be kicked out of Michigan, gone the chance to reconcile with his wife and remain in the same state as his daughters.

At this low moment, Streeter took the call that he hoped would break this case wide open.

# CHAPTER 27

*FBI Efforts in Monroe Kidnappings Intensify as Reward Seekers Respond.*
– National News, Thursday, June 18

Cliff Hunter flipped the tab off his Bud, turned on the TV, and scrolled though the channels to ESPN. His life may have turned to shit, but he still had cable service. Baseball had been his life, and baseball was still his life. A spectator now, not a hotshot star, thanks to Scott Monroe. The Yankees, the team he despised among all other professional baseball teams – and with good reason – were playing the Washington Nationals. He hoped they would lose as they had last night and sink to the bottom of the league.

On his way though the channels to find the game, he passed CNN, then flipped it back on. He recognized the voice first, before the familiar face, a beautiful one, even he had to admit it. The face of Scott Monroe's sister, Monica. He'd once asked Scott if he could get him a couple of tickets for a show she was doing in Tampa. Scott had come through and he'd taken *her,* the seventeen-year-old bimbo that ended up ruining his life. That was when Scott had been his buddy, or his mentor, they now called it.

He needed to concentrate on what Monica Monroe was saying. Then he heard the words, "A reward of a hundred thousand dollars for the safe return of my nieces, Alex and Sammie." There they were again, the faces of the Monroe girls, appearing almost nonstop in the news programs and the newspapers. Those angelic-looking faces. Cliff turned down the volume. He didn't want the sound going down to the basement. They didn't have air-conditioning, and his mother preferred the coolness down there.

As he listened to the talking heads that followed Monica's brief and teary-eyed announcement, Cliff raked his curly hair, considering the impact. The famous, rich bitch was *offering* a hundred grand. He was *demanding* a million. Should he stick to his plan?

He thought about his mother down in the basement, depressed, he knew, because they were going to lose the house. He'd moved back in with her nine years ago, back when his baseball career had been ruined by Scott Monroe. Monroe had him kicked out of the Yankee minors and blackballed him in the American League. He'd tried the National League, had a run in the minors with the Pirates. When that ended, he had nowhere to go but back home to Dayton. In the meantime, his mother had taken out a second mortgage and later one of those home equity loans. Now she couldn't make the payments and property values were at rock bottom. He'd tried to help out with a job at a sporting goods store, but that didn't work out. So he had to come up with a plan. Ironic, how the bastard that had ruined his career, was now going to make him a wealthy man.

But with the Monroes ready to give a measly hundred thousand to just anybody, he'd have to make his move first. He couldn't afford some kook coming up with information. To hell with the Yankee game. Cliff clicked off the TV, not bothering to check the basement. He was off to Auburn Hills to stake out the drop-off site. He'd call it in to Don Plese at the Yankees later that afternoon.

# CHAPTER 28

*The Tampa Bay Rays Pause in Prayer for the Safe Return of Sammie and Alex Monroe at Today's Game in Colorado.*

— Sports Network News, Thursday, June 14

Special Agent Emmitt Rusk, FBI, Tampa field office, took the police artist's sketch of the unidentified female subject from Michigan, dubbed "frumpy," and headed for the palatial former home of Maxwell Cutty. At Streeter's suggestion, the Tampa field office had hastily assembled a cast of characters with known relationships to Cutty. They'd identified neighbors, friends, acquaintances, contacts out of his address book and requested them to show up for a brief interview late that afternoon. Treating them as volunteers, not suspects, the FBI wanted their reactions. Did anyone know who this woman was?

Immediately afterward, they repeated the process at Cutty's office. And when they did, they left with the same results. Fifty plus acquaintances of Maxwell Cutty denied ever seeing the woman. All Rusk got was snickers. The Cutty's acquaintances found the idea of Maxwell associating with a woman totally lacking in style ludicrous.

Last on their list of contacts that afternoon was Olivia Cutty's sister. Roberta Kendrick lived in nearby Plant City. She was the appointed, yet reluctant, temporary guardian of the orphaned Cutty children. From a prior interview with Roberta, Rusk had not considered her lifestyle preferences ideal mommy material. Once the estate was settled, the Cutty boys would be well off, but that didn't make up for loving parents.

At the time of Cutty's assassination, Rusk had gathered enough evidence for the Tampa police to hold Maxwell Cutty on charges of conspiracy to commit murder. He'd held back turning it over to the locals as the Monroe kidnapping scenario played out. The FBI accountants following the Cutty financial trail identified a suspicious withdrawal at the time of his wife's "accidental drowning," and another the morning after the Monroe kidnapping. Any murder charges were moot now that Cutty was dead, but the life-and-death question remained: Had Cutty taken the location of the Monroe kids to his grave?

Just the thought of Cutty made Rusk grimace. Molesting his children, killing his wife, kidnapping two little girls to prevent their mother from testifying against him. Had he merely taken the children or had he killed them? One thing now seemed clear. That he'd used a benign-looking, middle-aged woman to lure them out of the movie theatre into her car. The woman probably was from Tampa, where the girls lived. They must have known her from somewhere.

Plant City is less than an hour's drive north of Tampa. Rusk found Roberta's place in a neighborhood of small homes with sparse lawns, surrounded on two sides by a congested trailer park. Her place looked small, too small to accommodate Aiden and Jake Cutty, orphaned at age seven and five, respectively.

"Something's wrong with this picture," the agent driving muttered. "Kids going from riches to rags. How long have the boys been here?"

"Since the story came out that Daddy was abusing them," Rusk said. "Child Protective Services tries to place kids with relatives. And Roberta's it. She's eleven years younger than Olivia. Makes her twenty-seven. And light years different."

Rusk rang the bell, noting a couple of bikes on the scorched, skimpy lawn. One with training wheels. Both a shiny red.

The door opened and two little boys barged out. Both with brown floppy hair, plump, but not fat. They were poking each other and laughing. The smaller one tried to trip the older one. The older one faked a fall and grabbed the little one on his way down. Now they were tussling in the dirt.

"Quite a handful," Rusk said as Roberta appeared at the door. He recalled the photos of Olivia, polished and professional, contrasting them with her sister's unruly and wild appearance. Shoulder length frizzy hair going in all directions, wearing an ankle length skirt with a blend of colors, a knit top that emphasized an inviting bosom, and sandals.

"Hey, you guys, there's fire ants around here," she yelled, slamming the screen door behind her. "Jake, remember last time, I had to take you to the hospital."

"Agent Rusk," she said, "think about it. I mean, I have a job. Now I have two rowdy boys. I love them, yes. But it's not me. Hear what I'm saying."

"How are you doing, Roberta?" Rusk asked. She looked frazzled, and he wondered how she could be the administrative assistant to the editor at the *Tampa Tribune*.

She shrugged. "I know. I look like a disaster case. But those boys, I'm telling you — I had to take a leave of absence from the paper."

She led Rusk inside to a cluttered living room. Rusk showed her the sketch of the frumpy woman and asked whether she'd ever seen her. Of all those they had interviewed, Roberta's appearance was closest to that of the suspect, giving Rusk a flicker of hope. But Roberta was much younger than the woman in the police artist's sketch.

"Maybe," Roberta said, pushing hair out of her eyes. "Looks like a cleaning lady Olivia used to have. Babcock. Something like that."

Rusk's heart leapt in hope. Maybe they finally had something. A direct connection from Cutty to the woman the witness described in Detroit.

"Maybe the boys will recognize her," Roberta yelled out the door. "Little J. Big A. Come in here."

Rusk watched as the boys kept up their antics.

"Plug your ears," she ordered and let out the shrillest whistle that Rusk had ever heard.

This time they came, not walking, but bolting.

"Boys, do you know this lady?" Rusk asked.

"Yup," Jake said. "My kindergarten teacher. Mrs. Patches. All the kids thought she was ugly."

"Naw," Aiden said. "And, Jake, that's not a nice thing to say. Mom wouldn't like it."

"Well, she's dead and so is Dad. I can say anything I want," Jake yelled before breaking into tears.

"I can't take this," Roberta said. She scooped Jake into her arms. "I don't know shit about kids." Her eyes teared up. "I just took them to the shrink. The one they go to now that Dr. Katie's not here. The guy's a shit. When Maxwell got shot, he just told the kids that their dad was dead. Just like that. Then he does play therapy. Then he says time's up. And I don't know shit about what to do. I mean, are they supposed to cry? Or not cry?" Roberta slumped against her decaying porch. "And with Dr. Katie out of the picture, I just don't know. I even thought if her daughters are dead, maybe she would take my nephews. That's how desperate I am."

Rusk sneezed and pulled out a white handkerchief.

"Must be the cats," Roberta said, "and I guess you noticed, I don't have air-conditioning."

Rusk used the excuse to make his exit. He'd call in these two names from the car: the Babcock cleaning lady and the Patches teacher, new persons of interest.

After calling the Tampa field office, Rusk called Streeter in Detroit. He could sense the excitement in Streeter's voice and he prayed that he would not disappoint.

On his way back to headquarters, Rusk laid out his theory. Cutty arranged for the kidnapping, through an intermediary, using a local woman whom the girls would trust. Cutty had been under twenty-four-hour surveillance. He'd been followed into an Ybor City club the day of his death. He'd carried a bag going in. He'd not had the bag going out. He'd gone directly home and not emerged until late that evening when he'd taken an assassin's bullet. The FBI had saturated Ybor City, but nobody saw Maxwell Cutty meeting with anyone. Witnesses saw him come in and saw him go out, but they saw nothing else. He must have met with someone in that club, and Rusk swore that he would find out who.

# CHAPTER 29

*Third Monroe Triplet Rushed to Children's Hospital in Detroit.*
— Thursday News, June 18

Streeter waited five minutes for Scott to return with Katie before knocking gently on Jackie's hospital room door. He'd been told that she had fallen at her grandmother's home and that she'd been admitted for observation. *Fallen?* Then why would she be on the psychiatric floor? Was Children's Hospital that crowded?

"The little girl's room is sacrosanct, sir, the female agent who escorted him to Jackie's room said. "She needs calm and quiet. Nothing can be said about the missing ones, sir."

As Scott opened the door, Streeter heard the familiar music, *It's a Small World*, his youngest daughter's favorite.

"One of us should stay with Jackie," Scott said in a whisper.

"I really need you both," Streeter insisted. "This could be important."

"Jackie's asleep," Scott said. "I'll get Katie, but we can't stay out long, in case she wakes up."

*In case she wakes up*? Streeter looked quizzically to each parent as they walked toward a nearby conference room. Several agents were in sight, stationed to keep Jackie's hallway free of unauthorized personnel and visitors.

"Please," Katie said, her eyes darting toward Jackie's room. "I know that this is important, but could you hurry?"

Streeter started by telling them that a little before noon, the bureau had received a credible call. One that was now under intense investigation. Something in the caller's voice, a rapid-fire tone that signaled urgency and veracity had triggered the intake agent to pass the woman on to Streeter himself.

The caller was Sheila Gladksy. She'd been shopping last Sunday afternoon at the Hill Mall. Streeter explained to the Monroes that Mrs. Gladsky came in late last night to give her statement. She was very apologetic about not calling sooner, but she'd been camping in the Upper Peninsula, in a tent, no electricity. She called the instant that she found out about the abduction of your daughters.

Streeter opened his notebook. "I'm going to tell you pretty much like she told us. If you could listen closely for any connection whatsoever, for anything that strikes you, for anything that may trigger a memory."

Both Monroe heads nodded.

Streeter read, " 'Okay, here's what I remember. I was buying all that camping stuff. First time me and my girlfriend ever took the kids so far into the woods alone. I mean, I used to camp when I was married, but — well, it's different when you're on your own. But I wanted Brendan to learn how to rough it. We didn't go too far. Just across the Mackinac Bridge. But we were out of touch with the world. My Brendan — probably because he wants to be a Boy Scout — was okay, but my girlfriend's boys complained the whole time about no television. And you wouldn't believe the size of the mosquitoes. I thought they would eat us alive.' "

Streeter looked up. Katie and Scott were both trembling. He read on, "'Anyway about those girls, I want to get this right. I know exactly what time it was because I forgot my watch. When I saw that clock on the way out of the mall, I realized I was late.

"'It was 1:31 p.m. Precisely. I'm an accountant. A CPA, actually. So I'm very precise. Got to be.

"'I walked out the south exit coming from the pharmacy where I'd picked up some first-aid supplies, Band-Aids, disinfectant, that type of thing. I still have the receipts.

"'I was stuffing two bulky sleeping bags in the trunk of my Honda, which was parked next to the passenger side of a maroon sedan, or maybe brown, not a new model, but I'm not good with cars. That's when I heard a child's voice so I turned.' "

Streeter paused to assess the Monroes. Both were listening intently. Scott had grabbed Katie's hands to keep them from shaking. Streeter returned to his notes. "'I saw a little girl. What she had said was, plain as day was, 'Is she going to be okay?'

" 'It was the little girl in the pictures. The one in the multicolored pants, a geometric design, and a yellow top, the one with the ponytail and a red ribbon. She had cute red sandals with black trim. I thought she sounded upset. Not really scared, more like concerned. But not frightened. I did wonder what she meant. Like, was someone ill? But I never found out.' "

Katie gasped, said nothing, but her eyes started to blink.

Streeter read on. "'The other girl with no ponytail, in a very pretty lavender sundress with lacy straps crisscrossing in the back — I was sure they were twins — how could I have known they were from triplets — didn't say anything. I did notice her cute sandals, shiny white with a big yellow daisy.

"'Then the woman they were with unlocked the car with a key, and the girl with the ponytail got in the passenger side of the front seat. The woman had to kind of push the other girl into the backseat. Not shove, just sort of nudge. I did hear her say, 'Hurry up,' but I thought nothing of it.

" 'Once I got home and watched the news and saw the newspaper, I was sure that they were the missing children. Both had light brown skin and dark hair, very pretty. Made me wish that I had a little girl.' "

"They got in her car?" Scott interrupted. "They just got in her car? With no protest? Voluntarily?"

"Did either of them say anything else?" Katie asked, sitting on the very edge of her chair.

"No," Streeter said, returning to the written statement.

" 'Once they got into the car, I'd finished loading my stuff and I got in my car and drove away. I left the parking lot before they did.' "

"Unfortunately, she didn't notice the license plate and her description of the car was not very helpful. But she did have one crucial piece of information. She described Sammie's and Alex's shoes. The girls' shoe detail had never been disclosed to the media."

"Who was this woman?" Katie asked. "Was she white or black?"

"A white woman. Middle aged. Auburn hair, with some gray. Hair style described as poufy. She was wearing a dark blue dress, on the long side. White sneakers, white socks."

"Sammie got in the front seat, and Alex got in the backseat?" Katie said in a near whisper.

Scott's voice boomed in comparison to hers, "And they didn't seem panicky or even frightened?"

Streeter observed both parents intently as he answered, "Shiela Gladsky repeated over and over that the girls looked concerned, not scared. That leads me to ask, could Alex and Sammie have gone with a relative or friend of the family?"

"How old was this woman?" Scott asked. "And she was white?"

"Early fifties, the witness estimated. Definitely white. The witness described her as moderately overweight, not stylishly dressed."

"They would never have gone off with a stranger," Scott said.

"We asked Mrs. Gladsky to take a lie detector test. She did. She passed."

"Katie and Scott looked to each other, the obvious question on each face, "Do you know who this could be?"

Streeter scrutinized them. With this eye-witness report, it seemed more likely than ever that the abductor was known to the girls. The investigation would be taking a more inward look, unfortunately disrupting an already distressed extended family and circle of friends.

"And Sammie said, 'Is she going to be okay?'" Katie said. "What did she mean by that? Who is the *she*?"

"We don't know, Dr. Monroe, but we judge Mrs. Gladsky to be credible. Her description fits with Courtney Davis's report, the woman with two screaming kids whom Jake Plummer interviewed at the mall that Sunday. She said the woman wore a darkish blue dress that came mid-calf and sneakers. She described her as mid-fifties, sloppy, overweight, with teased auburn hair, streaked with grey. The woman had one child in each hand and they were walking fast. The Davis woman never saw the woman's face, only her backside."

"My God, Scott, who could she be? Two witnesses saw them with a *white* woman?"

"The description of the children met the description of Alex and

Sammie. But until Sheila Gladsky came forward, we had no description of the woman's face and we still have no idea where she may have taken the girls or who put her up to it."

Streeter handed Katie and Scott a police artist's sketch. An overweight, middle-aged woman in an unstylish housedress with auburn hair strewn with streaks of gray.

"Nobody I've ever seen," said Katie.

"Nor I," said Scott. "Can we have some copies to show to our families? Maybe somebody will recognize her."

Streeter handed him several copies and then closed his briefcase, preparing to leave. There was much to be done. "I'm afraid that we'll have to question your friends and relatives again on both sides of your family, and because the woman is Caucasian, we'll start with the Monroe side."

Streeter had already interviewed Scott's two brothers and their families as well as his famous sister, Monica, and her husband. Among them all, he'd found nothing but grief. Scott's mother had died thirty years ago and his father, Nick Monroe, was at Mayo Clinic, recovering from heart surgery. Today, he would dispatch Agent Juan Ortez to Rochester, Minnesota. If something evil was beyond the caring veneer of the Monroe family, Nick Monroe, the patriarch, would know.

In the back of Streeter's mind had always been the nagging suspicion that the girls' abduction could be related to some form of racial prejudice. Racial purists still existed. The election of a biracial president of the United States last year should have squelched that philosophy, but who knew what evil lurked in the minds of the modern neo-Nazi's? One of the worst, the National Socialist Movement, was headquartered in Detroit. He'd gagged when he'd read the twenty-five points of their creed – only those of pure white blood could be members of the nation. Very repulsive stuff.

Streeter had never addressed the race issue with the Monroes, and he decided to do so now. "You asked about whether this woman was black or white," he began. "Has there been any tension or any criticisms of the biracial aspects of your marriage? Any individuals that have expressed any objections or dissatisfaction with the marriage of a black woman to a white man?" Streeter knew he had to tread carefully here. He wished he paid more attention in the diversity classes the agency made them take.

Scott slumped forward, gripping the edge of the table so fiercely that his knuckles turned a starker tone of white. "You think that Sammie and Alex are in the hands of white supremacists?"

"I just raise the question," Streeter said, recalling the "one drop rule." Dating back to slavery, still pervasively embedded in American society to the point that in some communities biracial individuals are still considered black no matter what their appearance if they have even a fraction of African heritage. Case in point, Barack Obama, white mother, black father, almost universally classified as black. In reality, Barack Obama is a biracial American, obviously a powerful role model for the Monroe children.

"That doesn't make sense," Katie said. "Alex and Sammie went off without a struggle. How could a hateful racist get them to do that? A white woman simply leading Alex and Sammie away in her car? I can't see a racial angle here. And the answer to your question, Agent Streeter is no. We haven't been experiencing any racial unpleasantness. Don't you agree, Scott?"

"Yes, but what if—?"

"Look when we're out with the triplets, we get a lot of looks. We used to get them as a couple before we had kids. Curiosity, yes, but not bigotry. Nothing that would come even close to outright racism. But then again we refuse to raise our racial antennae out there. So we might have missed something. What do you think, Scott? That woman who took our daughters is white."

"I just can't see it. Yes, we know all about the theoretical implications for biracial families. And there are many: ideological, institutional, and individual racism. We debate all this with our friends, but none of that theoretical stuff has interfered with our lives. I can't think of a single incident over all these years. Could something have changed? Or maybe we didn't notice it?"

Streeter was becoming uncomfortable and wondered whether it had been wise to raise the racial issue. The Monroes had so successfully built their life devoid of racial prejudice and he didn't want to jeopardize that by pursuing a futile avenue of investigation. Earlier he'd consulted with the Department of Justice's Community Relations Service, the arm of the department that dealt with hate crimes. CRS had been created following the 1964 Civil Rights Act. It had no law enforcement responsibility, but intervened in suspected discrimination issues. He'd kept an open line of communication with them, but no hints of hate-crime motivation had surfaced from any source.

"There's one more thing," he said. "Before I go —"

"I have to get back to Jackie," Katie interrupted.

"Okay, Katie, but you and Scott have things to talk about," Streeter said, scrutinizing them, not able to shake the remote possibility that they were involved, individually or together. "Once you've had a chance to think about that woman who was seen with Alex and Sammie, maybe something will come to you."

"The ransom demand? Anything from Norman Watkins?" Katie said, once they'd reached Jackie's room. "Or Keith Franklin?"

"No," Streeter said, "but Agent Camry will be staying here, at the hospital. She'll let you know immediately if we have something."

"Thanks, Tony," Katie said. "We'll be with Jackie. They're setting up a couple of cots for us in her room."

"Is she going to be okay?" Streeter asked. The question made his heart stop. The exact words that Sammie had said four days ago before getting into a car with that woman, *Is she going to be okay?*

# CHAPTER 30

*Continental Flight 61 from Brussels to Newark, New Jersey, Lands Safely after Mid-flight Death of Pilot.*
— International News, Thursday, June 18

Marge Spansky clomped down the basement steps, carrying a large plastic bowl brimming with popcorn. She'd promised the twins that she'd be back after their dinner to read to them. Jennifer had asked for *Heidi*, Marge's all-time favorite, and Jessica wanted to read the next installment of the The Bobbsey Twins. Those two didn't know how good they had it.

As she passed the door leading to the outside, she looked to make sure that both the bolt and the chain locks were secure, and at the bottom of the steps, she unlocked the door to the basement with the key around her neck.

First, she blinked, then dropped the bowl of popcorn, when she opened the door. Strewn about were scraps of paper. Parts of board games, doll clothes, their clothing. What had they been thinking? Were they trying to play a trick on her? This was *not* funny.

"What have you two done?" Marge stared at the mess, her face turning shades of red. "You've trashed the place."

Before they could answer, she swooped inside. The girls sat on folding chairs at the twisted cardboard table, their faces sassy and fresh.

Marge lunged at them, unable to control the anger bubbling up inside. Such defiance could not be tolerated. Jessica swung out of the way, but Marge's slap connected with the side of Jennifer's face.

"Stop it," Jessica shouted. "You hit her!"

Marge reached out to grab Jessica, but Jennifer pulled on her arm, and Marge stepped backward.

"You're going to pay for this," she warned. "Now get the broom and clean up this mess. Forget me reading to you tonight."

Jennifer moved to get the broom, but Jessica stared at her with a sullen look. Before she unlocked and relocked the room, Marge lifted Jessica up by her hair and smacked her hard across the face.

"Double trouble," she mumbled on the way out.

Dr. Susan Reynolds and Lucy Jones were about to leave for the evening, hoping that Katie and Scott could get some sleep in the cots adjacent to Jackie's bed.

Since Streeter had shown them the police artist's sketch, they'd searched their memories again and again. The FBI had e-mailed the sketch to everyone in their professional and personal universe, but got no plausible match. The Tampa field office had promptly checked out the two new leads Agent Rusk got from his visit to Roberta and the Cutty boys. Camry had passed on the results: nothing."

"Waste of time," Rusk told Streeter from Tampa. "Babcock, the Cutty cleaning woman. Nice lady. Thinks Cutty was a pompous jerk, but she knows nothing about Katie Monroe or her family. The late Mrs. Cutty hired her just weeks before she died so she doesn't have much family history to draw on. She said the boys were sweet, but holy terrors around the house."

"What about the Cutty sexual abuse thing?" Streeter had asked.

"No inkling, or so she claimed," Rusk said. "Soon as Kaninsky moved in, Cutty fired her and hired a cleaning service. As you know, we've already checked them out. Before you ask, yes, the Babcock woman has an airtight alibi."

"What about the kid's teacher?"

"Vera Patches. The woman's never been north of the Florida state line. She's clueless about the Cutty domestic scene, but quite concerned about the boys."

"So if Cutty arranged to take Katie Monroe's kids, he went to his grave without disclosing where he put them."

"Shit, Streeter those little girls are probably dead. You know the odds. Going on five days without a trace?"

"They get in a car five miles from Grandma's with a white woman who looks like anybody's aunt or neighbor, and they disappear without a trace. God, let the statistics here *not* hold true."

"You're sure you'll be okay," Susan asked before leaving Katie that evening. "I am optimistic that Jackie will recover, but when I cannot say."

"I'll be okay, and thank you, Susan. We appreciate you driving Mom home."

On her way out the door, Lucy studied the sketch one more time. "No, I surely don't recognize her," she said. You *sure* that nobody in your family knows her, Scott?"

Scott shrugged. "The FBI has shown her face to all of them, even Dad at the Mayo Clinic."

"How's your dad doing?" Lucy asked. "With what's happened here, I've neglected to ask."

"The heart valve replacement went well, but he can't travel. Bobby was going to fly here from Rome, but I asked if he'd go to Minnesota to be with Dad. You know how close Dad has always been to the girls. What's happened can't be good for his recovery."

Lucy nodded. Scott and Katie had been one of those lucky couples whose families got along well. Lucy had a particular fondness for Bobby, Scott's brother the priest, stationed in Rome.

When the psychiatrist and her mother left, Katie placed a kiss on Jackie's forehead. "She hasn't moved," Katie whispered, adjusting the angle of the plastic bag of fluid hanging from a pole. For a while, Katie sat next to Scott, caressing his hand, as they both spoke in soft, soothing voices to their little girl. Jackie lay on her back against snow-white sheets, her head propped by a thin pillow. Her dark hair was brushed back, tucked behind her ears. Her skin looked lighter than usual and her eyes remained closed and her chest rose and fell rhythmically. They told her how much they loved her, how much they just wanted to see her beautiful smile.

Lucy had brought sweatsuits for Katie and Scott to sleep in. When they'd both changed, Scott kissed Katie gently on the cheek, said good night, and pulled the covers over his face. From beneath the covers, she could hear him sobbing. Falling apart would not help Jackie, but Katie could not stop her own leaking tears. Occasionally, she blew her nose quietly into a Kleenex as did Scott. What else could they do?

Katie knew that she needed sleep, that she was physically and emotionally drained, but when she closed her eyes, the horrors of what might be happening to her daughters burned her retina. And if she did close her eyes, she would miss Jackie, should she awaken.

When she thought that Scott had drifted off to sleep, Katie climbed out of bed, knelt, and prayed. She prayed that she and Scott would be strong no matter what happened. She prayed for Sammie and Alex, and she prayed that Jackie would emerge from this catatonia. Conversion disorder was a psychological diagnosis, made when there was no physical disorder but great psychological stress. She knew that it used to be called "hysterical paralysis" and that it was rare in kids younger than ten. What happened was that anxiety was converted to physical symptoms. There was no cure other than suggestive, supportive, psychosocial therapy, and sometimes hypnosis. All she could do was to keep Jackie surrounded by love and calm.

But in doing so, Katie felt as if she were caught in a trap, locked up in the hospital. But she didn't dare leave Jackie. Over and over, her mind cycled: who had taken her other two daughters? And why? Three distinct faces kept flashing from one to the other: Maxwell Cutty, Norman Watkins, Keith Franklin, plus a phantom face of whoever had sent that ransom demand. What if the kidnapper was Cutty, and he had been the only person on earth who knew the location of her daughters? Sammie and Alex could starve to death or die of thirst before anyone found them.

Katie crawled back into bed and tried to get the faces to stop flashing, and sometime in the middle of the night, she fell into a restless sleep.

# CHAPTER 31

*Monroe Kidnapping: Going into Fifth Day. Experts On Odds of Finding Sammie and Alex.*
– Friday Morning News, June 19

Streeter arose Friday morning after a decent night's sleep, the first in five nights. Not taking time to fix himself breakfast, he headed to his office. He lived in one of those renovated buildings along the Detroit river, an apartment that his daughters called "luxury." While it had all the modern amenities, there were only two bedrooms. He slept in the guest bedroom, leaving the large master suite for his daughters. That way they'd have a big closet and plenty of room for three twin beds. As he prepared to leave that morning, he picked up the eight-by-ten photo of his own daughters. *Where are you, Alex? Where are you Sammie?*

Streeter knew so much about the missing Monroe triplets that it was hard to believe that he'd never met two of them. Only Jackie. How tragic what was happening to that little girl. Survivor guilt? She was safe, but her sisters were – what would be going on inside Jackie's mind? He stared at Kloe, his eldest. Thin, like Jackie, about her height, dark eyes, dark hair but shorter. Kloe was so tan that her skin color almost matched Jackie's. What would Kloe feel if anything happened to her two sisters? How could anyone ever know what was going on in a kid's mind? If someone could, wouldn't it be Dr. Katie Monroe? He put down the photo, counting the hours since the abduction: one hundred twelve.

Camry, her short brown hair gleaming, her plum linen pantsuit meticulously pressed, was waiting for Streeter in his office. With a twinkle in her eye, she announced, "Guess who showed up this morning?"

Streeter's first reaction was anger. Could they have found Sammie and Alex and not called him? *Impossible.*

"Adam Kaninsky arrived fifteen minutes ago," Camry said. "We held him for you. But I've got bad news, too. Norman Watkins died last night."

"Shit." Streeter sunk back against the wall and set down his briefcase. "Did he ever say anything?"

"No," Camry said. "Not a word. And his wife is raising hell with the press. Wrongful death shit."

"Cutty dead. Watkins dead. Let's hope that Kaninsky has something for us. Let's go." Then Streeter hesitated.

"You okay, Tony?"

"Be better if I had some coffee."

"I've got that and something else you'll like. Follow me."

She led him into her office on their way to the Kaninsky interview. She pushed the button on her single-cup coffee maker and reached into a plastic container. "Orange walnut muffins. My neighbor made them early this morning. She felt sorry for me, knows how tough the Monroe case is on us."

Streeter inhaled the fresh-baked aroma and picked one. "Only good thing about all this is I've lost a few pounds."

Adam Kaninsky took the chair opposite Streeter and Camry. Streeter had seen his photo, but in person Kaninsky looked like a model for J. Crew in a cranberry golf shirt and slacks on the tight side. The guy was trim but plenty buff. Blond hair right out of a salon, blue eyes with expensive dark glasses perched casually on his head. What did this twenty-year-old kid know about the Monroe girls and why had he shown up voluntarily?

Streeter planned to cut to the chase, but was preempted.

"Look," Kaninsky said. "I've been out of the country. I didn't even know you were looking for me until I got here this morning. I decided to come talk to you. Okay? Not the other way around."

"Okay," Streeter said, forcing back a blink, not expecting this proactive stance.

"I'm going to come right out and say what's on my mind." Kaninsky did not flinch. "I've done nothing wrong. I have nothing to hide."

"Okay," Streeter wondered whether he ought to read this kid his rights.

"We're taping this. That a problem?"

"No problem." Streeter judged Kaninsky to be on the up-and-up, but could he trust his instincts? So far they hadn't contributed shit in this case.

"Okay, Adam," Streeter said. "You've got our attention."

Kaninsky began, "You know that I am gay. At least I think I am. I've been having sex with men for money since I was ten."

Camry actually gasped.

"Starting with my older brother. I was only a kid."

"How old?" Camry asked.

Ellen Camry's background was psychology, but Streeter didn't want to waste time exploring Kaninsky's psyche. He shot her a "don't interrupt" look, and she blushed ever so slightly.

"Three, four, I don't know. Brad, he was ten years older. Maybe someone was doing him, too. I don't know. All I know was that he started on me right after my dad left us. There was me, my mom, and Brad. Of course, Brad threatened me not to tell — all the usual stuff."

"Let's get to the point. What do you know about the missing Monroe girls?" Streeter's pulse quickened. Kaninsky could be the key to their whereabouts. Why else would he show up here?

"Nothing, man. Just that I heard the news when I was in Nevis. That's where I was. That's where Maxwell sent me."

Question marks appeared on the agents' faces.

"I'll explain," Adam said. "When I was maybe nine, my brother hurt me pretty bad. I wore light-colored pants to school the next day and my teacher saw the blood stain. She took me to the principal. You know the drill. Child protective services. Physical exam. Psychological therapy. That's where I met Dr. Katie. I got to know her and came to trust her. She made me understand that it wasn't my fault. Convinced my mom to get help for my brother. Bastard finally ended up in jail. He couldn't stop. Nobody should get away with doing that to kids."

"Tell us about Maxwell Cutty and Dr. Monroe and her children," Streeter repeated.

"First, I just want to say that I think that Maxwell murdered his wife, Olivia."

Streeter was losing patience. The dead bastard would never be prosecuted for that, no matter how horrendous that charge.*Tell me where Cutty hid the Monroe children.*

"Look," Streeter said. "That accusation is serious, but it's a matter for the Tampa Police to investigate. What we have to focus on now is finding Alex and Sammie Monroe. Do you know where they are? Because if you do — "

"No, Agent Streeter, I do not. All I know is that I made a terrible mistake. I told Maxwell what I told Dr. Katie — about him, how he was abusing Adam and Jake. I told him that she could never tell because I was her patient, but he went crazy on me. He sent me to Nevis, and told me to stay there. He wanted me out of the country just in case she, you know, didn't keep what I said confidential."

"Did he threaten her or her children?"

"Her, yes. That he was going to 'get even' " He flicked his index fingers into apostrophes. "Her kids? He said like — how would she like someone screwing around with her kids?"

"Did he say anything more specific?" Camry leaned in closer to catch every word.

"No. But I'll bet he used the same guy that he used to whack Olivia." Here Kaninsky looked around. "Am I out of bounds here?"

"Meaning?" Streeter leaned closer.

"Look, I had nothing to do with this, but when Olivia, quote, fell overboard, unquote, Maxwell opened a bottle of expensive champagne. I mean, of course, he'd be glad to get rid of her. Truth is she'd turned into a bitch. Constant bickering. Over money. Over the boys. Typical stuff for divorce, I figured."

Again, Streeter wondered whether he should advise the kid of his rights. He might be walking straight into a trap — an accomplice to murder? But Adam was not a minor, and he had showed up voluntarily. Streeter let him proceed.

"We ended up drinking two bottles. We were both pretty sloshed, and Maxwell was one of those loud drunks. On the way to bed he was slobbering all over me. "Vincent came though," he said. "Vincent drowned the bitch. Now it's just you and me, Adam."

"This Vincent, any last name?" Streeter flipped through notes. Had he heard that name before?

"In the morning I asked Maxwell who Vincent was. He looked at me strangely and said, 'Vincent who? What are you talking about? Just shut your mouth.' He never mentioned him again. That was a couple of months ago."

"So what's your take on this Vincent?" Camry asked while Streeter poured though the file.

"Just that if what he said about Olivia and Vincent was true. I'm not saying it is. But what if — well, maybe this Vincent is the one who has the Monroe kids. Like if he can make a drowning happen, maybe he could make the children disappear."

"When did you figure this theory out?" Streeter asked, wondering whether Kaninsky's hypothesis made any sense.Tampa agents had followed Cutty to a club in Ybor City in Tampa. They now knew that he met with a guy known as Manny. According to informants, Manny Gonzalos ran an exclusive, pricey hit business. Highly respected, efficient, and completely invisible. No amount of digging had unearthed his real identity, but the Tampa agents speculated that the professional killer lived in Clearwater, and they had staked out the address. But now Manny had disappeared without a trace. If Manny was Vincent, then Vincent was gone.

"When I was in Nevis, I heard on the news that Dr. Katie's kids were missing. That's what made me think. Maybe he used that guy — Vincent."

Agent Camry asked, "You ever hear him mention Vincent again since that night?"

"No, never. I forgot all about it until I heard about her missing children. That's why I left Nevis and came straight here to talk to you. I used my own money to buy my airline ticket. I respect Dr. Katie, and if there's anything I can do to help find her children — "

"Why did Maxwell send you to Nevis?" Streeter asked, trying to reconcile what Adam was saying with the scant information in the file. Why hadn't the Tampa office made a bigger deal out of Manny? They'd missed the connection between Cutty's former wife's death and this Manny — or Vincent, a suspected hit man.

"Maxwell was going to meet me there. He said his lawyer would get the case — you know — about what he did to his kids — dropped and that we'd unwind in the Caribbean. Maxwell had it all set up. A private plane to San Juan, then a yacht from there to Nevis. No customs. No nothing."

"You didn't think that odd, Adam?" Camry asked.

"Like I said, Maxwell did some bad stuff. I just did what he said."

"So when you got there, he was a no-show, and you used your own money to come here?"

"Yeah, but I flew back, Nevis to San Juan to Kennedy to Detroit. I wanted to help Dr. Katie. That's why I'm here."

Streeter asked him to go over in detail the timing. The clock in his mind was calculating. Could Cutty have gotten those kids out of Detroit to Nevis? If so, when and from where? He picked up the phone. "Find out the jurisdiction in Nevis," he said. "We need to get a search going on the island."

"He told you to go to a certain address in Nevis?" Camry asked.

"Yes." Adam pulled a scrap of paper out of his breast pocket. "But I never went there."

"What?" Streeter's head jerked up.

Adam handed over the paper. "I never went there because I got scared. I mean, with what he did to Olivia. Like he had her whacked. No way she drowned. Must have been pushed, man. Like I said, this guy Vincent. Maxwell wanted Olivia's money and he wanted that house. He loved that house, wanted to live in that house with *me*." Adam shivered and shifted in his seat. "That was before I 'betrayed' him. I got to thinking. What if Maxwell intended to off me? The Nevis thing could be a setup." Adam shrugged his shoulders, but the grimace on his face was anything but casual. "I found a bed and breakfast over by the airport and used my own money. Then I came back when I heard about the little girls. I wanted to tell you all this. I've got a soft spot for kids. As far as Maxwell and I are concerned, we're finished. I came to tell you what I know, then I'm going somewhere far away."

"Do you know where Maxwell Cutty is?" Streeter asked.

"Right now?"

Streeter nodded, observing carefully as Adam lifted his shoulders in a "who cares" gesture. Either the kid was a primo actor or he suffered from media deprivation. Hadn't the shooting in Tampa reached the island of Nevis?

"Home, soaking in the hot tub, I suspect. "

"He's dead, Adam." Streeter delivered the blow, and saw that it hit hard.

"Maxwell?" Kaninsky's reaction came out as a wail. Maybe the kid did have some feelings for his former sugar daddy. Then he straightened up in his chair. "You're kidding me?"

When Camry asked whether they should detain Kaninsky, Streeter shook his head. "Do a polygraph. If he passes, let him go, but keep him local and under surveillance. Focus on Nevis and how Cutty could have moved the girls there. Do an extensive search of the island — house-to-house — if we can get local law enforcement to go along."

As Camry led Kaninsky away, Streeter felt a surge of depression. The kid had guts coming in, but he offered little that would lead them to Alex and Sammie. Except a hit man known as Vincent. Could Vincent be Manny? If so, the Monroe children were in the hands of a professional hit man.

At eight Friday morning, Katie and Scott waited for Susan Reynolds to make rounds. They'd slept off and on, and as far as they could tell, Jackie had not stirred all night. The child seemed to be sleeping peacefully, her chest rising and falling in perfect rhythm. Every once in a while, Katie would lean over Jackie just to feel the egress of air. Now she and Scott were talking to her gently, about what they thought would interest her, had she been awake. If anything would entice Jackie, it would be Yankee baseball, but Katie knew that Scott had not been updated on the stats since he'd arrived in Detroit Sunday evening.

"I can't wait for us all to be home," Scott was saying. Katie thought she detected the tiniest motion at the corners of Jackie's mouth. *Home*, she thought, would they ever be able to go home? How could they ever leave Sammie and Alex in Michigan here and go home to Florida?

As Scott kept up an upbeat monologue, Katie reflected on how she and Scott were handling the immensity of their constant dread.

They each seemed to cycle in and out of paralysis. In and out of hope. In and out of despair. In and out of sanity. They were trying to stay focused on Jackie, but images of Alex and Sammie kept careening around in her head and she suspected in Scott's, too. She realized that all she could hope for, right now, was that either she or Scott would be in a coping part of the cycle of despair — hope — despair at any one time. If their despair cycles coincided, who would be there for Jackie? Would they lose Jackie, too?

Katie's thoughts and Scott's monologue were interrupted by a blend of female voices as the door opened, and Lucy, Susan Reynolds, and Katie's sister Stacy walked in. In an instant Katie was on her feet, rushing into Stacy's open arms. After the sisters' tearful reunion, Stacy hugged Scott, and Katie greeted Susan and her mother. When Stacy went to Jackie and stroked her forehead, Katie thought she saw a glimmer of response as Stacy told Jackie how she'd just come back from an awesome hike in New Zealand. How much she'd love to take her there with her sisters, of course.

A light tap on the door interrupted Katie as she was about to ask Susan about Jackie.

"May I interrupt?" Agent Camry appeared, and was promptly introduced to Stacy, the eldest of the Jones sisters.

Scott rose to pull back a chair for Camry to join them.

"Thanks, Mr. Monroe, but could I have a word with you and Dr. Monroe?"

"You go ahead," Stacy said. "Jackie will be fine with us."

Once they had relocated to the patient room they'd been using as a conference center, Camry requested coffee from the security detail. As they took their first sip, she informed them that Norman Watkins had died without regaining consciousness. Not waiting for them to ask questions, she told them about Adam Kaninsky's surprise visit that morning.

"Adam?" Katie's heart jumped. "Does he know —"

"He claims he doesn't know where your daughters are or even if Cutty arranged their abduction. But he does believe that Cutty had his wife killed. And that he used a professional killer, known as Vincent. Does he look familiar to you?" Camry showed them the police artist's sketch of a Hispanic-looking male based on the Tampa FBI investigation of the man they knew as Manny in Ybor City.

Both Katie and Scott shook their heads, their shoulders slumping in unison. They denied knowing this man.

Then Scott asked, "The ransom? Anything?"

"Not yet. And nothing credible yet on the reward. But the sketch of the woman who we think took them is in all the morning papers and on all the networks."

Katie and Scott asked a few more questions, but they realized that Camry would let them know if there was anything new. And there wasn't. Camry promised to update them immediately if something happened. Finally, she told them how sorry she was about Jackie. Was there anything that she could do?

"Could you bring us the morning paper?" Scott asked.

Camry left the room, returned with a stack of newspapers, set them down in front of Scott and Katie, and excused herself.

Katie and Scott sat across from each other, coffee in hand, silently reading the *Detroit Free Press* and *Tampa Tribune* version of what was going on in their lives. The tragedy of the abduction, the odds of finding the children alive after five days, speculation as to the hospitalization of the third triplet, the incompetence of the FBI. When Katie and Scott had scanned enough, they folded up the newspapers, and, hand in hand, left to join Jackie.

As they reached the door to Jackie's room, Agent Camry rushed up to them. She handed Katie a formal-style, engraved envelope. "This arrived from the White House. It's for Jackie."

Katie fingered the White House seal, afraid that any message from the president had to be bad news. She gave it to Scott to open. Inside was a note, written on the first lady's stationery. The letters were well formed and precise and there were two signatures at the end. In a voice that wavered, Scott read it aloud.

Dear Jackie,

We are praying everyday that your sisters Sammie and Alex are safe and that they come back home to you and your mom and dad very soon. We hope that they are not too scared. And we hope that you are doing okay while you wait. We know how special having a sister is. And we want you to know that our parents and everybody in our classes at school are praying for your sisters.

The note was signed by the two daughters of the president.

# CHAPTER 32

*Obama Family Reaches Out to Monroes as*
*First Daughters Pen Note to Jackie.*
– *News at Noon*, Friday, June 19

Marge Spansky squeezed her legs together and checked the wall clock. She had to go real bad and couldn't take a break for seventeen minutes. Thank goodness she'd broken down and got those adult diapers Dr. Steiner had suggested. She'd told him that she had these urges when all of a sudden she had to rush to the bathroom. A couple of times she hadn't quite made it. Once at work, and once at the mall. Each time she'd raced for the toilet, but before she got into the stall, hot urine seeped down her leg and onto the floor. In the mall, no one had noticed, but at the Ford plant where she worked on the assembly line, two of her girlfriends had seen the puddle and had helped her clean up enough to go back to her workstation.

Marge had been humiliated, but Janie and Elmira had sworn that they wouldn't tell a soul. She'd promised them that she'd go see a doctor since she hadn't been in eight years. What was the point? Pap smears and breast exams, who needed them? Dr. Steiner chewed her out before he did an internal exam and sent her to have her breasts mashed. He even took some blood. She was fifty years old and he wanted to check for high cholesterol. Sure. What he wanted was a bigger take from her health care benefits. One good thing about unions and the auto industry was decent health care. And what did Dr. Steiner do for her? Advise diapers and tell her to do those stupid Kegal exercises with the rubber balls. With her benefits, wasn't she entitled to surgery? Maybe she should get a second opinion. Somebody younger. Steiner must be pushing seventy. But he was the only doctor she'd ever seen. He'd delivered all her children. Told her that the stress of having twins had been too much for her pelvic muscles.

Marge looked at the clock again. Chassis still moved methodically down the line – 11:56 a.m. Four more minutes. Her stomach growled, and she thought about the chicken breast sandwich in her lunch pail. Mmm. And those chocolate chip cookies she'd baked last night.

Marge rushed to the ladies' room as soon as the foreman stopped the line, and emerged with a smile of relief. "Whew, I just had a close call," Marge confided to her best friend, Janie. "Oops here comes Beatrice. Remember, I don't want her to know about my pee problem."

Janie nodded, opening up her lunch bucket and slowly removing the contents. "Carrot cake. Enough for two if you give me one of those chocolate chip cookies."

Beatrice and Elmira had arrived and taken their usual places around the cafeteria table where the four girls had lunch every day. A quartet of Ford assembly line ladies well into their mid-fifties, they'd hung out for lunch and a weekly after-shift beer ever since they realized they had similar life circumstances. All had been divorced, raising kids on their own, too melancholy to attract men, and not motivated to change. As the years passed, talk of growing kids morphed into talk of grown kids – all had offspring with problems – and change-of-life issues became front and center.

For Marge this was her only social circle. She had no non-Ford friends and no outside interests. The others all had their hobbies and looked forward to the big "R." Marge never thought about retirement. What would she do without her job?

Elmira handed a piece of newspaper that was ripped out of a full page to Beatrice. "I clipped this out. Just in case you didn't see it. Front page of the paper. Now, doesn't this lady look like Marge?"

Janie leaned in to take a look. "No way. Marge isn't that fat."

"Hmm," said Beatrice, "looks like the kind of dresses you wear. I wouldn't be seen dead in one of those."

"Just 'cause you spend all your money on clothes. Some people actually pay their mortgages on time," Elmira said. "When you gonna pay me back that hundred bucks I loaned you last month? It was only going to be 'til payday and payday was two days ago."

When Beatrice handed her the wrinkled paper, Marge thought her heart would stop.

"That . . . woman doesn't look like me," she stammered. "She's . . . too . . . fat."

"Come on, Marge, Elmira didn't mean to insult you." Beatrice said. "Neither did I. That woman doesn't look anything like you. Look, your hair is much prettier, and you have such a nice smile. She looks awful. Now, what's the story here? Who is this Marge look-alike?"

"The woman who took those little girls. Two of the triplets. They have a witness who said she saw this lady put them in a car."

Marge tried to fold the newspaper in half, but her hands shook.

"Is this an actual photo?" Janie reached for the paper, unfolded it for one more look. "Or is it one of those police artist things? They never look anything like anybody."

Marge reached out to grab the paper back and started to refold it.

"Marge, defend yourself," Beatrice said. "It even said that those girls got into a brown Escort. Isn't that what you drive? I mean, you'd better clear this up."

Her voice shook, but Marge managed to repsond. "Escorts used to be . . . the best-selling car in the country."

"Very funny, girls," Janie added. "Now we'd better get back to the line."

Elmira put her arm around Marge's shoulder. "Can you imagine? Our Marge, a kidnapper? You know we were just kidding."

Marge did not say one more word. When her shift was over, instead of going out with the girls for their Friday beer, she went straight home to her daughters.

# CHAPTER 33

*FBI Press Release: New Witness in Monroe Kidnappings.*
*Identity Not Disclosed.*
— Friday newspapers, June 19

The ransom demand came, a letter addressed to Don Plese at his New York Yankee office.

Streeter studied the copy as it came off the scanner, amid the buzz of computers and printers and fax machines. The New York field office verified the postmark: Auburn Hills, Michigan; the date stamp, yesterday; overnight mail with no return address. A single sheet of white paper, computer generated, in a blank envelope inside the package. The content:

> Scott,
>
> Your daughters are safe with me as long as you bring the money and do not tell the cops or the FBI. That's why I sent this to your employer. To keep it between you and me. Bring one million dollars in hundred dollar bills to where I tell you. I will have your daughters. You get them only after I have the money. If I see any cops, I will leave with your daughters and you will never see them again. You have to trust me on this, man. If you want your daughters back, don't screw up.
>
> Saturday morning at eleven. Walk with the money in a roller bag to Hamilton and Woodward in Birmingham. Leave the bag with the money outside the door of The Blue Martini. Then go to the Caribou Coffee on Old Woodward and sip your chai tea. If the money is all there and clean of marks and

> bugs, I will release your daughters, unharmed. They will join you within the hour at that table. But if I see anything unusual or any cops hanging around, you will never see your daughters again. That, I promise, man. This time you are going to pay for what you've done.

"Whoever wrote this has a grudge against Scott," Streeter said, already on the phone to Camry at the hospital. Again, he second-guessed himself. His gut told him to push harder on Scott yesterday, but he'd backed down after seeing Jackie lying so still in that hospital bed.

"The Monroes will want to follow these directions exactly," Camry said. "No matter if we think it's a hoax. Those two are trying to hold it together, but they're an emotional implosion about to happen. Makes me glad I don't have kids. I mean, what could be worse?"

"If the girls were dead; I mean, that would definitely be worse. But the way it is, not knowing."

"It's almost like they're facing their death, over and over."

"Any way about it, the hostage team's ready to roll." Streeter gave an uncomfortable cough. "Meantime, I'm on my way to Children's Hospital."

"I'll wait until you get here before I tell them, but doesn't this have to be the work of an amateur? I mean, the setup is foolish. No offer of evidence that he has the girls. Just leave a bag of money, and 'trust me.' We'll get this guy, Tony."

# CHAPTER 34

*Sketch of Woman Last Seen with Alex and Sammie Monroe Released.*
— Breaking News, Friday, June 19

As Camry had predicted, the Monroe parents were adamant. They would go ahead with the ransom money. Scott would carry the money, leave it wherever he was told to. A million dollars in hundreds. Streeter and Camry explained all the reasons they thought this was a phony. The lack of an assurance that whoever wrote the note had the girls. All the Monroes asked is that the FBI not impede the safe return of their children. They wanted to believe that the exchange would occur the next day, that they would have Alex and Sammie back in twenty-four hours. Before Streeter left he inquired after Jackie.

"What Jackie needs is Alex and Sammie back," Scott said.

"A couple of things I'd like to ask." Streeter pointed to Scott's copy of the note. "The reference to chai tea?"

Scott's hand trembled as he read, his voice a raspy whisper. "How does whoever wrote this know I drink chai tea?"

"And why does he say, 'this time you are going to pay for what you've done?' " Katie said. "Baby, whoever wrote this knows you!"

"Chai tea?" Streeter asked. "Who all would know about that?"

"Everybody who knows me," Scott said. "Everybody gives me a hard time. I'm supposed to be a beer-guzzling jock."

"That doesn't limit the circle. Funny how that small detail worked its way into the note. Add that to the 'pay for' comment, and whoever wrote this note seems likely to know you. Does anything here ring a bell? Anything at all?"

"I must have done something to somebody, I just don't know — "

Scott raked his short hair with both hands. "I need to go over everybody. But, we don't want the FBI to jeopardize the safe return of our daughters."

"The credibility of this demand is low," Streeter warned. "No proof has been offered. The collection plan is amateurish. He provided unnecessary clues."

"Somebody from the Yankees. Somebody I must have harmed in some way."

"We have twenty-four hours to try to identify and locate this *somebody*," Streeter said. "Best if you came in to the field office."

# CHAPTER 35

*Ali Khamenei Announces Ahmadinejad Won the Iranian Presidential Election by 24 Million Votes.*
– International News, Friday, June 19

Marge drove straight home, not even stopping to check the mailbox at the end of her long driveway. She parked her car in the garage and, once inside, she went to her daughters' room and laid down on the daybed. This room was her sanctuary, a place she came to for solitude. But today there would be no solace. Today, Marge had to think logically.

She figured that she had two immediate problems. First, somebody must have seen her leave the mall parking lot last Sunday. Who was she kidding – that picture looked like her. Second, Spanky would be home tonight from his Miami run. She'd been hoping that he'd stay somewhere else, but he'd called from the road yesterday. She wondered if Spanky had seen the newspapers. Probably not, since he never read anything, but he did watch TV at those truck stops. Would that picture be on TV?

Marge's heart began to pound, and the harder she tried to think, the harder it pounded, spreading to her neck and to her head. She laid there for a long time, trying to reassure herself that she'd be able to handle her responsibility.

How easy it had been. Marge had spotted the girls just outside the entrance to the movie theatre. Three of them, all gabbing with an older black girl. She'd edged toward them, close enough to hear their conversation. She needed to take two of the three, but she wasn't clear how she'd do that. She listened carefully to catch their names. The older one was Danielle and the one in yellow was Sammie. Then as if reading her mind, they'd split up. Two went to one movie, and the other they called Jackie went with the older girl. Marge had been upset that they were dressed so differently. Shouldn't identical triplets be dressed alike? She thought so.

Marge had been clever. She'd waited about twenty minutes after the movie started. Then she worked her way through the dark theatre. The audience was mostly kids, and all eyes were glued to the screen. No one noticed as she made her way to the seat in back of the two girls. Leaning forward, Marge had tapped the one in the yellow top on the shoulder, gently so as not to spook her. "Sammie?" she whispered, hoping that she had the right name for the right girl. How shameful to name a little girl Sammie. Then she remembered *Bewitched*. Sammie, short for Samantha.

The girl handed the box of popcorn they'd been sharing to her sister and then both turned around, their dark eyes wide, questioning.

"Sammie?" Marge repeated in a whisper.

"What?" the child sounded annoyed. "Who are you?"

Here Marge had to be careful. She needed to get them quietly out of the theatre. She couldn't risk a commotion.

"It's your other sister," she whispered, inserting her head between the girls' shoulders, feeling her teased hair brush against their faces. "She got sick. Uhh, Danielle said to hurry. Come on. Both of you."

Again Marge held her breath, hoping that she'd gotten the Danielle name right.

The one in lavender, got wide-eyed. "Jackie's sick?"

The yellow top turned her attention back to the big screen. Something scary was happening in that museum.

"Yes," Marge said, trying to sound urgent, yet not loud. "We have to go. Follow me."

The one in lavender started to get up. "Sammie?" she tugged at her sister's sleeve. "Let's go."

Yellow top gathered her popcorn, kicking over her drink as she begrudgingly followed her sister. Marge met them in the aisle and ushered them out into the lobby.

"Who are you, anyway?" yellow top demanded. "Where's Jack?"

"They took her, uh Jack, to the hospital. I'm supposed to take you there. My car's out here," Marge said as her eyes darted around for hidden cameras. Whenever she thought back about that very moment, her head pounded louder.

"We can't leave the mall." Yellow top stopped dead, hands planted on hips. Marge had to think quickly. She inserted herself in between the twins. Grabbing a hand of each, she tugged them forward.

"Who are you?" Yellow top started to resist.

For a moment Marge hesitated, asking herself, *are these the ones*? Why was their skin so tan? "I'm a friend," she said, bending to face the stubborn little girl. "Look, I hate to tell you this, but your sister is vomiting blood. Lots of blood. They had to rush her to the hospital. We have to hurry to get to her. Let's not waste time."

"Blood?" both girls exclaimed loud enough that Marge again looked about. Was anyone watching? But her improvisation had the desired result. A look of horror passed between the girls, and they started to bolt for the exit, practically dragging Marge between them. Whew, thank God she had said the right word, *blood*.

Marge led the girls to her brown Escort and put one in the front seat and the other in the back. She locked the doors, cursing herself for not even knowing if she had those kid-safe locks.

"Did anyone call my mom?" the one in lavender asked, poking her head over the seat.

"Jackie wasn't even sick," interrupted yellow top. "What did you say happened to her?" Marge decided to call this one Jessica. She had known right then that this one was going to be a handful and she'd been right.

Marge had had to concentrate hard on the way home. On the way, she'd stopped at a Kmart. With the girls thinking they had a sister in the hospital, she'd told them that she had to pick up some pajamas and a bathrobe for their sister so she'd have something nice to wear in the hospital. "What's her favorite color?" she'd asked.

"Turquoise," said the one she'd call Jennifer.

"No, she changed to royal blue," corrected Jessica.

These two were going to be a challenge. Double trouble.

She'd been careful, driving right on by the Kmart in Auburn Hills, where she usually shopped and even past the ones in Southfield and

Troy. When she got to Mount Clemens, where she knew no one, she parked the car.

Mostly the girls had been quietly talking during the ride, but she'd been too busy planning to listen closely to what they were saying. When she stopped the car, they tried to get out. "You two wait here," she'd said. "We're in a big hurry."

Now, thinking back, her heart raced when she thought of how easily they could have escaped, but when she came back with a cart loaded with plastic bags, they were still there.

Again, they tried to get out, to help her. But she'd shoed them back inside and put the bulky bags in the trunk. She'd had to catch her breath. A woman her age, rushing up and down the girl's aisle and the toy aisle, grabbing matching outfits, pajamas, even underwear as fast as she could throw them into the basket. Two of everything. She should have shopped more carefully, but she'd had no time. Impulsively she pulled a couple of Barbies and some Barbie accessories off the shelf. Then she snatched two Disney comforters and two games. Two of everything, except for the games, the ones she used to play with Evan, Monopoly and Risk. She'd already decided *not* to treat these two as prisoners.

At the checkout counter she'd had to use her Visa. Counting her cash, she had only enough to stop at McDonald's. When she got back to the car, the girls both said that they had to pee. Tough, she had to pee, too, but she had not taken the time inside the store.

"They have bathrooms at Kmart," said the one in the back."

"You can wait. We'll be at the hospital soon."

"I gotta go real bad," the one in the front said. "I'm not kidding."

"Just hold it." All that talk about restrooms made her own bladder threaten to contract.

Then the one in back, the one in the dress, started to cry.

"That crying is not necessary," she warned. "You're not babies anymore."

Then before Marge had even started the engine, the one in front yelled at the top of her lungs, "Help!!!!"

Marge hurriedly started the engine, checked to make sure the back windows were rolled up, which they were, and turned on the air-conditioning to mute the crescendo of yells. Concentrating on her driving, Marge heard snippets from the backseat.

"You're a liar!"

"Take us back!"

"Stop at a phone. We want to call Grandma."

"Go back to the mall."

"My dad's gonna find us."

"You're gonna be in big trouble, lady."

That Marge had not liked. She did not like to be called "lady." She wasn't going to take disrespect. So she abandoned the plan to stop for cheeseburgers and fries and a shake and headed directly to Holly. Soon the blacktop ran out and the Escort bumped along unpaved roads.

As she approached the turn off Oakhurst onto Parker, both girls were screaming bloody murder. Marge slowed to a near stop, grabbing the one in front's arm, and turning to face the one in the back. "Stop that right now! You're my responsibility now!" To Marge's horror, the one in front bit her arm, drawing blood, and the one in back yanked hard on her hair. She couldn't reach the one in back, but she slapped the one in the passenger seat, hard. "You behave or I'm gonna beat the shit out of you!" Nice had not worked. She'd had to go to mean.

The girls shut up and settled back into their seats and Marge drove the short distance to her driveway, slowing at the approach to make sure that the coast was clear. Monday morning was trash pickup and this was about the time Sunday night that residents would be dragging their plastic bins out to the road. With that ruckus going on in her car, she'd been distracted. She couldn't swear that no one had seen her. Making her turn, she'd not dared to glance out, fearing someone might appear, catch her eye, and expect her to stop and chat. Marge might live in isolation, but she was not antisocial and she could do chitchat.

Of course, when Marge turned off Parker road into her dirt driveway, the girls realized that they were not to be reunited with their sister in a hospital. They started to screech louder than ever. Coming to a stop as close as possible to her house, she'd acted quickly, jerking one out of the front seat with one hand and reaching into the backseat for the other one. A girl in each hand, she shoved them toward the door. Both girls were jerking violently, trying to break loose. Too bad, they'd have some scrapes and bruises, something she didn't want. Shifting both girls' wrists to one hand, she freed the other hand to unlock the door. She yanked them both inside, locking the door behind her, and dragging them down the basement steps. Once down there, Marge didn't care how much noise they made.

Now five days later, Marge fingered her right arm just above the elbow, still sore from where Jessica had bit her. The bruises on her legs where both of them had kicked her were turning a purplish yellow.

Dwelling on how she'd gotten the girls in the first place seemed to calm Marge, but when she tried to focus on the here and now, that someone must have seen her, she felt numb and queasy, and the pounding in her head got worse. That's when she'd heard the crunching noise, the wheels of Spanky's pickup coming up the gravel driveway. If Spanky found the girls, there'd be complications. Those little girls were her responsibility.

# CHAPTER 36

*U.S. Treasury Department Confirms that Ten Big Banks Will Repay Funds.*

— Business News, Friday, June 19

Keith Franklin did not go home after his forty-eight-hour interrogation at the FBI office on Michigan Avenue. He'd had his share of trouble with the law, but not at the federal level. He wasn't going to fuck with those bastards. He'd answered their questions, even those that seemed to incriminate him. When the feds cut him loose, he hadn't had the guts to face his wife. So he headed directly to his mother's place on Clairmont Avenue on Detroit's near west side. She still lived near the epicenter of the 1967 Detroit riots, but in a small house rebuilt since the fires had devastated a twenty-by-twenty block area of shops and homes.

"Go home to Penny," Daisy Franklin had advised. "You have no right trying to track down Katie Jones. Now look at the trouble you're in. FBI agents have taken my house apart and yours, too."

"Stalking is what the FBI accused me of. Ma, you don't think I have anything to do with those children, do you?"

"I don't know what to think. I know that you used me to get information from Lucy Jones about Katie. I thought it was innocent, just you wanting to know for old time's sake. I didn't think you'd try to follow her. I just don't know what to tell Lucy. Son, is there anything you know? Anything that you can do to get those little girls back?"

"I would if I could, Ma, but I think that it's too late. The FBI thinks they're dead."

"Lord, Jesus," Daisy said.

"And Ma, it is going to get real ugly for me. I'm going to be staying with you for a time."

Keith had set the *Detroit Free Press* on the kitchen counter and pointed to the front page. "They're never gonna find Katie's girls after all this time. Look at what the paper's saying."

Daisy glanced down, for the first time seeing the police sketch of the woman who drove off with Lucy's granddaughters. "Look at this picture, Keith. Do you know this woman. Does Penny know her?"

"No," said Keith. The woman looked like most middle-aged white women, overweight and saggy. Now was the time he had to tell her. "I had to tell the FBI about a woman that I *have* been seeing. A white woman. When Penny finds out, she's — I'm fucked."

"A white woman?" Daisy reached again for the front page. "A white woman, you say. Not *this* white woman?"

"Ma, I hafta stay with you until all this blows over. Penny's going to make my life a living hell. She knows this white woman's name. Jane Wise. She's already called the Ford plant where she works. Raising hell."

"Son, you've given me so many worries. Why you carrying on with a white woman. Any woman? You've got a wife and kids. I just don't understand."

"It's not like I love Jane, it's just that, you know, Katie got herself a white man and I — I don't know, Ma. Maybe I deserve to go to hell, but I can't get Katie out of my mind. I would do anything. Anything in my power. And I would. I truly would."

Daisy started to say something, then backed off as Keith slumped back in the chair, covered his eyes, and started to sob. Finally, his mother said, "Son, you can stay with me."

# CHAPTER 37

*Father's Day Sales Lag Last Year.*
— National News, Friday, June 19

"Wonder what Jackie's gonna say when she sees us?" Alex asked, raking her hand through chopped off curls.

"She'll laugh," said Sammie.

All three of the triplets had prided themselves on their long black hair. They argued about a lot of things, but not how Mom wanted their hair, cut just below the shoulder and naturally wavy. Whenever they wanted to individualize, all they had to do was put it up in a ponytail or twist. Now, when Sammie looked at Alex, she felt like she would cry again. That woman had cut their hair short and ugly.

"What do you think Jack's doing right now?"

"She's home. Talking to Mom. Saying that she misses us. Even though she always used to try to get away from us. Mom is telling her that she can have a pet like she's always wanted. She's getting very spoiled. And look at us. Rotting in this smelly basement. We have to get outta here. I'm just trying to figure out how."

Sammie wouldn't admit it, but if Jack were here, they would have figured out how to escape. Jackie was smart. She got all *A*s in school and she read a lot of those girl-detective books.

"I really miss baseball." Alex swung an imaginary bat. "Wonder if the Condors lost a game yet? If Dad lets Jared play third, I'm gonna be so mad. Dad won't give away my position, will he?"

"Not to that Jared creep. He couldn't make a play at third to save his life. Dad'll keep him in the outfield. But he may bring Todd over to play short and make Jackie pitch."

"Yeah, Todd's not bad, and he's cute," Alex said. "What Todd wants is to pitch. I heard his dad ask Dad about it."

"What did Dad say?" Sammie asked, her mouth sticky with peanut butter.

"Don't talk with your mouthful," Alex stuck out her tongue. "He said that you're better and that he had to go with his best. But if you're not there, he'll either let him try or bring Jackie in from short."

"Jackie loves short, she's not gonna give it up to some boy, and she hates to pitch. I don't know what Dad is going to do." Sammie held up her half-eaten sandwich. "At least we get crunchy peanut butter. Mom only buys the smooth stuff."

"I sure do miss Jackie," Alex said, inspecting her apple for defects. "And piano."

"No piano here," Sammie proclaimed, the constant battle at the Monroe's home: mandatory piano practice. Alex loved her music. Sammie hated it, and Jackie simply endured it, even though she excelled and was several levels above her sisters.

"Yeah," said Sammie, reaching for the board game. "Let's play Monopoly. I can't believe we don't have TV. Can't go outside. How long can she keep us here? Mom and Dad just have to find us."

As she counted out the money, Alex said, "Do you think Jackie's really, really sick? Or do you think she's back home with Mom and Dad?"

"Mom and Dad would never go back to Florida without us." But Sammie was not that sure. The woman who said that her name was Maggie had told them that Jackie had gotten sick in the movie and that she had to go to the hospital. So, Sammie figured, maybe Jackie was dead. Sammie refused to think about that and she certainly was not going to freak out Alex. But tears started to seep out of her eyes thinking about how sad her parents would be.

"I gotta go to the bathroom." Sammie got up and hurried to the tiny room in the far corner so Alex wouldn't see her cry.

On the way she kicked a blonde Barbie doll against the wall. "Barbies are stupid," Sammie had told Maggie when she'd opened up the plastic boxes. "We're way too old for them."

"Sammie, we have lots of them at home," Alex had said. Sure, but they had all colors of skin: black, brown, and white. The ones Maggie bought them were all white.

"Shut up, Alex," Sammie had said. "Whose side are you on?" Sometimes Alex made her really mad, always trying to be so sweet.

Sammie had been pretending that she wasn't afraid of the woman who took them out of the movie, but she was scared to death. The woman did feed them, but she hurt them, too. She wouldn't let them have a clock, but they knew that five nights had passed. That would make it Friday.

"Maggie was really mad last night when we messed up everything," Alex said when Sammie came out of the bathroom.

"I still think we should have left it just like it was. If we act like spoiled brats, she'll get mad enough at us, she might let us go."

"She hit us, Sammie." Alex fingered the dusky patch on her left cheek. "We had to clean up. What does she want with us anyway?"

Sammie didn't know. She figured that it must be money. Wasn't that what kidnappers wanted? Did her parents have enough money? Surely their Aunt Monica did. Everybody kept saying how rich she was. She even had her own airplane. Sammie hadn't answered Alex's question. She didn't know what that horrible woman wanted or why she kept them locked up.

Sammie plunked down on the lumpy sofa, thinking that it smelled like a wet dog. She stroked the scar on her left knee. A dog bite from a pit bull. She'd disliked dogs even before that and now she tried to avoid all animals and even hated the smell of them.

For five days the same routine. In the morning Maggie brought Cheerios and a banana before she went out. A peanut butter sandwich in a brown bag paper bag for lunch. Dinner on a tray after she got home. Then she read them stupid books. Then it got dark. They played Risk for as long as they could see, but it wasn't fun without Jackie.

Most of the day they talked about how to get out. But they could not agree on an approach. Alex thought they should be good girls, pretend to be sweet, do what the lady wanted. Then, when she trusted them, she'd let them out and they could escape. Sammie wanted to make her mad, mad enough that she'd want to get rid of them. If that didn't work, she planned to attack her. Last night, messing up the place, was an example of Sammie's strategy.

"She's just going to get mad," Alex had predicted. And, she'd been right.

"I don't care," Sammie had said. "What's she gonna do? Beat us up? Not give us any food?"

"I just want to go home. I miss Mom and Dad so much. And Jackie."

Then they heard a motor outside and a door slam. Silent, they both listened.

"I hear a man talking," Sammie said. "Maybe he will save us. Sammie put her arm around Alex and they began to talk in whispers.

# CHAPTER 38

*Hunt for Sammie and Alex Monroe Focused on Oakland County.*
*— Detroit Metropolitan News*, Friday, June 19

During the week, Spanky drove an eighteen wheeler up and down I-75, but for weekends he had him a cool, white Ford F150. Marge marveled at how he loved that truck. She couldn't care less about cars even though she did work in the Ford plant.

She heard the big Ford's wheels on the gravel driveway and the slamming of the back door, familiar sounds of Spanky announcing his arrival. Marge did not get out of bed, lying prone, paralyzed by fear and indecision. Her head was aching, going back and forth, trying to figure out what to do about her son. This time, she decided, she had to protect the twins. Even if that meant taking them away. In twenty-two years, she had never, not once, spent a night away from this house. Could she bear to leave it?

Right now, could she just lay there, pretending to be asleep? Would he grab something to eat — the fridge was full of beer and plenty of that bologna that he liked — and go out to the bar like he usually did on Friday nights? Could she avoid raising his suspicion that something was wrong? She heard his clunky boots coming up the stairs.

"Ma? What the fuck you doin' in there?" Spanky said. "Shit, I was lookin' all over. Makin' sure you hadn't passed in your sleep."

"I have a bad headache," Marge said. "You know, a migraine."

She used to have them a lot when he was a little boy, but he probably didn't remember back that far.

"You know how you're always telling me to take a vacation. I was thinking about that, and then the headache came on so I just laid down."

"You gonna be okay? I wanted to take you car shopping. About time you got rid of that piece of junk out there."

Marge started to object. She didn't think it would be a good time to trade in her Escort. "Brown Escort," had been in all the papers. "No need —"

"But good idea, the vacation." Spanky hovered over her, putting his big hand on her forehead. "No fever. Seriously, Ma, you got a lot of seniority. About time you used it, but about that car, guess it's not a good time so I'm gonna go to town, get my pickup tuned. It's been runnin' rough. I need plugs, the works. Won't be home 'til dinner. How 'bout some of your deep fried chicken? You gonna be okay to cook?"

"I'll be okay," Marge said, trying to figure out what to do. Most important was keeping Spanky out of the basement until she could get the twins out.

Once Spanky left, she got up and pulled frozen chicken pieces out of the freezer. Spanky was right, she did deserve a break. While she was away, she'd miss her cronies at the Ford plant and her house on Parker Road in Holly, a suburb of greater Detroit, about seventeen miles from Pontiac. The town itself was small, but charming, peppered with antique shops and weekend out-of-towners. But Marge did not live in the town center. She lived in a plain two-story plank house, accessible only via a network of roads and situated so far off the unpaved road that it couldn't be seen through the foliage in the summer by passersby. Plenty of mature oaks and leafy maples completely obscured the neighbors' view on both sides. The house had been in Evan's family, and he had signed it over to her when he left. Most women would be too frightened to live in such isolation, but not Marge, she appreciated the solitude.

Marge was warming to the idea of a vacation. She had enough money saved up and enough time coming to her. Her boss would be pissed at the short notice, but she'd make up something about an elderly aunt. People did it all the time. Two years ago, Elmira went off with a man. Surprised everybody, but in two weeks she was back, glad to still have her job. In her case, that picture in the paper would be forgotten when she returned. She was sure of that. All she had to do was leave with the twins after dinner when Spanky left to go to the bar.

Now she had to fix a fried chicken dinner with all the trimmings. Marge loved to cook for Spanky, and he loved her home cooking. Who wouldn't, being on the road most every night? Then she remembered, she had to feed the girls before Spanky got back from the garage. Quickly she grilled two cheese sandwiches, opened a can of pears, and put everything on a plastic plate. Halfway down the stairs, she remembered their milk. Forget it. They could make do with water.

While Scott was at FBI headquarters, Katie stayed with Jackie, accompanied off and on by her mom, her sisters, and Monica. Dr. Reynolds dropped by every hour or so to monitor her patient's progress, or lack thereof. Katie was so appreciative of this calm, wise woman, who seemed to exude confidence. For the first time since Alex and Sammie were taken, Katie felt a tinge of rationality emerge from her shattered mind. She started to realize that she had to stay calm and logical and even optimistic. There must be something she could add, something she could do.

Throughout the day, Scott had checked in with her. She knew that he was as worried about her as he was about all three of their daughters. She was ashamed that her emotional instability had not only damaged Jackie, but she knew that it had also not been fair to Scott. He desperately needed her strength, as she did his. She wanted him with her, but she encouraged him to stay to help to identify the elusive white woman, and to try to solve the Yankee-related ransom demand. So far, no breakthroughs. At their insistence, FBI agents were guiding Scott through the money drop-off tomorrow morning, eleven a.m.

When Scott had asked about Jackie, Katie couldn't stop the tears gathering in her eyes when she said, "No change."

She and Scott had always insisted that they did not have a favorite among the triplets, but it was true that Jackie and Scott had a special relationship. What about her? Which of the three was her favorite? Alex, so sweet and loving and innocent. What about Sammie? That made Sammie neither of their favorites.

Balancing the food on the tray, Marge descended the steps. She pulled back the bolt, clicked open the lock, and walked into the basement. Nudging the tray against her ample hip, she balanced it with one hand.

She almost dropped it when Jessica said, "Let me help you." The child hopped off the couch, and Marge handed her the tray.

Marge carefully locked the basement door behind her then went to pour them water from the faucet. *Why so nice?* she thought, and *wasn't it about time?* After all, she had been good to the girls. It wasn't her fault that she'd had to gag them and tie them and hide them in the bathroom when that nosy guy delivered the twin beds. Then when they'd trashed the place, she hit them, and if they tried that in the future, she'd do so again. She was a kind person and it wasn't her nature to beat on kids, but they were her charges, a responsibility that she did not take lightly.

Jessica took a bite of her sandwich, then asked, "Are you married?"

Marge didn't know what to say. "Yes" that she was married. Or "no" that Evan had divorced her. But whatever God has joined, let no man put asunder. At least that's what she remembered from the Bible.

"Yes, I am," she decided, clenching her fists. She would have Evan back as soon as things settled down. And they would. There's no way that distorted picture of her face would be in the papers as far away as Toronto.

"Where's your husband?" Jennifer asked.

"Just eat." Marge said.

"We heard a man's voice today," Jessica said. "Was that him?"

"What?" Marge jerked her head toward the locked door. "Uh, no." Had they seen Spanky? Or just heard him?

Good thing she had a plan to get them out tonight. She'd do it after dark. After Spanky left to go out to the bars. She'd probably have to tie them up again, but maybe not if they stayed nice like this.

Marge watched Jessica and Jennifer exchange one of those twin looks. Like they were reading each other's mind. "What?" she asked. They'd tell her if they'd seen Spanky, wouldn't they? And what would he be doing in the basement? He kept all his stuff in the garage.

Marge headed for the door to let herself out, when Jessica asked, "Can we go with you? We always help our Mom. We can dust. Do the dishes. Lots of things."

"We need fresh air," Jennifer added. "It smells funny down here."

"I have a surprise for you later." Marge pushed back the bolt. It did smell moldy. She'd planned to spray the basement with Lysol, but now there was no point. Right now she had to gas up the car and make a stop at the pharmacy. And she had to do it quickly before Spanky got back from his buddy's garage. No way could she risk Spanky wandering into the basement. She had been worried that she'd have to gag the girls and tie them up with those rags, but they were behaving so well, she judged it not necessary. "You girls have to be real quiet. You're gonna love the surprise I promised you later, but you have to behave. Okay?"

"I just want to go home." Marge didn't like Jennifer's whiny tone.

"Is it a television?" Jessica sounded excited. The first positive reaction from her and it warmed Marge's heart.

"We'll see," Marge said. "Now quiet as mice. Promise?"

The twins exchanged another look, which Marge interpreted to be a promise.

# CHAPTER 39

*Sammie and Alex Monroe – Still No Clue.*
*Jackie Remains Hospitalized.*
– News Talk Shows, Friday, June 19

Alex didn't think that Sammie's escape plan would work. But all she could think about was getting back to Mom and Dad. Before he left, the man they heard upstairs yelled that he would be back for dinner. But would he help them or not?"

She'd posed the question to Sammie, the bravest one of all three of them.

"If he won't, we'll use these to knock him out." Sammie pointed to a shovel and a hoe that they'd found over by the washing machine and dryer. "And we can throw these at their heads."

Alex and Sammie each had a good arm. Better than any of the boys on their baseball team, but could they bean a man hard enough with the baseballs they'd found in a rotting athletic bag? The woman maybe, because she was fat and if they surprised her, maybe.

"First we try to knock them down so we can get out the door and then we run like crazy. If that doesn't work, then we'll have the baseballs in our pockets and the extras in this bucket by the door. See?" Sammie pointed to a plastic pail.

"Maybe the man will just let us go. Just because he's with her doesn't make him bad, too."

"Right. And maybe our fairy godmother will fly by to take us home. Alex, you're such a goody-goody."

"I just wanta see Mom and Dad."

"You do exactly what I tell you. I mean it. We're gonna escape from that bitch."

Alex felt her body shudder. If Mom ever heard Sammie use that word –

Marge had lingered too long and she was behind schedule. She'd packed both of her big suitcases. They'd fit in the trunk as well as some of the girls' things. But maybe not the two doll clothes wardrobes. If they didn't, should she take one or leave them both behind? She'd have to wait until the last minute to make that decision. In the meantime, what to do about gassing up the car? She did have half a tank. She'd planned to get some hair dye to make herself a dark brunette, but it was now six thirty p.m., too late. She had the chicken partially baked, ready to fry. Potatoes ready to mash. String beans ready to steam.

"Ma." Marge hadn't heard the crunch of gravel coming up the drive or the loud motor sound. He must have got his truck engine fixed.

Home already. Maybe that was good. They could eat earlier, he'd leave, and she could finish packing and wait until it was dark enough.

"In the kitchen, Spanky."

"Hey, Ma. I'm gonna take your junker. Where you got the keys?"

Marge went out into the hall. "What?"

"I wanta get an appraisal. For a trade-in. I'm gettin' you new wheels. Maybe one of those Porsches."

"You come in here." She didn't want him lingering by the stairs leading to the basement.

"Your Escort's a junker."

"Just a little rusted," Marge said. *Crap*. She couldn't have him driving around in her car.Thank goodness she hadn't started to put her suitcases inside.

"Rusted so bad you can't tell what the fuck color it is."

"Come on, Spanky, you know I don't like you talking like that. I don't care how you talk to your truck-driving buddies, but I didn't raise you like that. Another thing," she said, looking him up and down, "I wish you'd get rid of that moustache and that dinky beard." She especially didn't like the scraggly beard. It didn't look good with his completely shaved head. A big head, like his big body, six feet three, bulky muscles, and the start of a beer belly.

"Yeah, yeah. I need the keys."

"No, not tonight. Look, I got dinner about ready." Marge pointed to the chicken parts she'd spread out on the counter to dip into flour.

"Hmm, chicken. Guess I can wait until tomorrow. I got a buddy who's got a deal on an Impala."

"No way, Spanky. I'm only driving Ford cars. Chrysler and General Motors are both bankrupt. I've gotta show my loyalty. Besides, I can get a discount."

"You can't afford no new car. This one I got in mind's a beauty. Only got twenty thousand miles, a shiny red. Like you owe them any loyalty. What a crock of shit."

*Just feed him. Let him go out. Tomorrow I'll have left on vacation.*

Marge had the oil in the frying pan ready and when she began to drop in chicken legs, Spanky sniffed. "Guess, I'm not goin' anywhere."

"You're all sweaty. You go take a shower while I fry this up. Now, go along."

Marge breathed a sigh of relief as he went clomping up the stairs. She remembered how she'd always made him take off his shoes in the house when he was a little boy.

Marge didn't like to dwell on it, but Spanky had not been a very nice little boy. Even as a toddler back when they lived with her parents in that cramped house. Back before she'd married Evan. But hadn't it been all her fault? Getting pregnant when she was only seventeen by that no-good, pimply neighborhood kid. She'd brought shame on her family. Her mother, bless her soul, taking care of the illegitimate baby while Marge got a job on the production line at Ford.

Most kids were cuddly and cute, but Samuel had been mean tempered from the beginning, or at least that's how Marge remembered it.

Even when Marge's life changed so dramatically for the better, her son had been a constant worry. That's when Marge married Evan Spansky, a lovely man, who worked at the Ford plant. She met him when she worked the second shift and found out that he was going to college during the day to be an accountant. He was shy, but smart, and good looking with wavy dark brown hair and eyes the color of copper. From the first time he asked her out for coffee after work, she could tell he really fell for her. Samuel was then five years old, and once they were married, Evan had been eager to adopt him. Samuel had been called "Spanky" ever since then, after trying to explain his new last name to his kindergarten class. Once Evan graduated from Eastern Michigan University, Marge quit her job, and the Spansky family moved to Evan's place in Holly.

As always, when Marge thought of Evan, her mind jumped two years ahead to the birth of the twins. Identical, darling little girls with dark curly hair and copper-colored eyes just like their father's. Evan doted on them, as did she. Later, too much later, Marge realized that she and Evan had been so absorbed by the beautiful, delightful babies that maybe they did neglect Spanky just a bit.

Marge's last vision of the twins was as vivid today as it was twenty-one years ago, the two of them babbling away in their double stroller, dressed in matching fuchsia outfits with cute little visors. She'd parked the stroller in the sand along the shore of Elk Lake, where Evan's family had a log cabin.

Now, as Marge stood mashing her potatoes, she had to set down the masher to clutch her heart.

"You okay, Ma?" Spanky was at her side, shaking her. "You havin' one of those headaches again? Nothin' wrong with your heart, is there?"

Sometimes Spanky could be so sweet and caring. Like wanting to get her a new car. Like now, leaning over her to show that he cared.

All of a sudden Marge heard a loud clanging. It was coming from the basement. Not now, her mind screamed. Not now. But Spanky had heard it.

"What the fuck's that?" Spanky spun around. "Somebody at the door?"

"I'll take care of it, Spanky. Quickly Marge jerked open the refrigerator and pulled out a beer. "Take this. Go in the living room. Watch TV."

Marge hesitated a moment to make sure that Spanky would not follow her. The noise below was louder now. What were the twins doing?

Spanky opened the door and poked his head out. "Nobody out there," he said, reaching for the beer then turning. "Hey Ma, it's coming from — "

Marge held out both arms to stop Spanky as he bolted for the basement steps.

# CHAPTER 40

*Norman Watkins, Suspect in Monroe Kidnappings, to be Buried in Tampa.*
– *Tampa News*, Friday, June 19

"So if Cutty set up the abduction, he's gone to his grave with their whereabouts." Streeter ran a hand through his lengthening crew cut, wrapping up a detailed conference call summarizing the Monroe case. When the others hung up, Rusk stayed on.

"Same goes for Norman Watkins," Rusk added. "I don't think he's our man. Unless he had a streak of revenge that he'd hidden from everybody. Everybody we interviewed was all hero worship. It's like the joint turned the guy into a saint. The rumor is that his wife has a case against the feds? Like your agents up there provoked a police suicide?"

"The way this case is going, who knows? Watkins panicked, I guess. Either that or he did snatch the kids and – any way about it, it happened in Detroit, so I'm taking the heat. I've got three daughters in Michigan. They try to transfer me to a remote outpost, I'm out of the bureau."

"You divorced?"

"Yeah," Streeter said. "They live with their mom. Classic FBI. She couldn't take the job. I couldn't give it up. But if I don't break this case, I just don't know –"

"About the ransom tomorrow –"

"It's bullshit, but we have to go through the paces. So far we've kept it out of the press, but who knows what'll blow tomorrow. Chances are we'll snatch the guy and be no more the smarter as to what happened to those girls."

When Streeter terminated the conference, he took a call from Clarence Plummer at the Hills Mall. The two had kept in touch on a daily basis since this all started last Sunday, and Plummer was doing all in his power to find that middle-aged white woman who'd taken the Monroe girls out of his mall.

"There was a guy in the mall today who heard that I was still asking questions about the kidnapping," Plummer reported. "He stopped by my office and told my assistant that he had delivered a couple of twin beds on Monday. To a woman who lives out near Pontiac. Didn't give the address. He said that she looked a lot like the lady in the police drawing and that he saw a brownish Escort parked on the property and he remembered a couple of numbers from the license plate. He said that his wife had called the FBI hotline before, but that was before the picture of the woman was on the wire."

Streeter vaguely remembered the report. Thousands of callers, suspicious of something ridiculous. Something about twin beds. Nothing relevant, of that he was sure.

"I was off-site," Plummer went on. "This guy told my assistant that he remembered seeing me on TV and he wanted to talk only to me so the information wouldn't get ignored. He refused to identify himself, but said he'd call back in the morning. You can bet that I reamed out my staff for letting an informant leave without contact information. Of all things, dropping the ball – Streeter, you know how bad I want to find those little girls."

"I'll check into our database for that report," Streeter said. "We should be able to locate it and pinpoint the source. Sounds like a long shot, but we'll jump on it. And thanks, Plummer. If this guy gets back, give me a call, direct."

"You got it," Plummer said. "My wife and I are still praying that you find those little girls."

# CHAPTER 41

*Mystery Woman Who Left with Monroe Children Still at Large.*
— Evening News, Friday, June 19

Sammie couldn't tell by the light coming in from the small rectangular windows up by the ceiling whether it was getting late or whether it was just a cloudy day.

"Wish we had a Hershey Bar. Remember the first day down here, she brought us one."

If only Alex would stop talking about food. But what else was there to talk about? They didn't know anything about what was going on. Were their parents still looking for them? Was Jackie okay, or was she really vomiting blood like Maggie said? And what did Maggie want with them?

"Sammie," Alex interrupted. "I hear something."

Sammie jumped up. They were ready. They rehearsed like they were going to be in a school play. If only Alex didn't lose her nerve.

"Put your shoes on," Sammie said, leaning into the door. "I hear a man's voice."

"Okay."

Alex was at Sammie's side, sneakers tied, clutching the spade. Or was it a hoe? Sammie grabbed the shovel.

They both waited.

"It's that same man's voice." Sammie took a deep breath. Another look at Alex, and with her nod, they began. They'd figured hitting the shovel and the other garden thing on the pipes would make the loudest clamor.

They started to scream, "Help! Help Us!" That's what they'd decided. "Help!" over and over.

Beyond their shouts and the clunking of the iron, they heard Maggie's voice. Much louder than she'd ever talked to them. She yelled, "No, Spanky, don't go down there."

Sammie flashed Alex a hopeful look. Somebody was coming to help them.

Loud footsteps on the stairs and the girls stopped clunking the shovel and hoe. They kept calling for help. "Down here," Alex screamed. "We're in the basement."

Alex started to put the spade down, but Sammie shook her head, "No, remember, like we planned."

Before Alex could respond, the chain on the door clanked and they heard the bolt slide.

Standing on each side of the door, holding their implement, they waited for only an instant before a big man pushed though the door. Right behind him was Maggie. She had a scared look on her face, but the man looked surprised.

Sammie hesitated and Alex froze. Was this bald man with the ugly little beard going to help them?

"What the shit?" The man's mouth was so wide open that Sammie could see that his teeth in the back were black. She shrank back when his bulging black eyes stared at her. Still, she couldn't tell if this man was going to help them or not.

"What the —?" The man spun to face Maggie. "What the hell is goin' on here?"

Maggie stood perfectly still. "What do you mean, Spanky?"

"The hell you say! What're these girls doin' down here?"

Sammie was trapped between the man and Maggie, but Alex was close to the door, which was wide open. Sammie cut her eyes to the door. She wished she could yell, "Alex, run." But Alex was staring at the big metal thing the man held in one hand. Sammie had helped her dad around cars enough to know that it was a pipe wrench.

"Ma, what are you, crazy?"

Then with his free hand the man reached for Sammie's shoulder. Sammie tried to shrink back as far as she could against the wall, but before he could grab her, Maggie lurched forward and grabbed his arm.

"Spanky, don't," she yelled, but the scary man with the stupid name shoved Maggie back, toward Alex, pinning her against the wall.

"Ma," he said, grabbing Sammie's shirt and staring at her with really black eyes. "What the fuck are you up to?"

"Let us out of here," Sammie finally found her voice. "She locked us up in here. We want to go home."

"Well, you do, do you?"

"Look, Spanky, it's Jennie and Jessie," Maggie said, grabbing Alex's hand and leading her closer to him.

"No!" Alex opened her mouth for the first time. "We're Alexandra and Samantha Monroe. She locked us up down here, but we're not supposed to be here."

"What the fuck?" Spanky turned and stared at Maggie. "You're crazy as a loon."

"Spanky, let me explain." Sammie watched as Maggie took a step away from Alex.

If the big man would just let go of her shoulder, Sammie would jam the shovel into his knees. If only she had a baseball bat, it would work better.

"Let go of me," she cried, but the man only squeezed her more tightly.

If she could just make a move, Alex would follow. The door was still open.

"You're fucking crazy, Ma. I gotta give it to you though."

"Spanky, watch your language," Maggie said.

"You're the one that took them? Whole fuckin' world's lookin' for these girls. And I come home and find them in my basement. Holy shit."

Sammie looked at Alex. Her sister looked like she was paralyzed. Sammie wondered whether she'd heard him say that the whole world was looking for them.

"Let's just go up and talk, Spanky," Maggie said in a shaky voice. "You and me. We'll leave the girls down here. They like it here with me."

"No we don't! Please mister, make her let us go," Sammie said, trying to sound nice so he'd feel sorry for them.

"Well, well," he said. "You wanta leave my nice mama, huh?" The man let go of Sammie's shoulder and took the shovel out of her hand. "I gotta think about this."

Then he set the pipe wrench down and walked toward Alex.

"Give me that thing."

He stepped forward to take the spade Alex clutched protectively in front of her. Sammie stared at Alex. She looked so scared. She'd never seen her eyes so wide, but she didn't make a move.

"Give it over," he repeated.

Maggie moved closer toward Alex as the man demanded again, stepping closer, "Give it over."

Then Sammie saw just the tiniest flick of Alex's eyes toward the open basement door. She took less than an instant to react.

Marge's gaze fixed with dread on Spanky as he approached Jennifer with his brawny arms outstretched. When his back was fully turned on Jessica, Jennifer suddenly jerked the spade she was holding out of Spanky's reach. She raised it up and with one big gulp, swung it as hard as she could against the side of Spanky's knee.

"Oh my God," Marge screamed. What should she do? Spanky was so big; Jennifer so small.

"Little bitch!" Spanky yelled, shaking and rubbing his leg.

That's when Marge snatched Jennifer out of his reach.

Enraged, Spanky wrenched the spade out of Jennifer's hands and hurled it to the ground, smashing the card table, sending pieces of Risk flying.

Jennifer cowered behind Marge and broke into convulsive sobs. As Marge bent to comfort her, she knew that something was very wrong. Where was Jessica?

"Spanky," she cried. "Quick! Jessica got out! You have to find her. Hurry, hurry! You can't let her get away."

"What the fuck —" Spanky swung to face the open door. "Oh shit."

To Marge's relief, Spanky flew toward the door and clamored up the steps.

"You tie that one up," he yelled as the side door slammed closed.

What was Spanky going to do? Would he help her get the girls out of here to a place where no one would ever find them? Marge clutched the remaining twin tightly. Spanky had not been in her plan, but now she had no choice but to tell him. Maybe it was for the best, she thought, but deep in her heart, she knew better.

# CHAPTER 42

*Tragic Drowning of Eight-Month-Old Spansky Twins.*
— *Detroit News*, June,1977

Marge never imagined her little girls as twenty-six. That's how old they'd be. But in her mind, they were still children. She'd kept their room for them, the frilly curtains and the crib covers now faded and limp. Once in a while she'd buy them something new, an article of clothing, a new doll so that the small room was now crammed, leaving only the space for the daybed where she slept from time to time.

Margie Wisnewski had been an only child, growing up a Catholic girl in the Polish enclave of Hamtramck, a little city within the big city of Detroit. Had she been spoiled? Yes. Her girlfriends had siblings with whom they had to share the little discretionary income of their blue-collar fathers. But for Margie, every extra penny went to please her insatiable appetite for little girl paraphernalia. Her father toiled to construct her dollhouse. Her mother sewed doll clothes, the envy of all her friends.

Little Marge managed her doting parents well. So well that when she became an adolescent, she was not about to let overprotective parents stand in the way of a teenage romance with the boy two blocks over, a pimply boy, three years older. But Marge had not been a pretty girl, and she just wanted a boyfriend. Which she did not have anymore, once she became pregnant. And from then until she married Evan, she'd lived her life in shame.

Now, holding Jennifer closely, Marge brushed aside the child's tears. And she, too, started to sob when she recognized what she'd just seen. That look in Spanky's face when he rushed out the door after Jessica was the same look he'd had that day, when she'd come hurrying out of the cottage after checking on her cupcakes.

She'd parked the double stroller on a small patch of soft pine needles and she'd very carefully locked the brake. When she came back, the stroller wasn't there. She saw Spanky standing at the end of the dock, staring into the dark water. She'd screamed her son's name and ran.

It had been a windy day and the water was murky with weeds, but looking down, Marge could make out the outline of the overturned twin stroller. The wheels were facing her just under the surface and she could almost reach over and grab them. Evan was out in the motorboat, fishing somewhere across the lake. No one else was around. Marge had jumped in fully clothed, submerged to her shoulders, the stony bottom scraping her feet. Bending down, arms flailing, head submerged, she found the inert bundles trapped in the stroller. She pulled up one baby, struggling to heft her up onto the dock as Spanky stood passively by. She didn't know if it was Jennie or Jessie. Reaching back into the murky water she pulled up the second twin and dragged her straight to the shore before frantically rushing back to the narrow dock to carry the first twin to safety.

Hysterical, she'd knelt down in the sand between the babies and frantically breathed into their dark blue mouths, first one and then the other, like she'd seen demonstrated on TV, but Jessica and Jennifer, eight months old, never took another breath. The next thing Marge remembered was Evan forcibly dragging her from the two fresh mounds of dirt at the cemetery. She still had every article of their clothing, every little toy, all enshrined on shelves in their bedroom upstairs.

There could be no other explanation – Spanky had deliberately pushed the stroller off the dock. At seven, he was strong enough to push it the few feet through the sand and onto the wooden planks. She tried to concoct a story for Evan, but she knew that he knew how the accident had happened. Neither ever admitted it to each other or discussed it with Spanky. It was just too unthinkable, too unspeakable. If they'd taken him to a child psychologist, things might have been different. Instead, after the babies' funeral, Evan practically destroyed himself with heavy drinking before leaving Marge with the house in Holly – and with Spanky.

Truly, Marge tried her best to raise her troubled son, now a two-hundred-forty-pound hulk of a man with a protruding beer belly, a shaved head, and a mean temperament, but underneath she knew that Spanky's shortcomings were all her fault. She should have known something was not right with Spanky when he started torturing those frogs at the lake and chopping the heads off turtles. Why hadn't she realized he was crying out for love? She'd been too busy dressing up the twins like dolls. At least she and Evan had stood up for him when the detectives came around asking about how the accident happened. But then Evan walked out on them, and she'd had to go back to work.

Spanky now had a job driving an eighteen wheeler on the Detroit-to-Miami run. Not bad for a kid who hadn't graduated high school. And face it, he'd never done time except for when the cops kept him in the lockup after a bar fight. For his own good, they said. Drunk and disorderly, but nobody pressed charges or made a big deal of it.

But in the privacy of her heart, Marge had to admit her horrible, secret suspicions. Over the years, child molestation cases had been reported in Oakland County, all involving little girls. Marge was pretty sure that nobody else connected her son with these sordid reports, but she knew about the little panties he kept hidden in the small chest under his bed. The chest he took with him on the road. Whenever there'd been a report, she knew that Spanky had been in the vicinity. The last time she'd secretly checked his box. Panties stained with something brownish on a Mickey Mouse pattern had been added. She did feel bad about those little girls, but she could only blame herself.

But now, for Marge, things were different. God had answered her prayers. She must have paid for her sins because He was giving her a second chance. She had Jennifer and Jessica back and she had to protect them. She no longer even noticed that their skin was darker and that their eyes were not the color of copper. She'd been so happy, but she'd not planned to tell Spanky. She couldn't let him harm her little girls again.

Now Jessica had run outside, and Spanky was chasing her. Marge was all mixed up.

"We'll find her." Marge stroked Jennifer's forehead, hoping the child would stop shaking. "Everything will be all right."

# CHAPTER 43

*Yankees and Marlins to Hold Prayer Service for the Safe Return of Scott Monroe's Daughters at Land Shark Stadium in Miami before Tomorrow's Game.*
– News on Sports, Friday, June 19

Sammie ran as fast as she'd ever run in her life. Dad was always making them run and clocking their time. Although Alex was the fastest of the three, Sammie could almost beat her. But could she run fast enough to get away from the big man? He was fat and she hoped that he would get out of breath really fast. And what about Alex? She'd left her behind. For a split second Sammie slowed, wondering if she should turn back. That look on Alex's face, swinging that spade at the man, scared to death. She'd heard him yell a very bad word and she'd heard the door slam several seconds after. She was sure he was coming after her, and right now she couldn't think about Alex or anybody else. She had to find somebody to help them.

But run to where? She was surrounded by trees and scratchy bushes and she didn't know which way to go, but she kept on running. The sky had gotten darker and she felt a few drops of rain. She had to get out of the woods and find a road where there would be houses. Everything was too dark. Maybe being in that dim basement for so long was making her blind? That really scared her. How could she go on to be a baseball star if she was blind?

Sammie kept zigzagging through the woods until her legs started to sag and she had to lean over to catch her breath. That's when she felt the warm, stickiness on her bare arms. Blood, she thought with horror from all those prickly branches that tore at the skin on her legs and arms. Sammie was squeamish about blood, always had been. Alex and Jackie used to laugh at her when she freaked out about the sight of blood.

Then from far away, Sammie heard the bark of a dog. She dropped to a running stance and pushed off. She just had to find a street even though the streets out here were dirt, not cement like the city. And what if that barking came from a wild dog? Or a wolf? What if a wolf smelled her blood? She couldn't remember if wolves were like sharks. Whether they attacked when they smelled blood.

When Sammie was five, at a Yankee team picnic, she'd been bitten by a pit bull. She'd been petting it, when it turned on her, snarled, and ripped a piece out of her knee. She'd had to go to the hospital for stitches and she still had a big scar. And every time Jackie begged their parents to get a dog, she showed off her scar and said, "No way."

Sammie ran a few minutes then stopped to listen for the barking. She still heard it, but it didn't seem any closer. She stayed put long enough to try to figure out which direction the bark was coming from before starting out again in the opposite direction. She ran until her legs buckled at the edge of a cluster of bushes that came up to about her height. Her chest hurt with every breath and she had to lean over and pant as quietly as she could.

That's when she heard the man's voice. The man from the basement. The man that Maggie called "Spanky." And hadn't Maggie also called him "son"? One thing Sammie could tell, the man was mean. Totally holding her breath, she waited as his voice came closer and closer.

The voice kept repeating, "Come out, little girl. Wanna go home to Mama and Daddy?"

Sammie stood perfectly still, but she couldn't hold her breath any longer. Without moving a muscle other than her eyes, she strained to see where he was coming from. Should she stay here or would he stumble into her any second? Stay, she decided. If she moved even an inch now, he'd find her. Suddenly, she could make him out. His face and his bald head were but a shadow, but he was so close that she could hear his heavy breathing.

Something scurried on the ground within a foot of her white sneaker. The big man stopped short and fixed his gaze in her direction just as a striped chipmunk scurried out onto the rustling leaves.

"Fuck," the big man grunted. "Little bitch's gotta be out here somewhere." There were bushes in front of him, and he stepped over them coming within inches of Sammie's protective thicket.

"Spanky-y-y, where are you?" Maggie's voice cut through the soft droplets of rain.

"Hold on, Ma!" the man yelled. Slowly he turned away from Sammie's hiding place. "I'm comin' back."

Spanky banged back into the house and thudded down the stairs, tripping on an old duffel bag he hadn't seen in years. He was sweating like a pig and frustrated. He'd checked out Parker Road and Oakhurst all the way to Davisburg, then circled back. No sign of the little bitch. How long would it take for her to bring down the law? And what would happen to Ma?

Marge was sitting on one of the beds, cradling the other kid. "Ma, you gonna tell me what the fuck's going on? Every cop in the country is lookin' for these kids. Shit, you got Scott Monroe's kids? I always knew you were crazy, but this? You gotta be outta your fuckin' mind."

Marge placed both her hands over Alex's ears and glared at Spanky. "Watch your language. Okay?"

"Fuckin' okay?" Spanky stood over her, hands on hips. "You're in deep, deep shit and you're worried about cuss words. That's my fuckin' crazy ma."

"Find Jessica so we can leave here." Marge laid Jennifer down on the sofa and stood a moment before going about, gathering up toys and kids' clothes.

"You're in heavy doo-doo and you're worried about shit like that?" He took a pink doll clothes case out of her hands and set it down.

"The picture in the newspapers," Marge said. "It's not very good, but the girls at work were kidding around. You know, Elmira, Beatrice, and even Janie — What if — "

Spanky crossed the room and plunked down on the other bed. "Stubbed my goddamned toe," he mumbled, taking off his shoe to rub his foot. When he looked up, he took a closer look at the kid still sitting on the other bed. She was a cutie in those little red shorts and a snow-white polo shirt. "Hmm," came out, unplanned. "What if *what*, Ma?"

"What if they tell the cops? I have vacation time. I was gonna leave tonight. When all this blows over, we'll come back."

"So you figure this is gonna blow over? You're one crazy lunatic."

"Spanky, please help me. Please. Go find Jessica. I'll pack the car and we can go."

"Go where?" he asked, humoring her, clueless as to how to get her out of this mess.

Marge stopped stuffing things into plastic bags and came over to whisper something in his ear.

"That might just work," he said. "At least it'll buy us some time until I get this all figured out. But I got bad news for you, Ma. It's only gonna be this one. The other one got away. I spent forty-five minutes out there chasin' her down. She's outta here. And she'll lead the law straight back here. So we gotta go. Now."

Spanky put his shoe back on, stood to cross the room, and leaned over Alex. "I'm puttin' her in the car. You load up a few things. Food, as much as you can, cause we're not gonna be stoppin' to eat."

"I was gonna go out and get gas, but — "

"I'll siphon some out of my truck. That'll get us far enough. And I'll muddy up your license plate. Now, hurry, if that little bitch gets help, you're in a pile of shit."

Spanky knew that kidnapping was a federal crime. And this kidnapping was national news. But how could he betray his own mother? She might be crazy, but she'd always protected him. Didn't he owe her the same loyalty? And the feel of this little girl in his arms was nothing less than exhilarating.

# CHAPTER 44

*Heavy Rain Forecast.*
– Six o'clock News, Detroit Metropolitan Area, Friday, June 19

Sammie knew that he'd come back after her and she knew that her only chance was to hide from him. If he found her, he and his horrible mother would lock her up. She didn't want to leave Alex alone, but she figured her only chance to save her sister was to find somebody who would help them. But how in this dark, scary place?

She couldn't find the road, so she decided she had to move deeper into the wooded area. It was very dark now and she was soaked from the steady rain. Once in a while she'd stop under a big tree, where the rain couldn't get through the branches, but once the thunder and lightening started, she got even more scared. She knew that in a storm you were supposed to stay away from trees. She couldn't remember why, but growing up near Tampa, the lightning capital of the world, her science teacher told them that rubber was good. Like when you were in a car, the tires would protect you. Well, there was nothing rubber out here. Only tall, dangerous trees. And the barking she had heard had turned to howling. Probably a whole pack of wild dogs.

Sammie had no choice but to keep going. Now she just wanted to get out of the woods. It was dark enough that she didn't need the trees to hide her. Unless he came back with a flashlight. She was weighing the risk of lightning and the trees against the man with a flashlight when she saw the shadow of a building. She went back to the edge of the clearing and carefully worked her way forward. She could barely make out the outline of a two-story house. With the aid of a dim light inside the front door, she could see a large porch across the front. But that was the only light on in the house. Again, Sammie wondered if there was something wrong with her eyes. She backed up to get a better look and then she circled the outside of the house. In the back she noticed that she was stepping on smooth mushy ground, and she bent over to touch it. It felt like wet grass, cut just the way her dad liked it. When she straightened back up, she felt a bang against her head.

Her heart plunged. The man must have found her. She reached up to touch her head, holding her breath, waiting to be grabbed. But nothing happened. She stood perfectly still, noticing for the first time that the rain had stopped, and that the moon was starting to show though the clouds. Then she saw a frame in front of her. She still could not trust her eyes and she carefully reached out in front of her. Her hand encountered a smooth, wet pipe. Sammie let her hand explore the pipe, which extended all the way to the ground and up as far as she could reach. She slowly turned all the way around. No one seemed to be there. No breathing, only the barking. She thought it sounded louder now.

When she turned back, Sammie almost gasped in recognition. What she'd been touching was a swing set. She could see the outline now. They must have kids. They had to be good people. Hope poured out as she quickly retraced her steps to the front door. Pounding on it with one fist, she rang the doorbell with her other hand. She pushed and pushed and pounded and pounded with no response from within. Inside, the long narrow window pane beside the door was covered by a sheer panel, but there was a dim light on inside. In desperation, she pounded on the door, trying to open it, but it was locked.

Maybe there was a door in the back. Running around the house, she found one. Locked. Looking around, she saw the patch of grass and the lone swing set. All around it was woods. Except for the dirt driveway. But it would lead to the street. Before she'd been looking for the street, but now that she'd had time to think, she rationalized that that's where that man would be looking.

Sinking to her knees, Sammie realized that she'd have to hide in the woods in the dark. At least until morning, but she was so afraid of the woods — of wild animals and snakes and devils. She would never admit her fears to anyone — especially not Alex or Jackie — but afraid she was. Especially about devils. Sammie knew that she was naughty and she told lies and was sometimes mean to Jackie and Alex.

And now the devils were even more scary because this was all her fault. They wouldn't have gotten kidnapped if she hadn't insisted on going to *Night at the Museum* when they were supposed to go to *Star Trek*.

Petrified, Sammie righted herself and crept around the side of the house, heading back to the scary woods. At least it had stopped raining and there was no more lightning to worry about. But then she noticed something. Lined up against the house were three large trashcans. With the half-moon now exposed, she could tell that they were dark green. She peeked inside each one. The first two were crammed full of those white plastic trash bags. But the last one was not full. On the bottom was smelly garbage that was not wrapped in plastic bags.

Sammie stood there, hugging herself. Her shorts and her shirt were still drenched, and it was getting colder. Checking to make sure that the cuts on her arms had stopped bleeding, she made her decision. She lifted the cover of that last can again. "Ick. Disgusting," she said aloud, changing her mind, replacing the lid, turning again for the woods.

As she reached the edge of the trees, she heard something move in the bushes. Something big. Something very scary. She froze. Wild animals?

Quietly, she tiptoed back to the garbage cans. If only she could get inside one and hide. She didn't care how smelly they were. Maybe it would be warmer inside. And if the lightning started again, she'd be safe in rubber. But how could she get inside? If she tipped the can over, she could crawl in, but then an animal could get inside, too, in the middle of the night.

For the first time since she escaped, Sammie started to cry. She slumped down against the house. Why couldn't these people be home? She'd tell them to call the police and get Alex out of that house. Then her hand touched something cold and metal. A stepladder she realized, just like Mom used to get up into the top shelves where she stored the flower vases. She pulled it out just when a very loud sound that sounded like the howl of a wolf made her shake all over.

Sammie knew what she had to do. In one quick movement she jerked the ladder up. She had no trouble setting it up beside the partly empty trash can. Then she grabbed the green plastic cover placing it over her head as she scrambled up the ladder. Holding her breath, she jumped inside the smelly, squishy can. With the lid still held over her head, she dropped it loosely over the top to give herself enough air. The stench of rotting meat and vegetables filled her nostrils and she immediately vomited all over her legs and shoes. But it was dark inside, too dark to see the fat white maggots crawling all over her as she sank into her own vomit and the putrid garbage.

# CHAPTER 45

*Detroit Tigers Defeat the Milwaukee Brewers 10–4;*
*Yankees over Marlins 5–1.*
– Sports Nightly News, Friday, June 19

Late in the day, Scott left the FBI field office exhausted from nonstop brainstorming for any possible Yankee connection to the ransom note. After poring over hundreds of names, he was more disillusioned than ever. He'd always been well liked, he'd advanced many careers, and in cases where he'd had to make tough decisions, he'd made them with compassion and fairness. At least that's what he'd always thought. At the end of five grueling hours, they'd identified fifteen individuals with whom he'd had some degree of dissention and who had some connection to the Detroit area: two Detroit Tigers players, four women who'd had administrative positions with the Yankee organization, and a mix of players from the minor and major leagues.

The exercise had uncovered no serious confrontations; all were employment terminations, four based on use of illegal drugs, two based on breaches of moral conduct, the others either poor performance or unfortunate redundancies. Of the fifteen, Scott could not imagine any of these individuals capable of kidnapping. But Streeter had seemed encouraged, saying that by noon tomorrow, all would be thoroughly investigated.

Back at the hospital, the first thing he noticed when he walked into Jackie's room was a hopeful smile on Katie's face. As he sunk into the chair next to her, he immediately reached for Jackie's hand. This time he was sure, he'd felt the slightest pressure of a squeeze.

He had intended to call Streeter back and propose that he add one more person to the list, a blond, curly haired guy, Cliff Hunter. The guy whose face had kept popping up, but whose name he had not been able to remember until now.

"Please, Spanky, look a little longer. We must find Jessica. I *need* them both."

Spanky carried Alex over his shoulder as if she were a toddler. "We ain't got time to waste," he said as he leaned over to unlock the trunk.

"Spanky. No. You can't put Jennifer in the trunk."

Marge had followed Spanky out. She was beside herself. How could they leave Jessica here? Hadn't God meant her to have both her twins back?

"She can't breathe in there, and we have to find Jessica first."

"Get that food, like I told you. Hurry the fuck up. We gotta get outta here quick."

"No," Marge pulled at Spanky's arm as he laid Jennifer in the moldy trunk. "She can't breathe back there."

"Yes, she can, Ma. Don't be stupid. There's plenty of room back here for her and for the supplies you're supposed to be packin'."

It pissed Spanky off when Ma called those girls the names of the dead babies. Ma was crazy. But crazy enough to believe that the brown-skinned Monroe sisters were her dead twin babies?

As he filled Ma's tank from his own truck, Spanky thought of how lucky he was. He could fix any vehicle. He was strong and tough. Didn't take crap from no one. And goddamn it, he was smart. Didn't matter that he got mostly *F*s before he dropped out of school when he was seventeen. Street-smart trumped book-smart every time. How else could he be skimmin' off the top. Not enough that his asshole boss would notice. But enough to keep him and his ma "comfortably," as they say.

And now the pleasant prospect of his own little girl. In his mind he'd been calling her "Precious". Spanky interrupted the siphoning just long enough to pat his wallet where the key was tucked away. He wasn't dumb enough to put his cash in the bank. And now — beyond his wildest imagination — ransom for the kid. But only after he had a foolproof plan. Yes, he'd have Precious *and* the money. As for Ma, he'd take care of her, too.

But they had to get a move on. Any minute now the runaway bitch might bring down the heat.

"Ma," he yelled, "get the fuck in the car."

"I'm making sandwiches," she called from within.

"Just stuff the shit in a plastic bag and let's get out here."

Marge came to the door, arms full of plastic bags. "Oh, oh, it's raining," she said, dumping the bags in a heap by the door. "I'll get an umbrella."

Spanky stomped toward the door and picked up the heap of crap. "What you got in there?"

Marge held the umbrella out to him and she turned back inside.

"Just get in the fucking car." Spanky followed her to the kitchen. What was she doing? Making tea sandwiches? Grabbing a green garbage bag, he swept the bread, the slices of meat and cheese, the bottle of mayo inside. He opened the cupboards and stuffed two more bags with the contents of the refrigerator and the pantry. Then he bolted for the front door. No use locking it. The cops would be swarming soon. No two ways about it.

"What the fuck —" Spanky looked down at Marge trudging up the basement steps arms full of pillows and bedding with a teddy bear about to fall out of the load.

He set down his bags and grabbed the shit out of her arms. "Ma, just get in that front seat." Going around to the trunk, he shoved a Sleeping Beauty comforter, a pillow, and a fucking teddy bear in with the kid.

"That's Sammie's teddy," the kid whimpered. "Mine is brown. The gray one is hers."

Spanky shook his head. "Sorry, Precious." Then he slammed the trunk shut.

One more trip to retrieve the bags of food, which he threw into the backseat, and he started up the Escort's engine.

"Know what, Ma? I was gonna take you lookin' for a new car this weekend." He laughed over the sputtering of the engine. "Was kiddin' about a Porsche." As he backed down the long drive, he reached over to lightly punch Marge's shoulder. "But know what? A Porsche it's going to be."

"I forgot to lock the door," Marge responded.

Shit, she hadn't even been listening.

In the Detroit field office, Streeter was on his feet shouting orders. "All available agents to the thirteen hundred block of Parker Road, Holly. People, this may be it!"

His driver had the car ready to roll when Streeter hopped in, clutching his radio. When Clarence Plummer called about that guy who'd dropped by the mall, the FBI team had readily located the report that had come in three days ago, the delivery of twin beds to a specific address. They had the name and address of the woman who had called in and the report of the local police officer who had checked out the address of the delivery. No one had been at home at the residence, and a neighbor told the police officers that the woman who lived there had left for work like she did every day. End of story.

Now, Streeter and Camry headed directly to the address of the informant, after requesting SWAT team readiness at the Parker Road address.

The Talbotts were waiting for them on their front porch in the Detroit suburb of Fenton. Empty-nesters who'd held a yard sale after deciding to convert their son's bedroom into a room for a computer and a treadmill. The missus couldn't contain a heavy dose of smug as she confirmed that when she'd heard of the missing Monroe girls she'd become suspicious of a woman who'd purchased twin beds that day, the day after the girls had gone missing. Because the woman was clueless as to how to get the beds to her house, let alone reassemble them, she'd suggested that her husband deliver them in his truck and set them up for an extra twenty dollars. The deal was made. Eighty dollars. Paid in cash.

"Something about that woman made me suspicious," Mrs. Talbott said. "When I found out she had them put up in her basement, I told my husband that I was going to call the FBI. That was Monday, five days ago already."

"Did you see any trace of the Monroe girls?" Streeter asked, unable to keep the excitement out of his voice.

"Not them, that's for sure. But all kinds of girl stuff. Dolls, you know. And a Kmart bag with girlie sheets and pillow cases. Like Disney characters stuff. No crime in that, but my wife — "

"Did you hear anything suspicious?"

"Not that I can be sure, but I told my wife I heard some scratching sounds like I was afraid the basement was full of mice and it wouldn't be a good place for anybody to sleep."

"So I set up two beds in the basement," Mr. Talbott said. "So what? And the old lady calls in the feds. I hadda good laugh with my buddies over a few beers. I'm guessing you guys had a few chuckles too, but I'll be dammed. When I saw that face in the newspaper, I said first thing, 'It's her, the lady with the beds in the basement.' Said her name was Maggie Wise. I figured you'd ask about her car. A maroonish-brown Ford Escort. Ninety-four or ninety-five. License plate number ended in forty-eight. Year I was born."

"You didn't call the FBI?"

"Decided to report it to that Plummer security guy at the mall. He seemed real sincere about finding those girls when I saw him on television that first day."

"I told him to call the FBI," Mrs. Talbott said, "but he said that he'd rather deal with the mall. Can't blame him after what happened to me. Nobody did a darn thing. And those poor little girls. Oh, and what about the reward?"

Streeter didn't have time to defend the agency or get into the reward. He needed to get to Parker Road.

Streeter's radio buzzed. "We got the name for that address, sir. Spansky. Margaret Spansky owns the property. We'll have a vehicle check real soon."

"Not Wise?" She'd identified herself to the Talbotts as Wise. "Confirm the Gladsky composite sketch with the neighbors. Clear the proximate neighborhood. No tip-offs until SWAT's in place. And send somebody over to secure the Talbotts until this plays out."

Streeter felt his heart exploding. Five days, and now a big lead. Stay calm, he warned himself. Those girls could be anywhere by now.

At nine thirty p.m. the drive from Fenton to Holly was fifteen minutes. Streeter proceeded to the Holly address. Once there, he and his agents would stand back and wait for SWAT to take over the house.

That's what SWAT was trained to do and do it well. But Streeter would be first on the scene once they had the suspects contained and, most important, those two little girls safe and sound. Streeter couldn't help thinking how proud his own daughters would be knowing that he'd found Alex and Sammie Monroe.

Amid constant radio chatter, Streeter directed his driver to pass by the suspect's address in their unmarked car. Slowly, but not so slow as to attract attention.

"I can't make out anything through those trees," he muttered. "No light. Nothing. "

Agent Camry called in the status. "SWAT's fifty minutes from attack. They'll surround on foot. They have vehicular backup and emergency medical. Helicopter coverage. The works."

"I just did a drive-by on the rutted dirt road. I couldn't see shit."

Streeter took a call from SWAT communication. "We're approaching the perimeter. Starting the roadblocks. We've been waiting for this call for five days, sir. We're ready to rock and roll."

Streeter wished he could call the Monroe parents. But of course he'd have to wait. What if the girls weren't there? What if all this was a wild-goose chase?

"We got a hit on the car," a female voice blurted through the radio. "Brown Escort, Michigan license plate number ending in forty-eight. Registered to a Margaret Spansky, Parker Road, Holly. So she owns the car and the property. Driver's license picture matches the police sketch. Looks like the real deal."

Streeter checked the clock — 10:45 p.m. His driver had pulled off the road against a clump of leafy bushes within the perimeter they had blocked off, but out of sight of the target address. "Fifteen minutes till takedown," he mumbled. "God, let this go down on the side of the angels."

From his spot off the road, Streeter could feel, more than see, the SWAT team creep up to the house on Parker Road. His window rolled down, he heard the occasional engine, but not a human voice. Nor did he hear the helicopter yet, nor would he until the exact moment of impact.

Which happened at precisely the appointed moment. As soon as the targeted area came alive with floodlights, Streeter instructed his driver to position the car behind the emergency vehicles that were creeping into place. Although against protocol, he got out of the car and stood behind it, listening to the shout of "FBI" as the team in flack jackets surrounded the house, forced their way through the door, and poured inside.

Streeter listened so intently at first that he didn't hear the crackle of his radio inside the vehicle. His driver handed him the receiver.

"Sir, we're inside. Nobody's here. But they were, not long ago. You're clear to come in. Sorry, sir."

"Shit," Streeter's heart plummeted as he trudged up the muddy driveway. "Shit, shit, shit."

# CHAPTER 46

*Traverse City National Writers Series to Host Master Crime Novelist Elmore Leonard.*
*– Traverse City Record-Eagle,* June 2009

"Ma, will you quit yappin'. The kid's not gonna suffocate."

"You gotta stop for gas pretty soon. I'll just check her out then."

"Sure," Spanky said, just to shut her up. Like he was gonna let her open that trunk under the lights of a gas station. She was right that he'd have to stop for gas. Stations were few and far between on the back roads he was taking. There'd have to be one near Bay City. From there he'd drive north and west, avoiding I-75. If he drove nonstop, he'd pull into the cottage around eleven thirty. Maybe later, 'cause he had to keep the speed down to legal.

"I hear something," Marge tugged at his sleeve. If only she'd pay as much attention to the shit she was in. Instead she worries herself to death about Precious back there.

"The kid's just banging around. Means she's doing fine."

If the woman would just shut the fuck up. Give him quiet to think. This four-hour drive was nothing compared to his Detroit-Miami-Detroit run, but then he had peace and quiet.

Spanky had lots to figure out. Like how would he get the money? How much to demand? There was already a one hundred grand reward. So he'd ask for more. Maybe double. Not too much or they'd put more effort into stopping him. Scott Monroe must have socked away a load when he was catching in the majors. And everybody knew that psychiatrists charged hundreds of dollars an hour. He calculated mentally. What would they have in the bank? Then he just laughed out loud. It was the aunt that put the reward money on the table and that woman was loaded. She had her own plane. That had to cost her more than he was going to ask to get her niece back. Go with two hundred grand, he decided. He'd give it more thought when Ma calmed down, but for now that seemed a good number.

"Spanky, are you listening to me?"

"What?" he asked, distracted by his mental arithmetic, and reminding himself to look for a place to gas up.

"I mean it, Spanky, I gotta go. Real bad. I got this bladder condition, you know."

He did know because he'd seen boxes of those adult diapers.

"Gotta hold it, Ma, 'til the next station."

"I can't," she squealed. Seeing her squirm, he wondered if she had a diaper on now. Maybe not. What if she went in the car and he had to smell piss all the way?

"Okay," he said, spying a clearing ahead. He braked and pulled off the road.

"I need to go in a proper ladies' room."

Spanky couldn't help a chuckle at the horrified look on her face.

"Just get out and go," he said. "I'll close my eyes. And nobody's comin' down the road."

Facing her, he dramatically squeezed his eyes shut until he heard the car door open. Maybe he'd hop out and take a piss, too. That'd be safer than going in a men's room. Spanky swung his big frame out of the car as Marge had finished urinating. He'd just unzipped his fly when he saw her heading toward the trunk.

"Oh, no you don't," he said. "She waits till we get there."

"What if she has to go now?"

"Guess she'll have to pee her panties. Maybe you should have put one of your diapers on her? Now get back in the car while I take a leak."

"Spanky, that's not very nice," she said. "How do you know about that?"

"We don't have any secrets between us, do we, Ma? Oh shit," Spanky said, banging his fist on the fender. "Fucking shit." For a moment he stood beside the car, not getting in. "Secrets" and "panties" had triggered something.

"Spanky, is something the matter?" Marge hesitated before opening the passenger door.

*Yes, something is the fucking matter. We are in the middle of a kidnapping scam, number one. Number two, I left something behind in my truck. Stuff I'd been savin' for a while, my collection; twenty of them now.*

He knew that his mother knew about his stash. When he was home, he stored his trophies in a chest under his bed, and he could tell whenever someone peeked inside. But Ma had never said a word about it. So was it really a secret? Didn't matter. He wouldn't have to collect panties anymore. He'd buy those day-of-the-week pastel ones for his little Precious and he would wash them out by hand in the sink. He could feel the touch of the fabric in his hands. It made him want to jerk off right then. But he'd have to wait until Ma went to sleep. Then he'd slip into bed beside Precious.

"Everything's cool, Ma," he said. "Just hafta figure out what we're gonna do next."

Spanky prided himself on two skills. There wasn't a vehicle that he couldn't fix. And once he looked at a map, there wasn't a road that he couldn't follow. In his mind he had the itinerary memorized up until they had to take a series of private dirt roads. He'd need Ma to navigate those. He hadn't been to the log cabin on Elk Lake since he'd been an eight-year-old kid, twenty-five years ago.

Alex fell asleep in the trunk of Maggie's car. Luckily, she wasn't afraid of the dark, like Sammie. She even used to practice walking around in the dark, pretending she was blind. She'd been crying for a long time, her eyes burned, and it felt good to close them. Before she drifted off to sleep, she arranged the stuff surrounding her in the trunk. She put everything with sharp edges in the back and she piled the softer bundles in front of them. She took the Sleeping Beauty bedspread and curled up inside, propping her head on the pillow and hugging Sammie's teddy. Now she was glad she had Sammie's. The gray teddy made her feel like Sammie was not that far away. And Sammie would get the police, and soon she and Sammie would be back with Mom and Dad. But what about Jackie? Had she already died of some terrible disease?

Alex woke up when she felt the car stop. It was totally dark and for a moment she didn't know where she was. Then she heard voices outside and remembered. She couldn't hear what they were saying, but she could tell it was Maggie and that man. She held Sammie's teddy very close to her chest, and tried to think of what Sammie would do. Sammie would fight, that's what she'd do.

Alex crawled out of her cocoon and felt around her. For what she didn't know, but her hands found what felt like a canvas bag with a zipper. She fumbled to unzip it, and when she did she reached inside, feeling something cool and hard, like metal. For a minute she thought it might be a flashlight, and her fingers frantically searched for an off-on switch. She couldn't find one, so she used the object to bang on the side of the trunk. She made a lot of noise, but no one came and opened the trunk. She hoped that Sammie would have found help, but how could anyone know where to find this car? Then she heard two car doors slam and the car started moving again.

Marge was so mixed up. She'd waited so long for her two little girls, and now she'd lost one. Spanky should have tried harder to find Jessica. That's what her heart told her, but in her head she knew that they had to take Jennifer and run.

What would she have done all those years ago if only Jessica had drowned and if Jennifer was still alive? Wouldn't she have loved Jennifer and done anything in the world for her? Marge silently shook her head as Spanky drove the last twenty-five miles from the resort atmosphere of Traverse City to Elk Rapids, a sleepy town between Grand Traverse Bay to the west and Elk Lake to the east. The skies were dark with rain as they'd left Detroit, but up North there was no rain, she could make out every star.

"We're almost there," she said as Spanky took the turn leading to the shores of Elk Lake. The roads were deserted, and Marge hoped the cottage was as pristine and isolated as it had been twenty-six years ago.

"What do we do if someone's there?" Spanky asked. "It's the middle of the season."

"Evan swore he'd never go back. His sister lives in Europe somewhere, and she'd only come in August. I remember there's something about the deed. Like they have to keep it in the family."

"Fucking family."

Marge wished that her son did not use such bad language, but now wasn't the time to scold him.

"We're close to the turn-off," she said. "Go left on the gravel road about a mile."

Marge let out a deep breath as she recognized the Spansky property. She instructed Spanky to slow down and take the turn into the dirt driveway. There was so much overgrowth that she felt sure that no one stayed there. "I don't think anyone's here," she said as the one-story log cabin came into view.

"Not much traffic on this path," Spanky stated the obvious. "But somebody could be in there. No lights, but it's late. What if they're asleep?"

"Try the door." Marge's voice shook and her heart raced. Not with fear, but with the flood of anguish. Here was where she had lost her babies. "If it's locked, I remember a secret way in."

Spanky tried the door. "Locked," he said.

"Okay," Marge stepped out of the car onto the pine-strewn path, the headlights being the only source of light.

"Lord almighty, this looks exactly like it did back then. The air smells so fresh."

"Just get going." Spanky walked beside her along the side of the house until she paused at a certain point and bent low to the ground. She brushed aside saplings and thick clumps of weeds obscuring the recessed handle of a trapdoor leading to the basement. Marge gave a strong tug and the door creaked open. Then she brushed away enough debris to extend the opening wide enough for Spanky to crawl through.

"Go down there, take the stairs up, and sneak around and check the bedrooms. There're two. One on each side of the main room, the one with the fireplace."

"Hold this," Spanky said, handing Marge the tire iron that he'd taken from his truck. "Shit, how am I supposed to fit through this space. Marge squeezed her eyes shut as he maneuvered his bulky frame through the rusty trapdoor. "Lemme have that back," he grunted, holding out his hand for the iron.

"Remember, you're in the basement," Marge said. "When you go up the steps, tiptoe to the bedrooms."

Marge was wondering whether she should get Jennifer out of the trunk when Spanky appeared at the front door.

"Ain't nobody here," he called.

"Don't be so loud," Marge whispered a warning. "Can Jennie come out now?"

"I said, ain't nobody here, Ma. Let's unload the stuff first, then I'll get the kid. Gonna hafta ditch this car." He jerked his head toward the nearby moonlit woods. "Any place to hide it around here?"

"Let me think," Marge considered as they hauled plastic bags of groceries into the cottage. "But Spanky, we need a car. How will we get to the store?"

"Got enough to hold us a few days. Maybe we'll have to 'borrow' a car. Shit, Ma, what the fuck do I know? I need time to figure it out, but the cops'll spot the car right off. I'll hot-wire some wheels once we get a plan."

"There's a swamp along the road. Evan always made us stay away. Maybe the car would sink enough so nobody'd see it, but it's too dangerous tonight."

"I'll park it in back for now. But Ma," he glared at her, "once I get that kid inside, you be sure to tie her up good. I don't wanna run all over hell lookin' for her, too."

Marge took in a sharp breath. "Oh, my poor little Jessie. I hope she's okay."

"Your precious little Jessie, or whatever the fuck her real name is, is rattin' on you right now. Forget about her. One will be just fine."

Marge was too distracted by the baby carriages and high chairs and cribs in her mind to see the grin that spread over Spanky's face.

# CHAPTER 47

*FBI Action in Holly, a Detroit Suburb.*
— Breaking News at Eleven, Friday, June 19

Streeter bolted out of the car and pushed past a clutch of agents with FBI emblazoned on their flak jackets. They'd done their job, invaded the suspect property and secured it. Now the case was back in his hands, at least until the director called the SAC again to question his competency. What did the SWAT commander mean, *nobody's there, but they were, not long ago*? What had gone wrong?

Barging into the crushed door of the shabby frame house, Streeter demanded a report.

"Lot of shit in here you have to see," the team leader started. "Hell, I don't know where to start. This is real fucked up."

"Get on with it," Streeter said, following the agent down a flight of cement stairs.

"That informant, Talbott, looks like this is where he delivered the twin beds that your guys thought was a crock of bull."

Streeter felt his face turn red from anger, or was it embarrassment?

"Didn't mean for it to come out that way. We're all just frustrated, that's all. My men have been on call night and day. Then we get here too fucking late."

"Just show me what you've got." Streeter had no time to indulge his ego. "Geez, this is where they were?" He stared at the twin beds. One covered by a Cinderella comforter. The other bare except for the fitted sheet. Sleeping Beauty design. Just like Kellie's, his youngest daughter. "How long ago?"

"Don't think it was long. Found a carton of ice cream left out on a counter upstairs. Almost melted. Maybe three to four hours."

"Shit."

Streeter tried to focus. Agents from the field office had joined the SWAT commander at the site, and they relayed what they knew of Margaret Spansky, age fifty, and her son, Samuel, age thirty-three. Owner-occupants of record. Margaret Spansky, confirmed as the owner of brown Ford Escort; Samuel Spansky, as the owner of the Ford pickup parked at the side of the house. She was employed by the Ford assembly plant in Flint. No police record. Just an ordinary citizen. He an independent trucker, nonunion. Petty arrests, drunk and disorderly. No convictions.

"Check this out," one of the agents said.

"What?" Streeter's attention had lapsed momentarily. When he looked up, his whole body shuddered at contents of a plastic box held out for his inspection. Streeter felt a surge of bile fill his mouth and both hands flew to cover his mouth lest he vomit here in front of his peers and subordinates.

"We found this in the truck, tucked under the front seat along with a half-empty box of forty-four magnum hollow point shells." The agent handed Streeter the case, made of clear plastic, like something you'd keep a baseball card collection in. Or a paper doll collection like his middle daughter, Kassie's. She had a box just like that. As Streeter took the box, he sensed all eyes were on him. An agent handed him a pair of gloves.

He heard himself groan. "Oh, God, no." Inside the box was a collection of little girls' panties. Gingerly, with a gloved hand, he counted the individual items. "Twenty."

"Other strange things," the SWAT commander said. "Come on upstairs. This you gotta see."

Streeter climbed two flights of stairs with several agents in his wake. En route, the commander pointed out the living room, nothing unusual. The kitchen, in disarray as if someone had thrown food around quickly. Like packing to get the hell out.

"Upstairs, you're gonna see what appears to be the woman's bedroom. Neat, nothing unusual. The son's bedroom, also unremarkable except for a collection of child porn. Guy's a real pervert."

"Oh, God," Streeter said again. *How was he going to tell Katie and Scott Monroe?*

"But now for the weirdo thing. There's a third bedroom. Check it out."

Streeter had peeked into the other two bedrooms, still shaking his head, but as he peered inside the third, he stopped short. A room decorated almost completely in pink: candy-striped wallpaper, carnation pink carpets, wall-to-wall shelves on two sides painted magenta and displaying a collection of eighteen-inch dolls in colorful, international costumes reminiscent of Disney's "It's a Small World." Two identical cribs in hues of pink and lavender, tented with yards of hot pink satin canopies, dominated the room. Each crib held cuddly stuffed animals, all in soft colors. The closet door was open and inside he saw frilly dresses in pink, white, and yellow. There seemed to be two of each, ranging from toddler sizes to sizes that would fit his own daughters, Kloe, eight; Kassie, seven; and Kellie, five. And the Monroe triplets?

"She's got kids?" Streeter asked. "Babies? But keeps the Monroe girls in the basement? Can somebody tell me what's going on?"

Scott heard a soft knock on the door of Jackie's room. He jumped up, hoping not to awaken Katie. At a quarter to one in the morning, he did not expect good news. In his sweats, he eased out the door, closing it quietly behind him. Streeter stood facing him, his expression grim.

Scott's jaw dropped and his chest constricted. "What?" he whispered.

"We found the place where Sammie and Alex were taken."

"You —" Scott slumped against the door. His bowels felt loose and his heart started to race out of control.

Stepping forward, Streeter grabbed Scott's arm.

"Are they okay?" Scott knew they were not by the contortion of Streeter's face.

"We don't know. They've been moved from a house in Holly."

Scott's brain did not register the location.

"Holly's about fifteen miles from the Auburn Hills Mall. But we know who has them."

"Come in. I'll get Katie," Scott said. As reluctant as he was to wake her, she needed to hear this. Would either of them know the person that Streeter was about to divulge? Was it the kidnapper who'd sent the ransom note? Is that why Alex and Sammie had been moved? To exchange them for the money in the morning?

Streeter followed Scott into Jackie's small hospital room where Katie stirred on her cot.

Scott gently tapped her exposed shoulder. "Katie, you have to wake up."

"What?" She opened her eyes, focused on the two men, and bolted upright. "What happened ?" She groped for the switch on the bedside lamp. "Scott, what is it?"

"Agent Streeter has something to tell us, babe." Scott put a finger to his mouth and cast a glance at Jackie's sleeping form.

Throwing off the sheets, Katie leapt out of bed and pulled a robe over her floor-length nightgown.

Scott took her hand. "Let's just step outside," he said, drawing her toward the door.

Streeter wasted no time. He spoke as they stood in the hall outside Jackie's room. "Tonight we got a tip that led us to the woman who took your daughters. We went to her place. Sammie and Alex had probably been there, but they were not there when we got there."

"Then they're alive?" Katie slumped backward, against the wall.

Scott stared at Streeter, not daring to look at Katie lest his terror accelerate hers. "Who was the woman?" he asked. "We must know her since they got into the car with her. She must be related somehow to someone we know?"

Both listened silently as Streeter explained how they'd found the Spansky home. When he finished, each answered his anticipated question with a shake of their heads. The names meant nothing to either Scott or Katie.

"Margaret Spansky? Samuel Spansky?" Katie kept repeating, her eyes blinking as the looked back and forth from Scott to Streeter. "That name does not ring a bell. Scott, are you sure?"

"No, it does not." He was sure of that. Scott never forgot a name. "Is there any tie to Norman Watkins's sister and mother?"

"Or to Ken Franklin?" Katie added. "Why would Alex and Sammie willingly get into this Spansky woman's car?"

"We'll run down any connection. We have the car ID. We don't have them yet, but this is a big break. I have to get back now, but I'll be in touch the instant I hear anything. Think hard about any connection."

Streeter turned to leave, and asked, "How's Jackie?"

"About the same," Scott said. Maybe Jackie was responding just a tiny bit, or maybe it was his imagination.

During the drive, Spanky tried to figure something out. To get the reward money outright, he'd have to rat out his own ma. She might be loony, but she'd always stuck by him. She knew stuff about him and she never said nothing to nobody. And the more he thought about having Precious for himself, the more sure he was that he could pull this off. So he worked out a ransom plan. The singer-aunt had offered up a hundred grand, but she'd probably go for more so he'd already decided to double it. That sounded like enough. Where he was headed he wouldn't need that much.

His next decision was where to send the note and how to send it. The Monroe family address in Florida? That didn't make sense because they were staying with relatives in Auburn Hills. If only he'd paid more attention to the missing girls' story when he'd been driving his rig, innocent as a lamb.

Back then in Spanky's wildest dreams, he never could have imagined that Ma had those girls. That Scott Monroe's daughters, the ones the whole world was looking for and praying for, were locked up in Ma's basement? What a fucking piece of work. Now all he had to do was take advantage of her fucking craziness.

When they'd taken off with the remaining kid, he figured it'd be easy, but he still didn't have a good plan. With Ma snoring on the opposite side of the house with Precious tied in beside her, he could finally think. In the car she'd been yapping the whole way about the kid suffocating. And once he decided where to send the note — or should it be a phone call — where would he tell them to put the money? Of course, it had to be cash. He had his stash with him: $34,350. Money that he'd skimmed off the top of his trucking contracts. More money than he knew what to do with even without the two hundred grand.

Before the Monroe kid popped onto his radar screen, Spanky had developed his own long-term plan. He was sick and tired of running his rig up and down I-75, that ribbon of concrete, crowded with asshole drivers. Once he had enough money, his plan had been to cross the border into Canada by way of the Upper Peninsula, somewhere near Sault Ste. Marie. From there, he'd make his way north and west to Alaska. He'd head to the rough, remote territory north of Fairbanks, where nobody could find him. He'd pay cash for his patch of wilderness and live off the land, hunting his meat, fishing in the pristine streams. He couldn't stifle a chuckle. Add the ransom money to his stash, he'd be comfortable for life. Wouldn't have to take no shit from no one. And even better, just the thought of Precious made his blood tingle with anticipation.

When Spanky first came up with his Alaska plan, he hadn't been sure whether Ma would go with him. He'd figured that when she heard she'd have to live in a cabin in the wilderness, maybe she'd decide to keep on working in the assembly plant. But now, with the kid, Ma was in like Flynn.

Spanky had no one he could trust as an accomplice. Should he get Ma and Precious to Canada first, and then come back and arrange the ransom drop somewhere? How best to do that with the cops looking for him once they found the other triplet? Not daring to risk crossing the Mackinac Bridge, he decided to steal a boat, cross Lake Michigan, and hang out at a campsite he knew.

The way things were working out, he'd have his dream life in Alaska, be able to take care of Ma, have Precious for himself, and more money than he ever dreamed. But first, he had to figure a way to get the money.

Unable to sleep, he got up, deciding to ditch the car in that swamp Ma pointed out. He couldn't be too careful. He had to be crafty. He thumped his head with his fists. He had to figure out a plan.

# CHAPTER 48

*Monroe Girls Spirited Out of House in Holly, Michigan.*
— National News, Saturday morning, June 20

Sammie woke up to her own screams. She was trapped in a dark, stinky hole, things crawling on her skin, in her hair. "Mom," she screamed, "get me out of here!"

She was afraid to open her eyes. But if she didn't, how could she make the dream go away, get out of bed, go down the hall, and crawl in bed next to Mom. Then she remembered. She and Alex were still locked up in Maggie's basement. Okay, she would just go lay down next to Alex, not wanting to wake up her sister or to let Alex know how scared she was.

Sammie opened her eyes slowly and moved her hand to brush aside a stray lock of hair. But it wasn't hair, it was a soft spongy thing stuck to her face. She yanked it off in the dark. She tried to swing her legs out of bed. They met immediate resistance, and in a flash, she remembered running from the big scary man, hiding in somebody's garage, and jumping into a dirty trash can. Propped up in a sitting position, her legs crossed beneath her, she realized that this was not a dream. She was still in the smelly trash can. She was sitting in garbage and in her own vomit. Her legs were covered in it, her jeans soaked to her underpants. Something squished between her toes when she tried to move. The stench turned her stomach and she gagged, then retched, but nothing came up. Thirsty, she was so thirsty.

Nobody had found her. Was it morning? She attempted to stand in the big plastic container and struggled as she reached upward, lifting the plastic cover over her head. When she dislodged it, she saw daylight. Everything was quiet. The rain had stopped. The man must not have followed her in here. She needed to get out. Find help. That big horrible man and that crazy lady still had Alex, and Sammie just knew he would hurt her. Trying to forget her own terror, Sammie struggled to think, to do the right thing to help find her sister.

She stood upright in the garbage can and began thrusting her weight from side to side, hoping to topple it over. After only a few tries, the plastic container fell with a thud. Sammie hit the ground and as she did, she felt a terrible pain in her right shoulder. Ignoring it, she scrambled to her feet. She glanced at the inside of the container and froze. Fat white maggots were everywhere. Most of the garbage was semisolid or liquefying. As her eyes moved from the disgusting slop in the can to her own body, she started screaming. The maggots were all over her. She could feel those horrifying white things crawling on her. With her good arm, she tried to swat them off. Underneath she could see the scratches and dried blood from running through the woods last night.

She finally stopped screaming and started groaning with disgust. She stank so badly and those horrible things wouldn't brush off and she was covered with puke. Would anyone help her looking and smelling like this? She wished it was still raining. Slumped against the house, she decided she had to try to go for help. No one had been home last night and there was no car in the driveway.

Shivering and wet, she clutched her hurt arm more tightly against her and took off down the muddy driveway leading to the dirt road. Running faster now, she searched for a house, a house with people who would get help for Alex.

Sammie had always hated trips to the countryside. It was Jackie and Alex who begged to go hiking in the woods to pick wildflowers. Not Sammie, give her the city. Baseball fields and people living in houses close together. Once she reached the road, she saw a house a ways down on the other side. Her shoulder hurt so bad that she had to slow down. And for the first time it hit: her right arm was injured. And she was the Condor's pitcher. She stopped and kicked the ground as the tears came. Tears of anger and defeat. Dad would have to bench her.

A car slowed, and Sammie cringed. She didn't want anyone to see her crying. Still hugging her arm close to her chest, she started out again. Wiping her eyes with the back of her filthy hand, she noticed that the car was backing up. Panic made her jump into a clump of bushes. Her eyes stinging again with tears as sharp thistles tore into her legs. Was that bald man driving the car? Had he recognized her?

She'd give away her position if she moved, so she held perfectly still, not even breathing. When she dared to peek out, she saw two men walking toward her hiding place. They were ordinary looking men, not giants like Maggie's son. They were dressed in suits like men wore to work or to cocktail parties. She looked down at herself and sniffed the air in disgust. Would they help her?

The thought of Alex made up her mind. "Could you help me?" she asked, stepping out of the clump. "I need to find my sister. She's in a house back — "

She didn't finish. One of the men had scooped her up while the other talked into a radio like the police do on TV.

"Honey, what's your name?" the man who held her asked.

Sammie didn't know whether they were good or bad. "Ouch, my shoulder," she said as the man shifted her in his arms. He didn't seem to care that she was so smelly and dirty.

"Oh, I'm so sorry," he said, loosening his hold.

His kind tone reassured Sammie. "I'm Samantha Monroe. Can you help me find my sister?"

She didn't think he meant to do it, but he squeezed her and she gave a yelp of pain.

"Oh, didn't mean to hurt you," he said. Grimacing, he turned to his partner, "Patch me through to Agent Streeter."

"Shit," the other man mumbled, "we almost passed her up. Wait'll Streeter hears we have her."

Sammie was about to ask the man to put her down when he spoke, "Agent Streeter. We have the one named Samantha. She's okay, but there's something wrong with her shoulder."

Sammie heard a voice come on, "Get her to Children's Hospital quickest way possible."

"That'd be in our car, sir."

"The other sister?"

"Negative. Haven't questioned the child yet."

"Priorities: make sure she's safe, then find the other one."

One guy was talking and the other holding Sammie in his arms. She figured that they were policemen.

"Will you put me down?" she asked. "I can walk."

"Who are you?" she asked once the man lowered her gently to the ground.

"We're the FBI, little lady. We've been looking high and low for you and — " Sammie didn't like the way he stopped talking.

"Did you find Alex?" she interrupted. She didn't like the way he avoided her question. "She's in a house. I don't know exactly the street. It's on a dirt road. We have to go get her out of there."

"Right now we're getting you to a hospital. Take a look at that arm and all those cuts. Okay?"

"No!" Sammie stomped her foot, her good arm flailing in the general direction of the woods. "You have to find my sister. A bad man is hurting her. Back there. I know he is." And Sammie did know. At times, not always, the triplets had a sixth sense, a sense of the emotional status of one or both of the others. With Sammie, the sense was very strong about Alex. But all of a sudden, she felt sickened by a horrible sensation. It had nothing to do with Alex. It was about her other sister. Tears filled her eyes. "Jackie?" she asked. "Is Jackie dead?"

Both the FBI men looked at her funny. Then they turned to each other. Sammie knew that look. They were afraid to tell her the truth. Jackie must have been so sick that she died. She'd left Jackie at the movies and now she'd left Alex alone with a horrible man. Everything was all her fault. She was the bad one, just like everybody always said. She had to get back to that basement to find Alex.

Sammie took a deep breath, gritted her teeth, lurched forward with all her strength, and started to run. The FBI man talking into his radio put his arm out to stop her, but it was too late.

"Shit," she heard him say into the handset, "the girl got away. We'll get her."

Sammie got a few feet before tripping over an exposed pipe. She fell hard on her knees, scraping them on gravel. Before she could get back up, both FBI men tried to pull her up and she had to yank her hurt arm away. Before she could say anything, the one who was already grimy and stinky picked her up again.

"No! "Sammie scrunched up her face and yelled as loud as she could. "Find Alex! I think the house is that way."

As she pointed, an EMT van appeared in the distance, lights flashing but no siren.

"There will be lots of police here to look for your sister, Samantha. Right now you're on your way to the hospital."

Sammie wriggled, but couldn't get loose again. The ambulance had stopped and she could see more cars coming toward them. As the FBI man carried her to the big square van, a voice came out of his radio. "Streeter here. Do you or do you not have the child?"

The man walking beside them answered. "Affirmative. Just getting her inside the EMT van. She's a handful. Keeps trying to tell us where she left her sister."

"If she's physically okay, drive by the place now. I'll meet you there. Maybe if we let her walk though, something will pop up that we missed."

"Yes sir," the man said. Turning to Sammie he said, "We're going to take a ride up the street. Check out the house where they kept you two."

Sammie couldn't see out of the windows of the van. But when the back doors opened at Maggie's house, she stiffened.

A tall man with short brown hair in a really nice suit greeted her. "I'm Agent Streeter," he said, taking her filthy hand in his. "I've gotten to know your parents pretty well the last few days. Man, are they going to be glad to see you!"

"What about Alex and Jackie?" Sammie asked, tilting her grimy face to study his. "Nobody will tell me."

"Sammie, we haven't found Alex yet," Streeter said. "So we want you to take a look around this house. She's not here, but maybe you'll find a clue. Is that okay with you? Then we'll take you to your parents. Okay?"

Sammie nodded. She'd to do anything to help them find her sister.

"This is where they had you and Alex?" Agent Streeter asked. He seemed friendly and Sammie immediately trusted him.

"Yes, we got here at night and went straight inside. That lady – Maggie – made us stay in the basement. Then when that big man came, I ran out that door." Sammie pointed to the side door.

"Can you come down there with us and show us?" Streeter asked, as another agent held back a strip of crime-scene tape.

Sammie took the lead and descended the steps. Agent Streeter kept his hand on her good shoulder. When she reached the bottom step, she could smell the mildew. She hesitated, not wanting to step into that basement ever again. But she had to. She stepped forward and showed the FBI agents where she had last seen her sister. She showed them the twin beds where they'd slept, the small refrigerator, and a scattering of toys.

"Alex didn't take her teddy," Sammie said. "The brown one's hers. I had a gray one."

Agent Streeter took her upstairs and Sammie told him that Maggie had never taken them up there. When Agent Streeter showed her the room with the two cribs, decorated in so many shades of pink, Sammie gasped. "Did she keep babies up here?"

"We don't know, but you're never going to have to come back here again, Sammie. Now let's go see your parents. Then I bet you'd like to have a bath."

# CHAPTER 49

*Hunt for Mother and Son Intensifies. Marge Spansky and Samuel.*
— Saturday News, June 20

Evan Spansky nodded off while perusing the business section of the Friday edition of the *Toronto Star*. Normally he'd have read it in his office at Canada Life. But today his new manager had taken all the actuaries on a golf outing. Even though Evan didn't play the foolish game, he'd hacked away through the course with three guys unfortunate enough to get stuck with him. He'd ended up with a sunburned bald spot and an ignominious score. Worse yet, he'd pay the price Monday when he faced the bulging stack of computer printouts on his desk. Given his choice, he'd have chosen a boring day in the office to the stress of having to make awkward conversation with men and women he hardly knew. Evan was a private man, shy actually. But a happy man, content with his job and his family and his home.

The slam of the door jarred him awake.

"Hi, Mom. Hey, Dad, you awake behind that newspaper?"

Pamela, Evan's wife, muted the television and checked her watch. "Five minutes past curfew," she announced in a voice that was unable to disguise her pleased relief that he'd been so close to target. "I just turned on the ten o'clock news."

Tim headed toward his mother to bestow the nightly peck on the cheek before retreating to his room upstairs. "Dad, just so you know. I am the only guy who has to be in by ten on a Friday night."

Evan peered over his reading glasses at his youngest son. Tall for his age with a bulky build, he could pass for older than his fifteen years. "After your birthday," he said. "Just like Craig. Once you're sixteen, we'll extend curfew."

Evan thought he heard "shit," as Tim hit the stairs. Maybe he was too strict with his two boys, but he had his reasons.

Pamela clicked off the mute and Evan adjusted his glasses when he heard, "Breaking news: the FBI has just disclosed that the missing two of the Monroe triplets, abducted from a mall outside Detroit six days ago, had been held in a home in Holly, Michigan, a suburb of Detroit. All branches of law enforcement are cooperating in the search for Margaret — Marge — Spansky, a fifty--two-year-old white woman and her son, thirty-three-year-old Samuel Spansky."

Evan dropped the newspaper and rushed to the television to turn up the volume. As he did, Marge's picture flashed onto the screen. Evan reeled backward, banging his head on a bookcase, causing Pamela to jump to his aid.

"Evan? What's wrong?"

Evan righted himself in time to see the woman, recognizing his ex-wife even though he had not seen Marge in twenty-five years.

" — thought to have escaped with her son." The picture of an unshaven hulk of a man of indeterminate age followed that of the woman. The man must be Spanky, grown up.

"Spansky? Evan, did you hear that?" Pamela said. "Something about those missing triplets?"

Evan took advantage of his tumble to buy some time. What was he going to tell Pamela? He thought of Tim upstairs and of Craig, his oldest, who was away with parents of his friend, checking out colleges in Ottawa.

"Evan, are you okay? Did you hear what they said? About those triplets?"

"Yes, I heard."

"About *Spansky*?"

"That woman, Marge Spansky. She's the one I was married to. Back when I lived in the States. Back before I met you." There, he'd said it.

"Oh, no, how horrible." Pamela's hand flew to her mouth. "Is this for real?"

Pamela had always known that he'd been married, was divorced, and had no contact with his former wife. What she did not know was that he and Marge had had twin daughters, Jessica Ann and Jennifer

Marie. The most precious of babies. He could still see them as they had been that day. Eight months old, bubbling over with laughter, their dark curly hair flouncing in the summer breeze, their copper brown eyes the exact color of his. He'd never told Pamela. His loss was too painful to discuss, but now he must.

Pamela fingered the lump forming on the back of Evan's head and then took him in her arms. The television still running in the background, Evan told her the story of Marge and Spanky. It came out in staccato fragments. She did not interrupt.

"Met when we worked at Ford — I'd been a bookkeeper going to night school for my accounting degree — she worked on the assembly line — she was raising an illegitimate son — we married — I adopted Samuel — the boy was a brat — thought he was just spoiled — Marge quit working — got pregnant —"

Here Evan started to cry, and Pamela led him to the sofa where they sat hand in hand. Evan told of the twin's birth. How ecstatic he'd been, how the identical babies were rays of pure sunshine. He had to stop to blow his nose. "Marge and I both adored our daughters, little Jennie and little Jessie. So much that, I guess, we stopped paying enough attention to Spanky. That's what the kids in kindergarten started calling Samuel once his last name got changed to mine. I guess we didn't notice how much more hostile the boy had become. You know what the kid did?"

Pamela shook her head and pulled Evan tighter to her.

"Marge had a cat from the time I first knew her. Anyway, the cat had a litter of kittens and when we woke up one morning, all the kittens were dead in their basket. The necks had been snapped."

"My God, Evan," Pamela breathed and drew back. Pamela loved all animals. They had a cat. And three dogs.

"Marge loved that cat and was heartbroken about the kittens. We both knew that Spanky had done it, but neither of us brought it up. We just buried the kittens. Pretended it hadn't happened."

Pamela sank back against Evan and he went on. "A few months later we were at my family's place on Elk Lake. I was fishing in the rowboat. Marge was making cupcakes or something in the oven and went in just for a moment to check on them. All three kids were outside. When Marge came back out, the babies were in the water, their stroller overturned." Evan's chest started to heave as waves of sobs made the rest of the story halting as he described Marge's frantic efforts to resuscitate the babies. How he found her drenched and shaking. How Marge refused to leave the bodies until finally the undertakers called for a doctor to give her something to knock her out.

"Spanky?" Pamela asked.

"When Marge left in the ambulance, I found Spanky in the twins' bedroom, slamming their baby dolls against the wall. I tried to get to him to calm him down. He kept screaming, 'She's *my* mama!' At that moment, I knew. Spanky had pushed their stroller to the edge of the dock and tipped it over. Logically, there could be no other explanation."

"Was there an investigation?" Pamela asked.

"Yes, the local authorities did investigate. Ultimately, they ruled the twins' death accidental. Their position: that Spanky innocently pushed the stroller onto the dock and didn't know how to work the braking mechanism. I'm sure they had their suspicions, but with Marge and me so tragically distraught, the Grand Traverse district attorney did not want to charge a seven-year-old with homicide."

"So what now?" Pamela asked.

"I don't know what to make of this," Evan said. "Pamela, I'm very sorry to bring this all on you. And the boys."

"Evan, I can't believe that you kept this from me for all these years," Pamela said, edging away from him. "Why? You couldn't trust me?"

"I don't know," Evan said, massaging his head as if the answer might come. "Shame that I let that boy kill my babies? That I hadn't done anything to protect them? God, Pamela, I still wake up and think of my baby daughters, drowning in that cold lake."

Pamela had moved back close to Evan. He didn't want to cry, but all those memories. How could he make Pamela understand?

"Marge is a good-hearted woman," he said, wiping a lone tear from each eye. "We both fell apart after the babies' funeral. We were tearing each other up."

"That's when you divorced?" Pamela's voice lost the momentary hard edge, and Evan wanted to tell her everything. If only it wasn't too late. If he lost her, the boys –

"Yes. Marge got the house. All of our savings in lieu of alimony or child support. I made a clean break. I was lost and miserable until I met you. Pamela, I don't deserve you."

"Evan, I can't deny that I'm hurt that you never told me this, but I'm not going to question your motives." She lifted his head up out of his hands. "I love you. We're a team and we can face anything together."

"I guess you know now why I've always seemed overprotective with Craig and Tim." Evan knew that Pamela thought it odd that he watched over his sons more closely than most dads. "I just wish I'd told you before. I wanted to, but it never seemed the right time."

"The boys will be fine. What you have to think about are those missing little girls. Why would Marge and Spanky, who's no longer a kid, have kidnapped them?"

"I can't believe Marge would do that. She's not a *criminal.*"

"Let's think about it. So she got the house, the same house where she kept the kidnapped girls? Whatever happened to that cottage in Northern Michigan? After your mother died, I remember something about it in the will. But we've never been there."

"Something about the title, a trust that specified that it had to remain in the family. I suppose my sister in Chicago still spends the month of August there. As for me, I never want to see that place as long as I live."

"But what about Marge?" asked Pamela. "Suppose she goes up there?"

"She has no legal right to be there," Evan said, "but she does know that it's vacant most of the time."

"Do you think you should call the FBI in the States. What if — ?"

"I just don't know. It's too late tonight." Evan glanced at the ancient movie now playing on the television. "Let's sleep on it. My head is reeling. We can decide in the morning."

# CHAPTER 50

*Sammie Monroe Safe. Alex Still Missing.*
Breaking News, Saturday Afternoon, June 20

Agents Camry and Streeter accompanied Sammie to Children's Hospital. Along the way, Streeter called Scott and Katie, a bittersweet call. He told them that Sammie was safe, if filthy. Before they could ask, he added, "Alex is still missing."

"Is Sammie really okay?" asked Katie. "I mean, psychologically?" Her voice faltered, and Streeter knew why. Just before they'd got the call that Sammie had been found on that dirt road, he had shared with the Monroes, Samuel Spansky's suspected sordid background. "She wasn't — abused?"

"She's favoring one arm and she has scrapes and bruises and she needs a bath, but nothing else. Neglect maybe, being kept in a basement, but let's not speculate."

"I'm calling Dr. Reynolds to help with her. This may be my field, but with my own daughters, I'm helpless and incompetent."

"That would be a good idea. How is Jackie? Sammie keeps asking about her, but I've been evasive."

"The same. Still not communicating, but maybe seeing Sammie — "

"Sammie should be there in a half an hour."

"Please find Alex," Scott's voice. He must have grabbed the phone. "Katie and I *have* to have all three of our daughters."

The media was held back by the Detroit police as Katie and Scott sprinted toward Sammie, racing each other to sweep her up into their arms when she arrived at the ambulance bay near the emergency room. Scott prevailed, but Katie's hands were all over Sammie's smelly, stained body as he carried her inside. All three were talking at once, until finally the nurses had to pry Sammie out of her parents' grasp.

Over and over Sammie had asked about Jackie, but in the chaos of reunion, her questions went unanswered. Hospital and FBI personnel swarmed her, nudging Scott and Katie back to photograph Sammie from every angle. Then they took samples of the grit embedded in her skin and the debris covering her. The forensic experts worked efficiently, explaining to Sammie what they were doing and why. All the while Sammie answered their questions about the woman and the man who must have taken Alex somewhere else. She didn't know where. They didn't stop until she started to cry, and both Katie and Scott pushed everybody back.

At the suggestion of Dr. Reynolds, the hospital had arranged to keep Sammie under surveillance in Jackie's room. Katie wanted to take her there immediately, but she was overruled. What the FBI needed from Sammie as the highest possible priority was any scrap of information that might lead to Alex. Sammie understood that and with each parent holding one of her hands, she told them how she and Alex had been lured out of the movie, how they had been kept in the basement, how they'd only seen the woman who they knew as Maggie until the big man – Maggie's son – Spanky – came down into the basement last night, how she got away, hiding all night long in that stinking trash can.

Once the FBI finished questioning her, the nursing staff removed Sammie's filthy clothes, bagged them, and treated the worst of her scrapes and scratches. She was then sent to radiology for a shoulder X-ray, Katie at her side, Scott returning to Jackie.

When they returned from radiology, the spiked-hair pediatrician on call was waiting outside Jackie's room, conferring with Susan Reynolds, reviewing the sexual abuse protocol, reassuring her that he'd be thorough, yet gentle and rapid, and that this was forensically necessary. Susan repeated this for Katie who reluctantly let this too-young pediatrician take Sammie into the treatment room, watching her disappear behind the examination curtains.

True to his promise, the cool doctor bounced out of the examining cubicle, Sammie in hand. She didn't look traumatized at all.

"Mom, I need a bath," she said. "I stink. I can still feel those horrible white things crawling all over me. What if some are still in my hair?"

"We have a room waiting for you with a shower," the nurse said. "I'll take you up there as soon as your parents talk to the cute doctor here."

The pediatrician motioned for Katie to follow him into the hall. Katie's heart sank, expecting the worst even though his bouncy step and crooked smile made him look like he had the world on a string.

"Susan, you better come, too," she suggested.

"Here are the shoulder X-rays," the pediatrician explained. He pulled a film out of an envelope and slapped it against the light. "Negative. Based on the description of the trauma and her symptoms, she might have had a dislocation with the humerus slipping spontaneously back in place." He looked over at Sammie sitting in a wheelchair and winked at her. "Sammie sure did perk up when I told her she'd still have a baseball career. Like her dad. You know, she's quite a kid. Ingenious how she got in and out of that hiding place."

"Were there any other injuries?" Katie asked, holding her breath.

"Good news," the pediatrician said, tucking the X-ray back in its jacket. " No evidence whatsoever of abuse. She denies anyone touching her inappropriately. Of course, Dr. Reynolds may want to go over that with her, but I don't believe that your daughter was a victim of sexual or physical abuse. All her injuries seem related to her escape. You've seen the scrapes and scratches."

"Thank you, God," Katie breathed.

"Okay, Sammie, we're going to get you cleaned up now," Susan said, motioning for a nurse. "That sound good?"

"Then what?" Sammie asked, her hands gripping the handles of the wheelchair. "Why won't you tell me?"

Katie's heart plunged at the stricken look on Sammie's face. *What about psychological damage*? She had so underestimated what had been going on with Jackie, and now Sammie looked so terribly disturbed. Just a few moments ago she had seemed okay, but now —

"What's wrong, Sammie?" Katie and Scott asked at once.

"Mom, Dad, you gotta tell me. Where is Jackie? Is she *dead*?"

Katie looked first to Scott and then to Susan for help. Sammie had been through so much. She'd kept asking about Jackie. No one must have told her. How would she react to Jackie's catatonia?

Susan nodded her head for Katie to respond.

"Jackie's here. In the hospital. We're going to take you to see her. Just as soon as we get you cleaned up and smelling good. But she is sick —"

"Then that horrible Maggie woman was telling us the truth. Jackie did get sick in the movie. Alex and I didn't believe her. Jackie didn't look sick to us."

"She wasn't sick then, Sammie. The woman did lie to you," Scott explained. "But she got sick later."

"I want to see her right now." Sammie started to get up out of the wheelchair. "Before I get a shower."

Katie looked to Susan for guidance.

"You know what?" Susan said. "You're going to be just the medicine Jackie needs. But really, you stink. Shower first, then Jackie. I promise."

"Okay," Sammie said, "just let's hurry."

# CHAPTER 51

*Hunt Intensifies for Marge Spansky,*
*Alleged Abductor of Monroe Triplets.*
– International News, Saturday, June 20

Spanky awoke after a restless sleep, alone in the double bed. After Ma had fallen asleep, he'd gone out, found the swampy area she had described, and pushed the car as far as he could into the muck, and covered it with branches. The site was about a fifteen-minute walk from the log cabin and he made his way back with the aid of a flashlight. Not that he needed it, Spanky had a flawless sense of direction, but it did prove useful. About half way back, parked under a weeping willow toward the back of a dark, secluded cottage, Spanky spotted an aging panel van with one flat tire. He crept close enough to the house to peer into the windows and inspect the front porch. He saw no signs of recent residents. No windows open, no trash in the container, no footprints around the front door. Spanky passed up the van, but he'd return in the morning with his toolbox and air pump. There wasn't a vehicle that Spanky could not fix.

During the night, the temperature had dipped into the low fifties, and he'd shivered on and off all night under the thin bed covers. Twice he'd gotten up and traveled from the master bedroom, across the living-dining area to the guest room where Ma slept with Precious pressed tightly to her bosom in one of two twin beds. As much as he'd wanted to pry the girl off his mother and take her to his bed, he'd opted not to upset the silence of the night. The drive from Detroit to Northern Michigan had sapped everybody's energy. Besides, he needed time to think. He'd have to make his move today. Once he made that ransom call, the cops would know where to start looking. But he figured it would take some time for them to get organized, and by then he'd be far enough away.

He padded out to the kitchen and rummaged through their bags of food. He found a banana and ripped open a pack of cherry Pop Tarts. When they'd arrived, the refrigerator had been turned off, but there was electricity. By now the jug of orange juice was cool, and he poured himself a tall glass. He needed something in his stomach before he went over his plan. He'd worked it out while tossing and turning last night. Now he had to expose it to the light of day. He grabbed a second banana and a Twinkie.

Okay, the plan. Wander down the road. Find that van. Drive to Traverse City, about fifteen miles away, a city big enough to give him some cover. He'd place the ransom call on a pay phone, and disguise his voice. He hadn't been sure where to call, but he figured he'd call the Monroe house in Florida. The FBI would be tapped in to all the phones. He'd get the phone number simply by calling Tampa information, asking for Scott Monroe. But once he made that call, he'd have to move quickly.

Spanky had given a lot of thought as to where they should leave the money. At first, he'd been stumped. No way was he giving up Precious. No, she was going with him to Alaska. And he didn't dare go anywhere near Detroit. So that left his other stomping ground, Miami. He'd tell the Monroes that he'd give them until next Wednesday to drop the money in a marshy place he knew near the Everglades. Guy who worked one of those tourist airboats used to let him stay there and hunt gators illegal-style until the dude got busted. The place was remote enough that he could monitor incoming traffic, and Spanky knew the channels well enough to get away fast. He figured the parents would want evidence that the kid was alive, so he'd record Precious saying that it was Wednesday and that she was scared and all that stuff that kidnap victims say.

He hoped he had the timing right. Today he'd get Ma and Precious to a campsite in the Upper Peninsula. Ma told him that when he was little, she and his stepfather would take him camping, but he had no recollection of that. What he did remember was the one time Ma's brother showed up to take him camping with his own kid. Spanky had been ten and his cousin a couple of years younger. They'd gone to a camp called Wells Park in the Upper Peninsula. He remembered driving to the place by going through Milwaukee, the first time he'd ever been out of the state of Michigan. And they'd returned by driving across the Mackinac Bridge, which connects Michigan's upper and lower peninsulas. The other thing he remembered was that the trip was cut short. His prick of an uncle told Ma that it didn't work out and no, he didn't plan to take Spanky on further outings.

A couple of years after that, Ma's brother and his wife were killed in an accident, and he never heard anything more about his cousin, a snotty little jerk. But he did love that campsite and he knew that he could get to it by boat and nobody, nobody would know where they were.

Then he'd make his way to Alaska, after he collected the ransom. He'd simply divert to Miami once he had Ma and Precious settled in that remote campsite, collect the money, come back for them, and cross over into Canada. He'd have to study the maps and choose where to cross. Wisconsin? Minnesota? North Dakota? Even as far as Washington? Or just cross over at Sault Ste. Marie only a four-hour drive from the campsite?

Yes, Spanky had a plan. He just had to keep Ma and Precious hidden while he made his way to Miami and back. He wasn't much worried about being caught. There were millions of cars out there, he knew all the back roads, and he knew how to keep changing vehicles. Just the thought made his chest puff up. With all that money, he'd buy himself a sweet piece of land. Spanky chuckled. Other than a healthy supply of beer, he wouldn't need much. And neither would Ma. And they could each share the girl, total privacy, and no assholes to hassle them, ever.

"Time to get the show on the road." Spanky grunted as he replaced the orange juice in the refrigerator. "Oops, not yet. I'd better write down exactly what I'm gonna say."

Searching in Ma's bag, he found a ballpoint pen. After a few futile scratches, he began to write:

> Scott Monroe: I have your missing daughter. If you want to see her alive you need to leave two hundred grand in twenties.

Spanky crossed out "twenties" and wrote, "hundreds." Then he went back to the "twenties."

> Put it in an unlocked, waterproof trunk. Bring it to the Miami area. I will leave you a message later and tell you exactly where to leave the money. You have to bring the money yourself. I can recognize Scott Monroe. Come alone. Don't bring anyone with you. I promise that if you don't come alone, I will kill your *PRECIOUS* daughter. She's a sweet kid, but I'll kill her, I swear. So bring the money. Alone.

Then he'd hang up. Spanky thought something was missing, but he couldn't think of what. He reminded himself to disguise his voice and hang up quickly no matter if anyone came on the line and started to talk to him. But was he asking for enough money? Going through all this trouble. Maybe he'd ask for two fifty, an even quarter million?

He changed the number, tore the paper off the pad, and tucked it into his shorts pocket. Then he headed for the second bedroom. Without knocking, he walked inside.

"Ma," he said, tapping her shoulder.

"Spanky?" Marge stirred and one arm went protectively around the girl.

Spanky could see that Precious was awake. Her eyes were red and a tear started to trickle down her cheek. He reached over his mother's hulk to wipe away the tear with his hand. Precious was wearing a Disney character nightgown that made his pulse quicken. Not now, he told himself. There will be plenty of time. "Just you and me, Precious," he murmured.

"What do you want, son?" Marge asked, bunching up the sheet and pulling it over the girl. "What time is it?"

"I hafta to go out for a while," Spanky said. "You and the girl stay here. Whatever happens don't open the door to any nosy neighbors."

"But —" Marge stopped.

"I got everything figured out. Ma, you got us into this, and I'm gonna get us out. You just do as I say." Spanky reached over to pull the sheet back off Precious, far enough back to tell that under the pink nightgown were little white panties. He could feel the child cringe, and with the same hand, he then covered her back up.

# CHAPTER 52

*Two of Monroe Triplets Reunited at Children's Hospital.*
*But Where is Alex?*
— Saturday News, June 20

Katie questioned the wisdom of letting Sammie see Jackie so debilitated, but Susan Reynolds overruled her trepidation.

"Jackie's not talking to us right now," Susan explained to Sammie once she had been shampooed, scrubbed from head to toe, and dressed in the extra clothes they'd brought in for Jackie.

"I think it's because she's so worried about you and Alex." Susan bent down to meet Sammie at eye level. "She's lying in bed and she looks like she's asleep. She's not really sick. She just has decided she doesn't want to talk."

Sammie's eyes went wide. "But why — "

"Sammie, just understand. Jackie is going to be okay." Katie tried to sound reassuring, but she was being torn in two: wanting Susan to work with Sammie and Jackie; and wanting Agents Streeter and Camry to question Sammie more extensively about where to find Alex. Having Sammie back and safe just intensified her desperation to have Alex back with them. How could any of them survive without Alex? She knew she couldn't.

"Mom, are you sure she's not going to die?" Sammie nudged closer to Katie, as Susan stood poised to lead the way into the hospital room.

Katie nodded, but her eyes filled with tears. Two of her daughters were with her under this roof, but Alex, the most vulnerable of the three, was with those evil people.

Finding Jackie lying still, Scott stroking her forehead, whispering to her, Katie checked her watch. Had it been the Spanskys who'd made the ransom call? Would they really return Alex, today, at the coffee shop in Birmingham?

"Sammie, come here," Scott said as Sammie started to shrink backward. "Jackie will be okay, I promise." He looked to Susan who nodded. "Why don't you come over and talk to her."

Susan took Sammie's hand and led her to Jackie's side. Katie and Scott stood behind her.

"Jackie?" Sammie said, creeping closer, leaning over her sister. "Jack, wake up, it's me. It's Sam. I'm here. I'm okay."

Katie held her breath, and she felt Scott hold his, too. They both exhaled slowly as Jackie's eyes fluttered open.

A knock interrupted, and all eyes but Sammie's turned to see Agent Camry standing at the door. "Sorry," she said softly, "Katie, and you too, Scott, could I speak with you both?"

"I'll stay with the girls," Susan said.

Reluctantly, Scott and Katie joined Camry in the hall, but Katie kept one hand on the door knob.

"I . . . I think that Jackie's eyes opened," Katie said. "Please, I need to be there for her when she wakes up."

"You both need to hear this," Camry said. "We've received another ransom message. This one came in on your home phone in Tampa. Male voice demanding two hundred and fifty thousand dollars for the release of Alex." Camry nodded at the tape recorder she held in her hand. "There's a brief recording. We need you to tell us if this is Alex's voice. Let's go across the hall and sit down."

"My God." Katie felt Scott's body slump and she reached to steady him. "What about the other ransom, the drop-off in Birmingham?"

"If you can identify your daughter's voice, we'll send a look-alike decoy there."

"So this new call may be real?" Scott breathed, as they followed Camry into a conference room across the hall.

Before Camry started the tape recorder, she insisted that they both sit down. They did, holding each other's hand so tightly that their knuckles turned pale.

When Camry clicked on the tape, they heard a male voice sounding muffled, yet gruff.

> I have your girl. If you want her back you gotta give me two hundred fifty grand. I know you can get the dough. Get it to the Miami area. I'm takin' her to Miami. You wanta see your girl again, *Mr. Monroe*, you be in Miami and leave that money where I tell you. Put it in a waterproof trunk. Small bills. I'll leave you a message same place. No foolin' around. Nobody else. No cops. I got your girl. You want proof? Here, Precious. Say somethin'.

Katie and Scott had to bend over the recorder to hear the small voice. "Daddy," it said. "Please find me. I'm scared . . ." Then a click and the machine went silent.

That sweet, innocent voice, so terrified, so alone. Katie felt a pain in her chest so intense that she thought she'd been stabbed. Then she felt a terrible trembling next to her. Scott's body was shaking violently. She grabbed both his hands as a wail, loud and plaintive escaped from his being.

"Yes. It's Alex." Katie nodded and Scott dropped his head and started to cry.

As the tape played, Camry's phone had vibrated. She listened briefly before terminating the call.

Camry nodded to Katie and said, "The call came from a pay phone in Traverse City. I know that hearing Alex's voice must be devastating, but we need you to focus. You're quite sure that this is Alex's voice?"

Both Katie and Scott said, "Yes."

"We now have something to work with. Who do you know in Traverse City?"

"Some of my family's friends have summer places up there," Scott's voice shook and his body still trembled, but the tears had stopped. "But why did he say to come to Miami?"

"We don't know, but Agent Streeter would like you to come down to headquarters," Camry said. "And we'd like for you to bring Sammie. We haven't had time to talk to her more than superficially. She may have the answers we need."

Then Camry's phone buzzed again. Katie detected accelerated intensity as the agent grasped her phone more tightly, got up, and started to pace. "Do you still want Sammie downtown?"

Katie felt her heart start to race way too fast. Why would she ask that question about still wanting to bring Sammie in? She'd been ready to tell Agent Camry that Sammie would stay at the hospital with Jackie and that the FBI could question them there. But now, she *wanted* Sammie to go to the FBI building. She prayed for a reason for her to go.

"Let me tell you about that call," Camry said right away. "We just got a call that we think is important. We want to put off bringing Sammie to the field office."

Katie felt her body slump forward onto the conference table, Scott's arm now encircling her, very tightly. "Just tell us — "

"We have a lead on a possible destination in northern Michigan where they might have taken Alex. I need to emphasize *might.*"

"Where?" Scott asked. "Can we go there? Now?"

*Please, God, let this be true. Let them find Alex, safe and* — Katie almost said *alive*, but couldn't say the actual words, not even to herself.

"Elk Lake," Camry said, "just fifteen miles from Traverse City, which is where the call with Alex's voice was placed. We have a SWAT team on the way and the area is being put under surveillance. Agent Streeter is on his way up there now, and he wants me to stay here with you. I would like to question Sammie though, to see if her captors said anything about where they may be heading."

"I need to go there," Scott said, standing up. "Katie, did you hear what Alex said? She said, 'Daddy, please find me.' My baby is so scared."

"No chance," Camry said. "We sit tight. Don't forget the message said to go to Miami. We need to keep all options open. Even if they did have Alex in Elk Rapids, they could have moved her to the Miami area. Or she could be anywhere in between northern Michigan and southern Florida."

Scott came around to massage Katie's shoulders. His hands were strong, but she could feel his body shake.

# CHAPTER 53

*Scott Monroe Will Not Be Home for Father's Day Tomorrow. Alex Still Missing.*
– *Tampa News*, Saturday, June 20

Marge rummaged through the plastic bags of food for something that Jennifer liked. So far the child had refused anything to eat or drink. The twins liked Hershey bars, but she'd run out. Finding a box half full of stale donuts, she took one over to her little girl. Jennifer lay facing the wall curled up in a little ball.

"It's okay," she said, caressing Jennifer's short, choppy hair. "I know you miss Jessie and so do I, but she's gone now so – "

The child stirred and Marge's heart filled with hope. "Jennie, it's you and me now. We'll be okay. I promise."

Marge mourned the loss of Jessica, but she had to pull herself together for Jennifer's sake. She couldn't fall apart like she had before. She needed to get Jennifer to Evan so they could raise her together. She reasoned that even if they'd lost Jessica, he'd still want to be there for their surviving daughter. But first she had to get Jennifer to Canada. She hadn't told Spanky her plan yet, but she felt that everything would work out since they were so far north and Canada was so close. Wasn't it just across the Mackinac Bridge?

Marge suspected that Spanky was cooking up some plan, but she didn't know what. Spanky was a good kid, always doing nice things like fixing her car. Hadn't he even said he was going to buy her a new one? And sometimes he'd bring her stuff from his trips. She liked to collect shells and every once in a while he'd bring her a new one from his runs to Miami. But she knew she had to face the facts. Evan didn't like Spanky, and she needed to get Jennifer to Evan. Spanky was a grown man now; he'd be okay on his own. And if he no longer had to take care of her, he'd be free to go off and marry a woman of his own. And, then, maybe he'd get over his one very bad habit. One she'd never dared discuss with him. One he didn't even know that she knew about.

Alex woke up after the first night ever that she'd been separated from both of her sisters. When she wiped that sticky stuff out of her eyes, she turned over to find Maggie just staring at her.

"Oh, you're awake, Jennie. Good, I've got a donut and orange juice for you. We didn't bring any milk. Afraid it would spoil, you know."

"I'm not hungry," Alex said. That was not true, but Alex needed time to think. She turned to face the wall and pretended to go back to sleep.

First, Alex thought, she had to figure out where she was. Just in case there was a telephone around. She remembered the long, bumpy ride in the trunk last night. So she wasn't near Detroit anymore. Could they be taking her back home to Florida? She had to try to think. What was wrong with Maggie that she kept calling her "Jennie"? And where was that big, ugly man? He scared her so much. She figured that she would have to pretend to trust Maggie to find a way to get out. She used to tell Sammie that's what they should do, but all Sammie wanted to do was fight her.

So when Maggie started touching her hair she turned over.

"Maggie," Jennifer began, sweetly. "Where are we?"

"We're in northern Michigan, my dear," she said. Her voice sounded kind, and that encouraged Alex.

"Oh, I was hoping we were in Florida. We had such a long ride. Why did I have to ride in the trunk?"

"I tried to tell Spanky to let you ride in the backseat," Maggie said, plumping the pillow next to Alex.

"Who is Spanky?" Alex asked. Just hearing that awful name made her want to cry, but she kept her voice as normal as she could.

"Why, he's your brother, my dear. Your half brother, really."

Alex started, "He is —" but stopped.

"I'm going to take you to Canada," Maggie said, "to be with your real dad. He'll be sad about Jessie, but he'll love you, Jennie. I just know he will."

"My real dad?" Alex could feel her eyes start to blink like her mother's did when she was upset. "In Canada?"

"Yes," Maggie said, "but I don't know if Spanky will go with us."

"I'm afraid of that man Spanky." Alex's voice had sunk to a whisper as she dared to speak the truth. The way he looked at her – his eyes looked like a pig's, mean and ugly.

"I won't let him hurt you, Jennie. I promise that I will not let him hurt you this time."

Spanky had no problem jump-starting the dirty old van he'd identified the night before. The tank was on empty, but he'd been smart enough to siphon gas from Ma's car before he buried it. Just as he'd planned, he'd driven into Traverse City, placed the call, and recited his script into the message machine, making his voice sound squeaky like a wimp, not a big tough guy. Then, according to plan, Spanky drove fifty miles from Traverse City to Charlevoix.

Charlevoix would put him roughly just across Lake Michigan from J. W. Wells State Park and Charlevoix would be the perfect place to steal a boat. The marina there catered to rich folks who seldom took out their expensive boats. He'd never been on a boat in Lake Michigan, but he'd gone out on the Atlantic Ocean off Miami Beach. Same guy who showed him around the glades used to take him out on the luxury boats he'd "borrow" out of the fancy marinas. That's how Spanky learned about boat engines and how to read a chart.

Spanky chuckled at how one good turn deserves another. Out of the goodness of his heart, he'd helped that redneck who'd been hauling that airboat piece of junk on a trailer that broke down at a truck stop. Spanky'd fixed the rig and the guy ended up showing him how to hunt gators and steal boats. Now the poor bastard was in the joint, but once he got out, Spanky would send him some payback bucks.

Before Spanky made the call to the Monroe house in Tampa, he stopped at a Traverse City camping equipment store. He'd only camped that one time and he tried to come up with a list of supplies. He'd need a tent, big enough for two, but not so big he'd have trouble setting it up. A camp stove, an ice chest, a coffeepot, a lantern, a few cooking utensils, forks and spoons, a couple of plates and mugs. He picked up the smaller items as he moved through the store, getting ideas of other odds and ends they'd need. He didn't want to ask the clerk, not wanting to sound like an amateur and raise any attention. He needed to get out fast, afraid that his picture would be in the papers after the other girl was found. He selected a tent from the "on sale" list, paid for all his purchases with cash, and insisted that he did not need help loading it all in the van. He wondered whether he should buy more food, but figured that Ma had hauled plenty out of Holly. Precious didn't eat much, and Ma could afford to lose some weight. But realizing that he'd forgotten to buy fuel for the lantern, he did stop at a smaller camping store for kerosene, or should he get propane? He didn't know, so he picked up a can of kerosene, some of those Sterno cans, and an assortment of breakfast bars and canned juice.

The drive from Traverse City to Charlevoix took less than an hour. Driving north on Route 31, he came to the perfect marina site. Approaching on foot, he tried to blend in as he located a boat. He'd need speed, and the Grady White with twin 300-horsepower outboards would handle the five-foot swells that he might get on the lake. The boat's slip, about halfway down the dock, gave him just the cover he needed to jump onto the deck. Peering inside the cabin, he could see the instrument panel, noting a global positioning system that he'd have to disengage. He saw a stack of charts, which he could sure use. As for fuel, he'd have to wait and see, but most skippers kept their boats topped off.

The boats here belonged to the very rich. Hell, they only used them a couple a days a year. With any luck, no one would miss this one until he had it far away. Spanky did not break into the cabin, but he'd made up his mind and would be back with his tools, and his .44 Magnum piece, should he need it. Returning to the van, he was glad he'd worn his overalls so that he blended in with the other service personnel as he strode along the dock with the confidence of belonging. Pleased that he hadn't attracted any attention, he climbed in the van and drove off at a moderate speed, calculating how long this operation would take: three hours, max, round-trip to the log cabin, including loading Ma and Precious into the van; another hour to get the boat out of the marina and to a boarding spot for Ma, Precious, and all the stuff.They'd be crossing the lake by three o'clock. With the wind out of the northwest at about twelve knots, and the course due west, there'd be some pitch and roll, but they should make it to the park in six hours. Nine o'clock, midsummer, there should be just enough light to stake out an isolated campsite, but he'd have to get a move on.

Marge bustled about the cabin dusting the rustic furniture, checking the inventory of ancient cleaning supplies, changing the bedding, and arranging the cutlery and dishes. As she worked, she chatted nonstop to Jennifer. If only her little daughter would open up to her. What could she do to cheer her up? She had to be sad, too, that they'd lost Jessie, after all twins had a very special relationship.

Marge jolted as she heard the door to the cabin slam shut.

"Ma, get packed." Spanky's voice. Where had he said he was going? And why were they leaving, they'd just got here?

As Marge turned to face her son, she reeled at the fright in Jennifer's dark eyes. A stab of concern momentarily paralyzed her. She needed to talk to Spanky. To tell him in no uncertain terms that he'd have to leave Jennifer alone. That he couldn't do the bad things to Jennifer that he might do to other little girls. That Jennifer was special; she was his sister.

"Spanky, come sit down," Marge said, ignoring his opening statement.

"Ma, get your shit together. All that food. All the warm clothes you packed. Get it in the van out there. Now." Spanky walked over to Marge, grabbing her shoulders and turning her head toward him.

"I don't understand," she said. "I thought we were going to stay here."

"Don't be stupid, Ma. We can't stay here. I gotta plan. Now get movin'. We gotta haul ass. Now move." He gave her a forceful shove toward the bedroom.

"But —"

"I'm gonna start shovin' your shit in the van." Then Spanky

leaned over Jennifer and reached to stroke her forehead, his fingers lingering to twirl the curls in her short hair.

Marge took that as a sign that he, too, was concerned about the sad look in Jennifer's eyes.

But as she stepped into the bedroom to collect their belongings, she froze. "Better start liking me, Precious," Spanky was saying. "You're mine now."

# CHAPTER 54

*Riot Police Clash with Protesters in Tehran.*
— International News, Saturday, June 20

Scott and Katie returned to Jackie's room. Agent Camry had made it clear that they had no immediate role in finding Alex, and they knew that both Sammie and Jackie needed them. When they walked hand in hand into the hospital room, they saw that another bed had been set up. And, on that bed, they saw Jackie and Sammie. *Both* girls sitting side by side, backs against the wall, in animated conversation.

"Scott," Katie's smile was wide and spontaneous, "look at Jackie. She's sitting up and she's talking. I can't believe it."

Susan beckoned them into the room with a smile. "Sammie turned out to be just the right medicine."

Katie felt Scott squeeze her hand and her own heart skipped a beat. Jackie, recovered, looking alert; Sammie, safe. *But Alex still out there, somewhere.* Katie's smile faded, her eyes blinked uncontrollably.

"Listen," Susan whispered. The three adults stood close enough to hear.

"Tell me again," Jackie asked. "Was the lady mean?"

"No, I think she was crazy," Sammie said. "Like she called me Jessie and she called Alex, Jennie. But the man is very mean. He's going to hurt her. I just know it!"

"Yeah, I think so, too," Jackie said. "What can we do? Mom and Dad said we have to pray, but there must be something — "

"They just have to find her," Sammie said. "I promised I'd tell the FBI lady everything about that place and those people, Maggie and Spanky."

"Agent Camry's right here, Sammie, and she has some questions." Scott had inserted himself between them on the bed, an arm draped over both thin shoulders. "Can you tell her everything that you know?"

"Yes, Dad," Sammie said. "I sure can. I don't want to leave out a single thing."

Sammie took Camry through the kidnapping, and through each day, ending in her escape into the woods surrounding the Spansky home. Once in a while Jackie inserted an insightful question of her own for Sammie.

Camry finished by telling both Sammie and Jackie how brave they were.

On Saturday, Cliff Hunter knew that the FBI would be out in force. Even though he'd warned Scott Monroe not to call the cops and to come alone to drop the money and wait for his kids, he knew it would never happen that way. The feds would be swarming. That's why he'd chosen a busy, public place to pick up the ransom money. The law would not shoot into the affluent shoppers that populated the tony Birmingham streets on a Saturday afternoon.

Cliff had simply planned to scoop up the bag of money as he approached on his motorcycle, the way purse snatchers do it in the streets of Rome. Then he'd gun the bike, taking it through a series of maneuvers that he'd worked out. His escape car, a rented plain-Jane Toyota, was in place three miles away, near I-75, his exit route out of Detroit to return the car to the airport in his home town, Dayton, Ohio, far enough away from Auburn Hills.

But all his planning was now down the toilet. One of the Monroe kids had been found. True, one was still missing, but now the feds would have enough information to know that his story was crap, and that he'd never had those kids. But there was one precautionary step he'd taken. He fingered the handle, felt the heft. A Smith and Wesson .45.

Scott Monroe had screwed him over with his career, and Cliff craved revenge, needed it to move forward in his miserable life. Question was: did he need it enough to risk doing time in the joint? He'd been an up-and-coming catcher in the minors when some underage bimbo had accused him of rape. He'd roughed her up enough to scare her away from the law, but she'd gone to Scott Monroe. Scott, who was supposed to be his buddy, believed her story and kicked him out of the league. After that, all he'd been able to get were menial jobs. He still blamed Scott, so when Scott's kids came up missing, Cliff came up with a plan to get back at him. Only now he wasn't sure. He didn't know the answer to his own question. He'd hang out where he said to pick up the money, but he'd not do the grab, that would be too risky. He'd wait and see how it all played out. If he didn't get back at Scott Monroe this way, he'd find another.

# CHAPTER 55

*Summer Solstice Art Walk Kicks Off a Celebration of Art and Summer Solstice.*
– Entertainment Events, *Traverse City Record-Eagle*, June 20

By noon Spanky had everything loaded into the beat-up van. Jostling along the dirt road, he tried to work out all the steps of his plan. He had to focus, but he was so pissed at Ma for giving him a hard time. Hell, she'd gotten him into this mess, now all she could do was bitch about poor little Jennie. Jennie was no more that kid's name than Precious was, but he'd have to go along with Ma's loony shit until they were safely in Alaska with all that money.

He was having second thoughts about Ma. She was like a hawk, watching over Precious. Last night when he'd gone into Ma's bedroom to check on Precious he'd had a hard-on to beat all hard-ons. Couldn't risk waking up Ma and her making a noisy fuss.That would change soon.

Right now he didn't have a choice, he'd have to leave Precious with Ma at the campsite. When he came back with the money, he'd take off with the girl. Leave Ma enough money for her to get her own place. He just hoped that she had the smarts to stay on the run now that they had her name and all. But she wouldn't have a clue where to find him and Precious. Or maybe he was wrong about Ma, and once the three of them lived far away from anybody else, she'd understand and be fine with him and Precious.

He couldn't see what was wrong with him and a little girl, but others didn't see it his way, and Ma was the victim of peer pressure. Once they got to Alaska, they'd be on their own and nobody else's opinion would matter. But for now he had to get them the hell out of here and haul his butt down to the Everglades. He'd leave Precious with Ma, and figure out the long term later. Right now Precious was tied up in the back of the van, covered with a mess of blankets they'd taken from the cabin.

Alex cried softly underneath the pile of blankets. She could hear Maggie in the front seat talking to that man about Jennie. *Alex,* she wanted to scream. *My name is Alex.*

"And it's not right to tie Jennie up," Maggie was saying.

"How many time do I gotta tell you to shut up," the man said. Alex knew his name was Spanky and that he was Maggie's son, but she refused to call him by name.

The van lurched and turned and bumped along. Alex didn't know how long they'd been driving when they came to a stop. Could they be in Canada? What had Maggie meant when she said that her *real dad* was in Canada?

"Where are we?" Maggie asked. "Why are we parking in all these weeds?"

"Look, Ma, I said I had a plan. All you gotta do is stay here, keep quiet and be safe. I'll be back soon."

Then Alex heard the door of the van open and click shut.

Maggie climbed over into the backseat. She reached back and uncovered Alex's face, but she did not untie her. She talked to her like she was a baby and even sang her a lullaby. There was something very crazy about this lady. Alex knew that her mom worked with crazy people sometimes and she wondered if they scared her, too. During the second singing of the lullaby, Alex looked up when she heard what sounded like a motorcycle. Maggie's eyes were closed so she didn't see him, but Alex did — Spanky, on a motorcycle, coming up alongside the van. With a little wave, he turned the bike toward the road. Alex prayed that she'd never see him again.

Alex must have drifted off to sleep because the next thing she heard was Maggie's voice. "Not a boat Spanky. What if she gets seasick?"

The back of the van opened and Alex squeezed her eyes closed until she felt hands pull her into a sitting position. Before she could react, a strong band was pulled over her mouth.

The scary man then picked her up and carried her down a dock and onto a white boat.

"Lie down and be still," he said, wrapping her so tightly in a bed sheet that she could hardly wiggle. Then he loaded other stuff in boxes and bags so close to her that she thought she might be crushed if the boat rocked back and forth. The man hadn't covered her eyes and when she'd looked around, she saw an old man fishing on the dock. Had he seen her? Would he help her?

"Satisfied, Ma?She's okay under there?"

"Okay, but I don't like the idea of a boat. Where are we going?"

"Camping," Alex heard. After that, the sound of a motor drowned out their voices.

Streeter landed on a makeshift helicopter pad prepared along the stony shores of Elk Lake. The report was bad. He'd been on the radio the whole trip between Detroit and the Spanksy family's cabin. Again, Marge and Samuel Spansky had evaded them. Yes, they'd been there. They'd found the gray teddy bear belonging to Sammie Monroe abandoned. They'd missed by an hour or so judging from the partially melted ice in a tray on the kitchen counter. The Spanskys had left not an inkling of a clue as to how they'd gotten out or where they were heading. Other than finding the brown Escort, covered with branches and stashed in a nearby swamp among tall reeds, they had nothing but nondescript tire impressions in the sandy soil.

"Shit, shit, shit." What else could he say? How had the Spankys known they were closing in? Had it been Spansky who'd called in the ransom demand? Were they on their way to Miami? But why had they come all the way up here just to turn south? Roadblocks already peppered Michigan, and now they'd have to be extended all the way south to Miami. A weird pattern for a kidnapping scheme, thought Streeter. Either this guy was very smart or very stupid.

Putting it off as long as he could, Streeter put the call through to Camry, briefed her, and asked to speak to the Monroes.

Scott picked up in the girls' room. "We found the cabin," Streeter said, "but Alex is not there. She was there, but they've gone now."

"Oh, no." Scott's voice, and in the background, a gasp from Katie.

Streeter could feel his shoulders slump in defeat as he fed Scott the few facts that they knew.

"The money," Scott said in a low voice. "We have to get the money to Miami."

"The Miami field office is in charge down there, but Alex could be anywhere between Elk Rapids and Miami. We have roadblocks everywhere. The whole country is mobilized on this, as I'm sure you've seen on all the news stations."

"The other ransom note, the one sent to the Yankees?" Scott asked.

"We had a guy looked just like you drop the bag of fake bills. No one showed to pick it up. We're sure that this was phony and has nothing to do with the Spanskys, but we had three hundred sixty-degree photo surveillance around the designated drop off site. Later, we'll ask you to take a look, but that's not our highest priority."

Streeter tried to reassure Scott, offering his regards to Katie with a heavy heart.

As predicted, the boat ride took six hours, but daylight was fading fast. Spanky chose a desolate area a hundred yards inland from the shoreline, protected by tall trees and heavy brush, close enough to the cove where he'd secured the boat. He figured it would take him an hour to haul in the supplies and throw up the tent. Ma and Precious would be okay here as long as they stayed put. There was a fee for camping, and he'd give Ma enough cash to cover it should park rangers intrude, warning her to act innocent, apologetic, and eager to pay. And to keep the girl out of sight.

His earlier plan had been to steal a car and drive back down by the Mackinac Bridge. But the more he thought about it, the riskier it seemed. Now he planned to take the boat back down the western coast of Lake Michigan to the Milwaukee area. He'd abandon it there, find a car, make the drive. He still had seventy-five hours. Enough time, but none to spare. He'd wanted to leave that night, but he'd been up most of the night before. Being a trucker he knew the importance of sleep. If you don't get enough, you make mistakes. And he needed to stay smart. He decided to stay overnight in the tent and leave first thing in morning.

Marge threw up three times as Spanky charged across Lake Michigan at full throttle. She'd never been on a boat except for Evan's rowboat and a boat from Detroit to Belle Island and back. That had been slow enough to walk around holding a drink, but this was a violence she could never have imagined. She had to hold on with both hands or she'd go flying out as the boat went up and down over the waves at the same time it rolled from side to side. All she could think about was Jennifer back there. Would she even be alive when they got there — wherever they were going? Jennifer's hands were wrapped inside that blanket so she couldn't hang on and the bumps were very violent. It was very mean of Spanky to make her suffer like that. Before they reached the shore, Marge had made a decision.

By the time Spanky pulled the boat close to the shore, Marge was covered in her own vomit. Nauseous, with a killer headache, she crawled to the back of the boat where Spanky had stashed Jennifer. A picture flashed in her mind, Jennifer, blue eyes, dark curly hair, only eight months old. Spanky had pushed her in the water the first time. Could Jennifer have fallen out?

Spanky finally found a broken-down dock in a protected inlet. As he threw out a rope, Marge rushed to check on Jennifer. When her hand felt her daughter's soft curly hair, she felt a surge of joy. "Oh, thank God," she kept repeating.

Once on the shore, Maggie pulled the cloth out of Alex's mouth and untied her hands.

"Oh, thank the Lord, you weren't drowned," Maggie was saying. "I was so scared I'd lose you again, Jennie."

Even though Maggie stunk like vomit, Alex let herself be pulled into a hug.

Okay, she thought, this makes me sick, and Sammie would never do this, but — "Maggie," she said, her face touching the woman's. "Is it okay if I call you 'Mama' or 'Mom' or something? Maybe 'Mother?' " Alex thought that she, too, would throw up. Not because of smelling vomit, but because of what she had said. Calling this evil woman anything that meant mother was like the most shameful thing. But would it help her get the woman to trust her so she could escape?

"Oh, my baby, of course. That would be the most wonderful thing. 'Mama' I think that would be best. My little Jennie — Yes, 'Mama' would be fine."

Alex held her breath as Maggie started to tremble. Trying to disentangle herself from the woman's arms, she saw the tears in her eyes. Alex didn't care. She just wanted to get out of there.

"Get your butts in gear. Stop that blubbering, Ma. Precious, you can carry the bags of food." The man motioned for her to hold out her hands and he filled them with two white plastic bags. "Get your asses in gear or you're gonna be sleeping on the ground."

Maggie and Alex ran about doing whatever the man told them to do until he finally got the tent up. He told them how to make a fire and how to light the lantern. He said there were berries around but not to go too far. He told them not to talk to anyone. Maggie asked him how they were supposed to go to the bathroom.

"In the woods," he said. "Here, Precious, let me show you where."

Alex had been sitting on the camp bed, and Spanky came to offer her a hand.

"No, Spanky, just tell me where. I'm the one who has to pee."

Spanky pointed to a clearing in back of their campsite and Maggie hurried off.

No longer had she left than Spanky unzipped his pants and pulled out his penis. Alex had never actually seen a penis except in science books. Were they supposed to be that big? "Look at this, my Precious, this is just for you. Come Precious, touch it, before Ma gets back." Now he was right in front of Alex. Her face came within an inch of what looked like a huge, hairy sausage. "Touch it, Precious, or do you want to put it in your mouth? You can, you know. You can lick it, too. Oh yeah, that would feel real good."

Alex didn't know what to do. Should she touch it? Would he hurt her if she didn't touch it?

She shook her head. She knew what a penis was for. Boys had one. That's how they peed. She couldn't imagine why he was showing her his and why he wanted her to touch it, but she knew it must be something bad. *What would Jackie or Sammie do?* But they were not here and maybe she would never see them again. Alex started to cry, but Spanky took her hand and placed it on his hairy, throbbing penis just as Maggie came charging back inside the tent.

"Stop it, Spanky. I said, stop it. I told you not to do that to your sister. It's not natural."

"I surrender, Ma," Spanky said with a grin, zipping up his pants. "Won't be long and you're gonna stop telling me what I can and cannot do. I'm a grown man, Ma, and I'll be the one takin' care of you."

# CHAPTER 56

*FBI Questions Sammie Mònroe. Where is Her Triplet Sister?*
National News, Saturday, June 20

To Katie's relief, Jackie's recovery seemed genuine and complete, and Sammie's injuries only superficial cuts and scrapes, her arm in a sling as a precaution. Once Agent Camry had completed a thorough interrogation of Sammie, Katie had called her mom to give her the okay to visit. The girls were working on chocolate ice cream sodas when Lucy arrived, and Katie felt a rush of mixed emotions when they both leapt out of their wheelchairs to hug their grandma.

"Your hair, Sammie," Lucy exclaimed. "At last, I'll be able to tell you two apart."

"But not from Alex," Sammie said. "Hers is short now, too."

Katie's momentary pleasure at seeing her two daughters reunited with her mom evaporated as reality hit hard. She squeezed Scott's hand knowing, too, that he would have had the same reaction. Alex was still missing.

For Lucy, Sammie and Jackie retold the story of Alex and Sammie's abduction. "We have to find Alex, Grandma," they each kept repeating.

"Katie?" Lucy intervened. Katie had zoned out, asking herself over and over, *Was Alex safe*? Of course, there was no answer.

"Mom, we were thinking," Jackie was saying. "Can we go back to Grandma's. We don't need to be in a hospital. I'm okay now, really, Mom."

"As soon as Dr. Susan comes back to check on you, we'll ask her," Katie said. Yes, she wanted both girls out of the hospital, but could she cope, going back to Mom's without Alex? Somehow that felt like she was giving up.

As they all chatted and commiserated and went about reassuring each other, Scott responded to a knock on the door. Agent Camry asked to speak with him and Katie. "Nothing about Alex," she forewarned in a voice loud enough for all to hear.

"Agent Streeter thought you may want to know this," Camry said. "Roberta Kendrick, Olivia Cutty's sister, was found dead today, an apparent heroin overdose. She left a note, said she couldn't cope with the responsibility for Jake and Aiden. She hoped that someone would take care of them. She said that they'd be better off without her."

"Those poor kids," Katie felt profound sadness, mixed with guilt. "They have no one. I tried to protect them, but now —"

"They got a raw deal," Scott said, "but Katie, none of this was your fault."

"I'm the one who insisted that it was Cutty who took Sammie and Alex. How wrong I was."

"But, to grow up in the custody of a man who murdered their mother and who sexually molested them? Those kids never did have a chance."

"Where are the boys now?" Katie asked.

"Hillsbourgh Protective Services. Adam Kaninsky offered to take them, but I doubt that the courts will let that happen."

Before they went back to rejoin the family, Scott pulled Katie aside. "Babe, we have to stay focused. For us and for all three girls. We can't worry about anybody else."

Katie nodded, pressing her body against his. "Scott, I love you," she said.

# CHAPTER 57

*Search for Alex Monroe Moves to Northern Michigan.*
— Evening News, Saturday, June 20

The crime scene investigators who'd scoured the Elk Lake cabin briefed Streeter as he prepared to board the FBI helicopter that would take him back to Detroit. Indeed, the fingerprints there matched those found in the Holly house: Alex Monroe, Margaret Spansky, and Samuel Spansky. An hour earlier Streeter took a call from the director. Based on the ransom demand with Alex's voice verified, assignment for the Monroe rescue command was shifting to the Miami field office. Streeter would remain in charge of Michigan operations, but would take orders from Miami. The powers that be were convinced that the kidnappers would show up to collect the money in South Florida and that they'd keep Alex alive for demonstration purposes.

He'd just climbed into the bureau aircraft when the pilot announced, "A call for you sir. We'll hold takeoff so you have better audio."

"Agent Streeter," he said, flipping to the communication channel.

The Charlevoix, Michigan, chief of police identified himself then went on to report an incident. He apologized for bothering him in the middle of such a high profile case, but –

"Go on," Streeter said.

"I'm sure that this is nothing, but with all the police chatter today about the hunt for the Monroe kid, I thought I'd let you know about a report we got late this afternoon. A concerned citizen came across an older model panel van parked along a remote stretch of lakeshore. He walks his dog on the same path when he gets home from work every night, and he thought it strange, particularly because it had no plates, so he called it in. When we responded, we found the vehicle half hidden in heavy dune grass. It couldn't have been there long, based on the condition of the grasses. No plate, but we did find the registration info underneath the passenger floor mat. Registration address was Elk Rapids. When I tracked down the owner, he said that it must have been taken from his cottage on Elk Lake. Owner hasn't been in the area for three weeks so he doesn't know how long it's been missing."

Streeter was not impressed with this missing van, but arranged for fingerprints to be compared to the Holly house and Elk Rapids cabin. But this information did give him an excuse, however flimsy, to keep his small team in northern Michigan. His gut told him that the Spansky couple had not ventured far with Alex. He'd postpone his trip back to Detroit until the Charlevoix police had completed the fingerprint analysis from the abandoned van. He told the pilots and instructed them to find a place in Traverse City for them and Streeter and two agents to stay the night. He'd inform the SAC in Detroit later.

Streeter then returned to the log cabin. A few guys from the SWAT team were hanging around, bitching about poor communication. If they'd been called out an hour sooner, they would have the kid, the bad guys would be locked up. Same old bitch session that followed every failed SWAT operation. Streeter and his two agents may be able to delay going back, but no way could he persuade the elite team leader to stay. As of now the SWAT effort would be focused on Miami, and the case would be directed from there. Streeter would go back to Detroit, having failed Alex.

At the height of the season, the FBI team of five was lucky to find three rooms at a motel on Grand Traverse Bay. They had no luggage, but they headed toward their rooms with laptops and communication equipment. They'd use Streeter's room to set up and the four men would share the other two.

# CHAPTER 58

*Michigan's Upper Peninsula Temperatures Running Several Degrees Colder than Average this June.*
— Michigan Weather, Sunday, June 21

Spanky was gone when Marge woke up. He'd told her that he had things to do and that he would return to get her and Jennifer. She had enough supplies to last a week and she was not supposed to leave the campsite, no matter what. She hadn't slept well, yet she hadn't heard Spanky leave. Twice during the night, she'd gotten up to pile more blankets on Jennifer. She'd always liked camping when she and Evan had taken Spanky before the twins were born, but now she felt exposed and abandoned. Where had Spanky gone and why had he left her and Jennifer here?

But the main reason she stayed awake most of the night was to figure out what to do about Spanky. Marge realized that she could not trust her own son. For years now, she'd known that he did bad things to little girls. She wasn't sure of the word. Was it rape? Did they call it sodomy? Whatever, he collected their little panties in a chest. He even took them on the road for his runs. But with his own little sister? That was unnatural.

Marge lay on the blow-up mattress until Jennifer began to stir. She'd been thinking about work. What were the girls saying? Had the FBI or the cops questioned them? She imagined they had. If only she could go back to that easy, friendly, supportive life. But she couldn't. Simple as that. She'd made her move. And she'd lost one twin. But she still had Jennifer.

"Mama, are you awake?" Jennifer said in a voice so sweet that Marge thought her heart would melt. So many years she'd waited for this. This time she wouldn't let Spanky ruin things for her. She'd tried her best with him, but Spanky had turned out to be a pervert. There, she had said it. Pervert was the right word for him.

Marge had to chose: Spanky or Jennifer. Jennifer was Evan's child. Not an out-of-wedlock child like Spanky. The word bastard came to mind, a word her father had used when she first admitted she was pregnant, but a word that Marge had never said, even to herself, until last night when she was thinking things through. In contrast to Jennifer and her twin sister, Jessica, both legitimate children. And even if she didn't have Jessica, Evan would want to take her and Jennifer back, she was sure of that. All she had to do was find him. She knew that he lived in Toronto.

"Yes, Jennie, I'm awake. Were you warm enough last night?" Marge had skimped on her own blankets to make sure Jennifer wouldn't be cold.

"Yes, but why do we have to stay here? When it got a little bit light this morning you looked cold so I took a blanket over to you." Marge looked around. Surely, she had. What a perfect child. Shy at first, but really opening up.

"Hungry?" Marge eased herself off the mattress and stood, stretching her arms in circles until she felt a stitch of arthritic pain in her neck.

"I guess so," Jennifer said. "Want me to go look for some of those berries he told us about?"

"First let's go pee," Marge said. "For now we have to go in the woods, but maybe we can find a toilet. Campsites are supposed to have restrooms, and Spanky said that this is a state park. "

During the night Marge had finalized her plan. She would take Jennifer to Toronto to reunite with Evan, and they would resume their life together. No one would look for them there. Not even Spanky. In her purse she had $430, and they had plenty of food. She would pack as much as she could carry into a large black garbage bag, and then they'd start walking. She didn't know which way to walk, but Marge figured it didn't matter. She'd stick to the edge of the lake. People always camped on lakes. She'd tell them that – Well, she'd think up something depending on the circumstances. Like she lost her wallet and needed to get home to Toronto. At least she wouldn't have to worry about Jennifer kicking up a fuss. The child seemed quite content.

As Alex trudged alongside Maggie on the shore of the lake, she reminded herself to act nice but to stay alert. They hadn't seen another person and she didn't know what she'd do when they did, maybe yell, "Help me!" and run from Maggie to the person. As she practiced in her mind, she heard a dog bark. She stopped a step behind Maggie and turned around as a large dog ran to her side. Alex liked dogs, but her family had never had one because Sammie hated most animals. But this one seemed friendly with floppy ears and thick yellow fur. She didn't know what kind of dog he was, but as she put out her hand to pet him, Maggie grabbed her other hand and jerked her forward so hard that Alex felt a jolt of pain in her shoulder. Before she spun around to face forward, she looked for the dog's owner, but she saw no one. After that Maggie made her stay right next to her. When the dog scampered off, she asked Maggie whether she liked dogs.

"Yes, Jennie, I'll get you one if you want one, but not today."

For a while Alex wondered whether she should have made more of a fuss over the dog. Maybe its owner would have come after it, and she could have been rescued. But too late now, so she followed Maggie. What else could she do? No way was she going to run away into the scary woods, but the next time, if she saw anybody, she'd run to them and beg for help. She also reminded herself to drink plenty of water. Dad was always telling the team to stay hydrated. They didn't have bottled water so she soon drained the cans of lemonade and Sprite.

They kept going after stopping to sit on a log and eat a salami sandwich and an oatmeal cookie. When she asked Maggie about running out of water, Maggie just laughed and pointed at the lake.

"That's salt water in the ocean," Alex said, twitching her nose in distaste.

"No, Jennie, not an ocean, a lake. Lake Michigan or Lake Superior, I'm not sure. One of the Great Lakes. Didn't you learn about them in school?"

School seemed such a distant life to Alex that she simply shook her head, hoping Maggie was right about the water.

⁂

Leaving the boat in the same secluded spot as yesterday, Spanky headed for the tent. He was disgusted with himself. He had forgotten to get Precious to tape the message that it was *Wednesday* and *please rescue me, Daddy*. Now he had to recalculate his timing and perhaps move the ransom pick-up to Thursday. No problem there, he could use some slack, and he'd be able to get another night's sleep on the road.

At first he thought they were both asleep. All was quiet. Ma liked to sleep late on her days off, that's why he hadn't awakened her when he had left an hour and a half ago. But the campsite was empty. Okay, he told himself. Hadn't he suggested that they pick berries? All kids love picking berries. He knew he had. A glance about confirmed that nothing looked disturbed. No choice now except to wait for them. While he waited, he'd get some sleep.

Spanky awoke to the bark of a dog. He had no idea how long he'd slept. Looking around he did not see Ma or Precious. They must still be out there. He rose groggily from the floor to peer out the tiny flap window. He saw a yellow dog scamper along the path in the woods that led to the cove where he'd stashed the Grady White.

"Shit," he mumbled. Spanky felt the heft of the Taurus .44 Magnum revolver in the wide pocket of his cargo pants. Where there was a dog, there'd be a human. He checked his watch. Noon. He needed to find Ma and Precious, get the kid to tape that statement, and get the hell out of there.

Spending fifteen minutes circling the campsite, Spanky found no trace of either Ma or Precious. He went back in the tent, hunger gnawing at his stomach. He'd only taken a ham sandwich and a Snickers bar, but he'd left them enough to eat for a week. He poked around in all the bags. He found cans of sodas, apples and bananas, loaves of bread, peanut butter, but where were the energy bars?

# CHAPTER 59

*Happy Father's Day to All You Dads Out There.*
— Sunday Radio, June 21

Streeter had arranged to meet his team of four for breakfast at eight a.m. As he exited the elevator his face registered surprise and suspicion as a paunchy man in a uniform approached. Streeter figured the guy must have been waiting for them in the lobby.

"You Agent Streeter? FBI?" the man asked.

Streeter planned to come off as Mr. Nice Guy, not The Jerk as most agents presented themselves.

"Yes, I am." Streeter pulled his badge, holding it out for the man to examine.

"Chief Bagley," he said, pulling out his own credentials. "Just put a call into your room. Figured maybe you were on your way down. I came down from Charlevoix. Following up on that van I called you about."

Streeter was embarrassed that he'd forgotten the small-town chief's name.

"I got the report," he said. "Thought you needed to know. There's a match. Prints in that abandoned van match the cabin on Elk Lake. All three, match. That little Monroe girl was in that van. I'd like to escort you to Charlevoix. It's about a forty-five-minute drive with the sirens on."

Streeter's heart pounded. *Alex was in that van.* Miami had never made sense. His gut had been right. *Where was she now?*

His two agents and two pilots had arrived, and the six men clustered in an alcove adjoining the bank of elevators.

"I've got a vehicle waiting that'll hold all five of you," Bagley said. "So let's roll."

"Should we go in the copter?" Streeter asked the lead pilot.

"I think I can get you there faster," Bagley said. "But it's up to you."

Bagley, Streeter, and his two agents climbed in the sheriff's van, leaving the pilots to make arrangements to land at the Charlevoix airport. True to his word, Bagley made the fifty-mile drive along Route 31 in less than forty-five minutes. On their arrival at the Charlevoix County Sherriff's office, they were met by a cadre of deputies and two State Police officers.

"Put the word out," Chief Bagley ordered. "House-to-house search if need be. Concentrate on the lake shore, but I'm worried about a boat — "

Streeter followed Bagley into his small office and asked if his agents could set up camp there. He had to call this finding into the agency and have the FBI confirm the print matched. As Streeter waited for e-mail confirmation of the prints, he watched as local police fanned out to canvas the small resort town. Bagley had ruined Father's Day for a medley of town, county, and state law enforcement.

It didn't take long. Confirmation. Alex, Marge, and Samuel Spansky's prints all over that stolen van. Not sure what to do next, Streeter was interrupted by an excited Bagley.

"I'm on my way to the marina. Manager there just got a phone call of interest. Come with me. It's just a couple of minutes away. We can talk on the way. Let's go."

An officious looking man in pressed khakis and a white tee shirt with a sailboat emblem was waiting at the entrance to the Sunset Marina office. Streeter noted that the clipboard in his hand shook as did his voice when he walked toward them. "Can you turn off the flashing lights?" he asked. "And can you all come inside. I'm Mike Gates, the manager here, and I can't afford to raise any panic about stolen yachts."

*He's worried about a boat when a little girl's life is at stake.*

"I've got a problem," Gates started. "A stolen boat, Grady White thirty-foot center console with twin three hundred-horsepower outboards, Yamahas. Owner's name is Dale Bole. He's from Chicago, but traveling out of the country. He left no permission for someone to use his boat, so I can only assume that it's stolen. He's the type of guy who never lets another human being so much as touch his watercraft. Best I can tell is that the Grady White's been missing since between yesterday morning when I made my routine security rounds and about ten this morning when I first noticed it missing. Could have been anytime in between. This is my busy season and — "

"Anybody see anything unusual?" Bagley interrupted.

"I've asked around, but nobody saw anything out of the ordinary. Nothing like this has — "

"Camera surveillance?" Streeter asked, glancing around at the expensive watercraft that made Sunset Marina their home.

"I've been going to put in a camera system," Gates said, Adam's apple bobbing, "but there's not much crime in Charlevoix."

"Not unless you have my job," Bagley said with a smirk. "You telling me that kids don't fool around and 'borrow' these luxury boats?"

"That's what I thought might have happened, but when the officer came by to ask about anything out of the ordinary, I told him — "

The van and now the boat? Why a boat? And where? Streeter had no answers, but decided to wait for the results of the immediate area search before calling in reinforcements. But he'd have to do so soon, and the search would include the rough waters of Lake Michigan.

When the sun got very hot, Jennifer asked Marge if they could go up by the trees and rest for a while in the shade. She'd agreed and the two of them sat leaning against a huge fir tree. Marge was sweaty and her back ached something fierce, but it felt so good to have Jennifer, so contented, sitting beside her. But Marge knew that she didn't dare drift off to sleep unless she tied Jennifer up. So she sat awake, panting for a while as she cooled down, relaxing only when Jennifer dozed off.

When Jennifer woke up with a start, Marge realized that she, too, had fallen asleep. She checked her watch, three hours had passed.

They each ate an apple and started walking again. They didn't talk much, but enough that Marge knew that Jennifer was afraid of

Spanky. And with good reason, she knew. Once she found Evan, he would protect them both. But what to do now? She started to feel the raindrops landing on her head and the sky had turned dark and threatening. She'd have to find them shelter. Was she still on park property? She didn't know.

Marge, with her arm around Jennifer, regretted that she hadn't brought warm clothes, not even a sweat shirt. "You're shaking, Jennie," she said, drawing her daughter into her ample breasts.

Bagley had pizza delivered and the dozen or so men gathered in the too-small police headquarters gobbling quickly, anxious to be on the street, looking for any trace of Alex Monroe. Streeter had called his boss at home with an update and the SAC said he'd check with Miami, and get back to him.

Streeter had just dialed his ex-wife's home in Grand Rapids, when the marina manager ran through the door, shouting something. Hanging up, not sure whether Marianne had picked up, Streeter met him in the middle of the room. "I tried to call," he said, "but the phones were jammed, so I ran over."

Streeter could see sweat seeping through the preppy shirt.

"I got a call from a man." Gates's Adam's apple bobbed when he swallowed, and he referenced the notepad. "Rudy Conover. He said he saw the Grady White, that's the missing boat I reported. I wrote it all down.

"Go on," Streeter said when the man hesitated and swallowed again. "When? Where?"

"A state park in the Upper Peninsula. He's a pilot that flies his own plane and he likes to, you know, get away from phones, television. He and his wife have a special spot. Only his wife died and now there's just him and his dog."

"When did he see the boat?" Streeter interrupted.

"This morning, ten o'clock. He'd been walking on the beach and took a shortcut back to his camp. His dog barked and started to sniff a boat pulled up to shore at an inlet at the far end of Wells State Park. When he got closer, he recognized it as belonging to a guy who eats in his restaurant."

"Where's that?" Streeter asked.

"Chicago. The guy that owns the boat lives in Chicago and has a summer home in Charlevoix, and Mr. Conover's restaurant is in Chicago. They'd talk about going to the U.P. and such, something they had in common. Anyway Mr. Conover was pretty sure that my client, Dale Bole, would never leave his boat untended on the shore like that. So Mr. Conover steps back into the trees and waits just to check out what's going on." Again, a glance at the clipboard. "Waited about fifteen minutes. He said he didn't go too close, but close enough to keep an eye on the boat, half expecting to see Dale Bole appear on the scene. But no, he sees a big man, definitely *not* the owner, leave a nearby campsite, get into the boat, and take off."

"Alone?" Streeter asked. "No woman? No child?"

"You have to call Mr. Conover yourself. Gates checked his watch and extended the clipboard to Streeter. "He said that he'd stay by a pay phone for fifteen minutes in case the chief here wanted more information. He left the — "

Before he could finish the sentence, Streeter had his phone out. "Read me the number."

Streeter's hands trembled as he punched the numbers, praying that this Conover would still be there.

"Hello," a man's voice picked up at the first ring.

"Mr. Rudy Conover?"

"Yes."

"Special Agent Tony Streeter, FBI. I understand you have some information about a boat that may be linked to the Monroe girls' kidnapping."

"I don't know for sure. But I got suspicious when I saw the Grady White abandoned in that inlet. Not a very safe thing to do. Dale Bole would never leave his boat unattended. I waited a while, out of sight, thinking something was fishy. I didn't know whether I should interfere, but I thought if that were my boat, I'd sure as hell want someone watching it for me. In about fifteen minutes a bald man — not old, I'd judge in his thirties — with a mustache and a goatee, comes along on a path leading from a campsite. I stayed back and tried to keep Duke from barking. Successfully. After that I walked back to my campsite, got in my car, and drove to a pay phone over by the park entrance. I called information in Chicago, looking for my customer's phone number. Unlisted, they said. Then I got the bright idea to call the restaurant. We like to confirm reservations so I figured we might have this guy's number in the computer. My lunch hostess was there; she found the number right off." Conover paused to take a long breath.

"You're doing well, sir," Streeter said, wishing he'd minimize the embellishment.

"I called immediately. Housekeeper answered. Said Mr. Bole was out of the country. Said that he would never loan out his boat. Gave me the name and number of Sunset Marina. I made the call and told them I'd wait around the pay phone for a call back. My cell service doesn't work out here."

"You're at the Wells State Park right now?" Streeter asked, checking coordinates on a map the sheriff had given him.

"That I am."

"Sir, we have evidence linking your story to the Monroe kidnapping case. Could we ask you to stay right there until we arrive? We desperately need your help, Mr. Conover. Please?"

"I left my campsite unsecured —"

"Sir, we're looking for a nine-year-old girl." If necessary, Streeter would have him detained by the park rangers, but he'd have a much more cooperative witness if he agreed on his own.

"If you put it that way, of course. Sure, I'll stay."

"We're on our way to the park," Streeter said. "Stay there. We'll call the rangers and brief them. Don't talk to anyone else, and, thank you, sir."

Streeter knew very little about state parks, another one of his shortcomings. As Marianne had pointed out, the girls needed to experience the great outdoors. She'd grown up in Grand Rapids, Michigan, spending every holiday at one of Michigan's many lakes. He wondered if she'd ever been to J. W. Wells State Park. The park, located on Green Bay, not far from the Michigan-Wisconsin state line, comprises almost seven hundred acres of near wilderness and has an extensive shoreline. Some of the campsites were remote, others clustered closer to the main beach area.

Having arranged for the FBI helicopter to move on from

Charlevoix to the park, he studied the map while waiting for the pilots to refuel. The driving distance to Cedar River, a tiny town a mile from the park, was about 230 miles. The drive would involve crossing the Mackinac Bridge, going west and then south. By boat the park was directly west of Charlevoix, some 150 nautical miles.

Streeter contemplated the timing. Samuel Spanksy had stolen a boat in Charlevoix. He must have crossed Lake Michigan, heading due west to that state park. Had he stayed the night? Was Alex with him? According to Conover, he'd left the campsite about three hours ago. He'd left alone, without his mother, without Alex. Had he left them somewhere in the park? Or did he plan to pick them up somewhere along the way? Or were they already on their way to Miami to trade Alex for money.

Should he have the park rangers immediately check out the site where Conover had seen the stolen boat? His instinct said, "no." He would personally lead this search. There had been so many mistakes along the way. He prayed that this decision would not turn out to be yet another one. Too many mistakes, too many dead, Maxwell Cutty, Norman Wade, and Camry had texted him that Cutty's former sister-in-law, Roberta, had taken her own life. By holding back the rangers, was he risking another screw-up?

Streeter had alerted the head park ranger that he'd be arriving, but he had not shared the reason for the highly unusual descent of federal agents into the middle of nowhere. He did ask that there be fast boats and extra personnel on standby. He had emphasized to Rudy Conover that he not disclose the possible Monroe child connection. All he needed was a bunch of cowboys trying to be heroes.

The weather got progressively worse as the helicopter crossed Lake Michigan and descended onto the makeshift tarmac near the park office. The forecast included falling temperatures, a thunderstorm, and seven-foot swells. As Streeter and his two agents jumped out of the cabin, they were met by a cadre of six uniformed park rangers and Conover, a rugged looking guy in his seventies. Streeter detected a mix of curiosity and hostility, but when Conover, without a trace of hesitation, indentified Samuel Spanky's photo as the man whom he'd seen,

Streeter had their full allegiance.

A team now, they discussed options as to how to approach the campsite described by Conover. Since no road led to the site, they decided to go by police boat. The hovering of a helicopter would be too loud, but it could be called out at a moment's notice. Streeter with Conover, the senior park ranger, and one junior ranger took the lead boat. His two agents and the remaining park rangers would follow in the second, leaving the student ranger behind to handle park functions, the most important of which would be communications. Before climbing aboard, Streeter hesitated. During the helicopter ride, he had briefed Agent Pentero, from the Miami field office and now the lead FBI special agent in charge of the Monroe kidnapping. He'd gotten the go-ahead to proceed to the park, but it had come in a tone dripping with derision. Streeter's competence with the agency was at a crossroads. Should he call in SWAT? No, he decided. That would take too long.

A young ranger took the helm as Conover guided the craft toward the exact spot in the woods where he'd watched the man motor off in Dale Bole's boat. Streeter hadn't realized that the waves of Lake Michigan matched those of the oceans, and by the time the boat approached shore, they were all drenched in frigid water.

Streeter was the first to jump onto the shore. "Can you lead us from here to the campsite?" he asked Conover. "Or would you rather wait here?"

"Follow me," Conover said. "Single file. Path's narrow."

Streeter looked at the rough, overgrown terrain, then down at his pressed charcoal gray suit and polished dress shoes. Not optimal attire for a takedown in the woods, he thought as he followed directly behind Conover.

When Conover hesitated, Streeter could see a rather small tent. Nothing else. No activity. No vehicle. No ancillary camping equipment. He put up a hand for the others to halt and he readied his weapon. By now the second boat would have dropped off agents to fan out in a four-point circle around the site. Streeter led, approaching cautiously. Kneeling on the pine-strewn ground, he lifted the main flap of the tent. It rose without resistance. Still on his knees, he crept inside. The light inside was dim, and he flipped on his flashlight. He circled the inner perimeter with the bright light. Nothing moved. Nor was there a sound. The tent had no human occupants. Had the occupants heard them coming? Or had they left earlier?

Streeter signaled his two agents. "No one inside," he said, "but somebody's been here. I'm going to check around the tent. Meantime, get the scene secured."

The lead ranger waited at the open flap when Streeter stumbled out, a bundle of garments in his hands. "Clothes." On the top was a small pair of jeans. "A child's."

"The Monroe child?"

"Alex was here. But they're gone." Defeated again. For the third time now, Streeter had been too late for Alex. The house in Holly. The cabin on Elk Lake. And now this goddamned tent. Was it him? Was he jinxed? Was he incompetent?

One of Streeter's agents had gone into the tent and emerged holding a list. "Agent Streeter, we made a list of the contents. A few clothes: man's, woman's, a little girl's. A lantern. A pot and a frying pan. Paper plates. Some food. There's a plastic bag of trash. Ripped food wrappings, empty cans, that's all."

Streeter sent the rangers to search the area. Then he got on his satellite phone and called in their coordinates, reported their findings, and requested crime-scene investigators. After that he sat down on the ground with Rudy Conover.

"Got any ideas?" he asked the older man. How pathetic was that, an FBI special agent recruiting a restaurateur as a crime consultant?

"Here's what I'd do," said Conover. "Let's assume that the women got away from the man I saw. They didn't use a boat. At least there's no sign of that. What if they walked out of here?"

"Go on," Streeter said. A city boy, never comfortable with the vast outdoors, he valued the outdoorsman's insights. Then suddenly Conover gasped and clutched his chest like he was having a heart attack.

"Are you okay?" Streeter grasped the older man's shoulder.

"Oh, my holy Lord," Conover's voice sounded ragged. "This morning. I'd forgotten all about it. I was taking a leak behind my campsite near a clump of bushes when Duke, my dog, started to bark and run off toward the shore before I got my thingee zipped back up. By the time I followed him to the shoreline, he had chased down the beach in the opposite direction that we'd been heading. In the distance — why didn't I remember this before — a little girl had reached out to pet him. She was with a plump woman who seemed to be urging her forward. I don't usually see anybody when I walk along the beach, but I didn't think much of it, this being the tourist season. Later, I was so distracted by finding Dale's boat that the woman and girl simply slipped my mind."

"You've seen pictures of Alex Monroe and the Spansky woman?" Streeter asked, his heart starting to pump out of control.

"Who on the planet hasn't? Especially the little girl and her triplet sisters. Beautiful kids."

"Could the child you saw have been Alex?"

"Could have been. She was too far away to see her face. She had short, dark hair that was blowing this way and that. Sure could have been, but I only saw the back of the woman. Something like a hundred seventy pounds, medium height."

Both men rose at the same time. "How far could they have gotten assuming they walked on along the shore?" Streeter again felt that surge of hope, this time more powerful. He *would* find Alex.

"Know what?" said Conover. "I'd find that bright young ranger who piloted our boat. He has a map of our surroundings etched in his brain. I'll get him, and we can make a plan. I'm good with these woods. If that was her and she's in this park, we'll find her."

*Alex, where are you?* Streeter asked of the darkening sky.

# CHAPTER 60

*Today Marks One Week Since Alex Monroe*
*Was Taken Out of That Movie Theatre.*
– Morning News, Sunday, June 21

Scott had immediately disliked Special Agent Jason Pentero, the new agent in charge of finding Alex, out of the Miami field office. "Arrogant," "flip," "shifty" were the words he'd used to describe him to Katie after their first phone encounter. Pentero had advised Scott that he'd be transporting him to Miami, first thing in the morning so they could strategize over the ransom exchange.

Scott had balked. He'd have to consult with his wife.

He did and Katie said, "No. Tell him we all go. If we have to, and I guess we do. But I got the idea that Agent Streeter does not think that they'll have Alex there. Not that he said it in those exact words, but I think that he thinks she's still in Michigan. Up north. I wish he'd call us with an update."

"Agent Pentero said that I wouldn't personally have a role in the drop-off, but they want me there anyway. And when Alex is released, shouldn't we both be there? And Sammie and Jackie?"

"Yes, we should," Katie agreed. She sounded reluctant, but what else could they do?

Scott called Agent Pentero back to tell him that he would only travel with his wife and daughters. Pentero hemmed and hawed before agreeing to send an FBI plane to pick all four of them up the next morning, Monday, two days in advance of the anticipated exchange.

Katie was asleep in the bed between Sammie and Jackie when Scott returned to their hospital room. Tenderly he kissed each forehead before lying down on the fourth bed. Tossing and turning all night he thought of nothing except getting Alex back. Would he and Katie be holding their missing daughter by Wednesday night? Would Alex be sleeping between her sisters? Would he and Katie leave their daughters in the care of another ever again? He drifted off to sleep with a dream that had all three girls back out on the diamond. Sammie the pitcher. Jackie at short, and Alex, with her arm, the best little league talent at third base that he'd ever seen.

Spanky hemmed and hawed, then fell asleep on the limp air mattress. He awoke with a chill and the ping of rain on the tent. Still no Ma and Precious. They must be waiting out the rain in some kind of a natural shelter. Ma would return to the tent soon. She would surely understand the trouble they'd be in if anybody recognized the girl. Hell, she'd hid both of those girls for five days before anyone caught on.

Bummed he wouldn't have the kid on tape, Spanky knew he couldn't wait much longer. He needed to get to the Everglades to set things up. The Monroe parents would be desperate enough to drop the money even without their daughter's voice. But why take a chance? He'd go to plan B. On the way to Miami, he'd find a little girl, grab her for a few minutes, make her cry and say, *"Please don't kill me!"* Didn't all scared kids sound alike? Then he'd let the girl go and he'd haul ass. No time to start a new collection on this trip.

Emerging from the tent, Spanky sprinted off to the Grady White, secured in the inlet. Glancing at the sky, he cursed himself for his decision to leave by boat. The waves were really rolling now and Spanky reached for the life jacket, then tossed it aside. He was bulky enough, he didn't need more.

As he motored south, the temperature fell and he felt cold. Looking around, he saw a heavy flannel jacket and he put it on over his sweatshirt.

# CHAPTER 61

*Chase from Holly to Elk Rapids in Search of Nine-Year-Old Alex Monroe Ends in Disappointment.*
*– Northern Michigan News*, Sunday, June 21

Alex shivered in the crook of Maggie's flabby arm as they ate a cheese sandwich and finished the last of the plastic bottles of warm lemonade. All she had on were the pants and the short-sleeve cotton shirt that she'd worn as they'd left the tent that morning. The sky was getting dark and it had started to rain. She heard thunder in the distance. Alex hated thunder and she knew how dangerous lightning could be. Every year in Tampa, people died from bad lightning. Where could they go to stay safe?

"Jennie, I'm going to make a little nest back behind the dune grass. We can cover it with branches and stay dry. Just like the birds," Maggie told her.

Alex had argued that birds had nests in trees.

It had started to rain harder now, and Maggie was singing. Mother Goose stuff. "Twinkle, Twinkle, Little Star," songs like that. Songs for little kids. Alex didn't know why Maggie treated her and Sammie, when Sammie had still been with her, like babies. Thinking of Sammie made Alex think of Mom and Dad and home and Jackie. She didn't know if Jackie was still sick or if Sammie had found their parents.

She started to cry and Maggie wrapped her tighter in her arms."It's okay, Jennie, I'm not going to let Spanky get you. I don't think he'd hurt you again, but I can't take that chance."

"Is that why we left the tent?" Alex didn't trust Maggie to tell the truth, but she asked anyway.

"Yes. But it's so cold and a storm's coming. I thought we'd find someone to help us get to Toronto by now. Once we're there, we'll be safe and happy."

*Find someone to help them?* Alex thought that sounded strange as Maggie steered clear of the few people that they had seen today.

The first strike of lightning was huge, followed by deafening thunder. Maggie held Alex more tightly. But after the thunder, Alex heard something else. A faint motor sound. More lightning; more thunder. And the motor. Rain now poured heavily, and she and Maggie were both drenched. Alex shook from the cold and from her fear. Could there be a boat out there? What if someone in that boat would rescue her? Was there enough light that they could see her? She had never been so scared. She thought, *What would Sammie do?*

*She'd fight.*

Alex tensed her body and jerked herself out of Maggie's hold. She ran, as fast as she'd ever run toward the shoreline and the crashing waves.

"Jennie, get back here!" Maggie's screech pierced the rain.

Another bolt of lightning. More thunder. Alex thought of Sammie that night. How it had rained then, too. She imagined that Sammie had run really fast that night she got away, but Alex knew that she was the fastest runner of the triplets. She'd always bragged that Dad gave her the sign to steal more often than her sisters.

With her feet sinking into the sandy shore, Alex heard the motor get farther away. She moved back to the firmer soil along the trees and followed the noise. That way Maggie could not see her very well. Then she remembered that you should stay away from trees when there's lightning so she ran back out closer to the beach, stopping for an instant to listen to the sound of the motor. Yes, it was closer now. Which way was it coming from? She listened just long enough to be sure. The left. She started off in that direction. Behind her, she could hear Maggie's voice calling, "Jennie! Come back, my baby!"

Keeping her eyes focused in the direction of the rumbling sound of an engine, she almost called out when she saw a light that must be from a boat, moving up and down on huge waves. She ran left toward the boat and the light. Her heart was pounding so hard in her chest that she thought Maggie would be able to hear it, but Maggie's calls were getting farther and farther away. And the light was getting brighter and closer, highlighting the gigantic waves.

Alex kept running until she realized that that the light was going back and forth, like it was searching for something in the dark water. Then her heart started beating even harder. What if that was the bad man? Spanky, Maggie's son. He had a boat. He must be back looking for them. Alex ran back toward the dune grass, knowing that she had to go farther back into the woods to hide. Alone in the woods at night would be better than getting into that boat with that man.

Tears filled her eyes as Alex pulled back into the protection of the trees. Silently she watched the disappearing searchlight. The noise of the boat engine became fainter and fainter. Crying full out now, Alex almost missed the change in the pulsating sound. The motor rhythm had started to speed up and when she looked out to the shore, she saw the boat heading directly toward her. She'd have to hide farther back in the woods and hope that there were no wild animals back there. Thank goodness this wasn't happening to Sammie, she thought, with a smug smirk. Sammie, always so tough, was scared to death of animals.

But before Alex had wended her way among the pines, a scurry of movement made the brush at her feet crackle. Something furry rubbed against her leg and she let out a scream.

Streeter was the first to spot the lone woman on the shore, running frantically in one direction and then another. She went to the edge of the water and then moved back whenever a wave crashed. She was pointing into the surf. The ranger swung the boat toward her, and Streeter radioed the park office to call out the helicopter. The weather might keep the copter grounded, he didn't know. The woman on the beach could well be Margaret Spansky, but through heavy rain and darkening skies, he couldn't be sure. She appeared to be alone. Where was Alex? Had she eluded him again?

When the ranger cut the motor, it became apparent that the woman was yelling something at them and gesturing with both arms. Streeter jumped into the breaking waves and chilly water. The woman motioned hysterically into the waves, screaming something. When he got closer he could make it out, "My baby! She's drowning! You have to save her!"

Streeter approached, gun at the ready, but the woman was unarmed. Clearly distraught, she stumbled toward him. Streeter yelled at the others to take the boat and search for a child in the turbulent waters. To the helicopter he radioed, "Search the water; prepare for rescue."

To Streeter's surprise the woman had thrown herself, face down, onto the wet sand, moaning loudly, "Jennie's drowning again."

Jennie. The name that Margaret Spansky called Alex. Sammie was Jessie; Alex, Jennie; the names of her dead twin daughters. Where was Alex now? Was she actually in the turbulent lake? As he was about to bend down to interrogate the Spansky woman, Streeter heard something, a call, like a scream coming from the wooded area across the sand and the dunes.

"That sounded like a child," he said aloud.

Leaving Margaret Spansky writhing in the sand, he raced in the direction of the voice, praying that it was a child, not an animal or a bird.

Alex could hear Maggie yelling out there, but she didn't dare move after she'd felt that furry thing on her leg. Sammie was right. The woods were very scary, but she had to stay there until the boat was gone. Then she'd run away as fast as she could.

"Alex!" Her *real* name. A man's voice. Could it be her imagination? More than one voice. From above she heard a clomping noise. Could it be a helicopter? Was someone looking for her, Alex, not Jennie?

"I'm here!" she yelled as loud as she could.

Ignoring the sharp prickles of bushes, she ran out of the woods, through the dunes, toward the beach. It was still raining hard, but there was a bright light coming from a helicopter. She could see a form, lying on the beach near the shoreline. She saw a boat in the water with men shining flashlights onto the waves. That was when a tall man with a crew cut grabbed her as she was about to stumble. He picked her up, and instantly, Alex knew she was safe.

"Alex," he said, "we've been looking high and low for you. Will your Mom and Dad ever be happy to see you. And Sammie and Jackie."

Since Sammie left Maggie's house, Alex had worried so about her sisters. Jackie, so terribly sick that they had to take her out of the movie theatre. Sammie, running away that night into the dark woods.

"Are they okay? Sammie and Jackie?"

"Yes, and you'll see them soon. And you know what? You're going to have a ride in a helicopter."

"Tonight? I can see Mom and Dad?"

"Yes, and your sisters."

The man said her sisters were okay. Wait until she told them about riding in a helicopter.

Other men had landed in the boat and rushed toward them. "Are you okay?" they all asked. Alex saw they all had smiles, and she smiled back at them.

"I got some scratches from the bushes, and one of my arms hurts where Maggie pulled me," she said, showing them her wrists. "Hey, it's cold out here and raining real hard. When can I get in the helicopter?"

# CHAPTER 62

*Beginning of Summer in the Northern Hemisphere,*
*Summer Solstice.*
– Sunday, June 21, 2009

Neither Scott nor Katie could sleep, so they made tea in the corner of their one-room hospital quarters, whispering to avoid waking the girls. Katie was trying hard not to share her terror with Scott. She, herself, had an instinctive fear that this was the night. The night that Alex would be what? Tortured? Abused in a sexual way? Her triplets had always had a sixth sense among them, and tonight she had overheard Sammie and Jackie articulate identical predictions that the bad man was "hurting" Alex. This she had not shared with Scott. What good would it do?

She tried to reason that the Spanskys would have to keep Alex alive to collect the ransom, but what if they collected the money and did not release her daughter? Neither she nor Scott trusted the new FBI Agent, Jason Pentero, not with Alex's life.

"Don't trust him –" Scott was saying something.

Katie nestled closer to him, juggling her mug of tea as they sat side by side on the bench by the window. "Sorry, baby. Guess I was lost in my thoughts."

"I wish Agent Streeter were here. He probably went to Grand Rapids to visit his own daughters. Hasn't seen much of them, but still –"

"He's done such a good job of keeping us informed. Didn't he say he'd call us tonight?"

Scott nodded. "Yes, but I don't understand the politics of the bureau. It's like he's been demoted with Pentero now in charge."

"At least Agent Camry is still here with us. Let's check with her to see what she knows," Katie said. Then the phone rang.

Katie and Scott lurched upright to pick it up, knocking heads, causing Katie to fall back a step.

"Yes, we're both here," Scott said. Momentarily he covered the mouthpiece and whispered, "Tony Streeter."

Katie looked over to Sammie and Jackie, still asleep, thank goodness.

"What's he want?" she whispered back.

"He's *here*," Scott said. "He wants us to wake up Sammie and Jackie. He says he — "

Katie leaned into Scott, her heart racing. *Why would he say that: wake up the girls?*

"Okay," Scott sounded tentative. "Sure, she's right here, but we don't have a speaker. Sure." Scott pulled Katie closer. "He wants to tell us something. Together."

"I have a little girl out here who's very anxious to see her family."

Scott dropped the phone, and Katie didn't even try to modulate her scream. "Oh, my God. Thank you. Thank you, God."

Scott and Katie each grabbed a triplet and pulled them out of bed.

"Is Alex here yet?" Sammie asked.

"We knew she'd be back tonight," Jackie said. "Right, Sam?"

"I dreamed that she got to ride on a helicopter," Sammie said, pulling loose from Katie to put on a hospital robe.

"Not fair," said Jackie. "That's what I always wanted to do."

The door opened and Alex, a huge smile on her face, walked in between Agents Streeter and Camry.

"Mom?" Alex sounded so normal. "Mom, are you okay?"

Blinded by tears, Katie ran to Alex. "Alex, oh sweetie, is that really you? We've missed you so much. We were so worried. So very scared."

"I was scared, too, but I'm okay, Mom. Really. I escaped."

Katie could feel Alex try to wriggle out of her iron hold. She could feel Scott's arms around the two of them before she felt his hot tears trickling down onto her forehead."

"Oh Scott, it's really her," Katie said relinquishing her hold on Alex.

"Dad, are you crying?" Alex stared at Scott. "Dad, I never saw you cry. Are you okay?"

"You bet. Tears of joy," Scott said, swiping his arm over wet eyes. "We missed you, kiddo. The Condors have their third baseman back."

Then Katie and Scott as one, backed away as Sammie and Jackie flung themselves on Alex and in an instant all three were tumbling on a hospital cot.

"I have to call Mom," Katie said, pulling her cell phone out of the charger. "She'll get the word out. Oh, I am so happy that I can't believe it." She turned to Tony Streeter and Ellen Camry, "How can we ever thank you two. If you hadn't been there for us, I just don't think — "

"They're all okay," Streeter said, then repeated. "They're all okay. Just look at the three of them."

Scott's voice was hoarse. "How can we ever thank you. You gave us our lives back." Then he flung his arms first around Streeter and then around Camry.

Once the girls had sorted themselves out, Sammie said, "Alex, I didn't want to leave you. I just wanted to get help. Hey, you know what? Jackie was really sick. But she's okay. I mean, she was in the hospital and all."

"Jackie, you don't look sick to me," Alex inspected her sister. "But you do look different from Sammie and me now with our short hair."

"I'm not kidding, Alex," Sammie said, "Jackie was in a coma. That's what Dr. Susan said. Hey, did that Spanky guy hurt you?"

Katie gulped. Alex looked thinner maybe, but not hurt.

"No, not really," Alex said, but Katie noticed her expression change to near panic. And in an instant change back. "Hey I got to ride in an FBI helicopter. They let me put on the earphones and hear them talk And guess what? I decided. I'm going to be a pilot."

"See, Jackie," Sammie said, "I told you about the helicopter. You didn't believe me."

Katie and Scott exchanged a grateful look. The triplets were going at it again.

"I hate to interrupt this reunion," Streeter said, "but the director would like you to do an impromptu press release. The media is already swarming. We could have it right here, if you wish, or in a more formal setting in the hospital conference room. Very brief. Just a thank-you gesture for the efforts that the media made to find Alex and Sammie."

"That sounds fair," Scott said.

"I've already been on television," Jackie said with a smug edge. She flipped her long hair, "And I still have my long hair."

"Alex, guess what?" Sammie grinned. "We're famous. They even wanted me to go on TV."

"Alex, the whole world was so worried about you and Sammie." Jackie beamed with this announcement. "I even got a letter from the president's daughters."

"President Obama?" Alex's eyes widened. "Jackie, you did?"

"Yes." Jackie's smile widened. "I saved it for you to see 'cause you were telling everybody to vote for him."

"Okay, girls, Jackie, pull on a robe like Sammie, I'll brush everybody's hair, including mine. And let's do it here. But first, Alex, come here, I just need to look you over."

Streeter watched as Katie did a visual examination of her daughter, checking out scrapes and scratches and bruises. She seemed pleased with the first aid he'd administered during the helicopter ride from Wells State Park to Detroit. Now all three girls were talking at once. Streeter thought that was a healthy sign, but what did he know? He wasn't exactly the ideal father.

"Alex, you feel so hot," Katie was saying as she swiped a hand against Alex's brow.

"Ouch, Mom." Alex winced and took a step back. "You know how you make us use sunscreen when we go out. Well, I had to walk all day long on the beach. That woman didn't have any. I asked."

"Sunburn," Katie murmured. "Okay, that'll be okay. Yes, that'll be okay."

"We're going to need forensic samples from Alex," Agent Camry said. "Right after the press conference. Then you can all get some sleep. All of you. Together."

"I just want to get us all home," Katie said.

"We've arranged for you to stay one more night here," Streeter explained. "We still have security issues to work out. Getting Alex to you was our highest priority, but there are other loose ends. But, for you, they can wait until tomorrow."

Camry had left the family to check with the FBI public relations people. They'd want to milk this for all it's worth. Streeter would be a star, but all he wanted now was to be surrounded by his own daughters. He had called Marianne, and she had promised to drive the girls from Grand Rapids to Detroit, first thing in the morning. For that he was grateful. Just the vision would get him through another sleepless night.

Camry returned with a change of plans. "There are way too many reporters to fit in here," she said. "We're going to have to do this in the auditorium. Even then, it'll be crowded. That okay, Dr. Monroe? Mr. Monroe?"

Arms enclosing their three daughters, the Monroe parents said as one, "Anything you want is okay. We are just so, so happy."

Streeter insisted that the press conference be short, and the Monroes promised to include the girls in a more comprehensive one the next day, as did Streeter, speaking for the FBI.

When the family, Lucy, and Dr. Susan now with them, returned to their hospital room, they noticed a new bed had been wedged in. The hospital kitchen had sent up an assortment of sandwiches, cookies, and drinks, and Katie lobbied successfully that Alex be able to snack with her sisters before being led off with Susan for the required forensic examination.

The same young pediatrician who'd examined Sammie came by, and Alex went off with him willingly, all three girls giggling how cute he was. When Alex was returned in fifteen minutes, Streeter could see the relief in Katie's eyes as she beamed a smile at Scott. Alex had denied any sexual abuse, and the examination must have just confirmed that.

After Susan volunteered to drive Lucy home, Streeter and Camry adjourned to the field office for a full night's work. As Streeter closed the door he heard Katie say, "One more thing for tonight, let's call Grandpa Monroe. It'll only be ten o'clock in Minnesota. And this news will be the best medicine in the world."

While with the Monroes, Streeter had turned off all communications. He did not know the whereabouts of Samuel Spansky. Mother Spansky was in custody, and based on her babbling story, would most likely end up in a place for loonies.

# CHAPTER 63

*Storms Cast Gloom Over Great Lakes.*
Weather Forecast, Sunday, June 21

Spanky had trouble navigating the rough lake in the torrential downpour. He'd never been out on Lake Michigan, and he'd never captained by himself on the Atlantic Ocean. The sooner he could dump this boat and get on land the better. He could drive any vehicle over any terrain, that he knew. He had disabled the GPS as a precaution, and now he floundered, unsure of his position. When he came perilously close to a bridge abutment, he decided to hunker down in an inlet until the storm passed. He'd then figure out where he was and be on his way.

As the weather eventually broke, Spanky figured that he was past Sturgeon Bay. While he still had some light, he moved back out into the lake, heading south toward Milwaukee. Checking the chart, he picked Manitowoc, a big enough town in Wisconsin to abandon the boat and pick up an ordinary, older model car and head south on the back roads.

The waves were still gigantic when Spanky took the boat back onto the lake, but the rain had stopped, giving him decent visibility. It was close to eight o'clock and he'd only have another half hour of good light to select a landing site.

He heard the drone of helicopter engines before he saw powerful searchlights illuminate the lake around him. He was a sitting duck. A helicopter dropped to hover just over his boat. Over the crest of waves he heard a deep voice, "Michigan State Police. Samuel Spanksy. Come out on deck. Hands up."

The pigs had him. He had only one chance. Spanky pulled the .44

Magnum out of his cargo pants. Stepping down from the cabin onto the deck, he took his aim. A direct shot at the head of the operator, but before he got the shot off, a rogue wave knocked him off his feet.

Spanky felt his body, in one prolonged motion, slide across the smooth, wet deck, under the rail, and into the lake. He was going to drown. He knew it. Even so, he struggled to keep his head above water in the powerful wave action. As he took his last gasp of air and his bulky body started its descent to the bottom, he thought of the babies, his half sisters, Jennifer and Jessica. So this is what it must have been like for them.

The nightmare over, Katie didn't care what happened to Marge Spansky. In a way she felt sorry for her, a woman unable to recover after the drowning of her eight-month-old twin daughters. And now, her son, however evil he may have been, a victim of drowning. If asked for her opinion, Katie would advocate a plea of insanity, followed by psychiatric care. That woman had caused her indescribable pain, but she bore her no ill will. She had not mistreated Sammie and Alex, and in the end she had protected Alex. Truthfully, had she lost any one of her daughters, Katie wasn't sure if she'd be able to cope with reality and lead a normal, sane life.

Katie had received a letter of apology from Ken Franklin. Poor guy, said he was sorry for involving her in a crime twenty-five years ago and for stalking her recently. He would always love her, but he promised never to try to see her again — unless she wanted him to — like that would ever happen. He wanted her to know that he was living with his mother, just in case.

The Yankee connection had finally been resolved. Of that she was glad. Now Scott wouldn't have to second-guess some unidentified enemy out there. What would happen to the buff, blond guy that Scott had suspected and later identified in the surveillance video surrounding the ransom drop site in Birmingham, she didn't know. Cliff Hunter was a bitter, vindictive man. In a way she was relieved that all the crazies that had surfaced could not be traced to her psychiatric practice.

Her sister-in-law, Monica Monroe, had resumed her tour for her new CD release, but only after writing four one hundred thousand dollar checks. One to Sheila Gladsky, who'd described Marge Spanky;

one to the Talbotts, who'd led them to the Spansky home; one to Rudy Conover, who'd led them to the state park; and the fourth to Adam Kaninsky. But Adam had not been found. Katie prayed that he was safe.

Now as Katie sat in the bleachers at the little league park in Tampa, mopping the sweat, watching her expanded family take their places around the baseball diamond, she said a silent prayer for all the children hurt by Marge Spansky's abduction of Sammie and Alex at that movie theatre. Alex and Sammie seemed to be fine, but Jackie still had despondent moods, which worried Katie. But of all the children, she worried most about eleven-year-old Tina Watkins who'd waited so long for her father to be released from prison only to have him so terrified that he, in effect, took his own life. She'd already set up a trust fund for Tina's college and she would help Connie and Tina the best she could along the way.

Scott had just corralled the team for the pregame pep talk and Katie smiled and waved. She focused on her two adopted sons. The Cutty boys, Jake and Aiden, were adjusting well and had learned to throw and catch a baseball. Maybe with time, they'd give the girls a run for their money. Then there was Scott. There he was out there, face animated, saying whatever coaches say to motivate their players. Scott was a one-in-the-universe kind of guy. She not only loved him beyond words, but after all those years and all those troubles, she was "in love" with him.